# Kill the Puckers

# Also by Sam Evans

### **Standalone Novels**

*Kill the Puckers: A Dark Hockey Romance*

### **Stevie Diaz Mysteries**

*In the Woods Somewhere*

*Down by the Water*

### **Love & Lawlessness Trilogy (written with Travis Walter)**

*Boom Boom Bang: Love & Lawlessness 1*

# Kill the Puckers

## A Dark Hockey Romance

**Sam Evans**

Super Gravity Press

Published by Super Gravity Press

This is a work of fiction. All characters, organizations, and events portrayed in this novel are products of the author's imagination or are used fictitiously. Any resemblance to actual persons, living or dead, is entirely coincidental.

KILL THE PUCKERS

Copyright © 2026 Sam Evans

All rights reserved. No part of this book may be used or reproduced in any manner without written permission, except in the case of brief quotations embodied in critical articles and reviews.

ISBN-13: 979-8-9985201-5-0

*For everyone who speaks up despite the odds.*

# Content Warning

Listen Linda, you're a grownup (hopefully). You're reading a *dark* hockey romance. It says so on the cover. So don't complain that you didn't know what you were in for. But fine. You want more details? Here you go:

- Sex. There's lots of sex. Like so much sex. (Really, what did you expect?)
- Discussions of rape. While not depicted on the page, it's a central theme of the book.
- Murder. (It's on the cover. In words *and* in pictures.) But everyone who's killed deserves it. Pinky promise.

# Kill the Puckers Playlist

## Because every book should have a playlist

Each song corresponds to a chapter on a 1:1 basis in accordance with its number on the playlist and the associated chapter number in the book. Enjoy!

**Apple Music**

**Spotify**

1. *Don't Give Up* by Southern Avenue
2. *Boom Boom* by John Lee Hooker
3. *Born Under a Bad Sign* by Big Momma Thornton
4. *Cross Road Blues* by Robert Johnson
5. *Done* by Ruthie Foster and Larkin Poe
6. *Float Away* by Ian Moore
7. *Hold On I'm Coming* by Ruthie Foster

8. *You Got It Bad* by Samantha Fish
9. *Deep Stays Down* by Larkin Poe
10. *Death Bell Blues* by Cedric Burnside
11. *Every Chance I Get (I Want You in the Flesh)* by Dan Auerbach
12. *Ain't No Sunshine* by Bill Withers
13. *Different Kind of Love* by Adia Victoria
14. *Death Roll Blues* by The Curse of K.K. Hammond and David & the Devil
15. *Turn Me Loose* by The Record Company
16. *Troubled Man* by The Reverend Shawn Amos and Ruthie Foster
17. *Baby Did a Bad Bad Thing* by Chris Isaak
18. *Hard to Stay Cool* by Cedric Burnside
19. *Bad Woman Blues* by Beth Hart
20. *Deathwish* by Samantha Fish and Jesse Dayton
21. *Keep Diggin'* by Larkin Poe
22. *That's All* by Southern Avenue
23. *Dope Queen Blues* by Adia Victoria
24. *Paris (Ooh La La)* by Grace Potter & the Nocturnals
25. *Sometimes* by Larkin Poe
26. *Me and the Devil Blues* by Robert Johnson
27. *Dead Eyes* by Adia Victoria
28. *Oh My My* by Bad Flamingo
29. *Kill of the Night* by Gin Wigmore
30. *1947* by The Deadbeat Cousins
31. *Hangover Blues* by Amythyst Kiah & Her Chest of Glass
32. *I Just Want to Make Love to You* by The Righteous Brothers

# Kill the Puckers

# Chapter 1
# The Inciting Incident

"Are you nervous?" I ask, squeezing Katie's hand in mine as we walk down the long hallway. There are just a few people here at the moment, but it won't be long before it's filled shoulder-to-shoulder. The only reason it's not jam-packed right this second is because they gave Katie advanced notice to get to the courthouse prior to the verdict being read. As soon as everyone else knows it's going to happen, this hallway will be overrun with journalists, hockey fans, and the same kind of rubberneckers who slow down on the highway to get a peek at the carnage any time there's an accident. They're parasites. All of them. And they've all been salivating for a verdict for the four and a half days the jury has spent deliberating.

"I'm fucking terrified, Alyssa. What if they didn't believe me? What if they let them all go?" Katie asks, her honey-blond hair swaying as we walk.

"They won't."

"But what if they do?"

I sigh. I wish Katie's mom, Jeanette, was here, but she got called into work three hours ago when the hospital ended up short-staffed and couldn't make the drive from Portland to Seattle with us. Katie told her it was fine, but I don't think it is. Not really. Nothing is fine right now. I think Jeanette should've blown off work entirely. Being on call is a big part of why I went straight into private practice. Fuck that shit.

"Then you will feel unbelievably sad and frustrated. And on the way home, we'll buy every ice cream flavor the grocery store carries, and then we'll go back to my place and eat until our stomachs explode. But either way, *you* will be fine. It might not look like it, but there's more than one way to put things right, and you've already lived through all the worst parts of this hellscape."

"I'm pretty sure they're going to let them all go. Nothing is going to happen." Her blue eyes are bright, and her fear is apparent in the way her eyes move over our surroundings.

"Is that why you're in head-to-toe black today?"

"Yes. I feel like I'm going to my funeral."

"Even if this goes badly, Katie, they won't get away with it," I promise. The air feels heavy, and I'd like to chalk it up to the fact that it's near the end of August and the courthouse is an old building, but I know that's not why.

She nods, squaring her shoulders as I release her hand and pull the courtroom door open. All five sets of defense attorneys are already seated on the other side of the bar, as are the prosecutors. The defense attorneys look like a freaking army. Their clients aren't here yet, though. I'm sure they plan to make an entrance. They've turned every part of this trial into a media circus and defamed Katie as much as they possibly could while narrowly skirting the gag order put in place by the judge. I'm certain that many of the tabloid articles came about directly from them. If they have no qualms about gang-raping an unconscious, drugged woman, they won't have any qualms about speaking to the so-called press just because the judge told them not to.

I fully expect them to be among the last to show up today. I'm certain they want to parade up the courthouse steps, like they're the victims in all of this. Fuck them all. I'm not sure how they could possibly get away with it. But I've thought that so many times about so many rapists, and these ones are professional athletes. Hockey players. Scum.

Katie and I sit down on the hard bench, and the prosecutor turns to talk to Katie, explaining what will happen. Telling her that regardless of what the verdict is—guilty or not guilty—she has to remain composed.

*Sure,* I think. *Let's add insult to injury.*

The prosecutor must pick up on my fury, because he says, "That goes for you too, Ms. Reed."

"Doctor," I state.

"What?"

"It's *Doctor* Reed," I reply shortly. Normally I wouldn't care, but I don't like this asshole and his 'remain composed' bullshit. I want to burn this fucking building down, and I want to do it with Katie's rapists locked inside. I want to hear them scream, and I want to smell their skin charring as the fire cooks them from the outside in. And then I want to douse them in ice water and put them into the burn unit. That way, if they recover, we can do it all over again.

The prosecutor nods but says nothing else.

The minutes tick by with agonizing slowness, and Katie takes my hand again. Her palm is clammy against mine, and I can feel a small tremor in her fingers. I wish Jeanette were here. I wish her dad, Craig, hadn't died three years ago. I wish I'd gone with her to that concert in Seattle and been at the bar with her afterward, that night last year when all of this happened. I wish… Fuck. I wish I'd at least thought to bring a few Xanax for Katie.

The noise in the hallway on the other side of the courtroom doors has been steadily increasing for the past twenty minutes. It sounds like a dull roar. Like waves crashing in the distance. Another few minutes pass before the door opens and the noise comes flooding in more rapidly than the people. I check my watch. Five more minutes until they're supposed to read the verdict.

The first of the hockey-douchebags walks past the bar railing dividing the courtroom to sit next to his attorneys. Garret Fischer. A center for the Black Bears. He's tall and thin with dark blond hair and blue eyes. He's the one who initially hit up Katie at the bar. The one who bought her a drink and invited her back to his hotel room, where the other four were waiting. Katie might've been up for having a one-night stand with Garret, but she never had the chance to make that decision because the last thing she remembered before waking up naked on the hotel floor in a puddle of piss, was leaving the bar and walking across the street.

When she woke up, she found her clothing scattered around the suite, and as she was gathering it, trying to make her escape from the room, one of the assholes cornered her with his phone, and demanded she say she agreed to sleep with all five of them on video. She was still half-naked at that point. A five-foot-three-inch half-naked woman, with her back to a literal and figurative wall, with a six-foot-five-inch fully clothed man boxing her in. I saw the video. He had her pressed into a corner, wearing only her bra. You could see the whites of her eyes all the way around her irises. She was terrified. She would've said anything to get out of that room and away from him. Once she said it, though, he edited the video down to just that part and deleted the part where he told her she couldn't leave until she said it.

When she made it out of the hotel room just after noon, she was wearing only her jeans and bra. She was unable to find her underwear, shirt, socks, or shoes. She got into an Uber barefoot and topless and went straight to the nearest emergency room—the one at Harborview Medical Center—to report the rape. The hospital performed a rape kit and called the police. After the police showed up, Katie made an official statement accusing Garret Fischer—the one she left the bar with—and Rhys Steichen. She also accused Matt Davidson, Joey Carmichael, and Brandon Miller, whose names she only knew because hockey-douchebag and confirmed idiot Rhys Steichen gave them to her when he forced her to make the video saying she willingly had sex with all of them.

They found semen from all five men as well as signs of vaginal tearing. What they didn't find was any sign of date-rape drugs, because it had been too long between when they'd drugged her and when she'd woken up on the floor of the hotel room for them to still be detectable in her system. More than twelve hours, and all bets are off. But absence of evidence is not evidence of absence—regardless of what the defense attorneys tried to say.

Hopefully the jury is smart enough to understand all that. But a single woman against five of the Black Bears' star athletes, who've never had rape accusations publicly leveled at them? It doesn't matter that it's most likely because the other women they've done this to were too afraid to come forward and stand up to the scrutiny of trial with no guarantee that justice would be served.

Not Katie, though. Katie decided to scream it from the rooftops, figuring that at the very least it would warn other women about what kind of men they are.

But the odds aren't great. I know it's true, even if I'm unwilling to say the words out loud to Katie. I don't see how anyone could possibly believe this is what consent looks like, but... People don't believe women. I see it personally and professionally *all* the time.

Matt Davidson walks past the bar next. He's got dark hair that's just this side of black, and he's the most muscular of the bunch. Then Rhys Steichen. He and Matt are both defensemen—apparently the team's top defensive pair. Rhys is missing one of his upper front teeth, and he looks like shit. I want to pull the others out, one by one, with a pair of pliers. Fuck that asshole in particular for making my little cousin record that video. If they let these bastards go, I'm going to do it. I don't know how and I don't know when, but I'm going to rip every fucking tooth from his mouth.

Brandon Miller and Joey Carmichael—the left and right wing, respectively—show up together. They're both tall, generic-looking white guys with slim builds and brown hair.

Another minute goes by, and there's smothered laughter, followed by glances in our direction from all five rapists. I want to leave Katie sitting on the bench so I can go wipe the smirks off their faces, but I don't. I might have six inches on Katie, putting me much closer to their sizes, but every one of them is still bigger than me. Plus, it'd be five on one, and they're professional brawlers.

If they get off, none of that will matter, though. I'll make sure of it.

Judge Withers enters the courtroom, distracting me from my thoughts of revenge, and we stand as the judge makes his way to his seat. Once seated, he explains to the room that the jury has reached decisions for all five men and we'll hear their verdicts momentarily, however he expects everyone to remain calm and composed regardless of the outcome.

That finished, the judge looks at the bailiff. "Please bring in the jury." The door on the side of the courtroom opens, and he says, "All rise for the jury." Twelve people come shuffling in and take their seats. "The jury has reached a verdict?" Judge Withers questions, looking at the foreman.

"Yes, Your Honor," the foreman says as he stands. He's a fifty-something-year-old white man who's balding and slightly overweight. His eyes have been looking everywhere but at Katie.

*Fuck.* My stomach drops and bile rises in my throat. *It's 'not guilty,'* I think. *'Not guilty' for all of them.* My grip on Katie's hand tightens.

"On the count of Rape in the First Degree against Joseph Carmichael, how do you find?" the judge questions, apparently going in alphabetical order.

"Not guilty."

Katie lets out a quiet sob, and her hand clenches around mine. I think I might throw up. I decide I'm going to aim for those assholes if I do.

"On the count of Rape in the First Degree against Matthew Davidson, how do you find?"

"Not guilty."

The questions continue and, each time, the response is 'not guilty.' When the last charge is read and the last answer is also 'not guilty,' the courtroom erupts in cheers.

The judge bangs his gavel. "Order!" he demands, sounding pissed as he casts a sympathetic look in Katie's direction. It seems like at least Judge Withers believed her, even if the idiots on the jury didn't. "Would the state like to poll the jury?" he asks.

The prosecutor glances back at us, where Katie is quietly sobbing. "No, Your Honor."

"Very well. Ladies and gentlemen of the jury, you are free to go. Thank you for your service. Gentlemen," Judge Withers says, looking at the defendants with distaste, "you are also free to go."

After another raucous outburst, and a glare from Judge Withers, people begin filing out of the courtroom. The piece-of-shit scumbags smirk as they walk by.

Katie and I sit on the bench until the room empties, and the prosecutor eventually turns to us and says, "I'm sorry, Katie. I can escort you out the rear of the courthouse if you want to avoid the media."

Katie says nothing for a moment. Finally, she uses her sleeve to wipe away her tears and responds, "No. Thank you." She looks at me and says, "Let's go crash their celebratory press conference, Alyssa."

"Are you sure?"

"Yes. If they can talk to the media, so can I," she answers defiantly.

"Alright. Let's do it."

We get up and walk out of the courthouse into a sea of reporters, all of whom swivel their cameras and microphones away from the rapist assholes the second they see Katie.

"Katie Stanton! Katie Stanton!" is shouted through the crowd.

Katie waits until they quiet and then says, "Let me tell you what those men did to me."

# Chapter 2
# Honey Traps

I walk into the coffee shop searching for Vaughn. I find him near the back, away from the windows, in the darkest corner. "Hey Vaughn," I greet when I drop into the chair across from him.

"Hey Alyssa. Good to see you," he replies, and I nod. "How's your dad doing?"

"He's fine. He'll be out early next year," I tell Vaughn, who's sporting a full head of white hair these days. He's trim, and the white hair, coupled with the beard, kind of makes him look like The Most Interesting Man in the World. With the stories Vaughn has about smuggling drugs from Mexico to Portland and Seattle back in the eighties, the comparison really isn't a stretch.

"Time off for good behavior?" Vaughn asks.

"Yup."

My dad was arrested when I was twelve. Our house was swarmed, my dad was handcuffed and thrown into the back of a cop car, and I was left standing in our front yard, crying. It was a big thing—made the national news for months. Before his arrest, we'd lived in a nice house in the Queen Anne neighborhood of Seattle. The sort of house that would list at over three million these days if it were to go up for sale.

Prior to the cops slapping handcuffs on my dad, I was under the impression that he was an entrepreneur—which wasn't wrong, exactly. Every con man is an entrepreneur. Right up until they get caught. Then they're a criminal.

So, my dad is a con man turned entrepreneur turned criminal, who's currently serving a thirty-year sentence for convincing people with too much money and too little common sense to invest their excess wealth into his nonexistent real estate developments. It was a good living while it lasted. After he was arrested and sentenced to spend the rest of my childhood in prison, I went to live with my aunt Jeanette, my uncle Craig, and my cousin Katie—who was nine—in Portland, Oregon. Overnight, I was living in a new city with a new family and sharing a room with Katie, who more or less ended up becoming a little sister. It could've been worse. They all loved me, and I loved all of them, even if I never quite fit in.

"What've you got for me?" I ask. Vaughn is an old family friend and business associate of my dad's who used to provide my dad with whatever forged paperwork he needed to convince his marks that the real estate developments were legit. When my dad went down for fraud, theft, and half a dozen other crimes, he never named names, which means Vaughn owes him—and by extension, me—in perpetuity. Vaughn moved from Seattle to Portland not long after I did. Ostensibly it was a fresh start for him, but really it was so that he could keep an eye on me. Vaughn has always been an odd combination of an uncle meets surrogate father—even before my dad went to prison—never mind the fact that we're not related. After the verdict was read at Katie's trial, Vaughn was the first person I called when we got back to Portland.

"I went through the entire team—excluding the five assholes who raped Katie—and all the supporting staff who work closely with them. You said you didn't care if it was a man or a woman, so I looked into all of them, focusing on the ones who aren't currently in any public relationships, which left fifteen people. Of those, six appear to be in undisclosed relationships, so I ruled them out, dropping us down to nine—seven men and two women. I know you said you don't care, but as far as I can tell, both women are straight, which rules them out. Plus, women are harder anyway."

"What do you mean?" I ask.

"If you want to run a honey trap, which is what I'm assuming you're aiming for, men are an easier mark. They're less suspicious by nature, and they're generally idiots. They're usually so convinced that they're smarter than everyone else that they never see it coming."

"Okay, any luck with the remaining seven guys, then?"

"Well, two of them are gay. So we're looking at these five," Vaughn says, setting five folders in a stack on the table before me, opening the top one. "First is Topher Anderson." There's a photo of the guy. He's in his mid-twenties, with longish dark blond hair that looks like it could stand to be washed. "Originally, he's from Connecticut, but he's been living out here for the past two years. He's a forward for the Black Bears. You're not his type, though."

I raise my eyebrows, waiting for an explanation.

"He likes large-breasted petite blonds who don't seem to have a brain between their ears. Think Dolly Parton, but dumb. You fit absolutely none of those criteria."

"Okay."

Vaughn sets the first folder to the side and opens the next. "Then there's Elliott Sinclair." The photo in this folder is of a square-jawed, dark-haired guy. "Another forward. Rumor has it he's looking to be traded, meaning he probably wouldn't bite hard enough to make it worth the effort."

I nod, trusting Vaughn's assessment. Although I know a lot about cons theoretically—having read about them extensively after my dad's arrest, while I was trying to make sense of things—I've never actually run one before. Vaughn has.

He moves this folder to the side as well. "The last three are all real contenders." Vaughn pushes the remaining folders closer to me. "Take the folders, read about the guys, think it over, and let me know what you want to do."

"Alright," I agree, picking up the folders and sliding them into my bag without looking at their contents. "I'll call you. Thanks Vaughn."

He nods. "Anytime, Alyssa. Especially after what they did."

Katie is sprawled across the living room couch when I step into my condo. She's been living here since we got back from Seattle three weeks ago. She can't stand to be alone knowing the scumbags who raped her are still out there, gallivanting around the same city we live in without a care in the world. Jeanette's hovering drives her nuts, and I just treat her like an annoying little sister who hasn't *quite* overstayed her welcome. So she's here with me instead of at her mom's.

"Hey Alyssa, you're home late," Katie says.

"Yeah, I had a coffee date with a friend. What are you up to?"

"A friend or a *friend*?" Katie asks, ignoring my question.

"Just a friend."

"Well, that's no fun."

I roll my eyes. "Sorry. Anyhow, what are you up to? Did you make it to therapy today?"

"We did it on Zoom."

"Okay. Well. That's something."

Katie hasn't been big on leaving the apartment alone recently. I don't blame her. There are over six hundred thousand people in the city, so the chance of running into one of those rapist assholes at the grocery store or in a gas station might be low, but it's not zero. Not yet, anyway.

"What are you watching?" I ask, tracking the antelope moving across the TV.

"*Planet Earth.*"

I nod. Katie's been all about nature documentaries recently. Less chance of being triggered by anything. Or everything. She's been putting on a brave face, but I know she's struggling. Sitcoms are out—you never know when a joke is going to land badly, or some intimate moment will pop up on screen. Romcoms are out for the same reason. And dramas and reality TV? Just no. So, nature documentaries are where it's at.

"Want to join me?" she asks. "I can make some popcorn."

"Sure, as long as you don't mind if I'm working and not paying attention to the TV."

"I always thought psychiatry seemed like it would be fun, but you work too much, Alyssa."

I shrug. "Just some patient files I want to review before tomorrow's sessions," I lie, taking a seat on the couch as she gets up to stick a bag of popcorn in the microwave.

I pull the folders Vaughn gave me from my bag and open the top one. It's for Clark Thomas. According to Vaughn's dossier, he's an athletic trainer for the team and a Portland native. He's thirty-two. One year older than me. The picture Vaughn included shows a thin man with light brown hair and a smattering of freckles staining his face. It says he broke up with his last girlfriend nine months ago, so he's probably ready to start dating again. His interests are listed as the gym and *Star Wars*. Not my favorite things, but still. He's definitely a possibility.

Katie returns to the couch carrying a bowl of popcorn dusted with seasoned salt and sets it between us. I idly grab a handful, shoving it into my mouth with a distracted, "Thanks."

"Mhmm," Katie says, focusing back on *Planet Earth*, leaving me to my 'work.'

I move to the next folder. Adam Klaussen. He's a goalie. The picture depicts a man with close-cropped black hair, dark eyes, and a five o'clock shadow. He's not unattractive. According to Vaughn's notes, he's twenty-eight. He seems to have a tendency to date women for a couple of months before abruptly breaking things off. Though it's unclear if he's the one ending things, I'm betting he is. Most likely, every time one of his girlfriends lets the L-word slip, he panics and dumps them. His interests are listed as classic cars and old movies. Also not my favorite things.

Physically, he's more my type than Clark Thomas, but if he has a new relationship every few months and suffers from commitment issues, Clark is still the better choice. It's not like I'm going to move in with any of these men anyway, so who cares? They're all just a means to an end.

I go to the last folder. Mark Eriksson. *A mark named Mark*, I think, my lips curling upward. It says he's the Black Bears' head coach. *Well. That's promising.* Mark Eriksson is thirty-six. Apparently, this is his first year as the team's head coach, although he served as their assistant coach the previous year. Vaughn's notes say he's one of the youngest head coaches in the NHL. He's attractive with short, mahogany-colored hair, hazel eyes, a square jaw, and broad shoulders. *Yeah. I'd hit that,* I muse as I continue reading. The write-up says he's dated casually since relocating to Portland from Louisiana a few years ago—*do they even have hockey in Louisiana?* I wonder. He doesn't appear to have been in any serious relationships since being here. Before that, though, he was evidently in a long-term relationship, and I wonder if he moved here because the relationship ended or if the relationship ended because he moved here. His interests are listed as blues music and kayaking, which is better than classic cars and *Star Wars*.

I think Mark Eriksson is my guy. My mark. Go big or go home, right? I need access to the Black Bears—their players *and* their facilities—and of everyone, Mark seems like my best shot. The fact that he hasn't been dating much bodes well for me, too. He's probably looking for a serious relationship. Most likely with someone who's interested in him beyond his profession, which will work well for me, since I know fuck all about hockey.

I'll talk to Vaughn again tomorrow. I'm pretty sure he'll agree that Mark is the best choice, though. Hopefully, Vaughn will be able to get me more info about Mark's past relationships as well as his current routine. Then all I have to do is become exactly who he's looking for. If I can pull that off, gaining access to the hockey-douchebags who hurt Katie will be easy. And then I'll make sure they never hurt anyone else.

# Chapter 3
# Stronger than Portland Cement

"Hey kid," Vaughn says when I answer my phone.

"Hey Vaughn. What's up?" It's been two weeks since I sat across from him in a coffee shop and told him I thought Mark Eriksson was the one. Vaughn agreed. He's been gathering background information on Mark since then—following him, figuring out his routines, his likes and dislikes, his favorite foods, and where he does his grocery shopping. You know. Everything a woman could want to know before a first date.

It's not stalking if someone else does it for you. It's just business. At least that's what I'm telling myself.

"Check your email. It has everything I've been able to dig up about Mark Eriksson over the past couple of weeks. It should be more than enough to get you started. But I'd recommend you still spend a few days following him yourself before bumping into him. Literally. Unless someone has a dog you can steal and then heroically return—which he doesn't, it was the first thing I checked—running into them bodily is your best cold opener. If you can do it in a way that makes it seem like it's his fault, more's the better. If not, I'd recommend that you be carrying something when you bump into him. Makes it more dramatic. Don't ever let anyone tell you men don't love drama. They do."

"Okay," I say with a laugh. "Where are you anyway? I thought we were going to meet up tomorrow."

"I've got a new client. I'll be out of town for a few days, but let me know if you run into any snags. And Alyssa?"

"What?"

"Take your time. Don't rush this. You only get one chance. He's your best shot, so don't blow it."

"Vaughn, if there's one thing in this world I know how to do, it's manipulate a man."

"Everyone thinks that. But trust me. It's going to be different than whatever you're expecting."

"I'll be fine, Vaughn."

"I know. You're your father's daughter. Bye kid," he says, ending the call, his words echoing through my head.

I am. If there's ever anything that worries me, it's that. Once I've made a decision and settled on a course of action, I have exactly the same ability to shut off my feelings and do what needs to be done that my dad does. It landed him in prison, though. Hopefully I'm smarter than that.

IT'S SATURDAY MORNING, AND I'M SITTING IN A DINER that calls itself a cafe, making my way through my second cup of coffee, waiting for Mark Eriksson to show up. According to Vaughn's notes, whenever Mark is in the city, he has breakfast here. His hours vary, I guess depending on the team's training or game schedules, which I haven't put any effort into figuring out. I'm betting if Mark were interested in dating someone who gave a shit about hockey, he'd already be doing it.

It's closing in on ten-thirty when he finally walks in. He's bigger than I thought he'd be. He probably has six inches on me. We're both in the one percent. Hopefully, he's not one of those guys who only dates short women. That would be just my luck. His mahogany hair is a few inches longer than it was in the picture Vaughn had. He's wearing khakis and an unbuttoned flannel shirt over a grey T-shirt. It's like he was born and raised here. Looking at him, there's not a single hint of Louisiana remaining. Even his skin is the pasty white of a native Portlander.

He takes a seat at the counter and greets the waitress behind it like an old friend. She smiles when she sees him and quickly brings him a cup of coffee.

I watch him surreptitiously as I pretend to work on the Saturday *New York Times* Crossword Puzzle. Saturdays' puzzles are always the hardest. He orders a Denver omelet with a side of hash browns, and when a tall woman with medium-length black hair walks in and takes a seat at a booth near the windows, his head turns as his eyes track her.

Half an hour later, he tosses a twenty on the counter and leaves. I do the same and then follow him out. According to Vaughn's notes, he'll hit up a farmer's market next. After that, his routine seems to vary.

His height makes him easy to track from a distance as he meanders through the stalls, stopping briefly to talk with people. I get the impression most of them have no idea who he is, so he probably isn't a fan of the spotlight despite his position forcing him into it often.

He buys a jar of local honey at one stall, some apples at another, and two bunches of chard from a third. I wonder if he actually cooks, or if he's just planning on shoving it all into a blender and making a smoothie.

After a few more minutes, Mark leaves the farmer's market opposite the side where we entered, then makes his way along the city streets another couple of blocks before he pulls a set of keys from his pocket. A black Audi twenty feet ahead chirps as he unlocks it, and then he gets in.

# Kill the Puckers

*Damn it!* I'm parked about three-quarters of a mile in the opposite direction. I'll never make it back in time to tail him to wherever he's headed next. With any luck, he'll simply return to his house near Forest Park, and I'll be able to resume following him there. I walk past his car and turn left at the corner to loop around the block before beginning the return journey to mine as he pulls away from the curb.

Ten minutes later, I finally make it back to where I parked. It's almost noon. I drive the twenty minutes up the hills toward Forest Park, moving down progressively smaller, more shaded neighborhood streets. Based on the map, it looks like Mark lives halfway down a dead-end street. By the time I turn off the main road and onto his, I'm questioning whether the directions are accurate. There are so many trees around his house that I drive past without seeing it. It's not until I reach the end of the road that I realize I must have missed it. I turn around and creep by more slowly. I catch a glimpse of the deck, and a small break in the trees that marks his driveway, but unless I drive right up to his house, there's no way to tell if he's there.

After a second of indecision, I park on the street and pull out my phone, opening Zillow and typing in his address as I consider my next steps. The house sold last year for $1.8 million. *Damn. I should've become a hockey coach,* I think. My condo is nice, but it's not $1.8 million nice.

I bet there are no female head coaches in the NHL. I Google it to see if I'm right, and unsurprisingly I am. There's one woman in the league who's a full-time assistant coach—the first woman to have the position in NHL history. She must be a badass.

I put my phone away with a sigh. I can sit here waiting indefinitely for Mark to come or go… but that seems like a waste of time. I shift my car into drive, heading away from Forest Park, back toward civilization, deciding to come up with a better plan.

"What are you *doing?*" Katie asks, her eyes meeting mine in the bathroom mirror as she looks in from the doorway.

"Dyeing my hair," I reply.

"I can see that. But why? And is that *black* hair dye?" she probes, her eyes moving to the discarded box sitting on the bathroom counter. "You know you're never going to get that out, right?"

I shrug. "I felt like a change."

"So you're channeling your inner goth?"

"Something like that," I tell her with a smirk as I smear some dye over an uncoated section of light brown hair.

Katie huffs. "Sit down. Let me help you. You're going to miss a spot, and it'll look ridiculous."

I glare at her reflection, but she merely stands there waiting until I turn and hand her the bottle. Then I take off the overly large plastic gloves that came in the box and pass them to her too. Once she has the gloves on her hands, I sit down on the lid of the toilet. She sections my hair and begins diligently ensuring each section is coated in dye before moving to the next.

"So why are you really dyeing your hair?" she questions after a few minutes.

I shift my weight, trying to decide how to answer, and Katie 'tsks' at my fidgeting. I don't want to tell her the whole truth, but I also don't want to lie to her about it. "Promise not to laugh?" I ask.

"No, but tell me anyway."

I groan.

"C'mon Alyssa! Tell me," she whines in a singsong voice that I know means she won't let it go until she gets an answer. She'll spend the next three days pestering me if I don't give her *something*.

"Fine. I sort of..." I close my eyes, already cringing. "I sort of met a guy, and I think he likes black hair." I dig my nails into my palms so I have something besides the mortification I'm currently feeling to focus on.

"You... You're dyeing your hair for a guy? *You?*"

"Kind of?" I say lamely.

"Which guy? Why haven't I met him? Why don't I already know who he is?"

"Um… We're not exactly… dating… yet."

"I want to meet him!" Katie declares.

"No. No way, Katie. I don't need you scaring him off before I even have a chance!"

"Oh, so you're serious about him," Katie teases, and I don't contradict her, because I *am* serious about Mark Eriksson, just not in the way she's assuming. "Did you finally meet someone you're going to date for longer than a month or two before getting bored?" she asks, continuing to poke at me.

I roll my eyes, even though I don't really mind. This is the most animated I've seen her since she spoke to reporters on the courthouse steps the day the verdict was read. If ripping my love life apart is what it takes, I'll gladly let her.

"I'm not *that* bad!" I insist.

"Oh yeah? When was the last time you were in a relationship that lasted more than two months?"

"Med school," I admit.

"And even that was only because you were too busy to find the time to break up with him!"

"Whatever. It's not my fault people are boring."

"Uh huh. But not this mystery man you're dyeing your hair for?"

"I don't know."

"*That's* why I want to meet him!" she says in that same badgering singsong voice.

"I'll consider it. Maybe in a few weeks."

"Fine. But don't expect me to forget about this!"

"I won't."

"Turn around so I can do your eyebrows too. You'll look ridiculous otherwise." I spin around and let her coat my eyebrows in dye as well. "Wipe that off in a few minutes," she tells me. "If you don't—"

"I'll look ridiculous," I mutter. "I know."

Katie hands me a cup of coffee when I walk into the kitchen. She's always been a morning person. There's not a single day in my life I've ever been *that* awake at seven in the morning, let alone on a Sunday. Our entire childhood was like that—Katie waking up with the sun, and me hiding from it.

"You know, the black hair actually really suits you," Katie says. "I thought it would be too dark, but it makes you look like a green-eyed Krysten Ritter."

"Thanks."

"I kind of think you should keep it like that."

"We'll see."

"So what are you doing today?"

"I was going to go see about a guy. Why? Did you want to do something?"

"Nope," she replies quickly, her voice too chipper. "Go see about a guy."

"I can stay here if you need me to," I offer.

"Alyssa, your life can't revolve around me forever," Katie states. "Eventually, I'm going to have to… Eventually, I'm going to have to get over it."

"Kay—"

"No. You know it's true."

"You don't have to 'get over it.'"

"No. I do," she asserts. "And *you* need to get over feeling guilty for not coming with me that night." I open my mouth to protest, but she continues. "Don't even think about denying it. I know you do. It's not your fault any more than it's my fault."

"I know," I agree.

"Okay, then. Go see about your guy. By the time you come home, I'm going to have gone to the store and bought some flowers." The way she says the words makes it sound like she's giving herself a pep talk.

"Sounds good, but call me if you need anything?"

"Yes. Go."

I'M PEEKING AROUND A MAZE OF BOOKSHELVES, WATCHING Mark Eriksson browse for books in Powell's. Apparently he's a reader, which I wasn't expecting. He's got three books wedged under one arm, and he's reading the back of a fourth—*In the Woods Somewhere*.

*Maybe it's about his house,* I think with a quiet snort. His head jerks up, and I look down, pretending to read the back of the book that's at the top of the stack I'm holding—*Deep Blues: A Musical and Cultural History of the Mississippi Delta* by Robert Palmer. I grabbed it off the shelf along with a couple of others when Mark was perusing the music section, figuring it'd be a decent study guide for what he likes.

I've been following him for the past couple of hours. He started with breakfast at Wilma's Cafe again, then he hit up a vintage record store and spent a solid forty minutes flipping through old vinyl. He walked out with two records. One was *Stronger than Dirt* by Big Momma Thornton, and I wasn't close enough to make out the second. We've been wandering through Powell's together ever since—although he doesn't know that. It's kind of fun. It's like I'm pretending to be a spy, only I'm not really pretending.

Mark adds the book to his stack and then snakes through a few more aisles before stopping to consider another. I climb up onto a small step stool to get a better look at what he's doing. A burble of laughter escapes as a title on the shelf catches my eye. I grab it, scanning the blurb. I laugh again, and then someone clears their throat.

Mark. Mark clears his throat.

The step stool wobbles beneath me as I startle, and then I'm on the floor. My elbow is pulsating and tingling waves are spreading down my forearm to my fingertips.

*Ow. Ow. Ow. Ow,* is the only thought repeating through my head.

"Shit!" a voice snaps. Mark. Again.

# Chapter 4
# Don't Make Me Scream

OH YEAH. MARK, I REMEMBER.

A book goes sliding off my chest and falls to the floor with a dull thud as I sit up, cradling my arm. *He's taller from this angle,* my brain uselessly supplies.

"Shit," Mark repeats more softly, coming to crouch before me.

"What the fuck, dude!" I bark out somewhere between normal conversational volume and a full-on shout. I bend my knees, pulling my feet in, then shove myself away from him, until my back is braced against a nearby shelf, my right arm still cradled in my left. "You just make a habit of sneaking up on women in bookstores and scaring them?" I ask.

"No," Mark says as he begins gathering my scattered books, his mahogany hair falling across his forehead as he looks down. There's stubble from yesterday contouring his jaw. His eyebrows rise when he sees the title of the book I was holding when he snuck up on me.

"Give that back," I snap, snatching *Scary Stories to Tingle Your Butt: 7 Tales of Gay Terror* by Chuck Tingle from his hands.

"So you weren't following me?"

"No, I wasn't following you! Why would I be following you? I'm not the one who snuck up on you!"

"I thought I saw you following me a few aisles ago," he says before setting the now-stacked books beside me.

"Get over yourself," I grumble. "It's a bookstore. I'm here to get books, not to troll for creepy dudes." I try to pick up the stack of books using my somewhat-injured right arm. "Ow," I hiss, a new wave of pain shooting down it.

He closes his eyes and takes a breath as I awkwardly reach across my body, trying to pick up the books with my uninjured arm. "Are you okay?" he finally asks when he opens his eyes. I've resorted to taking the books from the pile one by one and stacking them in my lap.

"Yeah. I'm just dandy," I mutter sarcastically.

"Let me take you to the hospital."

"No thanks. I'm not letting you take me anywhere."

"Your arm could be fractured. You should really have a doctor look at it," he says, his eyes focused on me. They're hazel and flecked with green and amber.

"It's not fractured. It just hurts. I'll be fine. You can go."

"You don't know that. You need to see a doctor."

"I *am* a doctor. And, oh look. I've just consulted with myself. According to Dr. Reed, I'm fine."

"*You're* a doctor?" Mark asks disbelievingly.

"Jesus. Yes. *I'm a doctor.* Are you always such an asshole?"

"What kind of doctor?"

"None of your business," I tell him, wrapping my left arm around the books piled in my lap and then turning to pull my feet under me as I clumsily stand.

He grabs my shoulder, pinning me in place once I straighten up. "What kind of doctor?" he repeats.

"What the hell? Get your hands off me!" I try to slide to the side, to move out of his grasp, but he doesn't release me. "Let go, or I'll scream," I warn.

"Tell me what kind of doctor, and I'll let go."

"The kind that went to medical school."

"What kind?" he repeats, drawing the words out.

"I'm a psychiatrist, you dick!" I snarl, and his hand drops.

"So you know functionally nothing about skeletal injuries," he asserts.

"I guarantee I know more than you," I scoff.

"I doubt it."

"Whatever." I push past him, winding my way through the labyrinthine aisles toward the registers and the doors.

"Let me take you to the hospital."

"I already told you. I'm not going *anywhere* with you," I throw over my shoulder.

"Okay," he says, exhaling loudly. "Let's start over. My name is Mark Eriksson. I'm the Black Bears' head coach. Please let me take you to the hospital so you don't sue me."

"The head coach for the what?" I ask as I stop at the intersection of a few aisles, trying to remember which way I came from before turning left. "No. Whatever it is, I don't care. You could be the leader of the Roswell Aliens for all the difference it makes. Go away. I'm fine. It doesn't matter if you come in peace."

"Here," he says, shoving his phone in front of my face. "This is me." He shows me a picture of him standing behind the wall of an ice rink, surrounded by a bunch of hockey players.

I sigh. "You're not going to go away, are you?" I ask.

"Not until you let me take you to the hospital, and they take an X-ray of your elbow."

"Fine. Whatever," I say, making a show of giving in. "I need to pay for my books first, though."

Mark picks up his pace, moving ahead of me and spinning around to walk backward as he lifts the books from my left hand. "I'll get them," he says. "I have to pay for mine anyhow."

"I don't—" I begin, but he cuts me off.

"It's the least I can do. I did sneak up on you after all."

"Yeah. You did. Why?"

"Like I said. I thought you were following me," he states, as if that explains everything.

"So you suffer from paranoia then? Fear of persecution, perhaps? I can recommend someone if you're ready to seek treatment," I reply with a smirk.

"Ha. Ha. No. Like I said, I'm the head coach for the Black Bears, and—"

"Yeah. You mentioned that."

"And sometimes fans can be a little... invasive."

"Fans? *You* have fans? You can't be serious."

"Clearly you're not big on sports," he says drily.

"Not even a little bit," I tell him as we reach the register and he sets one large, combined stack of books—his and mine—on the counter.

"Yes. I have fans. Or stalkers. It's hard to say where the line is, or if they understand that there is a line," he tells me as the cashier rings up the books.

"Mhmm," I murmur as he passes his card over.

A minute later, he's rushing to get the door, and a small satisfied grin creeps across my face before I quickly wipe it away, replacing it with a look of general annoyance. Like I thought, Mark isn't interested in some adoring hockey fan. I think he might have a thing for not being fawned over, generally speaking. It seems like arguing might be his version of flirting, which I can definitely work with.

He holds the door for me and then leads the way west, over stained and uneven pavement. The sky is grey overhead, and it's much cooler today than it was yesterday. It's finally beginning to feel like fall, and it won't be long before the unrelenting drizzle starts.

We walk along in an uncomfortable silence for several minutes before I say, "How far away did you park? I'm not following you down any sketchy alleyways. I don't care who you are or what newspaper your picture is in," I tell him even though I know exactly where he parked. It didn't seem that far earlier. My arm is really starting to hurt. The pain wasn't that bad while I was sitting on the floor of the bookstore, but now that I'm up and moving, and my blood pressure is elevated, the pain is increasing. It's now a dull throb, pulsing outward from my elbow in sync with my heartbeat, and I'm beginning to think I did actually fracture something. It's probably an olecranon fracture if it's anything. Hopefully not. Hopefully, it's only a bone contusion or a subperiosteal hematoma.

He smirks. "Why? Is your arm starting to hurt?"

"You're mocking me? Seriously? You know I can still sue you?" I gripe.

The smirk turns into a grin. "It's not much farther. The black car ahead on the next block," he says, pointing.

"Fine." I fall back into silence.

When we reach the car, I go around to the passenger side, awkwardly fumbling for the handle with my left hand. Mark appears beside me. "Allow me," he offers.

I consider refusing, but the angle combined with the slope of the street is making it difficult to open the door, so I step aside and let him do it for me. He grins again, as if he knows *I* don't like it, which *he* does seem to enjoy.

I climb in, and he shuts the door behind me. Fortunately, I can at least buckle my own seatbelt. I wonder what Vaughn will have to say about all of this when I talk to him. Either he's going to laugh and call me an idiot, or he's going to be impressed by my dedication to landing the mark named Mark. I look out the window to cover my momentary smile as Mark slides into the driver's seat.

"Don't go to any of the downtown ERs," I tell him as he pulls away from the curb. "I don't feel like sitting around for five hours waiting for someone to come take an X-ray."

"So ordered," he says, navigating away from downtown.

Robert Johnson begins playing on the stereo, and I close my eyes and quietly sing along to *Cross Road Blues*.

"You're a blues fan," Mark comments.

I shrug, saying nothing. I'm in the process of *becoming* a blues fan. I've been giving myself a crash course over the past few weeks, and I actually really enjoy it. I have yet to find a blues artist I don't like.

"The books," Mark supplies, and I hope I'm not blushing. The damn books. Or, rather, the damn *book*. The one that had the audacity to distract me long enough for Mark to sneak up on me and then land directly on my chest when I fell. The one that he *very* obviously read the title of and definitely had thoughts about. "The fact that you know who Robert Johnson is, let alone the lyrics to Cross Road Blues. You are a blues fan."

"Okay. Yeah. I'm a blues fan. So what?"

"Nothing."

"Do you have any ibuprofen or Tylenol?" I ask. I was only singing to distract myself from the fact that my nervous system is catching up to how much my elbow hurts.

"Check the glove compartment."

I open it and begin rummaging through it. Vehicle registration, insurance, mouthwash, deodorant, toothpaste, hand sanitizer… "Do you live out of your car or something?" I ask, glancing at him before returning my attention to the glove box full of miscellaneous items. Band-Aids, antihistamines… Ah. Advil. "Can you open this?" I ask, passing him the bottle and noticing a faint blush across his cheeks.

"Sure," he murmurs, bracing the steering wheel with his knee while he removes the lid, then passes it back to me.

I shake seven into my hand. "Have you got any water? I'm shit at dry-swallowing pills."

"Just the bottle I've been drinking out of," he says, pulling an open bottle of water from the door.

"I'll take my chances. Give it here. Please." He unscrews the lid before handing it to me. His hands are big enough that he could palm a basketball. "Thanks." I swallow the pills. "What's with the mouthwash, deodorant, and toothpaste? You rent a lot of by-the-hour no-tell motel rooms?"

"No."

"Okay… so?" I prod.

"I like to be prepared."

"Uh huh," I reply but let it go.

"What's with the butt tingling?" he asks.

I snort. "Of course you'd ask about that," I mutter.

He shrugs. "Who *wouldn't* ask about that?"

I wait until we hit a red light, and he comes to a stop, and then I turn to stare at him. After a few seconds, he meets my eyes. Once I'm sure I have his full attention, I say, "I prefer reading my porn to watching it."

# Chapter 5
# Pineapple Belongs on Pizza

I've got a clipboard with intake forms balanced on my lap and a pen tightly gripped in my right hand. The tingling in my arm is making me feel like I might drop the pen at any second. So far, I've written my name. It's a race to see who's slower—the ER doctors having time to see me, or me managing to fill out these forms.

Finally, I give up and thrust the clipboard at Mark. "Here," I say as he takes it. Then I dig out my license and insurance card and pass them over as well. "Fill this out for me."

He sighs, like I've put him out.

"It's seriously the very least you can do."

"Mmm," he rumbles. "I'm pretty sure driving you here was the least I could do."

"No," I refute. "That was only to stop me from suing you, remember?"

"Ah. Yes. Well, in that case, any allergies?"

"No."

"Past surgeries?"

"I had my tonsils out when I was eleven," I tell him.

"Nothing else?" he inquires, his eyes moving to my face.

"Oh my god! Are you seriously hitting on me right now?"

"What?"

"You. Right now. You're wondering if my boobs are real, aren't you?" He's definitely blushing, and I laugh.

"Well, I wasn't—" he begins.

"You were totally checking them out!"

"That doesn't mean I was wondering if they were real. Anyway." He clears his throat. "Nothing else?"

When it's obvious I'm not going to answer, he mumbles, "Okay then. Nothing else. Medications?"

"Ocella."

"What?"

"Just write it down. O-C-E-L-L-A."

"Any of these conditions?" he asks before beginning to read from a standard list.

"Just check 'No' for everything."

"You don't even know what they're asking about."

"It doesn't matter. I know you can check 'No' for everything."

Mark finishes filling out the forms, then passes the clipboard back to me. I wince as I stand and my arm straightens—*Yup, still hurts*, I think.

I cross the scuffed linoleum floor, making my way to the desk. I pass my license and insurance card to the woman seated behind it when I hand over the clipboard. She's on the phone, but she flips through the pages to make sure I've filled everything out before scanning my license and health insurance card and giving them back.

"You can take a seat," she mouths to me, with no estimate of how long I'm likely to be waiting. Oh well. It's not like it would be accurate anyway.

Mark is on his phone when I return. He appears awkwardly large sitting in the hospital's plastic chairs, which were designed for someone closer to my height than his. I have no idea what his conversation is about, but it seems to have irritated him more than anything I've said today has.

"No. Tell that asshole that if it were up to me, I'd have already fired him, contract or no contract." He pauses, listening. "No. I can't. I'm busy," he replies. "No. I'm already sitting in the ER, and this isn't an emergency." He hangs up.

"Problems?"

"Just work," he comments, and there's a low growl in his voice which seems to only be present when he's pissed.

"You're blowing off work for me?" I ask, grinning ear to ear.

"Something like that. You know I can look up that medication you didn't want to give me details about?" he questions, changing the subject.

"Congratulations. You know how the internet works. I'm very impressed."

He folds his arms across his chest and scowls.

"Oh god," I say with a snort. "Just ask me out already. I know you want to."

"What?"

"You've been doing your version of flirting with me since you paid for my books. I already caught you staring at my boobs. You're definitely interested in me. Stop being a wuss and ask me out already."

His eyes widen, and for a split second I worry that I've gone too far. Then he laughs. "Do you know the last time someone called me a wuss?"

Immediately, I think, *Well, given the half of the conversation I heard, whoever you were talking about probably calls you worse on the daily,* but that absolutely would be too far, so I settle for a simple, "No."

"When I was twelve, and I beat the crap out of that kid," he replies, staring at me levelly, waiting to see if I'll blink first, I suppose.

"Don't make promises you have no intention of keeping," I warn.

A smile ghosts across his face. He's pretty when he smiles, but so am I. Appearances can be deceiving. "Alyssa, are you free this Friday?" he asks. It's the first time he's said my name. I don't even think I'd told him what it was prior to handing him my license and telling him to fill out my intake forms.

"Actually, I do have plans already that day." I pause long enough for doubt to creep into his expression, then follow up with, "I was planning to wash my hair that night, but I suppose I could rearrange my schedule for you."

"Alyssa Reed," a disembodied voice says over a staticky PA system.

"Well. That's me. Are you waiting around?"

"You have some other way to get back to your car?" Mark inquires.

"Uber?" I say with half a shrug.

"I'll wait. What do you like to eat?"

"Food?"

"What kind of food?"

"I'm not picky. I'll eat anything," I tell him as I stand. "Well. Not fish. I don't like fish."

The nurse is impatiently waiting for me near the doors next to the desk. I follow her through them, down a corridor, past screened-in beds, to my own, and then explain what happened, leaving out the part about Mark sneaking up on me. Eventually, they take X-rays of my wrist and elbow, ultimately declaring that there are no fractures. The attending physician expects it's a bone contusion, which will likely hurt for the next several weeks. *'Ice and ibuprofen'* are his suggestions. He does also offer to write me a prescription for naproxen, but I decline. If worse comes to worst, I'll have Jeanette write me one for something stronger than naproxen. Forty minutes later, I'm walking back into the ER waiting room, looking for Mark. He's outside the building, pacing. His phone is pressed to his ear once more. I bet it's related to the call from earlier.

The exit doors slide open with a hiss as I approach them, and the air smells faintly of exhaust fumes when I step outside. My elbow is wrapped in a compression bandage, and the attending gave me a sling I probably won't wear after today, but it's still throbbing. That's just going to be life for a while, unfortunately.

"How many ways are there for me to say no? If he doesn't sit down and shut the fuck up, I will bench him for the entire season opener," Mark snaps and then pauses, listening. "I would rather we lose. Tell him that so he knows I'm serious." He turns on his heel and sees me watching. "I have to go," he says, abruptly ending the call.

"Don't let me stop you," I remark when he comes closer.

"How's your arm?" he asks, eyeing the sling as he changes the subject from his very dramatic work life once more. His very dramatic work life, which I intend to make exponentially more dramatic.

"Not broken. Exactly like I said."

"Well, at least there's some good news," he mutters. "Are you hungry?"

"If you're trying to get me to come back to your place with you, the answer is no."

"I wasn't. I was trying to figure out if you'd be interested in going out for pizza with me."

"Oh. I guess I could eat."

"So, you're a psychiatrist?" Mark asks, sitting across from me.

"Yes. I thought we'd established that fact. Are you asking if I'm psychoanalyzing you?"

He shrugs as his eyes scan the menu.

"You're a hockey coach, right?"

As expected, Mark says, "Yes. I thought we'd established that fact. Are you asking if I'm evaluating your on-the-ice potential?"

"No. But you probably looked at me and immediately made some assessment of how coordinated I am—falling off step stools notwithstanding—right? Chances are you subconsciously do that every time you meet someone."

"So you're psychoanalyzing me."

It's my turn to shrug. "Only a little. Why? Are you worried I manipulated you into asking me out for pizza and whatever you have in mind for Friday?" I'm actually interested in his response.

"No."

"Okay. You're worried about something else then," I say innocently. "You want to tell me, or you want me to guess?" There's a bit of a dare to my words. I don't think he'll tell me. But he *is* right. I *have* been psychoanalyzing him the entire time. He thrives on conflict, and he values competence. He doesn't like easy, and he probably grew up in a somewhat abusive household. Most likely, he feels that love—like respect—isn't something that's given, but something that's earned. If someone shows him love or affection without what he deems to be a valid, worthwhile reason, he is suspicious of it by default. But when he falls for someone, he falls hard. He doesn't do anything halfway. He's driven, and even though he coaches a team sport, he prefers to succeed or fail on his own merits. It's probably why he coaches rather than plays. He likes to run the show.

"Go ahead and shock me with your insightful nature," he says, setting the menu aside and focusing on me.

I raise my eyebrows and wait, but he doesn't take it back. And like it or not, I need Mark to continue to be fascinated with me. "You like that I argue with you. You like that I'm not impressed by whatever it is that you do. It turns you on. You're probably wondering what I'm like in the bedroom. Will I turn soft and pliant and let you call the shots? Or will I fight back there too? You're wondering if I'm this mouthy when I'm naked. I bet…"

I consider my next words, but the slight forward lean to his torso and his eyes locked intently upon mine—pupils blown wide—tell me to keep talking. "I bet that if I stretched out a foot beneath this table, I wouldn't need to ask if you're happy to see me. I bet that you're wondering if I was serious when I said earlier that I wouldn't go home with you tonight. I bet you're desperately wishing that you were wearing pants that were just a little bit looser right now."

I fall silent, and after several moments, he clears his throat and shifts his weight. I smirk knowingly. "For the record, I was serious."

"About?" he asks, evidently so distracted he's already lost the finer points of what I said.

"Going home with you tonight. I won't."

"Why not? If you don't mind me asking. You're clearly as interested in me as I am in you. Arguing is obviously foreplay for you as well."

"For one, I don't know you. For another, my elbow might not be broken, but it does really hurt. Mostly, I'm not in the mood to screw someone who may as well have pushed me off a step stool today."

Our conversation is interrupted by the server asking if we've decided. Mark glances at me, and I shrug. He takes that as permission to choose for the both of us and orders a large pepperoni and pineapple pizza. He would. He likes being contentious. Luckily, I also agree that pineapple belongs on pizza.

"You know I wasn't intending for you to fall," Mark tells me when the server has left.

"I know. You're just a dick."

He scowls.

"What? Are you going to tell me I'm wrong? You are, and you know it. You *enjoy* it. Tell me I'm wrong." I wait a moment, but he says nothing. "That's what I thought. So. What are we doing on Friday?"

"How do you feel about concerts?"

# Chapter 6
# Joey Carmichael Dies First

"Hey Alyssa. What happened to your arm?" Vaughn questions, eyeing the compression bandage as he sits down next to me on the lichen-crusted park bench. This park is only two blocks away from my office, so it makes it easy to meet Vaughn on my lunch hour. We're both wearing jackets to ward off the damp chill in the air, but he's gotten some sun since the last time I saw him. Wherever his work trip took him, it must have been somewhere warmer than Portland.

"I took your advice about making an entrance. Turns out you're right. Men do love drama." I explain the circumstances of my first meeting with Mark. Vaughn laughs when I mention Mark spending his afternoon in the ER with me.

"Nice job," Vaughn says when I tell him about going to get pizza afterward.

"We have a date this Friday," I finish.

"Sounds like he's solidly on the hook. Now you've just gotta reel him in."

"I know."

"You're going to have to sleep with him," Vaughn comments softly, as if he's explaining something I either don't know or haven't thought of.

"I'm aware."

"And you're okay with it? Because there's a difference between being aware and being okay with it."

I shrug and take a bite of my sandwich, chewing and swallowing to give myself time to decide how to answer. "I'll do what needs to be done. Whatever it takes to get me close enough to rid the world of every one of those piece-of-shit rapists, Vaughn. If that means sleeping with Mark Eriksson, I'll do it a thousand times over. It's worth it. Besides, it's not for forever."

"What happens if you develop feelings for him?"

"I won't. Are you just asking me this because I'm a woman?"

"No. I'm asking you because I've been the honey in a honey trap before, kid. And unlike you, I know how hard it can be to separate who you are from who you are *with them*. I know how easy it can be to catch feelings. Regardless of what you believe, you're not a sociopath. You're not immune. So, what happens when pretending to have feelings for him turns into actually having feelings for him?"

"Vaughn," I say flatly. "That won't happen."

"Alyssa—"

"No. It won't happen," I assert. "Can you get me some cyanide?" I ask, wanting to get away from having to explain to Vaughn that I won't develop feelings for Mark. From having to explain that I seem to be incapable of falling in love with anyone, let alone someone like Mark Eriksson. Because while Vaughn is right, and I'm not a sociopath, I think standing in my pajamas in my front yard at twelve years old, watching my dad disappear from my life and into the prison-industrial complex via the backseat of a cop car broke something in me.

Katie was right about me getting bored in relationships, but getting bored in relationships is simply a defense mechanism. A way to keep myself from sticking around long enough to *'catch feelings,'* as Vaughn so eloquently put it. Half the reason I went into psychiatry was to figure out what the hell is wrong with me. Unfortunately, knowing the answer to that question does absolutely nothing to fix it, but hey. I was operating under the 'knowledge is power' lie. I'm smarter than that now.

"Cyanide is pretty tightly controlled. Can't you use something more easily available?"

"I could. But I would strongly prefer cyanide. It's more dramatic for what I have in mind, Vaughn. And I know your opinion about the drama," I quip with a grin.

Vaughn sighs. "When do you need it by?"

"Sunday. At the latest."

"That's only four days from now, kid. That's a big ask."

"But you can do it?"

Vaughn places his hands on his knees and leverages himself off the bench. "I'll let you know later tonight."

I nod. "Thanks, Vaughn."

"Yeah, yeah," he mutters as he walks away.

THE CONDO IS DARK WHEN I GET HOME, AND KATIE IS nowhere to be seen. She had a therapy appointment earlier in the day, so my first thought is that maybe she went somewhere afterward. I consider calling Jeanette to find out if Katie is with her, but I decide not to. I don't want Katie to feel like I'm checking up on her. She's lost enough throughout all of this without people constantly reminding her of it by treating her like she's someone who's fragile and breakable and can no longer be trusted to take care of herself.

Instead, I go to the fridge, pull out the tub of cookie dough, and pour myself a glass of pinot noir while hoping Vaughn can get me the cyanide I asked for. I know it's a big ask. The stuff is almost impossible to obtain legally, so hopefully Vaughn, with his many connections, can do it illegally. I want Garret Fi—

A loud thud comes from Katie's room. It used to be my spare

bedroom, but sometime in the past month I mentally reclassified it, and I now firmly consider it her room. I leave the cookie dough and the bottle of wine on the island, which divides the kitchen from the living room, and walk to Katie's closed door. For a moment there's silence, and then I hear faint snuffles coming from inside the room. I tap on the door. There's no response, and the snuffling stops.

"Katie? Are you okay?" I ask, but as with the tap on her door, there's no response. "I'm coming in," I state a second before opening the door. The room is dark, and I use the flashlight on my phone to navigate to the bed. "I'm going to turn on the lamp," I warn.

She's facing away from me, shrouded by blankets, but I can still see the shudders racking her body. I climb onto the bed to sit next to her, not touching her, and the mattress sinks slightly.

"What happened?" I ask. She's been doing pretty well lately. She's actually been leaving the condo to go to her therapy appointments instead of doing them on Zoom. She went grocery shopping alone the day Mark took me to the ER. And I know setbacks can happen any time, for any reason, but this isn't what I expected to come home to today. I'm almost positive *something* happened.

She says something garbled and unintelligible.

"Come again? I couldn't quite make that out over the sound of you choking on your own snot," I say lightly.

She wipes her nose with the back of her hand as she turns to face me, and I pass her the Kleenex box. She blows her nose loudly and then, so softly I almost miss it, she whispers, "I saw him today."

My stomach plummets. Through the bed, through the floor, through the condos below mine until it feels like it's bottomed out on the asphalt of the street beneath me. "Him who?" I know the name she says is going to be one of the hockey-douchebags. I just don't know which one.

"Joey Carmichael," she whispers.

"Where?"

"Outside of the pharmacy. When I was picking up my prescription."

"Shit, Kay. I'm so sorry."

"He waved at me, Alyssa," she says before breaking down sobbing again.

I wrap my arms around her, making a split-second decision and changing my original plan. I had planned to cut the head off the snake and kill Garret Fischer first. He was the one who convinced Katie to leave the bar with him. He was the one who drugged her. If I had to put money on it, based on what I saw during the trial and the way he interacted with the other four, I'd wager Garret was the driving force behind it all. Rhys Steichen would've been next on my list. He seems to have a vested interest—maybe by virtue of his position as a defenseman—in protecting himself and the others. It's why he forced Katie to make that video. The two of them dying would've likely introduced a fissure among the remaining three. But this changes everything.

Joey Carmichael is going to die first.

"How do I look?" I ask Katie when I come out of my bedroom. I haven't been this nervous for a date... well, ever. Half of my closet is currently covering my bed, and if I don't go home with Mark, I'm going to be sleeping on the couch because there's no way I'm putting all of that away tonight.

Katie lifts a hand and makes a spinning motion with her finger, so I oblige. I'm wearing a low-cut red bodysuit with a black tulle skirt. My hair is curled in loose waves, and there are five diamond studs in each ear, turning my head into an approximation of a disco ball.

"You look like you *tried*!" Katie says, and I immediately turn to go back to my bedroom as she launches herself off the couch, coming to stand between me and my door, stopping me from ripping off everything I'm wearing and futilely searching for another outfit. "No. I meant 'you look like you tried' in a good way! I don't think I've seen you do more than throw on a pair of jeans and *maybe* some red lipstick before a date in... what? At least a year? You look good, Alyssa!"

"It's not too much?" I ask, having second thoughts now for a totally different reason.

"No, it's not too much! Dyeing your hair for this guy was too much—even though it looks great," she hurries to add. "This is just a normal 'I like a guy' level of trying."

"You're sure?"

"Yes, I'm sure! What's wrong with you?"

"Nothing. I don't know. I'm just nervous, I guess. Usually, I don't really care if guys like me. I just... kind of expect that they will," I say, knowing it sounds horrible. "This guy is different though. He expects that women will like *him*, and he's not... interested in that."

"Well, clearly he's interested in you. He's been texting you all week. Don't think I haven't noticed!"

"I didn't realize you were paying attention."

"Of course I've been paying attention. How could I not? Plus, I don't exactly have my own love life at the moment. Or even my own life. I sort of have to live vicariously through yours. So, do I get to meet him yet?"

"No. Definitely not." Her face falls, and I rush to explain. "It's our first date, Katie. Let me make sure that he's going to be around after tonight. And then you can meet him," I promise, having absolutely no idea how I'll introduce her to Mark. Maybe I'll hire a fake boyfriend to hide my fake relationship with Mark for a day, but if I introduce her to him... she's going to recognize him, and she'll definitely have questions I can't answer. Or she'll hate me. Yeah. Both of those things.

"Promise?" she asks, and I swallow hard as I nod. "Okay. Are you coming home tonight?"

"I'm not sure."

"Text me and let me know?"

"Okay. I will," I tell her as the condo's intercom buzzes. *Shit! It must be Mark.* I'm instantly thankful that this is an older building and it doesn't have a video stream integrated in. I rush to the intercom, pressing the button and saying, "I'll be right down."

"Have fun," Katie orders. "Don't do anything I wouldn't do."

"Thanks. Love you. Text me if you need anything," I say, tugging on a pair of heeled boots.

"I won't, but thanks," she replies as I pull open the door and step into the building's hallway.

Mark is waiting for me on the ground floor, just outside the main doors. He's wearing black jeans and a navy-colored sweater, which contrasts nicely with his hair. His lips twitch upward when he sees me, and his smile grows as his eyes rove over my body. He extends his right hand to me—seeming to remember my right arm is injured—and I place my left hand into his, allowing him to tug me closer. He smells fantastic—like leather and wood smoke with a hint of burnt marshmallows.

His lips brush against my cheek, and he murmurs, "You look lovely," into my ear. I fight the urge to shiver as his words wash over me.

It really is a shame he's the Black Bears' coach. He's easily the most attractive person I've been on a date with in the past year. Hell, probably longer than that. "Thank you," I say, remembering my manners. "So do you."

Mark nods, then inclines his head toward his car, which is parked in the loading zone. "Shall we?"

"Yes."

"How's your arm?" he questions as he opens the passenger door for me, having noticed I'm not wearing the compression bandage or sling. I would've wrapped my arm, but it didn't exactly vibe with the sultry look I was going for.

"Still sore. Who are we going to see?"

"Austin Sharpe." The fact that I have no idea who that is must be apparent because he quickly follows up with, "You'll like him," as I get into the car. "Should I be offended that you didn't invite me up and offer to show me your place?" Mark inquires after he climbs in.

"Did you want to come up?" I ask, deflecting instead of answering the question.

"Yes."

I sigh. I was hoping for a less direct response. Something I could've continued to dance around. "I have a roommate, and she's been having a bit of a rough time lately. Inviting you up while she's there probably isn't the best idea."

"Huh."

"What?"

"I didn't figure you for the roommate type."

I shrug. "You're not wrong. We grew up together, though. She's more like a sister than anything."

"Ah."

"Yup. What about you? Any family nearby?" I probe.

"You didn't Google me?" he asks.

"No. Should I have? I figured you didn't kill me the first time I got into your car, so there was no need."

"No, it's... that's fine. Unusual, but fine."

"Ah. I see," I say softly.

"What?"

"You're used to an uneven playing field, so to speak. Everyone always knows more about you than you know about them." He nods when I pause. "Did you Google me?" I ask.

"No. Should I have?"

"I don't know. Maybe we'll play Truth or Dare later. Dig up each other's pasts. A secret for a secret," I suggest, falling silent.

Twenty minutes later, we arrive at the venue. It's a mid-sized bar with a section of wall that rolls up, extending the space out onto a gravel patio, which is strung with lights.

"Want a drink?" Mark asks. His question is accompanied by the sound of gravel crunching as it shifts beneath our feet.

"Yes. A double bourbon on the rocks. Nothing from the bottom shelf, please."

Mark nods, and I watch him walk away, admiring the view. This place is nice. I'd come back here. There's a volleyball court and horseshoe pits off to the right, and I briefly wonder how badly I'd do trying to throw horseshoes left-handed. I'd probably kill someone. *Maybe...* I consider the possibilities for a moment. *Could be the modern equivalent of a stoning,* I think.

A few minutes later, Mark returns, handing me a drink. Hopefully, he's more trustworthy than the players on his team. Hopefully, this isn't laced with Rohypnol. I should've gone with him to the bar. I force the thought away, and clink my glass against his, saying, "Cheers," as I do. If worse comes to worst, I can kill him too. I take a sip. "This is good. What is it?"

I take another sip as he says, "Pappy Van Winkle Family Reserve."

For a moment, I'm caught precariously between spitting my drink out and choking on it. "Come again?" I say once I manage to swallow.

Mark laughs. "I'm pretty sure you heard me."

"How old?" I force out.

"Twenty years."

"Jesus fucking Christ. This is a three-hundred-dollar drink!"

"More," he tells me with a hint of a smile.

"I hope you're not expecting me to sleep with you just because you bought me an expensive drink."

"No. I'm expecting you to sleep with me because you want to. And I bought you an expensive drink because I wanted to."

"Yeah, well I'm rethinking that desire," I mutter, turning away from him and his stupid grin as applause filters through the crowd. A tall white guy in his fifties with longish brown hair is on the stage with a guitar in his hands. He launches into the first song without an introduction, and I'm unsure if he's an opener or the main act since it's such a small venue.

"He's good," I murmur when the first song ends.

"He is," Mark agrees as the second song begins.

For a while, the world narrows to only the music and the stage, and I forget about Mark, the drink in my hand, and the rest of the crowd. After several more songs, the music stops long enough for the musician to introduce himself as Austin Sharpe, the main act.

Mark interlaces his fingers with mine, pulling my attention from the stage to him. "Enjoying the show?" he asks.

"Very much so," I reply. I'm not sure if the bourbon or the music is more intoxicating, but I only seem to be capable of focusing on one thing at a time, and right now, Mark has my full attention. I'm hyper-aware of his skin touching mine and the stubble on his jaw. In my heeled boots, I'm just a few inches shorter than he is, and when I turn to face him, we're almost at eye level with one another. "Are you?"

"Mhmm," he replies. His eyes are laser-focused on me, and I can see the pulse jumping in his neck.

The music starts again, but I keep my back turned to the stage, and my attention centered on Mark. I place my hand on his sternum and wait to see what he'll do. He freezes, and my smile grows broader as I slide my hand up his chest and over his throat until my fingertips are grazing his carotid and I can feel his pulse thrumming beneath them. I let them linger there for a moment before running them across his jaw. The stubble ever so slightly prickles the pads of my fingers.

"What are you doing?" Mark finally asks, his voice a husky whisper.

"Deciding if I want to kiss you."

"And do you?" His mouth is inches from mine, and the warmth of his breath envelops me.

"Absolutely," I tell him, closing the distance between us. As soon as my mouth finds his, his lips part, and I deepen the kiss as his free hand wraps around my waist, pulling me into him. I stroke my tongue over his and taste the same bourbon I've been drinking. It makes me want him more, as if I can get drunk from this kiss. I press my hips into his, and his hand drops from my waist, skimming down my body until it's cupping my ass. He's pressing into me through the thin tulle fabric of my skirt. He's rock hard, and he definitely wants more than this kiss in a crowded bar. I suck his tongue into my mouth, and he moans as his fingers dig into my ass. At this point, I know our mouths have been locked on each other long enough that we're making a scene. I'm just not sure I care. Or maybe I want to make a bigger one.

But if this gets any hotter, we're going to end up with our

mugshots plastered on the front page of the local news section for indecent exposure. I lean back to end the kiss, but Mark follows me until I place my hand on his chest and push him away.

He growls in frustration when our mouths finally break apart, and his eyes have a wild look to them.

"Been a while?" I ask with a smirk, which is apparently a step too far, because the next thing I know, he's thrusting his empty glass into my hand, forcing me to take it or let it fall to the floor and shatter. As soon as his hands are free, he pulls me back to him, one hand wrapped around my hips, the other wound into my hair, and his mouth finds mine again, more insistently. This time, he's fully in control of the kiss, dominating my every move. I could shove him away if I wanted to, but that would defeat the purpose, and I don't want to. He kisses me until we're both breathless, then abruptly retreats, leaving me unbalanced and stepping toward him in search of more.

"Been a while?" he says, throwing my question back at me.

"You're a bastard, you know that?"

"Yeah, you already told me. Last week." His own breathing is still ragged, and fuck me if I don't want more.

"Ask me to spend the night with you," I demand.

# Chapter 7
# Sorry About All the Screaming

MARK'S CAR MOVES UP THE DARK, WINDING ROAD THAT leads to his house. The same road I followed days ago, trying to find him, only to discover that while his house isn't technically within Forest Park, it may as well be. The trees seem to press in on the car, and the headlights illuminate only a narrow strip of road before us. It feels more claustrophobic than cozy. I've never been the biggest fan of the woods at night. It sets off some primal instinct that makes me uneasy. Or maybe that's just nerves.

I already texted Katie to let her know I won't be coming home tonight. She responded with a GIF of Sandra Bullock in *Miss Congeniality* singing, and I immediately put my phone on Do Not Disturb. She's continued texting me, but I haven't looked at anything she sent after that.

"Why do you live all the way up here?" I ask Mark, finally breaking the silence.

His eyes flick to me as he says, "It's quiet."

"The better to hear you scream, my dear," I murmur to myself.

"What?" Mark asks, and I'm not sure if it's because he heard me or because he didn't.

"Nothing. So. Truth or dare?"

His eyebrows rise as surprise flickers across his face. "I didn't think you were serious."

"I'm always serious. So?"

"Truth."

"Why do you really have all that shit in your glove box?" I know there's a reason, and it's not that he likes to be prepared.

His hands tighten on the steering wheel, and a long moment passes where it seems like he might not answer. Finally, he says, "When I was a kid, my mom and I lived out of our car off and on, and I got in the habit of making sure necessities were stocked, just in case."

"In case you had to leave in a hurry?"

"Yes."

I nod. Abusive dad then. Or stepdad. Probably the sort of guy who was nice enough until he started drinking, but touch a drop of alcohol and all hell breaks loose. Then once he sobered up, he'd swear it would never happen again. I only say, "Your turn," though.

"What would I find if I Googled you?"

"Depends on how hard you looked." Part of me wants to leave it at that, but he answered my question, and fair is fair. "If you looked at the top few results, most likely just stuff about me being a psychiatrist and my practice. Maybe some patient reviews. If you kept looking though, on the second or third page of the search results, probably—I'm not sure, it's been a while since I checked—you'd find some articles about my dad with my name briefly mentioned in them. Maybe some pictures of me as a kid."

"Why?"

"My dad stole a lot of money, and the police raided our house. It was in the news for a while." I still remember what it felt like the next day, seeing the pictures of me standing barefoot in the grass in front of our house, wearing only a nightgown with tears streaming down my face plastered in the newspapers. Pretty little girl, crying for the camera while police swarmed her house and tore her life apart. Prior to my dad's trial and the availability of courtroom photos, those were the ones the media used most often when talking about him. It didn't matter that he wasn't in them anywhere. They simply put a much, much smaller picture of his mugshot below and called it good.

"What's his name?"

"Randall Reed."

"Where is he now?"

"Prison. My turn. Truth or dare?"

"Truth," he says again.

I could ask him about whatever man it was in his life that routinely sent him and his mom fleeing to the safety of their car. I could ask him about how he wound up as a hockey coach. I could ask him about how he ended up here, of all places, because I'm sure there's a story there, but I don't. I don't ask any of those questions. Instead, I let the combination of alcohol and my own insecurities get the better of me.

"Have you ever been in love?" I regret the words as soon as they leave my mouth.

"Once. Why?" he asks.

"What's that like?"

He considers it for a moment before asking, "Have you ever been skydiving?"

"No."

"Well, before you jump out of the plane, it's a mixture of fear and exhilaration. Then, once you've jumped, all you can hear is the wind roaring past you as you plummet toward the ground at two hundred feet per second. There's no time to think—not really—so the fear disappears."

"What happened?"

"I don't know. I guess you could say I pulled the ripcord, and my parachute didn't deploy. And when I tried to deploy the backup 'chute, it was missing." He's quiet for a moment. "It ended badly, and I ended up here. Why do you ask?"

"You have to say truth or dare," I remind him.

"Truth or dare?" he asks with a sigh.

"Truth," I reply, deciding to be nice, since he clearly wants to know.

"Why did you ask?"

"I've never been in love. Not really. I've dated lots of people—men and women—but... I guess when I'm standing in the plane's opening, waiting to jump, every single time, I look out at the ground and think, 'Nah. I'm good.'"

"You've seriously never been in love?"

I shake my head, deciding not to ask him any more questions. A few minutes later, he turns down his driveway. Lights flicker on as we near the house. He must have some kind of smart home setup that detects when he's nearby. I bet there's a pretty elaborate security system too.

As the lights come on, I'm presented with a large house that can only be described as mid-century modern meets treehouse.

"*This* is your house?" I ask as we get out of the car. I don't know what I thought his house would look like, but definitely not this.

"Not what you were expecting?" he replies, seeming to read my mind.

"No. This is... whimsical. You do not strike me as being full of whimsy." There's a deck that wraps around the house, and it's hard to say for sure, but the exterior square footage must be nearly as large as the interior.

"I have a thing for architecture."

"And what? This was some famous architect's house?"

He looks a little sheepish as he says, "Yes. Would you like to come in?"

I nod as I move toward the front of the car, and he takes my hand. Heat seems to flow through his skin to mine and up my arm. I'm surprised that my admission of never having been in love didn't give him second thoughts. But maybe he doesn't care because he's intending that this will be a one-night stand. I don't think so, though. He doesn't strike me as the type to bring people back to his house for that.

We pass a small carport filled with shelves of turpentine and stain, and he leads me up a series of steps toward a small bridge, which connects to the deck and house. There's a large entry door made almost entirely of glass, and he stops to unlock it before pulling me into the house. He gives me a quick tour. It's floor-to-ceiling glass windows, vaulted ceilings, and light-colored wood. It's completely unexpected, but gorgeous.

"You're showing off, aren't you?" I ask as we return to the living room, and he smirks. "Okay, well just to warn you, my condo looks nothing like this, and I should probably ask you for the number of whoever did your interior design." I grab his hand and tug him closer to me until the space between our bodies vanishes, and all I can feel are the hard lines of his pressing into mine. His hands circle my waist, gripping it. "Truth or dare?" It's still my turn.

"Truth."

"What is it you want from tonight?"

His fingertips slowly trace up my spine, making me fight the urge to shiver, as his eyes bore into mine. "I want to take you out on my deck, where anyone can see us, and I want you in my lap, writhing on top of me, until I'm so close to coming that I'm worried about it happening before I've even had you. Then, I want to tear your clothes off and plunge my tongue inside you. I want to feel you clenching my tongue while you climax, so I can imagine how good it'll feel when you're coming around my dick, screaming my name."

My breath catches as he presses his hips into mine, and I feel exactly how much he wants me. I respond by pressing against him with the same amount of force, and the friction makes me gasp slightly. His gaze, locked on mine, intensifies. I couldn't look away even if I wanted to, and I don't want to.

"I want to bury myself so deep in your mouth that you're gagging on me, tasting the pre-cum dripping from me. Then I want to bend you over the railing of my deck and fuck you until you're screaming my name so loudly, for so long that the neighbors call the police, and when they show up, I'll look them straight in the face and say, 'Sorry about all the screaming, officers.' And once they leave, I'll look at you and see my cum running down your thighs. After that, I want to bring you back in here and do it all over again."

"Damn," I whisper, clearing my throat, still unable to look away from him. "I don't know what I was expecting you to say, but it wasn't that. You want to see your cum running down my thighs?" I question.

His fingers move to my face, pushing my hair back. "I know you're on birth control," he says with a smirk. "And I'm clean, so assuming you are too, yes. I'd like to see my cum running down your thighs."

Thoughts spin furiously through my head. I'm trying to decide what to say next. To determine which words will get me closer to my goal, but he's right here. He's all I can see, all I can feel, and my cunt is throbbing, begging for release, shouting at me to say yes. To agree to everything he just said. Finally, I settle on the truth. Winning gets him off. It'll probably take me further than any lie ever could.

"Ask me how many people I've fucked without a condom. Ask me how many people I've ever let come inside me," I demand. My nipples are so hard I want to rub my chest over him simply to get a little relief.

"How many people have you let come inside you?" His voice is a low, husky growl. It's full of sex and possession, and I'm certain in that moment I chose correctly.

"None. You would be the first."

"None?"

"No," I say with a shrug. "I'm big on safe sex. I've never wanted to let anyone do that before."

His eyes are almost entirely black, and his breath hitches when he says, "Truth or dare?"

"Truth," I answer, already knowing what his question is going to be.

"Do you want to let me?"

"Yes. I want to know what it feels like to have you come inside me. I want you to do everything you said you wanted to do."

"Yes?" he verifies.

"Yes," I agree.

"Get your ass out onto the deck, Alyssa," he orders, a mixture of need and demand straining his voice.

"Make me."

"Oh, this is going to be fun," he states as he bends and scoops me up, throwing me over his shoulder in a fireman's carry. A slight 'oof' escapes as my stomach hits his shoulder. He carries me across the room, through the door, to the deck, and as he does, I slide my hands over his ass, applying more pressure as I snake one hand between his legs, massaging him through the denim of his jeans. "Fuck," he groans before setting me on my feet in front of an outdoor couch, which he drops onto, tugging me with him until I'm straddling him. My skirt is fanned around us, and only the thin layer of fabric from my bodysuit—which snaps apart—and his jeans are separating us. I bring my mouth to his, and his hands slide under my skirt, up my legs. His thumbs stop just shy of where I want them—caressing my inner thighs—as I rock my hips into him.

I'd say I was dry humping him, but there's nothing dry about this. I am so wet that I'm going to leave imprints of my labia and cunt stamped on the front of his jeans. The friction of his fly brushing over my clit feels amazing, and I do it again, moaning. I'm no longer uneasy about the trees pressing in around us. The idea that someone could be out there watching us is clearly a turn-on for Mark, and I find myself enjoying it too.

"Your skin is so soft," he says into my mouth, his thumbs continuing to tease me, refusing to touch me where I want to be touched.

"I want you, Mark," I breathe, rhythmically rubbing against him. "I'm so wet, and I need you to touch me. I want to sit on your face. I want to feel the head of your dick stroking my clit and teasing the opening of my cunt. I need you to fuck me." I drop my hands to his fly, but he grabs them, stopping me.

"No, not yet. Keep going, Alyssa. Just like this. Please."

I grind my hips into him more forcefully, my nails digging into his palms, which have my hands trapped between us, and bite his bottom lip. He moans my name again.

"I want to taste you," I say. "I want to see your face when you come inside me. And then when your cum is dripping down my legs, I want to watch you lick it off me."

He lets go of my hands and drops one of his between my thighs, ripping the snaps of the bodysuit apart, and then one of his fingers is circling around my opening.

"Yes, Mark. More," I plead, as I move my hands to undo his fly and slide my hand into his boxers, gripping him. There's already a bead of pre-cum on the head of his cock, and I want to lick it off him as I stare into his eyes, but he said something about going down on me first, so I don't. If I wrap my lips around his dick right now, neither of us will stop. He is so hard, and so thick, that I know having him inside me is going to feel amazing.

He twitches and gasps as I stroke his shaft. "God, I want you," he says as he plunges his fingers into me, and my hands tighten around him. "You're so wet," he continues, his fingers thrusting into me, over and over. "You want me too."

"Yes," I moan as I ride his hand.

"Say it."

"I already did," I tell him, knowing that arguing with him is a turn-on for both of us. And doing it while his fingers are stroking the walls of my cunt and my hand is wrapped around his dick is just icing on the cake.

"If you want me to keep going, say it again," he demands.

"I want you, Mark. I want you to fuck me in ways that I've never wanted anyone to fuck me." I place my lips next to his ear and whisper, "And I'm going to fuck you in ways that you've never been fucked."

He pushes me away. "Off. Take it all off," he orders, ripping his sweater off.

I wait until his eyes are focused on me, and then I stand in front of him and turn around. I unzip the skirt and shimmy it off over my hips, glancing behind me as I do. Mark's eyes are locked on my ass, and there's a stupid grin on his face. I think it's safe to say Christmas came early this year. When my skirt falls to the floor, pooling around my ankles, I bend over and slowly unzip my boots. I'm still wearing the bodysuit, but the crotch is unsnapped, and he has a full view of everything. The deck creaks as he stands, and suddenly the length of his dick is pressed between my cheeks, and his hands are on either side of my ass, holding me in place. I grind myself against him, and his sharp intake of breath is so hot.

"Is your ass tingling?" Mark asks, his voice a low rumble of unmet need.

I grind into him again. "My entire body is tingling."

"Take it off," he repeats, tugging at the bodysuit.

I stand up, trapping his cock between my cheeks, and wriggle out of the bodysuit, enjoying every twitching gasp I wring from him. His hands wrap around me. One hand goes to my boobs, teasing my nipples, and the other drops between my legs, making lazy circles around my clit. I let my head fall back against his shoulder, going almost boneless in his arms, whispering his name as he brings me to the edge and backs off, again and again, until I'm whimpering, "Please."

Finally, he drops his hand from my tits and thrusts two fingers from one hand inside me as the other strokes my clit. I grind my ass into his cock as I come around his fingers, screaming his name for the first time. When rational thought returns, I turn in his arms, reaching to slide him inside me. I want all of him filling me.

He realizes what I'm trying to do and grabs my hands, stopping me. "No. I want you on my face. I want to bury my tongue in you and taste every inch of you, and I know you want me to."

"But—" I begin, ready to have him now.

"No," he repeats, tugging me toward the couch and lying down on it. "On my face. I want to watch you touch yourself while I do it. I want to hear you scream my name when you come. Again," he says, with a glint in his eyes. "After that, I'm going to fuck your face until I can't take it anymore. Then we'll really have some fun."

I move into position, my knees framing his head. His hands wrap around my waist, pulling me down onto his face, his tongue thrusting inside me, stiff and warm and wet. I trail my hands over my boobs, playing with them as he takes in the show. Initially, I let Mark control the pace, his hands around my waist setting the speed, but as desire builds, I drop a hand to my clit, touching myself as I ride his face faster and faster.

"I'm so close," I pant, increasing the speed. "I'm going to come. I'm—Mark!" The scream that tears from my throat this time is even louder than last time, and lights appear, filtering through the trees in the distance. I fold over him, my body crumpling as I whisper, "I think I just woke up your neighbors."

He shifts me off him, sitting up, pulling me to his chest. "Good," he says, his mouth finding mine. Our kiss is slow and languid this time, and I taste myself on his tongue. I can't wait for him to taste himself on mine, and I reach my hand between his thighs. He's still hard, and he groans as I begin stroking him.

"It's your turn now."

He stands, and my hand falls away. "Get on your knees."

I look at the hardwood deck. "No," I reply and watch the confusion flit across his face. "I will happily blow your brains out, but I will do it from the comfort of this couch. Kneeling on this deck would hurt, and not in a fun way."

His eyes scan my naked body.

"Yes," I reply, giving voice to his very obvious thoughts. "I *am* still that mouthy naked."

He growls in frustration and rips a cushion from the couch, throwing it on the deck. "Get on your knees," he repeats.

I look at the cushion, then back at his face, a grin spreading across mine as I move onto it. "Yeah. Okay. That works. I like a problem solver," I manage to get out before his hands wind their way into my hair and his dick fills my mouth, hitting the back of my throat, making me gag and my eyes water. I cup his balls, massaging them as he thrusts into my mouth like its only purpose is to get him off. His hands are in full control of my head, and I have no say about the depth or the speed or anything, and it's incredibly hot. I want all of him so badly. I can taste the salty, acrid flavor of semen leaking from his cock, and if I weren't so desperate to feel him come inside me, I'd stay here until he blew the entire load straight down my throat. Maybe some other time.

Instead, I slide a finger between my legs, inside me, lubricating it, and then before Mark can object, I slide it into his anus and begin massaging his prostate. The look on his face quickly goes from surprise to confusion to pure bliss, and he shoves me away.

"Damn it, Alyssa!" he gasps, pinching the base of his penis, and I grin. Knowing that I had him so close to orgasming that he had to make me stop feels just as incredible as anything else we've done tonight. He closes his eyes, gathers his composure, and then pulls me to my feet. His cock is pressing into me, and I grind against it, fighting down a moan as I stare into his eyes. "I want you to do that again later," he tells me, and I kiss him, aware that he can taste himself on my tongue. "Turn around and put your hands on the railing," he orders when I finally break off the kiss.

I immediately comply.

"Tell me if this is too much for your elbow," he says as he nudges my legs further apart and steps between them, the head of his dick rubbing my clit—slowly, rhythmically.

My hips jerk. It feels amazing. I don't care about my elbow. "Mark," I groan, "I want more."

"What's the magic word?" It sounds like the restraint of not burying himself in me and fucking me senseless is causing him physical pain, and maybe it is. I've already orgasmed twice, and he's been denying himself the entire time.

"Please. Please give me more."

He changes the angle so that the head of his penis is lined up with my opening, and I try to press back into him, but he pulls away. "No. I'm in control right now. You only get what I decide to give you, when I decide to give it to you."

He strokes just the first inch of himself in and out, in and out of me, over and over again, until the only sound I can make is a keening moan of, "MarkMarkMark, please."

"Tell me you want me to come inside you, Alyssa."

"I do," I beg. "I do want you to come inside me." I might explode if he makes me wait any longer. "Please," I plead one more time, and he slams into me. A guttural shout that's a mixture of pleasure and raw need tears from my throat as he bends me further over the railing, pounding into me. I'm screaming his name, and I'm screaming for more, and I'm just screaming because of how good it feels to let him have his way with me.

He pulls out and spins me around roughly, my back digging into the wooden railing as he slides inside me again. One hand snakes into my hair, and he keeps my face focused on his. "I'm almost there, Alyssa." He wants me to watch him come. Or I said I wanted to watch him. I don't even know. But I do want to watch. Like I've never wanted anything.

Our screams merge as his hips jerk and hot, wet cum fills my cunt, deepening everything and pushing me over the edge. The look on his face can only be described as rapture. I'm screaming his name, and he's screaming mine, and I don't even know what the hell just happened, but I've never had an orgasm that was anywhere close to as good as that one, and I've slept with a lot of people.

"Holy fuck," I whisper as Mark drags me over to the couch, cradling me against his body. "What did you do to me?" I ask as his fingers make slow circles on my ribs.

"I could ask you the same thing."

"I think you just ruined sex for me forever."

"What do you mean?" Mark asks.

"I'm going to compare anyone else I ever sleep with to this—to you—and they're always going to come up short," I murmur as I stare up at the stars. They're very bright out here.

Mark's hand stills on my waist. "I wasn't anticipating you were going to be having sex with other people," he says cautiously.

"What?"

"I wasn't intending this to be a one-night stand. I wouldn't have brought you back here if I just wanted to hit it and quit it."

"Are you suggesting that this is a thing? You and me? We barely know each other."

"I'm suggesting—" Mark's words are cut short by the rumble of an engine and headlights approaching his house. "Shit," he mutters, scooping his clothes up and tossing his sweater at me before pulling on his boxers. "We're not done talking about this, but you may want to put that on. We have company."

I tug his sweater over my head at the same time a car door slams. Then a flashlight switches on.

"Hi," Mark greets, and the beam swivels to him.

"Are you the property owner?" the voice behind the flashlight questions.

"Yes, that's me."

"We received some noise complaints."

"Ah. Yes." Mark's eyes dance to mine, and then back to the flashlight below. "Sorry about all the screaming, officers."

# Chapter 8
# A Parade of Shame

I WAKE UP SPRAWLED ACROSS MARK'S TORSO WITH morning light filtering through the trees into his bedroom. None of the windows have curtains. I know you can't see anything from the road, having tried and failed to do so myself, but still. The man seems like he might have a bit of an exhibitionist kink. I file the thought away for later. I expect it will come in useful at some point.

He's passed out beneath me, and I study the lines of his face for a few moments, then drop my gaze to run over his body. In the morning light, he's very pretty and very hard. I wonder if I could get him off before he woke up. I want to wrap my hand around him and find out, but I know it's a bad idea.

The police left last night after they realized who Mark was, and he signed some autographs for them. I had no idea anyone cared about sports coaches at all—let alone that they wanted their autographs. Once the police left, he tried to redirect the conversation back to the two of us. However, I successfully diverted his attention to the cum dripping down my thigh, and watching him lick it off me while I ran my hands through his hair was easily as hot as anything else that happened. I know I won't be able to escape the conversation this morning, though, and I'm already dreading it.

On the one hand, I'm usually trying to help people *resolve* their issues, not give them new ones. And I know if Mark were to find out I'm using him to gain access to his team... Well. It wouldn't be great. He already has trust issues, and what I'm doing is so far beyond violating his trust. I'm basically going to douse it in kerosene, light it on fire, watch it burn, and then take the ashes and throw them into the sea. And for whatever stupid reason, he's decided to let me in. To trust me. Me, the one person who deserves it least.

But on the other hand, if having the conversation gets me closer to my goals and means I get to keep having the kind of sex we had last night... Well. I won't say no to either of those things. It was seriously the best sex of my life. And letting him come inside me, while definitely a stupid decision, showed me what I've been missing out on. If I'm lucky, he'll never realize I was using him, and I'll be able to figure out a way to end things amicably. Mark's not an idiot, though. So the chances of that seem low.

If I didn't *need* to be here, I would gather my clothes, which are still on the deck and probably soaked in dew from being there overnight, and sneak off.

His chest noticeably rises and falls, shifting my body atop his, and he opens his eyes, blinking them blearily a few times. "Good morning," he says, and his voice is rough with sleep. "How long have you been awake?"

"Not long. Maybe ten minutes," I supply, slipping a hand down his stomach, my self-restraint at an end.

The sound he makes when my hand wraps around his dick is like the purr of a large cat. He lets me stroke him for a couple of minutes, and then he pulls me onto him. I can't help but wriggle atop of him even though things are still tender. It doesn't take long until I'm reaching down to slide him inside me, and the sex we have this morning is unhurried and sensual in a way that's totally different from last night. It leaves me wanting to find out all the ways Mark and I can enjoy each other's bodies, and all the feelings it can evoke.

By the time we finally climb out of bed, I have been so thoroughly fucked that it's like I'm riding on a drug-induced high. Mark gives me a pair of his sweatpants and a T-shirt because, as expected, my clothes are damp from sitting outside all night.

Then I'm seated at his kitchen table with a cup of coffee, and he wants to talk. He hasn't said the words out loud yet, but I can tell from the surreptitious glances he's casting in my direction that he does, and he's building up to it. I consider making an excuse about why I have to leave before he can, but I don't. Like it or not, to get to Katie's rapists, I need him. And I need him to feel like it's not too easy. Like he had to work for it. For me. Because it's what he likes. Plus, he'd be suspicious of anything else.

Finally, as he takes a seat across from me, he says, "So, hey. About last night..."

"The part where the police showed up?" I ask, like I don't know what he's talking about when he trails off. "Because that was actually hotter than I thought it would be. Especially the part where you licked your cum off my legs."

A hint of a smile tugs at his lips. "No, but I agree, and I'm willing to do that again anytime. Both parts."

"Okay. So, what about last night? Since you're suddenly acting like a boy who's never kissed a girl before, and we both know that's not true."

"The part where you mentioned sleeping with other people," he says.

"Oh." I let the pause draw on, waiting to see what he'll say, but he seems to have the same idea, so I give in. "Like I said, we barely know one another. I have no expectations of you. You're free to sleep with other people. It's not like—"

"I don't want to sleep with other people," Mark states, cutting me off. "But you're right that we've just met and don't know each other that well. However, I would like us to *get* to know each other and decide where we go from there. I meant it when I said I wasn't intending this to be a one-night stand."

"Okay," I reply, acknowledging that I'm listening.

"And when I said I wasn't anticipating that you'd be having sex with other people, I meant that too. I don't share well."

"No, I imagine not," I murmur. "You want me to agree to enter into a monogamous relationship with you so that we can find out if we want to be in a monogamous relationship?"

"After last night—and this morning—do you really want to sleep with anyone else?"

"No," I admit. "I don't."

"Then what's the problem?"

I want to say, *'What's the problem? Aside from the fact that I'm using you? Aside from the fact that you're going to end up wanting something I can't give you?'* but I don't, because I do actually need this. I simply feel terrible about it. Instead, I say, "You know how I told you last night that I've never been in love?" He nods. "I wasn't lying or exaggerating. I think it's not a thing that I can do, and I think it's very much a thing that you can do. You're going to fall in love with me, and I won't be able to reciprocate those feelings."

Mark bursts out laughing, and I'm sure he's laughing at me, but I don't know what the joke is. Eventually, he gets control of himself enough to say, "Two things. First, you have an extremely large amount of self-confidence."

"What's that supposed to mean?"

"You just walk around the world assuming people are going to fall in love with you? Please, Alyssa." He rolls his eyes. "You know exactly what I mean."

"Fine. What's the second thing?"

"Second, maybe you just haven't met anyone worth falling in love with yet."

It's my turn to laugh. "Pot meet kettle," I finally say. "Now look who's walking around the world assuming people are going to fall in love with him!"

"I merely want a chance, and you can't tell me you don't want the same. I saw the way you were looking at me when I woke up this morning."

"I'm sorry?"

"You were looking at me like you can't get enough of me. The same way you're looking at me right now. I could bend you over the counter and have you begging me to fuck you within three minutes."

"I'd like to see you try," I scoff. Then he begins moving toward me, and I'm afraid he might be right. I hold up a hand. "Not right now, though."

"Oh, so you acknowledge I'm right?"

"God. You really do love winning, don't you?" I say, and he smirks. "Yes, you're freaking right. I want you, okay? I look at you and I instantly think about you bending me over a counter! That doesn't mean I should let you. Great sex isn't the foundation of a long-term relationship."

"No, but it can be the mortar that holds it together. All I'm asking is that you give us the chance to find out."

"And what? Your only criterion is that I don't sleep with other people? And you'll do the same?"

"Yes. And we try it until one or both of us no longer wants to. That's all any relationship ever is anyway. Anyone who believes otherwise is delusional."

I take a deep breath, knowing I'm going to regret this. "Fine." I extend my hand. "Deal." He takes it and pulls me toward him, kissing me. He's such a dick.

"I GOT YOUR GIF," I SAY TO KATIE WHEN I WALK IN THE door. She's in the kitchen, making a smoothie or something. Somehow, I seem to be the only person in the world who thinks food should be eaten, not slurped through a straw. Mark had the audacity to ask me if I wanted a protein shake this morning. Evidently, the look on my face pretty quickly clued him in to the fact that I *never* want a protein shake. "And I hate you."

"So, you wanna watch *Miss Congeniality* tonight?" she asks, looking away from the blender to me. "Oh. My. God. Are you wearing his *clothes*? Does this still count as a walk of shame if they're not your clothes? I feel like the answer is yes."

"Okay. First, I still hate you. You're doing nothing to help your case. Second, yes, we can watch *Miss Congeniality* tonight. I do have to run an errand before that, though. Third, I would have to feel shame for this to be a walk of shame. And fourth, even if I *did* feel shame, I would feel it in style, Kay. It wouldn't be a walk of shame. It would be a parade of shame. Or maybe a sashay of shame."

"I take it he's really good in bed then?" Katie says with a grin.

"What makes you say that?"

"You and your freaking shame parade make me say that! You may as well have his name tattooed on your ass!" Katie states before immediately turning on the blender to drown out my response.

I leave her to her smoothie-making and go get in the shower. Mark raised the idea of taking one together, but that seemed unwise given he had some hockey training-coaching-practice thing to be at this afternoon. I'm honestly relieved that he hasn't tried to mansplain hockey to me. He doesn't seem to mind that I don't care about it at all. But whatever he has to do, I know it's not a game, because they have their first game of the season in a few days. And although no one but me knows it, it's going to be one for the history books.

Vaughn let me know Thursday afternoon that he'd be able to get me the cyanide I requested, and I need to go meet him to pick it up soon. It turns out that the USDA Wildlife Services relies upon it heavily. They use it in M44 devices to control the coyote population. It's a particularly nasty contraption that tricks coyotes into injecting themselves by biting on a lure that, when triggered, causes a canister to eject cyanide into their mouths, poisoning them. The M44 devices have misfired a few times over the years, occasionally killing people too, but they still use them extensively. And it also turns out that the USDA Wildlife Services doesn't pay nearly as well as they should if they don't want their employees to supplement their incomes by skipping setting up the odd device and selling the cyanide to people like Vaughn. And me.

"Each capsule contains a bit less than a gram of sodium cyanide," Vaughn tells me as he hands over a pill bottle. I already know this, but I let him continue talking anyway. He's worried I might screw up and poison myself. I won't. I've spent a lot of time buried in chemistry and toxicology textbooks lately. Unlike the internet, the research you do via a book's table of contents is untraceable. Sodium cyanide has roughly the same density as table sugar. For someone Joey Carmichael's size—reportedly a hundred and eighty pounds—fifteen grams of sodium cyanide, absorbed via the dermal layer, should be more than sufficient to kill him. I did my calculations based on a two-hundred-and-twenty-pound man just to be safe. "And there are seventeen capsules. You need to be careful not to let it come into contact with your skin, and even more careful that it's not exposed to water while you're around."

"I know, Vaughn," I say. Sodium cyanide is cyanide in a salt form. Mix it with water, and it produces hydrogen cyanide, a very, very deadly gas. Much deadlier than sodium cyanide. "I'll be fine. I'll even promise to call and let you know when I'm done."

"You do that. I take it things went well with Mark?"

"Yeah. To use your previous analogy, I believe it's safe to say I've reeled him in."

"And how do you feel about that?" Vaughn asks, looking at me, searching for something. We're sitting on the same park bench as we did last time we met. I was tossing bread to the pigeons earlier, and even though I've long since run out, there's still a small flock gathered around us, waiting to see if more will magically appear.

I shrug. "I don't know. How do you do it?"

"Do what?"

"Make someone fall in love with you knowing you're going to screw them over?" I don't bother saying so, but it's harder than I figured it would be. Or at least I'm feeling guiltier about it than I thought I would.

"Mostly you try not to think about it. Or at least that's what I did, for all that it ever worked out for me," he mutters.

"Meaning?"

"How do you think I met Marjorie?"

"Marjorie was a mark?" I question, not bothering to hide my surprise.

"Yeah, so when I tell you I know a thing or two about catching feelings, I know what I'm talking about, kid. Been there, done that, got the ring to prove it," he states, flashing his left hand at me. "No judgment. I'm only saying I get it. If you ever need to talk."

"I'm good. Thanks. How much do I owe you for this?" I ask, rattling the bottle at Vaughn. I'm sure this can't have been cheap, and I won't ask him to foot the bill for it.

"Don't worry about it. The guy owed me a favor."

"Do I need to worry that he'll hear what's happened and decide to pipe up about it?"

Vaughn snorts. "No."

"You're sure?"

"I'm sure."

"Okay. Thanks again, Vaughn," I say as I stand. I've got things to do. I have to go to the hardware store and pick up a respirator. Just to be safe. I shouldn't need it, but going a little overboard on PPE never hurt anyone.

"Anytime. Remember to let me know you're okay."

# Chapter 9
# Watch Out for the Zamboni Drivers

*Hey, when you have a sec, can you check to see if my license is in your car? I haven't seen it since Friday,* I text Mark. It's Monday morning, and I know my license is in his car because I shoved it between the seat and the center console during our date on Friday.

For a while my message shows as unread. It's a bit after eleven, and tomorrow is the team's first real game of the season. I guess there are some preseason games that don't count for anything because when I asked Mark yesterday how he was feeling about tomorrow's game, he mentioned something about those matches going well. He didn't supply any additional details, and I didn't ask any follow-up questions. He should be at their training facilities now though, which is why I'm texting.

About forty minutes later, my phone buzzes, and the responding message from Mark reads, *Yes, I found it. Want to get dinner later? I can bring it with me*

*Any chance I could come pick it up in twenty or thirty minutes and take a rain check on dinner? Maybe for Wednesday? I'm headed to Walla Walla tonight and visiting my dad tomorrow*

*Sure, that works. And yes on Wednesday*

*Okay. Where should I meet you?* I send back.

He drops a pin to what must be some kind of employee lot and replies with instructions to tell the guard that my name is on the visitors' list when I arrive.

*Damn. How am I going to get around that?* I wonder as I sit in my car, staring at Mark's message. I can't park in the employee lot. My car will end up sitting there all night long. It'll be incredibly obvious. Mark will see it whenever he leaves the building and wonder why it's still there. There will be security footage of it parked in an empty lot with me nowhere to be seen. When they start looking at Joey Carmichael's death as a homicide, which they definitely will because that is rather the point, it'll make me an obvious suspect.

I consider parking on the street near the arena and walking to the location where Mark said he'd meet me, but that would force me to leave my car on the street overnight and I'd either end up with parking tickets plastered to my windshield in the best case scenario, or with my car impounded in a tow lot in the worst case.

I run through different ideas about what I could tell Mark to explain why I'm showing up on foot, and the best idea I can come up with isn't very good, but hopefully it's good enough. Maybe he'll be too distracted by whatever preparation is required for the season's first game to give it much thought. I order an Uber and hope for the best. When it arrives, I grab my shoulder bag, which is stuffed with necessities, and climb in, shutting my phone off as I do.

"Are you a hockey fan?" the driver asks enthusiastically upon realizing Tofana Arena is my destination.

"No," I reply shortly, hoping to end the conversation.

He doesn't take the hint, though. "Oh. Well, Tofana Arena is where the Black Bears play. They're our hockey team," he supplies helpfully. "Tomorrow is their season opener."

"That's nice," I answer, looking out the window, taking a mental inventory of what's in my bag for approximately the fiftieth time. Multiple pairs of latex gloves, a baseball cap, goggles, an N95 surgical mask, a respirator, a snap gun for picking locks, a portable door security bar, a roll of tape, several sheets of blank printer paper, a Sharpie, the book I got about the Delta Blues, a water bottle, a couple of granola bars, a black plastic poncho, a penlight, and of course a bottle filled with capsules of sodium cyanide. It's the world's most random assortment of items, all carefully chosen. I shouldn't need anything else, but I also don't know what the non-public areas of the arena are like. I wonder if I should've brought some rope. I have no idea what I'd need it for, but they always find a use for it in the movies.

I make the effort to stop my mind from spiraling. I know it's just nerves making me second-guess my planning, and I know it's going to be worse once I'm sitting there, unmoving, for hours.

"Can you go around to West Basin Avenue?" I ask the driver, and he nods. "You can stop here," I say when the guard station comes into view. "Thanks."

I get out of the car and approach the small building. The guard is seated at a desk inside, flipping through a magazine, and he doesn't notice me standing in front of his sliding glass window. I tap on it, and he jumps. "Hey," I greet after he sets the magazine down and slides the window open. "I'm Alyssa Reed. Mark Eriksson said you should have my name on a list."

He pulls a clipboard from the wall and scans it. "You have ID?" he questions, seeming to find my name on his list.

"No. Sorry."

He doesn't roll his eyes, but it's clear he wants to. "Wait here," he orders with an exasperated huff, sliding the window closed and picking up a phone. A couple of minutes pass, then he opens the window again and says, "You can go through. Head down to the first level, then go left until you see the door. Wait there. Someone will meet you." The window closes. Apparently he's fulfilled his duty and *Popular Mechanics* is calling.

I go down the ramp to the underground lot on foot. It's surprisingly well-lit and doesn't smell of damp or garbage at all. Briefly, I wonder how much money the hockey team brings in. This arena is fairly new, with construction having finished five years ago when the city decided it needed a hockey team, and the however many millions or billions of dollars it took to build was the cost of bringing a franchise to Portland. I'm not sure why any city needs any sports team, but there must be projected financials online from the city planning and zoning meetings where they convinced the comptroller and whatever other officials to allocate tax money to it.

Mark is already waiting at the door by the time I find it. His face breaks into a grin, and my own face matches his. He wanted to get together yesterday, but I begged off, telling him I had some family commitments. I didn't, but after my conversation with Vaughn, my conscience was screaming at me. Much to my surprise, I actually like Mark. But I'm not Vaughn, and Mark's not Marjorie, and I don't see a happily ever after for the two of us.

"Hey, Terrance said you walked in?" he says when I'm close enough he doesn't have to shout.

"Yeah. My car is at the mechanic's right now getting an oil change before I head to Walla Walla. I didn't have time to wait for that or to come here after work, though, so I took an Uber."

"Ah," Mark murmurs once I'm close enough he can take my hands. I push my bag out of the way as he tugs me toward him. Once our bodies are pressed together, he releases one of my hands, weaving his into my hair instead and bringing his face to mine. When my tongue slides over his, I can taste the coffee he's been drinking, and a small groan escapes from my mouth into his.

Mark pivots us until my back is pressing into the cool concrete of the parking structure, pinning me there with his body. Part of me knows I should be smart and break this off, but I'm pretty sure the knowledge that anyone could come into the parking garage at any second is a turn-on for him, and I think he might be blowing off steam. Even though he said things are going well, I'm sure he must still be nervous. Tomorrow will be his first game as head coach—which would be enough to make anyone nervous—and, although he doesn't know it, I'm going to destroy it. I feel fucking awful, and I'm probably also using this to salve my conscience, which is all kinds of screwed up and isn't actually working. Nevertheless, kissing him feels good enough that I don't want to stop. I slide my hands under his shirt as I nip at his bottom lip, and his hips press into mine harder as a deep rumble moves through his chest.

Finally, I force myself to push him away. "We should stop," I say raggedly, watching the pulse jumping in his neck, even though I don't want to stop at all. What I want is to press my lips to his neck and roll my tongue across it at the same time I drop my hand to stroke him until he's coming in my palm. I push the thought away.

"Do you really want to stop?" he asks, sounding just as ragged when I meet his eyes.

"No, but neither of us has time for this right now."

"We could make time," Mark suggests, his fingertips tracing along my jaw, pushing a lock of hair back from my face.

I shake my head. "I really can't. I have patients to see before I leave this afternoon."

"Alright. Here," Mark says, pulling my license from his pocket. "It was wedged between the seats."

"Thanks for finding it, and sorry for disrupting your day," I reply as I take it from him, shove it into my pocket, and make a show of checking my phone. "My return Uber is still fifteen minutes away. Want to give me a tour?"

"You want to see where I work?"

I shrug. "Sure. Why not? Then on Wednesday, I can give you a tour of my office. It's much smaller, though there is a couch."

"A couch?" Mark asks, his eyebrows rising.

"Mhmm."

"You know I'm going to be thinking about that couch for the next two days."

"Wondering what color it is?" I tease.

"Something like that," Mark mutters. "Well, come on, then. I'll show you around." He holds a badge up to the card reader next to the door, and the door unlocks.

*Step one—access to the building—complete*, I think.

"There are two floors beneath the main arena floor," Mark says as we walk down a long, dark grey hallway. "This floor is primarily the team's floor. It has our practice ice, training and rehab facilities, practice locker room, my office and so on."

"Practice ice?" I question. "There are two ice rinks? Why?"

"Well, the one up above, on the arena floor, is typically only there on game days during the season. They do a lot of other events on non-game days, and they tear down the ice rink for that. Concerts mostly, but sometimes MMA, boxing, or wrestling events, and every now and again there will be some weird religious conventions. The practice ice is always here."

"Does that mean there are two Zambonis, too? Have you guys got a game day locker room?" I wasn't anticipating there being two sets of locker rooms. That's going to throw a wrench into things.

"Yes to both," Mark says with a hint of amusement. "Everyone is always so interested in the Zambonis."

"Well…" I start but trail off.

"Yes?" Mark prompts.

"No. Never mind. It's nothing."

"You were going to say the Zambonis are the only interesting part of the whole thing, weren't you?"

I shrug, but glance over when I feel his eyes boring into me. "Fine. Yes! But it's true. It's so true that you knew it without me even having to say it!" I assert.

He laughs. "Anyway, if you keep going down this hallway and hang a right when it ends, you'll get to the Zamboni room. I'd show you, but the last thing I want is for you to meet the Zamboni driver and decide there are better prospects out there."

"Whatever," I grumble, reaching out to shove his shoulder. He stumbles a step before regaining his balance with a smile on his face. "So, show me the other things you mentioned. Maybe the Zamboni will be out on the practice ice."

"It's not."

"How sad for me," I quip.

"Indeed. Anyway. This is the equipment room," Mark comments as he stops at a door and opens it.

"Is this what a hockey store looks like?" I ask as I look at a well-organized room filled with rows of sticks, skates, jerseys, and pads. There's a lot of black and amber, and the team's snarling bear logo is everywhere.

"Something like that." He shuts the door, and we continue walking down the hallway. "The locker room is up ahead on the left, and the drying and laundry rooms are—" Mark's words cut off when someone steps out of the locker room, and he grabs my hand, pulling me to a stop before taking half a step in front of me.

"Hi Coach," someone says. *Garret Fischer*, my brain supplies a fraction of a second later, and I have to fight to keep my hand from tensing on Mark's when the realization hits me. His tone is possibly the most disdainful I've ever heard one person use when addressing another. I'd be impressed if I weren't so busy trying to restrain myself from violence.

"Fischer," Mark begins with a warning note in his voice.

"Garret Fischer," he says, ignoring Mark and extending his hand toward me.

Mark steps between us before I can decide how to respond. "Why aren't you on the ice right now?"

"I pulled a muscle," Garret replies, not even trying to be convincing. "I'm headed to see the PT."

"Then go," Mark orders. Garret's eyes flick to me, then he turns and walks in the opposite direction.

"Friend of yours?" I murmur once he's out of earshot.

"The bane of my existence is more like it." Mark forges ahead, giving me an overview of a few other areas prior to ending in his office, but his mood has obviously soured. "When should I meet you on Wednesday?" he asks after shutting the door.

"My last pa—" I'm interrupted by the ringing of Mark's office phone.

"Sorry," he says before picking it up with a quick, "Hello." He pauses to listen. "No. That's not what…" He pauses again.

Seeing my chance, I whisper, "I have to go. I'll text you about Wednesday."

"Hold on," Mark interjects, cutting off whoever is speaking and placing them on hold. "You're okay finding your way out?" he asks.

"Yeah. I'll be fine. I'll be driving tonight, so I'll call you sometime tomorrow. Good luck."

"Thanks. Sorry about this," he says, gesturing vaguely.

"No problem. I'm the one who interrupted your day." I press a quick kiss to his cheek, then make my way to the door as Mark resumes his call.

I retrace our steps, remembering the public restroom we passed. Considering I have yet to see another woman, it's as good a spot as any to spend the remainder of the day hiding out. When I enter the bathroom, the lights flicker on. They must be controlled by a motion-activated sensor, and the fact that they were off proves this bathroom doesn't get much use. I open my bag, pinning it between the edge of the sink and my hips, and pull out the roll of tape, the Sharpie, and a sheet of paper. Then I write *Out of Order* on the paper and tape it onto the second to last stall before going in and locking the door. The stall is nice, as bathroom stalls go. It's one of the ones that has walls and a door that go all the way to the floor.

I take a seat on the floor and pull the book from my bag. It's going to be a while.

It's just after midnight when I finally unlock the bathroom stall and creep out. I finished *Deep Blues* by Robert Palmer a couple of hours ago and have been staring at the wall, bored out of my mind since then. I should have brought a second book.

During the time I spent hiding out, a grand total of two people came into the bathroom. It's safe to say the NHL is a boys' club. And it's never a good thing when a microcosm of men is fawned over by a mesocosm of women. All it does is make those men believe they deserve attention for existing. In the best case, you end up with a bunch of guys who have no clue how many misogynistic viewpoints they hold. In the worst, you end up with guys like Joey Carmichael and Garret Fischer who think they're entitled to women's bodies simply because they want them.

No one should ever be put on a pedestal. Especially not a professional athlete.

I open my bag, putting on my baseball cap and tucking my hair into it. Then I pull on the N95 surgical mask, a pair of gloves, and the black plastic poncho. I slide my bag under the poncho before stepping into the hall. The hat and mask will obscure my face, the gloves will ensure I don't leave fingerprints anywhere I shouldn't, and the poncho will obscure my clothes and body shape, just in case they're monitoring any of these halls with CCTV. The baseball cap has the California state flag—the Bear Flag—emblazoned on it. Mostly because I was feeling petty. California is adjacent to Oregon, and in a fight between a grizzly and a black bear, a grizzly wins every single time. It was the closest I could come to poetic justice without writing a manifesto.

The hall is quiet and dimly lit. I go to the practice locker room first, since it's on this floor and I know where it's located. I can use it to get my bearings before trying to find the one on the main floor. When I reach the door, it's locked with a keypad. I have the snap gun, but I only want to use that as a last resort, so I take out the penlight and shine it over the lock. The only number on the keypad that shows signs of use is the nine. *They really can't be that dumb,* I think, but I press nine-nine-nine-nine anyway, and the light flashes green. When I try the door, it's unlocked. I bet they use the same code for the arena-game-day-whatever locker room. There's almost no chance they're going to make them remember more than one code if the only code they can remember is 'just press nine for a while.'

There's a bench with stalls behind it wrapping around the room. The stalls are marked with both a last name and a number—presumably the same number that's on their jerseys, but I haven't bothered learning anyone's numbers, so I'm not certain of that. I find the one labeled *Carmichael* and then double-check that there are no other Carmichaels on the team. There aren't. I open his stall door and find exactly what I was expecting—a bunch of hockey gear plus some other odds and ends. I close it and decide to take the opportunity to do some recon on the other four players. I'm not going to poison them all

—that would be too easy—but I may be able to learn something useful while I'm here. There's nothing of interest in Garret Fischer's stall. There's an EpiPen in Matt Davidson's, and I wonder what he's allergic to. In Rhys Steichen's stall, I find an address book and shove it in my pocket. Either he'll assume he misplaced it or someone took it. Brandon Miller also has nothing of interest.

I leave the locker room and look for stairs to the next floor. At the same time, I'm starting to wonder how I'm going to get out of here. I'd been thinking I'd go out the way I came in, but if that guard station is staffed twenty-four hours, which it likely is, the chances of being seen are pretty high. Do I wait until daylight and try to leave via one of the main floor exits? That seems just as dangerous.

It occurs to me that this may be a terrible idea, and I consider abandoning my plan. If I leave now, everything will be okay. They'll only ever check the security footage if I give them a reason to. A reason like poisoning Joey Carmichael with cyanide while he's on the ice. I don't though.

I find the stairs and climb up them, wondering if there was ever a moment where my dad considered stopping, but didn't. I'll have to go see him tomorrow. Maybe I'll ask. I reserved a hotel room online and checked in using their app, so at least I'll have that to make it look like I spent the night in Walla Walla if anyone ever checks. It won't stand up to scrutiny if they look too closely, but hopefully no one ever will. I pause to consider my exit strategy again at the top of the stairs. As dangerous as going out the way I came in is, it's still the best option. I'll just have to hope that whatever guard is there now is as distracted as Terrance was. When I open the door, I place a wad of tape into the strike plate to ensure I don't get locked out. Then, I follow the same path as I did below, hoping the game-day locker room will be in an identical location on this floor. If it's not, I'm going to be aimlessly wandering around for a while.

I'm almost to the locker room door when I hear footsteps in the distance. I freeze, but the footsteps are moving away from me rather than toward me, so I hurry the last few feet to the door and press nine-nine-nine-nine into the lock. The light flashes green and I'm in.

# Kill the Puckers

The room is dark, and I find Joey Carmichael's stall in the same place as it was downstairs. I open the stall door, searching for his gloves and his socks. When I find them, I remove my N95 mask, replace it with the respirator from my bag, and put on the goggles. Then, I take out the bottle of cyanide pills and begin splitting the capsules apart. There are seventeen capsules, which means four are going into each glove and sock. That'll leave one extra. I'll smear a bit of it into his mouth guard and dump the remainder in his jockstrap.

The cyanide is like a powdery table salt, and he might feel it when he puts on his gloves or socks, but I'm counting on the adrenaline of the first game to keep him from examining things too closely.

Skin contact with sodium cyanide alone likely wouldn't be a big deal, but add some sweat into the mix—say the way Joey Carmichael's hands and feet probably do when he's in the middle of a hockey game, and it's suddenly a very big deal. If I planned this right, and Joey Carmichael is part of the second line this season, as everyone is predicting, he should drop dead on the ice before the first intermission. I wonder if they'll play the rest of the game or cancel it when that happens.

Initially, people will speculate that it was a heart attack. But within a few days, they'll know it wasn't. Then things should really get interesting.

After I finish emptying the last of the pills into his gear, I close the stall door and check the stalls of the four other rapists. These are much more impersonal than the ones in the practice locker room were. They're all filled with black and amber uniforms, but other than that, I find nothing. I remove my gloves, shove them into my pocket inside out, and replace them with a fresh pair. Then, I take off the respirator, shove it back into my bag, and put the N95 mask back on as I listen at the door. Finally, hearing nothing, I step into the hallway and make my way to the stairs once more. I remove the tape from the strike plate prior to closing the door, then leave the building, pausing before each intersection to listen for movement, but I don't encounter anyone else on my way out.

Less than ten minutes later, I'm standing in the parking garage, staring at the guard station. There's a light on, but I can't see anyone inside. I approach it cautiously, trying to keep to the shadows as much as possible, but eventually the exit narrows so much that I have no choice but to come into view of whoever is on duty. When I do, the guard is asleep with his head on the desk, using his arms as a pillow.

I sidle past the guard, out onto the street, walking a couple of miles—taking off the poncho, mask, and gloves after the first mile, putting them all back into my bag—before catching a bus back toward my office.

There are only a handful of people on the bus when I climb on—a couple of homeless people trying to be somewhere safe and warm for the night plus a few people probably going to or from late-night jobs.

# Chapter 10
# That Guy is Poisoned

I'M SITTING ALONE AT A TABLE IN THE PRISON VISITORS' room, waiting for my dad to be brought out. There are bored-looking guards standing against each wall. Their eyes scan the room, but I can't tell if they're actually paying attention or if they're lost in their own personal daydreams. I try to make it up here to see my dad once a month, but it's close to a four-hour drive each way. In the almost twenty years I've been coming to visit him, I've never seen the guards do anything more than lean against the wall or occasionally bark out some orders to make people move apart if they're too close for too long.

The room itself is nothing like you see on most TV shows. There are no glass panes separating the prisoners from their visitors. No plastic phone receivers. No one is handcuffed. The room looks more like a cafeteria than anything. There are even vending machines. The small windows are high above the floor and covered with metal grates, though, and the light that bleeds through them is torpid and weak. Between the windows, the guards, and the prisoners' beige uniforms, you can never quite forget where you are.

At the next table, there's a mother and daughter visiting with a man—likely the girl's father. Or at least I assume it's a mother, daughter, and father. I suppose it could be an aunt and her niece. Jeanette was the one who usually brought me here to see my dad when I was that age. By then, my mom was no longer around. She's probably still alive. Somewhere. I don't know for sure though, because the last time I saw her was at my fourth birthday party. She left to 'visit family' not long after that and never came back. She called on my sixth birthday, and again on my ninth—but I haven't heard from her since that last phone call. I could hire a private investigator to find her, I guess. Hell, I could probably even ask Vaughn to do it. But why bother? She could find me easily enough if she wanted, and clearly she doesn't want to.

There's clattering near the doors opposite my table, and then a minute later, my dad is escorted into the room. His eyes find me within a second. Not that it's hard. There are only twenty tables in the room. We're not exactly playing *Where's Waldo*. Visits are granted on a first-come, first-served basis and can last a maximum of three hours, so you never know how long you'll be waiting when you show up. Today's a Tuesday in the middle of the day, so I only had to sit in the waiting room for about fifteen minutes.

"Hey dad," I greet as he takes a seat on the bench opposite me, running a hand through his short-cropped, salt-and-pepper hair.

"Hey Alyssa. You look tired."

I snort. "Thanks dad. Just what every woman wants to hear." I don't mind, though. Not really. I'd prefer the truth to a lie any day, and it's true. I only got about three hours of sleep. After I made it back to my office last night, I immediately hopped in my car to drive up here. It was after five in the morning when I pulled into the hotel parking lot and then collapsed face down on the bed until my alarm woke me up at eight-thirty.

"The hair looks good," he comments.

*That's right*, I think. *I forgot he hadn't seen it.* "Thanks," I say again.

"Gotta ask why, though."

"I'll trade you. An answer for an answer. You don't bullshit me, and I won't bullshit you."

"Alright. You go first."

"Did you ever consider stopping? Before the police raided our house? Before it all came crashing down?"

"Honestly?" he asks, and I nod, already knowing I'm not going to like the answer. "No, not seriously. Sometimes I'd say it was the last one, but I never really meant it. I never really believed it. When all you see are the angles… well. I wasn't built to just sit around and notice them."

"Yeah. I know."

"You got a diagnosis for that?" he questions, only partially joking.

"About half a dozen."

"Want to tell me what they are?"

I raise my eyebrows. "Do you actually want to hear what they are?"

"No. I don't care. But I'll listen if you ever want to tell me."

"I know," I say. My dad's a high-functioning psychopath with both narcissistic and obsessive-compulsive tendencies. In another life, he could've run a Fortune 500 company. It's not that he doesn't love me. He does. But he literally can't help himself. Randall Reed sees the angles, and he has to prove he's the smartest person in the room. He loves me, but he loves the adrenaline rush of getting away with it—and it doesn't matter what *it* is—more. However, he's not lying when he says he'll listen if I ever want to tell him what's wrong with him. Because even if he doesn't love me the most, he does love me. "Your turn."

"The hair?" he says, inclining his head.

"I dyed it for a guy."

"I thought we said no bullshitting."

"No bullshit. I dyed it for a guy. I needed to get close to him, and he seems to have a thing for black hair, so here we are."

"Do I want to know more than that?"

I shrug. "No idea. Vaughn sends his best, though."

"Alyssa, what the fuck are you doing?" my dad hisses.

"Nothing you wouldn't do, dad. Only I'm going to do it better than you. Learn from your mistakes and all that. Did you ever think about trying to find mom?"

"Not really. She was gone, and I was busy," he says like it's that simple, and I'm pretty sure, for him, it was. "Why? Are you thinking about trying to find her?"

"Not really. She's gone, and I'm busy."

My dad smiles, and the corners of his eyes crinkle. "I hope you know what you're doing, Alyssa. I'd hate it if I were released just in time for you to get locked up. Wouldn't be much of a homecoming."

"Chess?" I ask, changing the subject. "If I remember correctly, I'm one up on you."

It's nearly three in the afternoon when I plop into the driver's seat of my car. The hockey game tonight is scheduled to begin at seven. I should be getting back into town right as it's starting. I haven't decided what I'm going to do tonight yet. Do I go to a sports bar so I can watch the carnage? Because there's no way I'll put the game on in the condo with Katie there. Or do I go home, act surprised when I hear the news, and then watch the highlights—or lowlights, depending on your perspective, I suppose—on the internet afterward?

I designed this train wreck, and I should be woman enough to watch it unfold. Some of these guys are sure to have families who love them despite the fact that they're scum. But the guilt I'll feel for putting their family members through an unexpected, untimely death is worth it to make sure they can't ever hurt anyone else. I guess I believe in the greater good, and the greater good says they need to pay. And if the judge and the jury had gotten it right, then I wouldn't have to play executioner, but they didn't, so I do. It's not like anyone else is signing up for the job.

I grab my phone and text Katie to let her know I'll be home around eight-thirty, and then I send Mark a quick message wishing him good luck tonight. I refrain from including the words *'knock 'em dead'* anywhere in my text. Because I'm thoughtful like that.

# Kill the Puckers

The sports bar is dimly lit, and the bulk of the bar's lighting is pouring out of the eighty-whatever-inch TVs on the wall. There's no sound coming from their speakers, though. It's an unwritten rule of sports bars everywhere: the TVs must always be on, and the sound must always be off.

It's a few minutes into the game, and it's hard to keep track of what's going on. The Black Bears are wearing black and amber uniforms, and the other team is wearing red and white. Aside from that, the figures are completely ambiguous and totally interchangeable—in fact, I'm pretty sure every single person on both teams is white. Mostly, the players just look like flies buzzing around the ice, and they keep climbing in and out of the bench, which seems like a misnomer. Presumably, Mark is somewhere among the sea of players crammed into the space, but I haven't been able to pick him out at all. The cameras are constantly moving and cutting and zooming, and I think I'd have a better idea of what the hell was going on if they simply held still and showed the entire rink. As it is, I'm wondering how people don't get motion sick trying to watch this.

Joey Carmichael is number thirty-four—I remember it from the label on his stall—and I'm trying to keep track of him, but between the camera jump cuts and how often who's on the ice seems to change, it's next to impossible. He might keel over on the bench for all I know. What a travesty that would be.

"Is the camera work always this bad?" I mutter, jabbing at the ice in my soda with my straw.

Vaughn laughs from his spot on the stool next to mine before saying, "You get used to it."

"Are you secretly a hockey fan?"

"Less a fan and more exposed by virtue of being in places like this."

"Can you tell what's going on?" I inquire.

"Some. The Black Bears' offense looks strong. And the other team looks under-conditioned in comparison."

"How can you tell?"

"Do you actually want to know?" Vaughn questions, side-eyeing me.

I consider it for a minute. "No." I jab my straw back into my drink and return to trying to keep an eye on jersey thirty-four, but the stupid cameras won't cooperate. It's pissing me off.

"Thought so. Besides. You can ask your coach about it if you want to know."

"He's not my coach," I snap.

"You want to tell me what's bothering you?"

"Everything. Nothing. No. I don't want to talk about it," I tell him finally. I'm dreading talking to Mark after the game, or tomorrow, or whenever. Do I pretend like I know what happened or do I act surprised? Do I pretend like I have no idea who Joey Carmichael was or do I say, *'Oh, that rapist?'* I shouldn't care about lying to Mark, but I think maybe I do, and I'm a bit disappointed in myself. It'd be best to steer clear of the topic entirely, but I can't do that without looking like I live under a rock, and I'm certain Mark isn't a fan of dumb women. It's not like I haven't considered this before, but as with those other times, there's no good solution, and this is the first time it's actually felt real. I could ask Vaughn. He might have some suggestions. I don't though. I change the subject, saying, "My dad says 'hi,' by the way."

"You told him what you're doing?" Vaughn asks, sounding surprised.

"No. Just that you said hello," I answer distractedly. Joey Carmichael is back on the ice. Or maybe he's been there all along. I seriously have no idea what's happening on this TV. I've seen stampedes that make more sense.

If I did my calculations right, he should be beginning to feel the effects of the cyanide right about now. He's probably starting to get a bit dizzy. Maybe he's feeling like he can't quite catch his breath. Cyanide is a COX inhibitor—meaning that in large enough doses, it interferes with the body's ability to utilize oxygen. On top of that, it interferes with ATP production via a related mechanism. In short, it causes chemical asphyxiation. And contrary to popular belief, diagnosing cyanide poisoning isn't obvious because cyanide is a tightly regulated substance, and it can look like so many other things. Things that are much more common. Things like a heart attack. Only no amount of CPR or defibrillation will save someone from cyanide poisoning. People believe the smell of almonds is a dead giveaway, but it's not—especially not in this instance—and the reason is twofold. First, when I was poking through Joey Carmichael's gear prior to slipping cyanide into it, it reeked. I don't think you could smell anything over that. Second—and again, contrary to popular belief—not everyone can smell cyanide.

I swirl my straw in my glass. The camera is focused on two guys battling over a puck when it suddenly cuts to a figure lying face down on the ice, unmoving. The number thirty-four is written large across his back. There's a handful of seconds where everyone is frozen and no one is sure what's going on. Then the players on the ice rush toward him. Next, the players from the bench are spilling over onto the ice. And finally—*finally*—the camera is holding still. Another moment goes by, and then there are medics rushing onto the ice, carrying med kits.

*It's probably hard to get electrodes on a hockey player,* I realize as I watch them moving toward his motionless body. Even if you cut off their jersey, there are going to be pads to contend with underneath that.

One of the medics drops to his knees beside Joey Carmichael—who's been rolled over and is now on his back—and pulls a pair of trauma shears from his kit. About ten seconds pass before someone with some common sense cuts to a different camera, and Mark dominates the screen, his arms folded across his chest, his eyes narrowed.

I lean forward without meaning to, studying his face. It's not like I've known him all that long, but still. I feel like I know him well enough to read the expression on his face, and right now he appears to be a combination of irritated and disinterested. It's not what I was expecting, and Mark suddenly got a whole lot more interesting. Not that he wasn't interesting before… but now? Now I'm interested in more than just his body and the access he provides me to Katie's rapists.

I turn to Vaughn, intending to ask him what else there is to know about Mark, but I close my mouth, leaving the words unsaid. Mark likes the fact that I haven't obsessively Googled him, so I might be better off letting him tell me the things he wants me to know. I decide to trust my instincts and grab my phone instead.

*You look pissed*, I text.

A few seconds later, he's on the TV, pulling his phone from his pocket. He glances at it, his brow furrowing before his eyes dart up, looking for the camera. He grimaces when he finds it, then turns away.

Vaughn is staring at me when I set my phone down, but he merely says, "What now?"

"I haven't decided. I'll let you know when I do. Thanks for keeping me company tonight, Vaughn. And for everything else," I state as I stand. The TV has cut to sports broadcasters. I have no idea if the game will resume or not, and I don't really care. I toss thirty dollars on the bar to cover my soda and Vaughn's Old Fashioned before walking out. It's not even eight.

It's eight-fifteen when I walk into the condo. Katie is sitting in front of the TV, with her eyes glued to it. She barely even looks in my direction. She just says, "He's dead." Her tone sounds almost awestruck.

"Who's dead?" I ask. I haven't told Katie what I'm doing, because I'd rather she think the universe has her back than me. There's something about believing karma is real and bad people will get what's coming to them that's healing in a way that having your older cousin even the score isn't. I have enough relevant experience to say this isn't conjecture so much as fact.

"Joey Carmichael!"

"How? When?"

"Just now. I got a Google Alert about ten minutes ago saying he was pronounced dead after collapsing on the ice at the team's opening game!" she tells me, grinning. "That motherfucker died with the entire world watching."

"Good," I say, coming to sit next to her on the couch. "You set up a Google Alert for him?"

Katie nods, pushing her blond hair back from her face. "For all of them."

"Why?"

"I just… I don't know. After he waved at me at the pharmacy last week, I got kind of paranoid, and… There wasn't anything else I could do, Alyssa."

"Okay. That makes sense. You haven't seen any of the others, have you?"

"No. But I still can't leave the condo without feeling like they might jump out of every doorway I walk past."

I wrap my hand around hers. "You know that's normal, right?"

"I know. But it doesn't help."

I sigh. "Yeah. I know. It usually doesn't. Well. How do you feel now?"

Katie hesitates before saying, "I don't know. Better? Does that make me a terrible person?"

"Absolutely not. The *world* is a better place without someone like Joey Carmichael in it, and you're allowed to feel better—*safer*—because he's dead. That's also a completely normal reaction."

# Chapter 11
# Not the Jealous Type

"How have you been since we last spoke, Nicole?" I ask. I've been seeing Nicole Menendez for the past year and a half, and we recently went from weekly to biweekly visits. The point of patients coming to see me is that they improve, they get better, and eventually—if I do my job right, and we're lucky—they *stop* coming to see me. Usually that takes years though, and typically the first time that visits become less frequent, everyone panics and regresses.

"My anxiety is getting worse," Nicole says. She's sitting on the couch opposite me, picking the red polish off her nails.

"Why do you suppose that is?"

"I don't know. I can't stop checking whether the stove is off and the toaster is unplugged. I've replaced the smoke detector batteries three times this week. I almost went and bought all new smoke detectors even though I did that a few months ago."

I nod sympathetically. Nicole started coming to see me after she developed PTSD following a house fire. She was lucky, and she made it out physically unscathed. Unfortunately, her dog didn't. The cause of the fire was suspected to be faulty wiring, but Nicole hasn't been able to get past the guilt or the fear that it could happen again.

Her experience, while completely different from Katie's, still has a lot of overlap. It's what so much of trauma boils down to, really. Guilt—rational or not—about whatever happened combined with the fear that it could happen again. And there's no easy way around it, unfortunately. I wish I could wave a magic wand and make it better for both of them, but I can't.

"I know it's not rational," she continues. "But that doesn't help."

"Why do you think you're feeling more anxiety this week?"

"I think it's because I didn't meet with you last week, which is also irrational."

"It sounds like you've been saying those words to yourself a lot," I state as neutrally as I can. Not judging yourself is one of the hardest things for most people to do. Now and then, you'll meet a unicorn who doesn't engage in negative self-talk, but they're rare.

Nicole and I spend the bulk of the next hour discussing her internal monologue and coming up with alternate coping mechanisms, but we schedule an appointment for next week, with instructions to call and cancel if she feels up to it. I want to get her down to every other week, but it needs to be on her terms, not mine.

When I walk Nicole out of my office, she stops and talks to Teresa—my receptionist, billing expert, and right-hand woman—long enough to be added to my calendar for next week, and then she's out the door. It's just after five-thirty.

"Ready?" Teresa asks. We usually leave the office together. There's not a lot of reason for one of us to be here without the other.

"No. You can call it a day, though," I tell her. "I'm going to stick around here a bit longer. I need to do some prep for tomorrow."

Teresa's eyes narrow, and her head tilts in question. I don't typically stay late to prepare for the following day, and she knows it. But I don't want to tell her I've invited Mark to stop by for a 'tour' of my office.

"Okay," she finally says, and when I offer no other explanation, she grabs her bag and jacket and heads for the door. "See you tomorrow."

"Yup. Have a good night."

The door closes behind her with a soft thud, and I turn to the mirror hanging behind the reception desk, studying my reflection. I go back to my desk to find some lip stain and reapply it. Then I finger-comb my hair and tell myself I look fine. I think I'm going to keep the black hair. Even if dyeing it regularly will be a pain, I like it enough to make it worth it.

I know I'm using my appearance to distract myself from the fact that I'm more nervous than I should be, but we all need our coping mechanisms. Mark texted me earlier this morning to confirm we were still on for tonight. He should be here within the next twenty minutes, but we haven't talked or texted beyond that and the message I sent last night warning him that the cameras were on him.

I have no idea what his mood is going to be like. It's not as if he knows I'm responsible for Joey Carmichael's sudden death, but still. I guess it's good to figure it out now, though. However he's feeling, it's only going to intensify as I make my way through the others. I imagine having your entire second line and your top defensive pair drop dead during your first season as head coach is going to be pretty stressful. They *shouldn't* blame Mark for it, but they probably will. There's a good chance he'll lose his job because of me.

I scroll through social media and do a quick search to see what there've been for official press releases. So far, there's only the one that was released by the team's media spokesperson giving the usual spiel: *The team is terribly saddened by the loss of such a rising star. He will be deeply missed...* blah, blah, blah. Nothing from Mark specifically, which is all I was really looking for.

The game was paused and then halted after Joey Carmichael was pronounced dead. Right now, everyone is still reporting that his cause of death is unknown, but an undiagnosed heart condition is suspected.

I check my watch. There's still about ten minutes before Mark should arrive, so I call Vaughn. He answers after the second ring.

"Hey Alyssa, what's up?" he says over music playing in the background.

"Hey Vaughn. Can you do some digging for me? I found an EpiPen in Matt Davidson's locker, and I'd like to know what he's allergic to."

"Sure. Should be pretty easy. When do you need to know?"

"By next week, if possible. Can I get one more favor?"

"What?" Vaughn asks.

"Can you find out where he hangs out? Bar, restaurant, gym, whatever?"

"Yeah. No problem."

"Thanks, Vaughn," I say before ending the call.

A few minutes later, there's a knock on the office door. I set my phone to Do Not Disturb, smooth my hair down, take a deep breath, and open the door. Mark is standing on the other side. His red-brown hair is tousled, like he's been running his hands through it, and the amber flecks in his hazel eyes look like they're glowing.

"Hi," I greet, stepping toward him and lifting my hand to run my fingertips over the stubble on his jaw.

"Hi," he replies, his hands moving to encircle my waist as he brings his mouth to mine. I have the good sense to tug him into the office as his tongue strokes hungrily across mine. We stutter-step backward, our bodies locked around one another until he's finally far enough into the room for me to push the door shut. I shove him back against it, flipping the lock into place and pressing my hips into his as he drops his hands to my ass.

As I fist my hands into his hair, part of me is thinking we should stop and actually talk to one another, but it's Wednesday evening. The last time we slept together was before I left his house on Saturday morning, and I don't want to wait. I want him now. And clearly, he doesn't want to wait either.

*Yeah. We can talk later,* I decide as I drop my hands, sliding them under his shirt and tugging it over his head. His skin is warm under my palms as I move my hands across his chest.

He pulls his mouth from mine long enough to growl, "I could fuck you right here, against this door."

"Do it," I gasp, dropping my hands to his fly as he spins us, reversing our positions so that my back is pressing into the door and his body is pinning me in place. I work his pants over his hips, my hands caressing his glutes, as I push them down, following them to the floor, kneeling before him, my mouth inches away from his very erect dick. I could wrap my lips around it, but I don't. "Tell me what you want," I demand as he runs his hands through my hair.

"No," he says, rubbing the head of his cock over my lips. "I told you last time. It's your turn. You tell me what you want."

I consider protesting. Mostly because every little thing I tell him about myself—down to what I want to do to him and want him to do to me—allows him to know me that much better, and I'm not sure I want him to know me at all. But ultimately, I start talking.

"I want to blow you for just long enough that you begin to think you'd rather come in my mouth than finish inside me," I answer, looking up at his face, far above mine. His eyes have a feverish look, and I'm certain that whatever words I utter, he's going to do his best to make good on them. "Then I want you to fuck me against this door until it's rattling in the frame, and it's all I can do to keep from screaming your name. I want your mouth locked on mine, and my legs wrapped around you as you come inside me. After that, I want to order a pizza and lie on the floor and eat dinner with you. Only this time, I decide what's on the pizza. And while we eat, we can talk."

"About?" he asks, sounding wary.

"Things. Then when we're done, I can show you my couch, and we can decide the best way for you to screw me on it."

"Okay," he agrees, and I wrap my hand around his shaft and suck him into my mouth.

"What did you order on the pizza?" Mark asks.

"You'll see when it gets here," I tell him, trailing my fingers over his thigh. He's sitting on the floor with his legs outstretched and his back against my office wall, and I'm sitting between his legs, reclined against his chest. The carpet is scratchy beneath my ass, and I wish I had a blanket, but I've never needed one here before.

"Fine. What did you want to talk about?" he inquires, resting his chin atop my head, his left hand stroking across the skin along my hip.

"You."

"What about me?"

"What's going on with you? I saw you on TV last night when that guy died, and you looked more annoyed that he did it mid-game than you did concerned that he was dying. Are you okay?"

Mark's hand stills on my hip, and he says nothing for a long moment. "Joey Carmichael," he mutters finally. "You recognize the name?"

I shrug but say, "He was on trial for rape recently, right?"

"Yeah. Him and four others. If it were up to me, I'd have fired all of them. I wasn't exactly heartbroken to see him die." He takes a breath. "Thanks for the warning about the camera. I didn't expect you to be watching."

"Well. Normally I wouldn't have been, but I was having drinks with a friend and the game was on."

"What did you think?"

"About what? I don't know anything about hockey." He waits, seeming to want more, so I tack on, "Vaughn said something about your offense looking strong. It just looked like a melee to me, though."

Mark snorts as he asks, "Vaughn?"

"Oh, that's right. I forgot that you're the jealous type. Vaughn is an old family friend. I've known him since I was born."

"I'm not the jealous type."

"Are you sure about that? The way you practically dragged me away from that hockey player who tried to introduce himself the other day would indicate otherwise," I say lightly, hoping to elicit more information from him.

"That had *nothing* to do with jealousy. Garret Fischer is the ringleader of that little group of rapists. I couldn't be jealous of that pissant if I tried. I just don't want him anywhere near you."

*Interesting. He called them 'rapists.' He believes they did it. The jury didn't believe Katie, but Mark did. Or maybe he just knows exactly what kind of men they are*, I think, though I say nothing.

"What makes you believe I'm the jealous type?"

"Well, that. But also your vague comment about your last relationship ending badly combined with you saying you don't share well, and your question about Vaughn. Plus, you just have that vibe about you. And there was the fact that you wanted to lock me down after a single date."

"That vibe?"

"That vibe that says 'mine.' I can't imagine you'd react well if you thought I was flirting with someone else."

"Well, first of all, I'm not the jealous type. But no, I wouldn't react well to you flirting with someone else. However, I wouldn't be here if I thought you were the sort of person who would do that. Second, I was only asking about Vaughn out of curiosity. To get to know you better. And third, it was at least a date and a half," he says, and the words vibrate through his chest to my back. It's almost soothing.

"You're counting the hospital?"

"And pizza. Yes. We spent half the day together. I'm pretty sure it counts."

"So you want—" I'm interrupted by a knock on the door. Pizza. I grab Mark's shirt off the floor, looking down at myself after I've tugged it on. You can see a whole lot of leg, but nothing else, and it's good enough. I double-check to make sure Mark won't be visible before I open the door. The delivery guy gives me a once-over and smirks as I take the pizza from him.

"You were saying?" Mark says when I return to sit next to him, leaning against the wall, my shoulder brushing his, the pizza box balanced across our legs.

"Um. I think I was going to say something about you wanting to get to know me without reciprocating. You've functionally told me nothing about yourself, but you want details about my friends and family. It doesn't seem fair," I comment as I open the box. Pineapple, pepperoni, and jalapeño.

"You've been to my house," he responds as he takes a slice of pizza. "I still haven't been to yours."

"Yeah, but you know all about my family. I know nothing about yours."

"I don't know *all* about your family. Besides, you volunteered that information," Mark reminds me. "By the way, how did your visit with your dad go?"

I shrug. "I don't know. Fine, I guess. Why? Do you want to meet him?" I ask, fighting down a grin. The idea is hilarious. Mark in a prison visitors' room.

"Wouldn't be the first time I visited someone in prison."

"Oh yeah? Who else?"

"My older brother."

"You have a brother? I pegged you as an only child. What was he in prison for?"

"You really don't know anything about me, do you?" Mark asks, sounding surprised.

"No. I still haven't Googled you, or read your Wikipedia page, or whatever, if that's what you're asking."

"I have an older brother. Well, half-brother. He's eleven years older than me. His name is Aaron. He's still in prison."

Eleven years older. That explains why he seems like an only child. It's a big enough age gap that—depending on their upbringing—he may as well have been. "What for?"

"Killing my dad. When I was twelve." He pauses to take a bite of pizza, chewing slowly before saying, "It was in the news for a while," repeating my words from last week back to me. "They still talk about it when they talk about me sometimes."

"Huh. Your dad abused your mom, and your older brother finally put a stop to it?" I ask. The fact that we both had traumatic events involving our fathers happen when we were twelve isn't lost on me, though I don't comment on it.

He nods. "Yup."

"That sucks." I don't say it, but I bet he still feels guilty for not doing anything about it even though he was a kid. He probably believes it would've been better if he'd killed his dad himself rather than letting his older brother do it, because he likely would've gotten out of juvie at eighteen.

"Yup. So where's your mom? You've never mentioned her."

"God. You weren't kidding about this 'get to know you' shit," I grumble.

"Nope. I wasn't."

"I don't know where my mom is. She split when I was four, and I haven't seen her since."

"What happened to you after your dad was arrested? Who did you live with if your mom wasn't around?" Mark asks.

"My aunt. His sister. That's how I ended up living in Portland and not Seattle."

"Ah. Are you guys close?"

"I guess. We usually have dinner together every weekend," I say, remembering that I told him I was doing some family stuff last weekend.

He nods. "I like jalapeños, by the way."

"Good. Let me know when you want to see the couch in my office," I tell him, hoping to move the conversation away from our families. I was right, though. When Mark falls for someone, he falls hard. This is going to end up being the messiest breakup of my entire life.

"You should spend the night at my house tonight," Mark says, apropos of nothing.

"Should I?"

"Yeah. I'm going to be gone with the team for the next week and a half. So you should spend the night tonight. When we leave here, we can swing by your place, and you can grab whatever clothes you need, but you should come home with me."

"I thought you wanted to find out what color the couch in my office is."

"I do. But I also want you to come home with me."

# Chapter 12
# Penguins Are Birds

I'M CURLED ON THE COUCH UNDER A BLANKET WITH MY laptop balanced on my thighs, a glass of cabernet on the coffee table in front of me, and Rhys Steichen's address book held open in my left hand as I awkwardly type addresses from it into Google Maps with my right hand so that I can look at them in Street View. Katie is on the couch next to me, and we're ostensibly watching *March of the Penguins*.

"Did you know there were people who didn't know penguins were birds before this documentary came out?" Katie asks distractedly.

"You're kidding, right?" I reply as I zoom in on the map.

"No. I was reading a conversation about it on Reddit earlier. That's what made me think to put this on."

"What did they figure they were?"

"I dunno. Mammals, I guess."

"Weird," I mutter. The house I'm looking at right now is large and gated. It's got to be worth a couple of million. I type the address into Zillow. The estimate is $2.3 million. It must be one of his teammates' houses. I keep looking and run across several more multi-million-dollar addresses. Eventually, I go to the county records website and try to look up the property owners for the addresses, but every address over a million dollars is listed as being owned by an LLC. The LLC varies based on the address, but no individuals' names are listed. I try to look up who owns the different LLCs on the Oregon Business Registry, but most of them don't provide any information about the LLC members, and the ones that do are filled with names I don't recognize.

I'll have to meet up with Vaughn and give him a list of the addresses so he can see if he can figure out which houses belong to which players. Vaughn has a private investigator's license, which gives him access to a lot of information I don't have. I'm guessing Rhys Steichen has every player's address but his own in here.

"Are you coming to my mom's for Sunday dinner?" Katie asks after several minutes have passed.

"Sure."

"Okay. Good. She's going to want to talk about it."

"'It' what?" I probe, glancing up to find her chewing on her lip, her eyes unfocused on the TV screen.

"Joey Carmichael dying," Katie says neutrally.

"Oh. And you don't want to?"

"No. Not with her. You know how she is. Once she brings it up... She'll just make me feel bad for being happy he's dead. She won't mean to, but she will."

"Okay," I acknowledge, making a mental note to talk to Jeanette prior to tomorrow night. Katie's not wrong. Jeanette will probably begin talking about how unexpected deaths in young people are always difficult to process. She means well, but Jeanette is an optimist with a bleeding heart who's made of steel. It's a rare combination that creates resilience that borders on fanaticism. I'm certain it's why she went into pediatrics. In med school, it was all I could do to survive my pediatrics rotation. It takes a special kind of person to go into work every day knowing they might see a child die, and I am not that kind of person. Unfortunately, the same characteristics that make Jeanette great at her job will likely end up making Katie feel guilty for wanting to throw a party celebrating Joey Carmichael's demise.

I continue flipping through Rhys Steichen's address book. The other addresses listed are all for normal-sized houses and apartments.

They're mostly local addresses, spread all over the city, but there are a few out-of-town addresses scattered throughout as well. I keep turning the pages, and toward the back of the book I find Katie's address—the address where she was living prior to breaking her lease and moving in with me—and my blood runs cold.

*That son of a bitch.* I bet at least some of these addresses belong to other women he and his hockey-douchebag friends have done this to.

I close the address book and text Vaughn. *Can we meet during the day tomorrow? I have something I need to show you*

A moment later, a response appears on my screen. *Sure. 1pm at Eastside Coffee Joint?*

*Yeah. Sounds good. Thanks*, I reply.

My phone vibrates as I drop into the chair across from Vaughn. I glance at the screen. Mark is FaceTiming me. I think they're playing somewhere on the East Coast today, so their game is starting in an hour or whatever, but I don't have time to talk to him now. I decline the call, then send a text telling him I'm busy. Vaughn's eyes are boring into me as he waits for me to finish.

*Are you free after the game?* Mark replies.

*What time will that be?*

*Around six for you. Maybe a little after*

*Yeah, I should be free then*, I respond before setting my phone down.

I won't be having dinner with Katie and Jeanette until seven, and I already called Jeanette earlier to ask her not to bring up Joey Carmichael's death around Katie.

Mark and I have talked every day he's been out of town, and I gave him a video tour of the condo yesterday when Katie ran to the grocery store. I'm hoping that'll buy me some time and stop him from wanting to see it in person, but it probably won't.

"Hey Vaughn. Thanks for meeting me," I finally say. "That was Mark," I explain, nodding toward my phone.

"Sure. No problem. What did you want me to see?" Vaughn asks, not wasting any time.

I pull the address book out of my jacket pocket. "I took this from the arena the other night. It's Rhys Steichen's." I flip the book open and turn it to face Vaughn. "And this," I say, pointing at an address halfway down the page, "is Katie's address. Or it was anyway. Before she broke her lease."

Vaughn's eyes move from the page to mine. "And they never met before that night and haven't talked since then," he states.

I nod as Vaughn pulls the book toward him and flips through the pages.

"Some of the addresses in there are for multimillion-dollar homes owned by LLCs. I'm assuming they're his teammates' houses. But there are a lot of regular-people addresses too."

"And you want to know who lives in the houses."

"Yeah. And maybe for how long. He probably added Katie's address that night last year when they raped her, so everything before that is most likely older. People could've moved."

"There are a lot of addresses. It'll take a while."

"That's fine."

"Okay." Vaughn pulls a beige folder from his bag and slides it toward me. "This is everything I've been able to find out about Matt Davidson. He's allergic to bees, so I'm not sure how helpful that is. There's also a copy of his daily schedule, as near as I've been able to nail it down."

"Thanks."

"Marjorie wanted me to invite you over for dinner on Saturday next week," Vaughn tells me.

"Yeah, I can do that," I agree. It's been several months since I last saw Marjorie.

"You should bring Mark."

"That sounds like a terrible idea. You seriously want him to know who you are—where you live—after this is all done?"

"If you do it right, it'll be nothing more than a standard breakup."

"And if I screw it up?"

"Don't do that," Vaughn says, like it's just that simple. "Besides, supporting characters help to sell the con. He's going to want to meet your friends and family before too much longer, and you're not going to introduce him to Katie or Jeanette, so unless you've got someone else in mind…"

I roll my eyes. "Okay. I'll come on Saturday. I'll let you know about Mark," I say as I stand.

AT SIX, MARK CALLS AGAIN. IT'S BEEN GLOOMY AND drizzly here all day, but it's still daylight outside my windows, however murky it might be. The windows behind Mark show nothing but gaping darkness. Evidently, the man doesn't close the blinds anywhere, ever.

"Hi. How do you not feel like people are watching you all the time?" I ask.

"Hi," he replies, his brows drawn together, confusion marring his face. "What are you talking about?"

"The windows behind you. You realize they have curtains, right? And you can close them, and then that way people can't look in."

"Oh. I don't care. I don't ever really think about it, honestly."

"So I see. How was your game? Did you beat whoever you were playing against?"

"We won in overtime."

"That's good. Do you get back into town on Friday or Saturday?"

"Late Friday night. Technically, early Saturday. Around two in the morning. Why?"

"I was having lunch with Vaughn earlier, and he invited me—well, us really, if you want to come—to dinner with him and his wife, Marjorie, on Saturday. You don't have to come if you don't want to. I just figured since you'd asked about him, and he said you were welcome to come…" I trail off. I'm still not sure this is a great idea.

"You talked to Vaughn about me?"

The question catches me off guard, and I can't completely fight down the grin that wants to stretch across my face. Mark has no idea how much I've talked to Vaughn about him. But I merely say, "Yes. Is that a problem?"

"No. It's just unexpected. You don't strike me as the type to…" Apparently it's his turn to trail off.

"The type to?" I ask, eyebrows raised. I'm sure he stopped talking because he thought better of whatever he was going to say, which makes me curious.

"Discuss your personal relationships with people. Even with people you're close to. You seem like the type of person who would move in with someone, and people close to you would only find out when they tried to visit you and found you were no longer living at that address," he tells me, apparently deciding to be honest about what he was thinking.

I see the opportunity to screw with him a little though and take it. "'The type of person who would move in…' Was that a veiled invitation asking me to move in with you?" I question innocently. By the time ten seconds have gone by with Mark frozen in place, unsure of how to extricate himself from this situation, I burst out laughing. "Sorry," I gasp between laughs. "You should've seen the look on your face."

"You know you're kind of a dick, too," he mutters.

"Yeah. I know. And I also know you like it."

"Yeah. Well." He clears his throat. "Yes, I'll come to dinner on Saturday."

"Okay. I'll let Vaughn know. And you're not wrong, by the way. That does sound like something I would do."

"But you told him about me anyway," Mark says, and the smile tugging at his lips sends guilt roiling through me.

"Hi Jeanette," I say, her arms wrapping around me as I step into the house.

"Alyssa! I swear it's been weeks since I've seen you!" she replies as she squeezes me. Jeanette has the same honey-blond hair as Katie, only hers is streaked with grey now. "You've dyed your hair!" she says as she steps back, fingering a lock. I guess this is going to be an ongoing thing—at least until every person who's ever seen me sees me again.

"Yes. Do you like it?"

"You know I think you look lovely with whatever hair color you choose, dear," Jeanette says.

Katie rolls her eyes from where she's standing just over Jeanette's left shoulder, and I stop myself from laughing. Jeanette means well, but that was definitely mom-speak for 'I don't like it, but I'm too polite to say so.' I'm used to Jeanette's mild disapproval though, and it doesn't bother me in the same way that it bothers Katie. I know she means well. Most of the time.

I've always found it interesting that she and my dad are only a couple of years apart in age and grew up in the same house with the same parents. Aside from their looks and intelligence, they have almost nothing in common. Meanwhile, Katie and I aren't siblings, and though we spent the second half of our childhoods together, we only saw each other a few times each year prior to my dad's incarceration. Despite that, we're much more alike than Jeanette and my dad.

"What have you been up to, mom?" Katie asks, taking the focus off me and my hair. We've always been good at running interference for one another.

"Work, mostly," Jeanette huffs before launching into an extended story about hospital politics—which is the other reason I went straight into private practice. A steady salary and a billing department sound nice, but not nice enough to put up with that headache.

We make our way to the kitchen as Jeanette shares the ongoing battle surrounding the hospital's employee shortages and the administration's latest staffing changes. We're gathered around the island picking at the cheese plate Jeanette set out when she abruptly changes the subject.

"Katie, I heard about this really cute one-bedroom apartment from one of the nurses! It's the unit right above hers, and I think you should check it out. Let me send you the address."

"Mom—" Katie begins, but Jeanette cuts her off. Jeanette has been subtly pushing Katie to *'go back to normal'* for a while, and each time she does it, it makes Katie feel a little worse.

"No, you'll like it. It's perfect for you, and you can't keep doing online tutoring and living with Alyssa forever. You've got to get a place of your own and go back to work sometime."

"Actually, Jeanette, I like having Katie live with me. She's welcome to stay for as long as she wants. I'd rather have someone using my spare room than have it sitting empty."

"But Katie has to—"

I cut her off, not bothering to hide my irritation. She hasn't brought up Joey Carmichael, but somehow she still found a way to tell Katie she's doing it wrong. Jeanette has good intentions, but that doesn't make her actions helpful. "Katie doesn't have to do anything. She *is* working, and she can stay as long as she wants. By the way, my dad says hi. He was hoping you might come to visit soon. He said it's been a while," I state flatly, staring her down.

She sighs but lets it go. Since I became old enough to visit my dad on my own, Jeanette has only bothered to make the drive twice a year —usually once around Christmas and again near his birthday. I suspect even those visits stem more from a sense of obligation than any real desire to see him, which is fine. My dad didn't actually mention her. Their indifference is mutual.

"Very well. How's work been, Alyssa?"

"It's been good. Thank you for asking. My days are booked more often than not."

"That's good. It's good to be busy," Jeanette replies with what I'm pretty sure is her personal mantra.

"And she's dating someone new!" Katie says, and I shoot her a glare. Mark is the last thing I want to talk about, not that I've told Katie that. It would only make her more curious, which isn't something I need.

"You are? What's his name?" Jeanette asks.

"Mark," I say, using his real name since odds are Katie has heard me use it when talking to him over the past week.

"And what does Mark do?"

Both Jeanette and Katie have their eyes locked on me, and I try not to squirm as I slowly chew my cheese and cracker to buy time. Eventually, I swallow and say, "He works with troubled youth." It's kind of true.

"Oh, he's a counselor!" Jeanette supplies. "You must have so much to talk about."

"Mhmm," I reply noncommittally. "Yup. Lots in common." I grab another slice of cheese and hastily assemble a cracker sandwich before they can interrogate me further.

"I still haven't met him. You should invite him over for dinner soon," Katie tells me.

*What is it with everyone wanting me to invite Mark to dinner?* I wonder as I say, "Yeah. I could do that. I'll mention it to him when he gets back to town."

"Where is he now?" Jeanette asks.

"Visiting family," I lie. "He's from Louisiana. He'll still be away for a bit yet."

The oven timer dings, and I release a pent-up breath as the topic changes to how good the food smells instead of my quasi-fake relationship with Mark.

# Chapter 13
# Pinned Against the Glass

I'M SITTING AT MY DESK BETWEEN PATIENTS, EATING A sandwich and reviewing the file that Vaughn gave me on Sunday. It's Friday now, meaning Mark and Matt Davidson will be back tonight, and I'm trying to figure out what to do about Matt. According to Vaughn, Matt spends the majority of his time either at Tofana Arena or at home, playing video games. He doesn't do his own grocery shopping. He doesn't seem to go out to bars regularly. He either works out at home or in whatever gym they have in the arena. It's unlikely I'll be able to bump into Matt in a way that won't set off alarm bells for him. It doesn't leave me with a lot of options.

I was hoping he'd be deathly allergic to something like peanuts, or even shellfish. Instead, it's bees. I can't exactly pack up a beehive and transport it to his house.

Matt lives in one of the multimillion-dollar houses from Rhys Steichen's address book, so his home is almost guaranteed to have some kind of security system, and whatever the PIN to disarm it is, it's bound to be more complex than nine-nine-nine-nine. Plus, if he has anything more than the most rudimentary of alarm systems, he probably gets an alert on his phone every time someone arms or disarms the system. He does have a cleaning service that comes by once a week, which may be my best shot at gaining access to his home.

But then there's the question of what I do once I'm inside. I don't own a gun, and I'm not stupid enough to think I'm going to win a hand-to-hand fight against someone with five inches and at least fifty pounds on me. A blitz attack is likely my best bet. A baseball bat will at least keep some distance between us. Maybe a taser? Probably not. I bet the movies oversell their effectiveness. Chloroform takes minutes to work, and it's not like Matt is going to hold still while I press a rag over his face. Heroin needs to be injected into a vein, which is easier said than done if the person you're injecting doesn't want to be drugged. I could use a benzodiazepine—something like midazolam, but unless I steal it, it could be traced back to me.

I sigh and look at Matt Davidson's house on Google Maps again. He's got a pool. Accidental drownings happen all the time. Even among adult men. If I can incapacitate him and get him into the pool, they might assume his death was an accident, which could be beneficial. It might delay the other three in figuring out someone is hunting them. The last thing I need is for them to go into hiding or hire bodyguards. *How many hockey-douchebags can you kill before they realize they're an endangered species?* I wonder.

The most sensible approach might be to sneak into his house when the cleaning service goes in and then rely on a blitz attack and more than my fair share of luck. The cleaning company comes every Sunday, according to Vaughn's notes, so I've either got a couple of days or who knows how long, depending on when and where the team is playing over the next several weeks.

I pull out my phone to check their schedule. They have a game tonight somewhere in Ohio, which is why Mark said he wouldn't be home until late. There's no game tomorrow, but there is one on Sunday, which is actually perfect. Sunday Funday. I wish there were time to watch the cleaners, but unless I want to wait five weeks—and I don't—this Sunday is my best chance.

I'll need to make sure I've got everything ready before Mark gets back. He texted me earlier to ask if I want to have breakfast with him tomorrow. When I asked where—assuming it would be at Wilma's Cafe since that's his normal haunt—he surprised me and said his place. Of course I agreed.

THERE'S A FINE MIST COATING EVERY SURFACE AS I KNOCK on Mark's heavy glass-paned door on Saturday morning. The beat of a bass and the higher treble of a guitar are faintly leaking out around it, which is probably why Mark didn't seem to hear my car as I drove up the driveway, or me when I got out and slammed my door.

I wait a minute, but there's no answer. I knock again, a little louder. The music quiets, and a few seconds later I can make out Mark's silhouette approaching.

He pulls the door open. "Hi. It was unlocked. You could've come in," he says with a smile. He's wearing a black T-shirt, grey sweatpants, and his damp hair is a hint darker than its normal mahogany shade. He looks amazing, and it's all I can do to focus on his face.

"Well, I'll keep that in mind now that I know I'm allowed to let myself in. You look happy. And relaxed," I comment as he tugs me into his house. "Did you win last night?"

"I don't know if I should be disappointed or elated that you still don't care about hockey, but no. We lost."

"You seem surprisingly indifferent to that," I remark as he shuts the door, and I slip my shoes off.

He shrugs. "I'd rather have won, but the team we lost to is outside our conference, so it doesn't matter as much in the grand scheme of things. Plus, I got to sleep in my own bed last night, and now you're here, so what's there to be unhappy about?" His hand slides over my cheek and through my hair as he lowers his face to mine. His lips are warm, and I shrug my jacket off as I press myself closer to him. It's nine-thirty in the morning, and I've been awake for a couple of hours.

I haven't eaten yet, but I'm willing to skip breakfast if it means I get to have Mark now.

Apparently, he feels the same because his hands are already slipping from my hair and moving under my shirt, stripping it off me. Our mouths break apart as my shirt goes over my head. "I dreamt about you while you were gone," I say, and it comes out breathier than I intended. Sharing that information was a split-second decision, and I sound like a teenage girl talking about her celebrity crush.

Mark growls as his hands slide down my sides and over my ass. He lifts me into the air, and I wrap my legs around his hips, locking myself against him as one of his hands reaches up to fumble with the hooks on my bra. I work my fingers into his hair, kissing him as he carries me toward the kitchen. He sets me on the island, stepping back just enough to remove my bra, and I remember his assertion that he could bend me over the counter and have me begging him to fuck me within three minutes. Honestly, he was selling himself short. There's no way I'm going to last longer than two.

*What the hell is it about this man?* I can't help but wonder as I pull his shirt off. Then I see the muscles ridging his torso beneath it and remember *exactly* what it is about him. But no, that doesn't fully explain it. I've been with other men just as attractive and—

He brushes his fingertips across my nipples—chasing every other thought from my head—then returns to pinch them until I'm writhing under his touch. After a moment, he threads his left hand through my hair and yanks my head sideways. Then, his mouth finds my neck as his right hand continues pinching and rolling my nipple between his fingers.

"God, I want you, Mark," I gasp as I fumble with the button on my jeans. I need them off now. Wearing pants was stupid.

"I love hearing you say that, Alyssa," he murmurs against my neck.

I finally get my jeans unbuttoned and unzipped, but I don't have room to get them off, and I don't want Mark to stop touching me. I can see how hard he is—the light grey fabric is highlighting every contour of his dick. He rocks his hips into my hand as soon as I wrap it around him, and I stroke him through the sweatpants. He groans into my neck, and it thrums through me. I pull my hands away from him long enough to push the pants over his hips, letting them drop to pool around his feet. He kicks them away, and I immediately bring my hands back to him, gliding one hand along his shaft as I fondle his balls with the other.

He groans as he draws his face away from my neck and releases his grip on my hair. "Tell me about your dream," he orders, his face inches from mine, filling my entire field of vision.

"Take my pants off first," I demand.

For a passing second, he looks like he might argue, but then he wraps an arm around my waist, pinning my hands between us. He lifts me slightly and drags my pants over my hips and down my legs with his free hand. The island's stone surface is cold against my ass, but the rest of my body feels like it's on fire.

Mark tosses my pants to land next to his and then slides the heel of his hand between my legs, pressing it into my mound until I'm shifting against it—ensuring the friction and pressure are hitting my clit exactly the way I need—and the tip of his middle finger is pressing through the fabric of my underwear, into me. I shift again, moaning softly. *Wearing underwear was stupid, too,* I think distantly.

"Tell me about your dream," he orders again, his dick pressing into my thigh as I resume stroking my hand from the tip to the base of his shaft. "Tell me, Alyssa," he growls through clenched teeth.

"It was on Sunday. That night after we talked, when I asked you about closing the curtains." I nip at his earlobe. His hand bunches the fabric of my underwear together, moving it to the side as the tip of his finger traces around the opening of my cunt. "More," I whisper, pulling back to watch his face. "Please."

"Keep talking."

"I was there with you. In the room." His finger dips into me a fraction of an inch. It's not enough. "More," I whimper. "More."

"Keep talking." His eyes are locked on mine. The intensity in them should terrify me, except I'm pretty sure my eyes look the same.

"It was dark outside, but the curtains were still open, and all the lights were on."

His finger moves ever so slightly deeper, but I want more. I try to slide forward onto his hand, but his other one is locked on my thigh, pinning me in place. The sound of frustration I make is somewhere between a plea and a demand as I continue stroking him. The first drop of pre-cum is beading at the head of his cock. It sends elation trilling through me. He's just as wet for me as I am for him. I continue speaking without being told this time.

"We were both naked. You were behind me, and you had me pinned against the window. You were buried inside me—screwing me—and I was plastered to the glass. Please," I gasp. "I need more. Give me more, or I won't tell you the rest."

"Keep talking," Mark says, finally sliding a finger all the way inside me.

"More," I demand. He slides another finger into me, and the walls of my vagina clench around them as he drives them deeper. "Yes," I moan. "You were whispering in my ear as you fucked me, telling me you were going to make me come where everyone could see. That you were going to make sure everyone knew how much I liked it when you came inside me."

He's rhythmically sliding his fingers into me, and as good as it feels, I want him to replace them with his dick. "Did you want me to show everyone?" he asks, and his voice has a deep raspy quality I haven't heard before.

"Yes," I admit. I've never been much of an exhibitionist, but part of what I get off on is him getting off, and in that regard I absolutely want him to fuck me against a window in front of everyone.

"What happened next?"

"I need you," I whisper raggedly. "I'm so close, I just need—"

"What happened next? Tell me."

"I woke up orgasming."

"What did you do then?" he questions as he removes his fingers from my cunt and pulls my hands away from his body, bringing them together behind my back. My right elbow twinges as he pins my hands in place with one of his before lining up the head of his cock at my opening, but not going any further. It hurts, but I don't care. I want him to keep going.

"Please," I moan.

"Tell me what you did after you woke up."

"I felt like I'd been robbed because you weren't there. So I grabbed my vibrator from my nightstand and fucked myself. It wasn't as good as the dream. Or you. Pl—" Mark slams into me, cutting off my plea and turning it into a scream. "Yes!" I'm stretched so tightly around him, matching his thrusts into me as best I can with my hands pinned behind me. "Harder, Mark! Harder!"

I'm riding the edge—pleasure and pain combining as I get closer and closer. He pulls my underwear further to the side and presses his thumb against my clit, stroking it like he knows it's precisely what I need as he drives into me. All at once, the orgasm rolls over me, and I'm convulsing around him, my cunt squeezing his cock in waves, my nails digging into his hand, which still has both of mine pinned, as I scream his name. Then he's coming too, filling me even more deeply, his hips jerking again and again as we ride the wave together. Eventually, he stills, pulling out of me as he releases my hands. I flop back onto the island, and he runs his hands gently across my body.

"Come on. Come lie on the couch with me. I'd carry you, but I'm not sure my legs could manage it," he tells me eventually.

"Did you dream about me?" I ask as I slowly sit up.

"Yes," he replies softly.

"Do you want French toast or a frittata?" Mark asks as he wipes down the kitchen island. He put the grey sweatpants back on—for all the good that does—but he's still shirtless, and I'm obviously admiring the view. Who knew I wanted a barefoot, half-naked man in the kitchen offering to be my personal chef?

"You can make a frittata?" I question, watching him from the couch where I'm wrapped in a blanket. We spent about forty minutes lying there, entwined in one another's arms, before he volunteered to cook breakfast.

He shrugs. "It's not much different than a giant omelet. Easier probably, since you don't have to fold it. If it were just me, I'd make a protein shake and call it good, but I know you don't like those," he teases.

I snort. "Alright. Let's go with the frittata, then. You can impress me with your cooking skills." I pause a moment before inquiring, "Do you guys have practice before the game tomorrow?" I know Mark will assume I'm asking because it'll affect the time we can spend together. In reality, that has nothing to do with it. I want to know when I should expect Matt Davidson to be out of the house. Even though I'm dependent on the cleaning crew to get in, it'll still be useful to have some idea about when he'll be gone.

"Yes. There's a morning skate at nine, then warm-ups prior to the game," he tells me as he puts the rag away and places a cutting board on the counter.

"Why?" I ask. It seems entirely unnecessary to practice that much.

"Why is there a morning skate and warm-ups?" Mark replies, clarifying my question, and I nod. "The morning skates on game days are optional, but a lot of the players like them. Some of the guys are superstitious, and it puts them at ease. The rest think it gets them more in the zone. Today is a mandatory day off, so I imagine most of them will show up for it."

Unfortunately, there's no way for me to inquire whether he believes Matt Davidson will. "What time do you have to be there tomorrow?"

"I'll be there all day," he replies, glancing up from the onion he started dicing. "Sorry."

"No. It's fine. I've got some personal stuff I need to do during the day tomorrow anyway, and then some family stuff during the evening. It actually works out well."

"What time do we have to be at dinner tonight?"

"Seven. Vaughn lives over near Powell Butte Park, so we'll need to leave by six-thirty."

"Earlier," Mark murmurs. "Do they drink? I should bring something."

"Are you nervous?"

"No," he asserts.

"Are you sure, because you sound nervous." Mark glares at me, and I laugh. "Vaughn is partial to Old Fashioneds. Marjorie likes Martinis. But we are *not* showing up with the most expensive bottles of bourbon and gin you can buy," I warn. "So don't even think about it. I'll never hear the end of it from Vaughn if you do."

VAUGHN LIVES IN A MEDIUM-SIZED, MID-CENTURY MODERN house. Mark is eyeing it as if he might change careers and go into real estate.

"What would you have done if you weren't a hockey coach?" I ask as we get out of my car and walk to the front door.

"Gone into architecture or civil engineering, maybe. Why? What would you have done if you weren't a psychiatrist?"

"Just wondering," I say, pressing the doorbell. "I'd probably have become a lawyer." I want to ask how he ended up coaching, but Marjorie opens the door before I can.

"Alyssa!" she greets, grabbing my hands and pulling me into the house. "I love the hair! It's very chic."

Vaughn is standing next to Marjorie, and he doesn't so much as twitch. I'm sure he mentioned what's going on, meaning Marjorie's comment about my hair is intentional, and I know she's up to something. I'm sure Mark will ask me about it later. Oh well. A lot of women dye their hair. It's not like he knows I dyed it specifically for him.

"Hi Marjorie. Thank you. This is Mark. Mark, this is Marjorie," I say, inclining my head toward her, "and Vaughn."

Mark reaches out to shake Marjorie's hand first. His hand engulfs hers. Marjorie is a few inches shorter than me with dark skin and a short pixie cut. I've never thought of her as being short, but seeing her standing next to Mark has me reconsidering my perspective. He releases Marjorie's hand after a moment and takes Vaughn's.

"Hi, nice to meet you both," Mark says. "I've heard a lot about you." He hasn't, really. The only thing I've told him about Vaughn is that Vaughn is an old family friend. All he knows about Marjorie is that she and Vaughn are married. But it's more than I've told him about anyone else in my life save my dad, who he can't meet unless he wants to make the drive to Walla Walla with me.

It's not like he's shared any more than I have, though. I guess we're kindred spirits in that sense.

"Yes, you as well," Vaughn replies as Marjorie says, "I can see why Alyssa is smitten with you."

Marjorie's gaze darts to me, and I open my mouth to protest, having said no such thing, but Marjorie continues talking. "Anyhow, please come in. Can I get you something to drink?"

"Actually, I didn't want to show up empty-handed," Mark says. "Alyssa mentioned you're a Martini fan and Vaughn likes Old Fashioneds, so I brought a bottle for each of you." He doesn't mention that he insisted we stop by what appeared to be—at least from the outside—a ridiculously snobby-looking liquor store on the way here. He didn't want me to go in with him, so I have no idea if the inside was as pretentious as the outside, and I also have no idea what he purchased. I just hope it was nothing insanely expensive. He removes a distinctive green bottle from the paper shopping bag in his hand and passes it to Marjorie.

"Tanqueray Number Ten," she says as she takes it. "A very good choice. Thank you."

He pulls a second bottle from the bag, handing it to Vaughn. It's a bottle of Glenfiddich Gran Reserva, and I breathe a sigh of relief as I take Mark's now-free hand and squeeze it. It's expensive, but only a couple of hundred dollars expensive. I won't have to hear about the time one of my boyfriends showed up with a two-thousand-dollar bottle of bourbon for the rest of my life.

"Here, let me take that," Marjorie says, snatching the empty paper bag from Mark's grasp as she and Vaughn lead us to the sunken living room.

"What year was your house built?" Mark asks.

"Fifty-eight. We've tried to remain as faithful to the original style as possible while still updating it," Marjorie supplies.

Mark nods. "You've done a wonderful job. My house was built around the same time—sixty-one."

"Would you like a tour?" Marjorie asks Mark as I take a seat on the couch.

"I'd love one."

Marjorie leads Mark down the hallway, discussing the finer points of the architectural style as Vaughn sits next to me. I wait until they're out of earshot, and then hiss, "What is she doing?"

"Playing matchmaker, I assume," he says with a disinterested shrug.

"What? We're already here together. She doesn't need to play matchmaker."

"Feel free to tell her that."

"She's *your* wife!" I fume.

"Yes. And that's why I won't bother. Listen, I told you how we met. She wants that for you and Mark too."

"First, I know nothing about how you met beyond that your relationship began as part of some con. Second, do you seriously think Mark is going to figure out what I'm doing and forgive me for it?" I scoff.

"You never know. Stranger things have happened."

"Not that," I assert. There's no way he forgives me for any of it. Least of all, lying to him about, well, everything. I'm playing with fire, and the part of me that likes Mark is really starting to hate it. But I wasn't built to just sit around and let creeps like Matt Davidson and Garret Fischer get away with it.

# Chapter 14
# Sunday Funday

According to the info in Vaughn's file, the cleaning crew shows up to Matt's house every Sunday at two in the afternoon. There are three people who stay for two hours. I have to assume Matt will be at the arena before they show up, meaning I shouldn't have to contend with him also being there.

It's currently one, and I'm parked in a neighborhood about three and a half miles away from where he lives. I should be able to walk to his place and arrive just as the cleaning crew does. Then I'll follow them through the gate and into the house. I'm assuming they leave it unlocked while they're cleaning so they can bring their equipment in and out without needing to constantly lock and unlock the door. After that, I'll simply have to find some place to hide until they leave and Matt gets back.

*Piece of cake,* I tell myself, knowing it's a lie.

I pull on the extra-large raincoat and wrap a scarf over my face to avoid being recognizable on any doorbell cameras without also drawing attention to myself by doing something stupid like wearing a ski mask. I have latex gloves, goggles, an N95 mask, and shoe covers in one pocket and the biggest canister of undyed, clear pepper spray I could find in the other. I tuck a baseball bat under my coat and get out of the car. Luckily, it's gloomy and rainy today, so the giant raincoat and scarf fit right in with the chilly weather.

The walk from my car to Matt Davidson's house seems to go by in the blink of an eye. I know that it's just nerves shortening and compressing time, but that doesn't make me feel any calmer. My plan isn't great, but it's the best one I could come up with. Like last time, I consider scrapping the whole thing, but then the cleaning company's van is coming up the street from the opposite direction, and I pick up my pace. The van stops at the gate in front of the house, waiting for it to open, which gives me time to get close enough to walk in behind them and then duck behind a bush as they continue up the driveway. I stay huddled behind the bush for the next fifteen minutes. Hopefully, they'll have brought in whatever equipment and cleaning supplies they need and started working by now.

Finally, I approach the house. One of the garage doors is open with the van backed up to it. I take a deep breath and walk into the garage, pausing to listen at the door leading into the house. All I can hear is a dull rumble that might be a vacuum. I take the gloves and shoe covers from my pocket, slip them on, and try the knob. It's unlocked. I'm in.

The first room is some kind of drop zone utility room. It's crowded with hockey sticks and bags as well as multiple pairs of shoes. The door between it and the hallway beyond is open, and the vacuum is louder now. I peek into the hallway. It leads to a kitchen, which is empty.

I gather my nerve and make my way down the hallway as quietly as I can, though I doubt whoever is in the next room will be able to hear me over the flat roar of the vacuum. For someone who probably doesn't do any of his own cooking, Matt Davidson has an exceptionally large kitchen. It's bigger than my condo's kitchen and living room combined. People think doctors make a lot of money, but we're usually just upper middle class. I could work for another fifteen years and not be able to afford a house this big. In terms of square footage, it's three times the size of Mark's house and six times the size of my condo. It's completely unnecessary. Especially for one person.

On the plus side, it's big enough to swing a baseball bat in.

There are two doors off the kitchen and a wide opening on the opposite side that leads to another room. No one is visible right now, but that won't last long. I try the first door. It's a small half bath. I doubt they've had time to clean it. They'll probably be back to do that at some point, so it's out as far as a hiding place goes. I try the second door. It leads to a large pantry that's mostly empty. If it were full, it could feed a family of ten for a month. I step in and close the door behind me softly. Chances are they'll ignore this room. I hope. I stand against the wall that will be behind the door if someone does decide to come in here, just to be safe. And then I wait.

It's a bit after four when the cleaning company leaves, and the house is eerily silent. Matt won't be home for another four or five hours, and I'm hoping he comes back alone. If anyone is with him, I'll be stuck waiting for them to leave before I can make my move.

I'd like to get out of this pantry and look around the rest of the house, but I have no idea if there are motion sensors that turn on when the security system is armed, and I don't want to risk it. He doesn't have a cat or a dog, so there could be. I opt to play it safe and remain where I am, reciting the diagnostic criteria of different mental disorders to keep my mind occupied.

I've been sitting on the pantry floor for almost seven hours. I really have to pee, and I'm dying of thirst. I'm running through the criteria for somatic symptom disorder, trying to distract myself from both of those needs—which are becoming more pressing by the minute—when I hear the distinctive chirp of the security system. I rise to my feet, forgetting every other thought that had been running through my brain, as the lights turn on, leaking under the pantry door. *Shit!* I'll have to wait until he turns the lights off and goes into the next room, or I'm going to be half blinded.

I put on the swim goggles and the N95 mask. Then, I start counting. The lights go off when I reach three hundred and five. I give it another few seconds, and then ease the pantry door open. There's a pendant light on above the kitchen sink, but the overhead lights are off. There are lights on in the next room, and I debate following Matt, but I want him to come to me if possible. Hunters like blinds for a reason.

I switch the baseball bat to my left hand and remove the canister of pepper spray from my pocket. I loop the lanyard attached to the can around my right wrist and make sure the nozzle is facing away from me. Then, I take a deep breath and open one of the cabinet doors below the island. I slam it shut as loudly as possible before pressing myself against the wall where I won't be immediately obvious.

"What the hell?" comes from the nearby room. A second later, footsteps are moving toward the kitchen. Toward me. My heart is pounding so fast and so erratically that I feel like it might explode. My hands are trembling. Hell, my entire body is shaking. *This is stupid, this is stupid, this is stupid,* keeps looping through my head, and I want to tell my internal monologue to shut up, but it's right. This is stupid. *I am stupid.* I don't know what the hell I was thinking. But then Matt's stepping into the room, reaching for the light switch.

"Hey Matt," I say as the lights come on. His head turns in my direction as I raise the pepper spray and hold down the nozzle. Only he's rushing toward me, letting out a scream of rage or pain—everything is moving so fast it's impossible to say which. Then he's tackling me to the floor. The stupid shoe covers offer no traction, and the baseball bat flies from my grip as I fall back, landing on the same elbow I injured a few weeks ago.

A grunt is torn from my throat. Tears fill my eyes behind the goggles, and pain shoots up my right arm. Matt Davidson's fist impacts my cheek hard enough that stars swim in my vision. I fumble for the pepper spray, which I dropped when my elbow hit the floor. It's still attached to my wrist by the lanyard, but it takes a second to get it back into my hand, then I raise it and spray it into Matt's face again. This time, the bottle is mere inches from his eyes, nose, and mouth.

He inhales the spray as it hits him. His body involuntarily curls inward as he starts coughing, unable to breathe. His hands go toward his eyes, and he rolls off me. The only things preventing me from sharing the same fate are the mask and swim goggles I'm wearing.

I scuttle backward, putting some distance between us, frantically looking for the bat. I have a couple of minutes at most. After what seems like forever, but I know was no longer than a handful of seconds, I spot the bat. It's a few feet away, next to the wall where it landed after I lost my grip. A moment later, it's in my hands, and I rise to my feet. Matt Davidson is on his knees, hunched around himself. I move to stand over him and raise the bat above my head, then slam it down on the back of his skull with the full force of my body behind it. The bat makes contact with his occipital bone, just below the lambdoid suture and perpendicular to his spine, where damage would be most likely to be present if he'd slipped and hit his head. There's a sickening thud, and Matt stops moving as pain explodes up my arm.

I strip off my raincoat, placing it next to him on the ground with the outside facing up. I set the bat on it, and then I roll his body onto it as well. As far as I can tell, there's no blood on the floor, and if I want to make this look like an accident, I need to keep it that way. There can't be a pool of blood inside the house, and he can't have drag marks on his torso—both will be dead giveaways that the scene was staged. They might figure it out anyway, but I don't want to make it easy for them.

Once I've got him positioned in the center of my coat, I grab the edges and start dragging him along. I need to find the door that goes out to the backyard, where the pool is. I'm not sure how long he'll be unconscious, so I need to get him into the water as quickly as possible.

Matt has got to be around a hundred and ninety pounds, and right now, it's all dead weight. My right arm is screaming at me, and I think my elbow might actually be fractured this time. It doesn't matter, though. I can deal with it later. I drag his body down the hallway on the far side of the kitchen, opposite where I came in. If his house has a somewhat standard layout, there should be a door leading outside there. About fifteen feet down the hallway, I find it. It's locked. I hope unlocking and opening it won't set off the security system, but at this point, I don't have any choice but to take my chances.

It's dark, but as soon as I step outside, motion-activated floodlights turn on, brightening the entire yard. There's a tall hedge all the way around the rear of the property, so I'm not concerned with being seen by the neighbors.

I drag him about thirty feet across the yard and position his body along the pool's edge. The night is still quiet. I pull my coat upward, rolling Matt's body into the water. He lands facedown with a small splash and doesn't stir. His dark hair is lazily floating in the water, fanned out around his head. He might already be dead for all I know. I didn't check for a pulse after I hit him. I grab his shirt, moving his body closer to me before pressing my hand to his neck. The water is warm, and there's a pulse. He's still alive. That's good. That means there will be water in his lungs when they do the autopsy.

I dab the part of my coat that's covered in Matt's blood on the concrete near the edge of the pool. With any luck, they'll believe it's where he fell and hit his head.

Then I sit down and watch Matt Davidson drown.

It's cold, but there's no wind. If my arm didn't feel like it was broken, and my cheek wasn't on fire, it would be peaceful. I remove the goggles but keep the mask on. Hopefully there aren't any external security cameras—because if there are, the game is up and they'll know it wasn't an accident despite my best efforts. Regardless, I don't want to take the mask off until I'm back inside and I can replace it with my scarf. I pull my coat toward me and shove the goggles into the pocket. The water should wash away all traces of pepper spray from Matt's body. It'll just be a tragic accident.

After ten minutes have gone by, I reach for the body again. There's no pulse this time. He's dead.

I swap my gloves for a fresh pair from my coat pocket. If I got any of Matt's blood on them, I don't want to risk transferring it to the doorknobs or surfaces in his house. And since my coat does have his blood on it, I don't want to risk accidentally brushing against anything when I retrieve my scarf from the pantry where I left it earlier.

The adrenaline is ebbing by the time I return to the house, and the air is pungent with the acrid scent of pepper spray hanging heavily in it when I swap my mask for the scarf. I crack the window over the kitchen sink open a couple of inches. If I'm lucky, it'll be long enough before his body is found that whatever breeze trickles in will dissipate the smell. The lights are still on, and I decide to leave them that way as I survey the kitchen to ensure it doesn't look like a crime scene. There's a faint sheen on the side of the island where some offcast mist from the pepper spray is visible. I grab the roll of paper towels, tear one off, and turn the sink faucet on, wetting it. There's no dish soap beside the sink, so I pump some of the hand soap onto the paper towel and use it to clean up the cast-off pepper spray. Eventually I'm satisfied that there's nothing visible to the naked eye, and I chose a pepper spray that was UV dye free, so even if they bring in black lights it shouldn't be obvious that it was ever used in this kitchen.

I do one final check to make sure I have everything I brought with me, which wasn't much, and then I return to the backyard to get my coat and the bat. I put the coat on and tuck the bat under my arm before going around the side of the house to the front where I can climb over the fence to get out. Even though it would be simpler, I don't want to leave the way I came in because I'd have to leave the garage door open, which would look suspicious. I don't have any way to rearm the security system, which is unfortunate. But they should assume Matt hit his head and drowned before he could do it.

I take off the shoe covers once I'm at the front of the house, but leave the gloves on since I have to climb the fence. If I open the gate, there will be a record in the security system somewhere. I throw the baseball bat over the fence and try to follow it. My arm screams and my head swims as soon as I put weight on my elbow to pull myself up. I count to thirty, then steel myself and try again. This time I'm better prepared for the pain, and I hook my leg on the top of the fence and use it to propel the rest of me over. I land on the other side and stagger a step before catching my balance. Then, I stand there panting for a minute. My face and arm are both throbbing in time with the beat of my heart.

Eventually, I take off the latex gloves, pick up the baseball bat, tuck it inside my coat once more and start the walk back, moving a lot more slowly than I did on the way here. By the time I make it to my car and open the trunk, it's eleven-fifteen. I remove the bat from inside my coat and shove it into the garbage bag I put in my trunk for cleanup purposes. I do the same thing with my coat before tying the bag shut. I'll throw it in the trash at my office building tomorrow, and it'll be carted off to the landfill on Tuesday.

Once I'm sitting in my car, I flip the visor down and open the mirror to take a look at my cheek. Damn. There's a small, one-centimeter cut along my cheekbone where Matt's fist made contact with my face. It's going to be impossible to cover up. I'm going to need a better plan for the others. Especially Rhys Steichen. He's huge. A baseball bat and some pepper spray won't cut it against that asshole.

I sigh, then close the visor and start the drive home. With any luck, Katie will have gone to bed before I get back, but it's hard to say—she keeps odd hours due to her tutoring schedule. Then I can spend tomorrow figuring out what lie I'm going to tell about how I got punched in the face.

# Chapter 15
# Pick Better Role Models

I PAUSE WITH MY KEY IN THE LOCK AND TAKE A DEEP breath. Katie was asleep—or at least in her room—by the time I got home last night, and I left for work before she came out this morning, so she hasn't seen my face yet. I tried to cover the bruise on my cheek with concealer, but the cut made it difficult. Teresa noticed it right away, despite my best efforts. I told her I'd been taking a martial arts class for a while, and the pads slipped during drills.

The bruise kept darkening throughout the day, though. By lunch, the makeup wasn't doing anything to hide the fact that I'd been punched in the face. It was just making me look like I was *trying* to hide it, so I went into the bathroom and scrubbed it off.

I can't tell Katie or Mark the same lie I told Teresa. Katie knows I'm not taking a martial arts class, and Mark wouldn't believe it. It would be equivalent to telling him I walked into a wall. There *is* a lie that they'll both believe. But it's a really shitty lie for me to tell.

I exhale, then open the door and step inside.

"Did you hear—" Katie begins before glancing at me. "Alyssa! What the hell happened to your face?"

I slip my shoes off as I raise my fingertips to brush across my left cheek. The cut has just started to scab over and is noticeably rough.

Despite holding an ice pack to my face for more than an hour last night, my cheek is so bruised and swollen that the lightest of grazes feels like I'm being punched in the face all over again. On the plus side, the compression bandage that's wrapped around my right arm is easy enough to hide. At least from Katie—Mark will be a different story.

I'm not sure if my olecranon is actually fractured this time or if I merely exacerbated the existing bone contusion. I still have full range of motion in my elbow joint—even if moving it through that range of motion makes me cry—so I'm taking my chances and hoping for the best. It's a better option than showing up to the ER and having to tell a completely different lie to the attending.

"A patient... sort of freaked out today," I tell Katie.

"A patient *hit you in the face?*"

I shrug.

"Why? What happened?" she demands.

"Kay, you know I can't tell you that. It's fine. I'm fine. They're fine. Everything is okay," I say as I walk to the couch and drop to sit beside her. "So, what were you asking if I heard?"

"About Joey Carmichael?"

I shake my head. "What's to hear? He's dead."

"They're saying it wasn't an accident. Apparently, he was poisoned. They're treating it as a homicide."

"Really?" I ask, feigning surprise. "Who do they think did it?"

"I don't think they know. At least it didn't sound like it on the news. Do you think they'll question me?" she asks.

"No. Why, did you poison him?" I joke, knowing she didn't.

"No, but I wish I had."

"Okay, well. If the police do come talk to you, maybe don't tell them that."

"I won't. I just wish I could give whoever did it a medal."

"Can I ask you something?"

"Sure," she agrees.

"Did you ever wonder if maybe you weren't the only person they'd done that to?"

Her jaw clenches as she nods. "Yeah. I think about it a lot. It's a big part of why I wanted to go to trial. Guys like that… they don't just do it once. Especially not if they get away with it. I don't think I was the first."

"Me neither." I pause before saying, "You know I'm proud of you for going through with it despite the odds?"

She reaches out and grabs my hand, squeezing it. Her skin is warm against mine. "Yeah. I know. I'm proud of me, too."

"Good. What are we watching?" I question as my phone vibrates.

"*River Monsters*. It's this series about insane freshwater fish. Did you know catfish could grow to be like seven feet long?"

"No. That seems…"

"Unnecessary?" she asks as I unlock my phone to read the text from Mark.

"Yeah. That," I reply distractedly. Mark wants me to come have dinner with him.

"Is that your boyfriend?" Katie asks, trying to sneak a peek at my phone.

I pull the phone to my chest, shielding it from her. "He's not my—"

"Oh, come on, Alyssa! He totally is! You guys have been dating for like a month now!"

"Three weeks," I correct.

"See! And you don't even seem bored yet," she states, her eyebrows rising as if she's daring me to contradict her.

"Okay. Fine. You're right. I'm not bored. I actually really like him, but I don't think it'll work out long term."

"Why?"

"Because none of my relationships ever have," I say, trying to deflect.

"Yeah, but that's pretty much always been because you haven't *wanted* them to work long term. You seem to feel differently about him."

"Maybe. I don't know. I don't want to get my hopes up."

"I still want to meet him! We should have dinner this weekend."

There's no way for me to explain to Katie why I can't introduce her to Mark. She'll recognize him, and he'll definitely recognize her the second he lays eyes on her. I'm sure the only reason he hasn't already made the connection is because we have different last names and I was never on camera during her trial. But if he sees her… he'll know right away. And then… Shit. I should've never mentioned Mark to Katie. It's not like I had much choice, though. She'd have figured out I was dating someone when I started disappearing half the nights every week. I'm stuck between a rock and a hard place, only I created both and then inserted myself between them.

*Maybe if I tell Mark before he finds out… But then he'll know I was lying about everything, and how long will it take after that for him to suspect I'm behind their deaths?* I wonder.

I think I need to talk to Marjorie.

"Are you going over to his house?" Katie asks, startling me from my thoughts.

"What? Oh. Um… yeah, if you don't mind."

"No. Go. But I'm serious about wanting to meet him."

"Yeah. I know," I grumble.

I'M PARKED IN MARK'S DRIVEWAY, BUT I HAVEN'T GOTTEN out of my car yet. I know I'm delaying the inevitable. It's just that there's so much 'inevitable' that I don't know where to start. If I were doing this over, I'd do it all differently. I have no idea what 'differently' would look like, but… not this.

I call Vaughn instead of getting out. If Mark has realized I'm here, he's probably wondering what the hell I'm doing, but that's the very least of my concerns. Vaughn doesn't answer, though, so I leave a message asking him to call me back when he has time.

Finally, there's no more delaying. I get out of my car, climb the stairs on the hillside, and walk across the miniature bridge to Mark's front door. He opens it before I reach it, meaning he definitely noticed me sitting in my car. Great.

"Hey," he begins, his silhouette backlit by the light streaming from the house. His face is in shadow, and I can't quite make it out, but he sounds tired. His tone immediately changes as I step into the pool of light cast by the lamp near the door. "What the fuck happened to your face?" he questions, sounding enraged.

"Nothing. I'm fine."

"That's not nothing," he says, grabbing my chin and angling my face toward the light. I can make out his expression now, and his eyes are narrowed to slits, but his fingers are gentle against my skin as he continues. "I know what being punched in the face looks like, Alyssa."

"You should see the other guy," I quip, fighting down a grin. Mark's jaw clenches. He releases my chin, and the smile slides from my face as I realize how badly my joke failed to land. "There was an issue with a patient earlier today. It's fine. I handled it. It's not a big deal."

"Who?"

I shake my head. "I can't tell you that." The guilt of blaming a nonexistent mystery patient is sitting in my stomach like a lead balloon, but I've never been so thankful to be able to fall back on doctor-patient confidentiality in my life. "Are you going to invite me in, or were you thinking we'd just stand here arguing about my face?"

He sighs, then grabs my arm to pull me into his house, saying, "Come in."

"Ow, shit! Don't," I gasp, and his hand falls away as I grip my right arm protectively with my left.

"What the fuck happened, Alyssa?" he asks more softly as I step through the door. I can see the pulse jumping in his neck and feel the anger pouring from him.

"I told you. There was an issue with a patient. I happened to bang my elbow again during said issue, and it hurts a lot right now. I'm fine. I promise."

"Yes. Because shrieking when someone touches you is a sure sign of being *fine*," he growls.

I glare at him as I repeat my last words. "I'm fine. I promise. But if you're going to keep arguing with me about it, I'll go home."

"Fine. I'll stop arguing with you about it," he says, walking toward the kitchen, away from me. I slip my shoes off and trail after him. "When did that happen?" he questions when we reach the kitchen.

"This morning."

"Hmm," he murmurs, staring at my face again in the brighter light.

"Hmm, what?"

"Nothing. It just looks older than that," he remarks. His eyes are still focused on my cheek, and I can tell he wants to press the issue.

"Because you're such an expert on being punched in the face?" I ask, rolling my eyes. It's beginning to seem like coming here tonight was a terrible idea.

"Yes. Personally and professionally. And that bruise is dark enough that it looks like it happened yesterday."

"Whatever," I snap. "I guess I bruise fast. Anyway. How was your day?" I ask, changing the subject.

"Not great," he says, and I feel like an ass for failing to consider that he might've already been having a bad day.

"Why? What happened?"

"Want a glass of wine?" he questions, already pulling two glasses from the cupboard.

"Sure."

"I spent all day in the middle of a group of about two dozen lawyers and nearly as many police officers and forensic techs," he tells me as he fills the glasses.

"What? Why?"

"You haven't heard?"

"Obviously, or I wouldn't be asking," I tell him, trying to keep my own irritation in check.

"They ruled Joey Carmichael's death a homicide."

I want to say, '*Oh, that,*' only I can't because I just told him I had no idea what was going on. Instead, I reply with, "And, what? They think someone on your team did it?"

"That's their working assumption, yes. They believe he was

poisoned sometime shortly before the puck drop, while he was in the locker room. And only the team and people who work directly with the players are allowed in there."

"Well, couldn't anyone have walked in regardless of whether or not they're supposed to?" I question as Mark hands me a glass, and I don't know why. I should just shut up and nod sympathetically.

"No. There are locks on the door."

"Oh. Well, damn. I'm sorry. That sucks."

He shrugs as if it doesn't matter, but then says, "It wouldn't be such a big deal if we didn't have a game tomorrow. But this has everyone looking at everyone else like they might've had something to do with it, which isn't great for morale, and there's not time to fix it before then. We had a player not show up for practice today on top of that, so it's been a crappy day all around. I'm sorry I snapped at you about your face."

"It's okay. I'm sorry I didn't think to mention it to you before you saw it. That was kind of shitty of me," I apologize, my voice softening. I should've said something, given his history with his parents. But it slipped my mind while I was obsessing over my own problems. Katie is wrong. I am objectively terrible at being in a relationship.

"Thanks." Mark pauses to take a sip, and something about the way he's looking at me tells me he's using the wine to buy time. Finally, he swallows, seeming to have reached some sort of decision. "Are you going to keep seeing the patient who hit you in the face today?" he asks, and though his words are neutral, the slight emphasis on 'today' at the end of his sentence makes my heart skip a beat.

He doesn't believe me. *Fuck.*

My phone vibrates, pulling my attention away from Mark. It's Vaughn. "Give me a second. I have to take this," I murmur, relieved to have an excuse to get away from this conversation as I stand and head for the door to the deck.

The wood is cold underfoot when I step outside. Fortunately, it's not also wet, or my socks would be soaked. "Hey Vaughn," I answer.

"Hey kid, what's up?"

"I only have a minute, but two things. First, can you start looking into Brandon Miller?" I ask, keeping my voice low, even though there's no way Mark should be able to hear me from inside.

"Yeah. Same deal as Davidson?"

"Yes. Daily routine and all that. Anything else you can find out would be great too. The sooner, the better," I tell him, since I'm feeling like time is running out.

"Alright, what's the second thing?"

I dig my nails into my palm and force myself to ask the question. "Can you text me Marjorie's number? I don't have it, and I'd like to speak to her."

I'M SITTING ACROSS FROM MARJORIE IN A SMALL BISTRO near my office. The tables are tiny and made of metal despite being indoors. As far as I can tell, the place is trying to recreate the scene of a Parisian or Milanese sidewalk cafe, and it's not quite successful.

I called Marjorie after talking to Vaughn last night to ask if she would have lunch with me. She said she was free today, so here we are. My actual parents might be absentee, but there's no shortage of surrogates willing to offer advice. Although in this instance, Marjorie is a much better sounding board than Jeanette.

"Did you want to talk about me and Vaughn or you and Mark?" Marjorie asks, cutting to the chase after the server has taken our order.

"Both. How much did Vaughn tell you about what I'm doing?" I know he told her *something* about me and Mark. I just don't know how much detail he gave her.

"Oh, everything," she says, waving a hand through the air as if underscoring the sentence. "It's part of our deal. I think you're doing the right thing. Well, mostly."

"Mostly?"

"We'll get to that. What do you know about how Vaughn and I met?" Marjorie asks, her eyes laser-focused on me.

"He said something about a honey trap gone wrong, and that he developed actual feelings for you somewhere along the way. That's it. But I only found that much out about a month ago."

"I was in my mid-twenties when we met, and he was in his early-thirties. He and your dad were hoping to use me to gain access to my father's money. Only it didn't quite work out the way it was supposed to. I got suspicious when Vaughn was a little too perfect. Liking all the same things I liked. Never disagreeing with me. It felt like he was blowing smoke up my ass. A couple of months had passed by the time I called him on it and told him I was breaking up with him. Imagine my surprise when he told me what was really going on."

"And you stayed with him after that? Why?"

"I almost didn't. Part of me felt betrayed, but that part had to contend with the fact that Vaughn was placing a lot of trust in me by telling me the truth, since the truth could've landed him in jail."

"Yeah well. What I've done is a bit more serious than that," I state.

"So maybe you don't lead with that part." Marjorie shrugs and takes a sip of water. "Anyway, to answer your question, I liked Vaughn. I'd already developed feelings for him, and his decision to be honest with me, even though it could've made things worse for him, made it clear his feelings for me were genuine as well. I was unwilling to tolerate being lied to, so once that stopped, staying with him wasn't a difficult decision. The fact that I didn't much like my father may have helped matters."

"You didn't feel like your entire relationship was built on a lie?"

"Hmm," she murmurs, considering it. "No. I don't believe so. It was simply the circumstances under which we met. He never lied about his feelings for me. And if he hadn't been trying to use me to con my father, we never would've met. Maybe that's me rationalizing things. Who knows?"

"I'm pretty sure Mark is going to feel like I betrayed him, no matter how I try to frame it."

"What was your plan going into this?"

I sigh, tapping my fingers lightly against the tabletop. "I figured I'd date him for a while, use him to get access to the arena and the team, and then break up with him when it was all said and done. I never thought I'd actually like him. I didn't expect that I'd get to the end of this and still want to be with him."

"But if that happens, he's definitely going to find out Katie is your cousin," Marjorie states knowingly, and I nod. "You know Vaughn invited you to dinner last weekend to buy you time to figure out what to do?"

"No. He said it was your idea."

Marjorie rolls her eyes. "Not that he'll ever admit it, but that man is a *hopeless* romantic. Anyway. You have one of two options. Either you tell him Katie is your cousin and you lied about knowing who he was because of that, or you say nothing, and eventually he finds out on his own. If you say nothing, and he finds out on his own, he's going to assume that everything, including your feelings for him, is a lie. The sooner you tell him the truth, the better he'll take it."

I let out a slow exhale. "I know."

The server interrupts us long enough to place our entrees on the table and ask if we need anything before disappearing once more.

"He's going to break up with me either way," I tell Marjorie as I spear my fork into a tube of penne.

"Maybe. I honestly can't tell you how he'll react, or what you should say to him to make him want to stay with you. You're not Vaughn, and he's not me. But he likes you as much as you like him. If you tell him who you are now, your odds are probably fifty-fifty."

"That seems incredibly optimistic," I mutter darkly.

"What have you got to lose?"

"Aside from him and my access to the three remaining players? Oh, and possibly my freedom? Absolutely nothing."

"You're smart. You can figure out another way to get to the others if you need to. And worst-case scenario, let's assume Mark immediately suspects you're responsible for the ones who have already died. Can he prove it?"

"No," I admit.

"Can *anyone* prove it?"

"Probably not. It's just that I'm putting my freedom up against a 'probably' for a man who might dump me as soon as he finds out Katie is my cousin."

"Well, I don't believe you'd be sitting here talking to me about him if some small part of you didn't think he was worth the risk." Marjorie takes a bite, mulling something over before saying, "You know Randall was pissed when he found out Vaughn had told me the truth?"

"No, but that tracks."

"Yes. It does. In a similar position, your dad wouldn't have told me. He wouldn't have told anyone the truth. Ever."

I nod in agreement. She's not wrong.

"I guess you've gotta ask yourself who's the better role model? Vaughn or Randall?"

# Chapter 16
# Straight Outta Jumanji

I leave lunch with Marjorie knowing I need to talk to Mark, but having no idea how to actually do it. I meant it when I told her I was sure he'd break up with me. But still. To give myself the best odds, I want to try to talk to him when he might be receptive to what I have to say, and hear me out before he *kicks* me out, but I have no idea when that will be. Obviously not today, since he has a game tonight—apparently one that matters, because games against teams in your division are more important than games against teams that aren't in your conference, which makes no sense since they're all part of the NHL.

He's already stressed because the team itself is the primary suspect in Joey Carmichael's death, which isn't something I could've predicted, but is incredibly satisfying. I *wish* I'd planned it that way, but all I really wanted was for everyone to watch Joey Carmichael die on the ice.

And at some point—probably today, maybe tomorrow—when Matt Davidson fails to show up for another practice or misses the game entirely, they're going to do a welfare check and find his body floating in the pool, which I'm sure is only going to add to Mark's stress level. Because of that, I'd like Mark to pick the time. But if I just call or text him and say, *'Hey, I want to talk to you about something important, when's a good time?'* either his answer is going to be, *'Now,'* or he'll be worrying about that too.

I should be better at this, but if experience has taught me anything, it's that fixing other people's problems is always a lot easier than fixing my own.

I opt for simple and benign, at least for now, and send Mark a text saying, *Hey, any chance you have time to get together in the next few days?*

Almost immediately, three dots appear. A minute later, I get a response saying, *If you don't mind it being late, you can come over after the game tonight. Otherwise, I'm free tomorrow evening*

I want to ask him how stressed he is, but that would definitely send up warning flags, so I don't. *Text me when you're on your way home if you still want me to come by tonight. Otherwise, we can get together tomorrow*

He responds with a thumbs up to my message but doesn't send back one of his own. I put my phone away, feeling the Doomsday Clock hovering above my head accelerate toward midnight.

"What are we watching tonight?" I ask as I take a seat next to Katie on the couch.

"*The Green Planet*," Katie tells me.

"How are you finding all these? Did you join some nature documentary club or subreddit or something?"

She laughs. "No. Mostly, I'm just working my way through the list of documentaries I've been meaning to watch for a while. Whenever we'd add a new one to the library's catalog, if it looked interesting, I'd put it on my list, only I never had time to sit down and watch them. So I'm finally getting caught up."

"Ah. I see."

"I'm considering going back to work," she says.

"Full time or part time?"

"I'm not sure yet. Maybe part time to start. I'm getting bored."

"Tutoring isn't cutting it?" I ask. Katie took medical leave from her position at the library after everything happened, when the panic attacks became too severe for her to be there. She's been working as a virtual SAT tutor for international students hoping to attend college in the US since then to supplement her income. The fact that she's thinking about going back to work is a big deal.

"It's fine, but... I guess I miss being around people."

"Cool," I say, not wanting to make her feel like there's any pressure or expectation from me that she should do so.

She nods, and we both focus our attention on the documentary. About ten or fifteen minutes have gone by, and I'm watching a giant water lily leaf unfold. It looks—and grows—like something straight out of *Jumanji*, and I couldn't be more fascinated.

"Holy shit!" Katie gasps, and I glance over to find her staring at her phone.

"What?" I ask, grabbing the remote and pausing the TV, trying not to be annoyed at the interruption.

"Matt Davidson is dead! They found his body earlier this afternoon. This says he drowned!" she says, a grin on her face. "This is the best month ever!"

"Good news for womankind," I reply, the grin on my face matching hers.

"Should I bake a cake? I feel like I should bake a cake!"

"I won't say no to that," I tell her, glancing at my watch. It's a bit after six. I have to assume they've already told Mark about this. I imagine the rest of the team knows too. Even if the other players didn't like Matt Davidson—and I have no idea whether or not they did—if morale was low upon finding out that Joey Carmichael was murdered, this will crush it. The game tonight is going to be a bloodbath.

I doubt I'll be hearing from Mark.

# Kill the Puckers

My phone rings as I'm walking into my office building. It's Mark. "Hey, good morning. How are you?" I ask.

"Sorry for not texting you last night. You heard what happened?"

I pause as I reach for the door, trying to figure out how to phrase my response. "About the drowning?" I probe. This is going to make telling him about Katie so much harder. He is *so* going to dump my ass, and I can't even blame him. I'd dump me too. "Yeah, I heard. I'm sorry. It's got to be difficult to lose two players that close together."

"I don't have any idea how I feel, if I'm being honest. I didn't like either of them as people, and personally, I'd prefer not to have them on the team, but they were both important for our success, and his death makes my job harder. It's a fucking disaster. They're saying it was an accident, but he's another one of the group who was on trial this summer, and it's got the guys spooked. Half the team is looking at the remaining three like they're contagious, and somehow that makes Fischer think he's entitled to be even more of a pain in my ass than usual. Sorry," Mark mutters. "I didn't call you to vent. You don't care about any of this."

"No. But I care about you, so I'll listen to you talk about it for as long as you need me to," I state as I head for the stairs, not wanting to risk losing the call by getting in the building's elevator.

"Thanks. Do you want to get together this evening? I promise I'll be better company by then."

I want to tell him not to make promises he won't be able to keep, but I only say, "Sure. What did you have in mind?"

"There's a barbecue place in Hosford-Abernethy that's supposed to be pretty good if you're up for it."

"Yeah, that works."

"Pick you up at six-thirty?"

"Let's meet there. I'm not sure I'll make it back to my place in time," I lie. If we arrive separately, and things go badly, he won't be forced to drive me home or make me take an Uber—which I'm almost positive he wouldn't do. He'd drive me himself, and it would be the most awkward, tortured drive either of us has ever endured.

"Okay. I'll text you the address later. And if you want to spend the night, I wouldn't say no."

"Okay," I reply noncommittally, because how the hell do I respond to that? *'Wait until you've heard what I have to say?'* If I did, he'd probably get straight into his car, drive over here, and demand to have the conversation right now. "I'm at the office though, so I have to run. I'll see you tonight," I reply before hanging up.

MARK IS ALREADY WAITING ON THE SIDEWALK IN FRONT OF Outsiders Barbecue by the time I arrive, and his face breaks into a smile when he sees me. Despite the terror curled in my stomach, I can't stop a similar smile from appearing on my face. This is going to suck so much. *I'll wait until we're done eating and tell him then,* I decide. At least that way I won't ruin his dinner.

Once I'm close enough, he grabs my left hand, pulling me toward him. He presses a brief kiss to my lips. I'm sure he intentionally avoided touching my still-injured right arm, and it makes me feel that much worse.

"Hey," he greets.

"Hey," I reply, suddenly having no idea how to carry on a conversation with him. "How was your day?" The question comes out sounding stilted.

"Could've been worse," he states, leading the way to the door. "No one died. So there's that at least."

"Is that the standard we're going with these days? No one dies, and it's a good day?"

"Right now? Yeah. Anyhow, how was yours? It doesn't look like you got punched in the face today."

"No," I snort. Although the bruise looks worse than ever, the swelling has finally started to go down, and the cut is fully scabbed over. I don't even think it will scar. "I didn't. I guess it was a good day for us both."

"Well, alright." He lifts my hand to his lips, pressing a kiss to the back of it. "To low standards."

Then someone is leading us to a table, and it feels like the room is simultaneously too hot and is spinning around me.

"Water, please," I mumble when I'm asked what I want to drink. The thought of adding alcohol to the mixture of guilt and nerves that's roiling through me would be a terrible idea. I already feel like I might throw up.

"What are you doing for Halloween?" Mark asks as my eyes scan the menu, not actually seeing a single word printed on it.

"I don't know. Why?" I ask, glancing up at him.

"Well, we're gone from the twenty-fourth through the thirtieth for road games, but we'll be back on the thirty-first. There's going to be a party at The Rose Room on Halloween, and I thought maybe you'd like to go with me."

"That sounds fun. I'm not sure if my cousin already made plans that night or not, though. Can I let you know in a day or two?" I ask.

"Sure."

Then the server is back, setting our drinks down and asking what we want to eat. Mark looks at me, indicating I should order first. "The ribs," I say, naming the first thing I see on the menu. "With the…" I search frantically for the list of sides. "Potato salad," I finish, once again reading off the first item.

Mark orders the pulled pork with the collard greens and, as soon as the server is gone, asks, "Are you feeling okay?"

"Yeah. Fine. Why?"

"You look paler than normal, and you seem a bit… distracted," he says in a way that implies it wasn't his first choice of descriptors.

"I… there's something I want to talk to you about, but I was going to wait until after we eat," I mumble, glancing away from him without intending to.

"Or we could talk about it now, since whatever it is, it's clearly bothering you," he says, folding his hands on the table before him.

"Hah," I reply humorlessly, looking around for a server to flag down, having changed my mind. Alcohol suddenly sounds like a fantastic idea.

There's a woman a couple of tables away. She's not our server, but she's wearing the same uniform. I wave at her, getting her attention. "Hi, sorry. I know you're not our server, but can you bring two double bourbons? One neat and one on the rocks. Anything from the top shelf is fine."

"Um. Sure. I'll put that in for you," she replies before walking away.

"I'm paying," I tell Mark.

"Okay. Why?"

"Because it's really the very least I can do."

"Alyssa, what's going on?" he questions, reaching for my hand. I let him take it, feeling the calluses on his fingers brush over my skin.

"My cousin, the one I live with—she's actually the only one I have, at least the only one I know of," I say, and I'm definitely babbling. "She wants to meet you."

"Okay. And why does that make you look like you want to throw up?"

"You remember the day we met? How you thought I was following you?"

"Yeah. It's kind of hard to forget," he replies, a smile flickering across his face, his amber-flecked hazel eyes steady on mine.

"You were right," I blurt out as our server appears and thunks two glasses of bourbon onto the table. "I was."

# Chapter 17
# Truth or Dare?

MARK YANKS HIS HAND FROM MINE AS IF I'VE BURNED HIM. Our server, perhaps noticing the change in Mark's body language and sensing the sudden tension at our table, makes a hasty retreat. I can't say I blame him. Running away sounds awesome right now. I slide the neat bourbon I ordered for Mark toward him, and pull the other toward me, picking it up and downing half of it. It burns going down. Whatever bourbon they brought to the table, it's not Pappy Van Winkle.

Mark still hasn't said a word, but the skin around his eyes has tightened, his jaw is clenched, and his knuckles have blanched. His hands appear to be so tightly clasped together that it looks like he may be forcibly restraining himself. So I start talking. It's the only thing I can do.

"I saw you that morning, and I recognized you. Not because I cared about hockey or you." His eyes have narrowed more—they're practically slits now—and his brows have drawn together. I don't know what he's thinking, but I know it's nothing good. So I keep talking. "But because of my cousin. You should ask me who my cousin is." I stop and wait. This needs to be a conversation. He needs to talk to me, even if it's in monosyllabic, one-word sentences, or we'll get nowhere.

"You lied to me," he spits out in a tone I haven't heard from him before. It sounds brittle and angry and hurt and mean. The closest I've heard him come to sounding like this was that day in the arena when he was talking to Garret Fischer.

"Yes. I lied to you. Ask me who my cousin is, Mark."

He picks up his glass of bourbon and downs the contents in one long swallow before pressing his palms flat to the table, shoving his chair back and moving to stand. I grab his right hand with my left, pinning it to the red and white checkered tablecloth. He has six inches and at least seventy pounds on me. I'm under no delusion that I'm stopping him. He could leave if he really wanted to, but he doesn't. He freezes in place instead. And I repeat my words again, hoping the third time is the charm.

"Ask me who my cousin is, Mark."

"Fine. Who is your cousin, Alyssa?" he asks, biting the words out flippantly, like he doesn't expect my answer to mean anything. Like he's already stopped caring.

I keep my hand on his, pinning it to the table, ensuring he can't leave without me noticing as I pull my phone from my pocket, glance at it to unlock it, and then scroll through my photos until I find one of Katie and me at her birthday party last year. I tap the image, zoom in on our faces, and spin my phone to face Mark as I say, "Katie Stanton."

Our server, with the timing of a vaudeville comedian, chooses that moment to appear and set our orders on the table without saying a word. He glances back and forth between us and disappears again. At least he can read the room.

The barest hint of tension leaves Mark's body as he mutters, "Katie Stanton. Katie fucking Stanton is your cousin?" His eyes are locked on my phone screen, and I withdraw my hand from his now that he doesn't seem like he's on the verge of walking out of the restaurant and away from me.

"Yes. The one I grew up with after my dad went to prison."

His eyes rise to mine. He still looks pissed. "Tell me what happened that day. What *actually* happened that day."

I take a deep breath, feeling like I'm playing the most important game of Two Truths and a Lie ever. "I was already at the bookstore, and I saw you. I recognized you, not because I knew anything about you specifically, but because I'd seen you in the background of pictures throughout Katie's trial—pictures they showed in the courtroom and in the news reports about the trial. I wasn't sure if it was you at first. I mean, I was pretty sure, but not positive, not at first. So I was following you, trying to decide if it was really you, and what I would do if it was. Only then I got distracted by that stupid book, and you snuck up on me. Then you insisted I go to the hospital and, well. You know the rest."

"You just happened to see me in Powell's?" He sounds skeptical, and there's a frown marring his face. He hasn't touched the plate of food sitting in front of him. I haven't touched mine either.

"Yes. It's a big bookstore. Lots of people go there." I shrug.

"And you knew who I was right away?"

"Not *right* away, but close enough."

"Why did you pretend you didn't?" His eyes are burning into me, and I wish I could read his mind instead of guessing what he needs to hear to not hate me.

"What the hell was I supposed to say, Mark? 'Hi, I'm Alyssa Reed. Five players on your team raped my cousin, Katie Stanton, and got away with it. What are you going to do about it?' Where would that have gotten me? You would've run in the other direction. Besides, it's not like I was planning on being here with you then. It's not like—"

"You've had weeks to mention this, Alyssa," he bites out, cutting me off. "So, why didn't you? You could've said something after the first night we spent together. You knew then that I wanted this to go somewhere. You could've told me after we had dinner with Vaughn." Mark closes his eyes and lets out a long breath before opening them, and the recrimination in his stare feels like it's burning a hole through me. "Jesus. He must have realized. You must've explained something to him about our relationship. Why the fuck am I only hearing about this now? Why am I—the first person you should've talked to about this—the last to know?"

"You're not the last to know," I state softly. "But you're right. I should've found some time before now to tell you. It's just... I never thought we'd be here. I didn't expect that we would get to this point and we'd both still be interested in the other. I told you that first day that I'm not great at being in relationships. That I've never been in love. I honestly never figured that there might be some future in which I would actually want to introduce you to Katie. Even if I have no fucking idea how I'm going to do it. How I'm going to tell her about you," I mutter darkly as I pick up my drink to wash down the bitter taste this moment is leaving in my mouth.

"She doesn't know you've been dating me?" he questions incredulously.

"No. She knows I'm dating someone. She knows that someone's name is Mark. She knows that I'm... more serious about you than I've pretty much ever been about anyone, which is why she wants to meet you. But that's it. I have no idea how I'm going to tell her, and I wanted to talk to you before I did, because if you're going to break up with me now that you know, I don't want to bring it up at all."

"She's the reason you haven't invited me back to your place."

It's a statement, and not a question, but I confirm it anyway. "Yes. If my feelings for you were any less strong—if I were any less certain—we wouldn't be having this conversation. If I wasn't sure I wanted to keep seeing you, I would've never brought this up. I would've just ended things with you. Telling Katie I'm dating you is probably going to go over about as well as... this," I say, gesturing to the space between us.

"I mean, I don't know. Maybe I'll tell her, and she'll no longer want to meet you at all. Then telling you who she is won't have mattered anyway, and you'll still dump me, and she'll feel like I betrayed her... My life is in shambles because I like you and I want to keep seeing you, but I can't keep doing that if you don't know who I actually am. So yeah. It makes me want to throw up." I'm babbling again. I pick up what's left of my drink and slam it.

"When was this picture taken?" he asks, inclining his head toward my phone on the table.

"Last year. On her birthday in July. We didn't really celebrate this year. For obvious reasons."

"When did you dye your hair?" My hair was still light brown in the picture.

"This year. I felt like a change, and then I ended up liking it and deciding to keep it black."

Mark glances at me. "That's what Marjorie was talking about," he says, seemingly to himself, and he's no longer clenching his jaw or scowling at me. "It looks good both ways," he murmurs.

"Thanks," I reply awkwardly.

"Why did you let me take you to the hospital that day? Why didn't you just tell me to get lost?"

"I did, remember? More than once. You were pretty insistent."

"You told me to get over myself," he growls.

"Yeah. Well. You surprised me. But I told you to leave me alone at least three times."

"And then you got in the car with me anyway."

I shrug. "I was interested. You weren't what I was expecting. Are you going to stay?" I ask, and I'm not sure if I mean here with me right now, to finish this conversation, or with me generally.

"I haven't decided yet." I'm not sure which he means, and I'm unwilling to ask. I'm not sure if he knows either.

"Great," I say dejectedly. "I'm going to order another drink. Do you want one? Please say yes."

"Yes."

"Thank you." I look for our server, catching his eye immediately. Evidently, he's been watching us from a distance. "I think he might recognize you," I tell Mark, inclining my head toward the server so he knows who I'm talking about.

Mark follows my gaze. "Whatever. I don't care."

"Okay." I lift my empty glass, point to it, and then put up two fingers. The guy nods and types the order in.

"What were you expecting?"

"Hmm. What?" I ask, my eyes snapping back to Mark.

"You said I wasn't what you were expecting. What were you expecting?"

I break a rib off the rack on my plate. He's still sitting here, and I haven't eaten all day. I was too worried about talking to him to stand the thought of food. My stomach is no longer churning quite so violently, and now that it's not, I'm starving. He might still leave and never speak to me, but right now he's here, which makes me feel a little calmer.

"I was expecting you to be like them. I've never talked to any of them directly, but I saw them during Katie's trial and, not only did they have zero remorse for what they'd done, but every single one of them wanted to rub it in her face. It's like they all knew they were going to get away with it before the trial was even over, and they were gloating. It was like that the whole time. I didn't show up every day since it was in Seattle and I had to work, but whenever I was there, that's how it was."

Our server sets two fresh drinks on the table, scoops up the empty glasses, and disappears without saying a word. This might actually be the best restaurant service I've ever had.

"Can you eat something?" I nudge Mark's food a little closer to him. "Please. I'm starving, and if you don't also eat something, it feels like you're staring at me, watching me eat, and it's uncomfortable."

"You don't like to be watched," he states.

"It's not my favorite thing ever. The same way you don't like people knowing more about you than you know about them. And for the record, I still haven't Googled you, or read your Wikipedia page, or whatever it is that's out there about you."

"Why not?"

"Because even though I lied to you about not knowing who you were when we first met, everything else I've told you about myself has been real. My feelings for you are real. And I'm a big proponent of trusting people regardless of how absurd it might seem for me to say that right now."

He finally picks up his fork and takes a bite of food. "What exactly did you know about me before you saw me in the bookstore?"

"I knew you were the Black Bears' head coach, and I knew you were the youngest—or one of the youngest—head coaches in the NHL, and that's pretty much it. Oh. I knew you were from Louisiana too. People love to mention that. I think they think it makes you seem exotic."

Mark rolls his eyes.

"So where do we go from here?" I ask.

"Is this why you wanted to meet me here? Why you didn't want me to pick you up?"

"Yes. I figured there was a good chance you'd want nothing to do with me after I told you, and I didn't want you to be stuck driving me home if that were the case."

"What about that day in the hallway with Garret Fischer?" He's frowning again, and it's making me uneasy.

"What about it?" I ask, setting the half-eaten rib down. It's impossible to say whether the food is good. I definitely ruined dinner for both of us, despite trying not to.

"You must've recognized him."

"Yeah. I did."

"But he didn't recognize you?"

"I don't know. I have no idea. You would know better than I would."

"No. I don't think he did. So you recognized him and, what? You were just going to let him introduce himself and shake your hand?" I hear the challenge, or maybe it's skepticism, in Mark's question.

"Honestly, I don't know. You stepped between us before I could figure out how to respond. I might've punched him in the face if you hadn't."

"But then you played it off like you had no idea who he was and accused me of being jealous," he says, sounding offended all over again.

"Okay. Yes. I did play it off like I had no idea who he was. That wasn't why I said something about you being jealous, though. Or at least it wasn't the only reason. It was that, plus the way you asked about Vaughn, plus your comments about not sharing well, plus your vague statements about the way your last relationship ended, plus your overall vibe, which I already told you. But for the record, I would like to apologize. I clearly jumped to an incorrect conclusion. And I like your overall vibe."

He says nothing in response to that.

"I'm sorry I lied to you about recognizing you. I never expected to like you as much as I do, and if I could go back to our first meeting and change it, I would. I know trust is kind of a big deal to you, and I would understand if you didn't want to keep trying it—this, whatever we're calling what we're doing—with me."

"Why did you agree to go on a date with me?"

"You want the full list of reasons or the short version?"

"Give me the full list."

I sigh. "You're going to have the hugest fucking ego by the time we're done talking. You're going to be so insufferable," I gripe.

He doesn't smile, but his lips twitch upward. He says nothing, though, and merely waits for me to continue.

"Fine. First, look at you. You're freaking gorgeous. Who wouldn't agree to go on a date with you? Second, I liked that you argued with me. I liked that you thought you could tell me what to do. That you thought I would listen just because you said so. And when I didn't, when I argued with you, it turned you on, which turned me on. I knew if I slept with you, it would be fun. Third, you kept flirting with me the entire time we were together, so you were clearly interested in me too. Fourth, you obviously had something going on with your job that day, but instead of rushing off to deal with that, you told them you were busy. You stayed at the hospital with me and then took me out for pizza afterward. Fifth, when I sat across the table from you in the pizza parlor and told you I was pretty sure you were already hard for me, instead of denying it, you asked me out on a date. Of course I fucking said yes. I'm not a masochist."

"Yeah. Well. That hasn't changed," Mark grumbles.

"What?"

"My reaction to sitting across from you in a restaurant."

I raise my eyebrows. "Are we playing Truth or Dare now?"

"Haven't we been playing Truth or Dare since we met?" he counters, and yeah. I guess we have.

"Okay," I agree.

"Truth or dare?"

"Dare."

Mark simply tilts his head and waits. I slip my foot from my shoe —knowing the tablecloth will obscure what's happening—and stretch my leg out under the table, running it up his, until it's resting on the chair between his legs. He's rock hard and his eyes flutter shut as I begin stroking him with my foot.

He really is a bastard, and I really can't get enough of him.

WE'RE BACK AT MARK'S HOUSE. I'M LYING ON HIS CHEST AS he runs his fingers up and down my spine, and we're both sheened in sweat. There was a moment at the barbecue joint, when my foot was on his cock, where I thought he might come in his pants. And then our too-observant server showed up with to-go boxes and the check.

I'm certain my face has never been redder than it was when I passed over my credit card to pay the bill, but Mark looked totally unperturbed.

"What the hell would I say to her if we met? Sorry doesn't exactly cut it," Mark says, breaking the silence.

"To Katie?" I ask, startled by his words.

"Yeah."

"I don't know. Sorry is a pretty good starting point. Not because she thinks it's your fault. She doesn't. She knows it's not anyone's fault except for theirs. But it's hard to go wrong with empathy and compassion. She may not want to meet you once she finds out who you are, though. I'm honestly not sure. Again, not because she holds you responsible, but…" I trail off, unsure how to end the sentence.

"Yeah. I know. I get it."

"Are we… okay? Should I talk to her?"

"Yeah, Alyssa. We're okay. Just…"

"I know," I murmur, already aware I can't keep that promise. I'm definitely going to lie to him again. I just hope he won't find out. Once the last three are dead, I won't have any more lies to tell. "I'll talk to her and let you know if she still wants to meet you. Sometime after Halloween, right?"

"Yeah. I'll make any night we don't have a game scheduled work."

"Okay."

# Chapter 18
# Dating the Enemy

"What do you think about doing a movie marathon or something for Halloween?" I ask Katie when I get home from work the next day. I figure I can spend the first half of the night with her, and then meet up with Mark at The Rose Room for the second half.

"What did you have in mind?" Katie questions from where she's hovering above the kitchen stove. "Also, I'm making grilled cheese sandwiches. Want one?"

"Yeah sure, I'll take a sandwich. I was figuring we could watch all the *Halloweentown* movies. Maybe *Hocus Pocus*, too. We could light some candles and make s'mores over them."

"I'm down. You don't already have plans with your boyfriend?"

"Nothing official yet. Plus, I was thinking I could go out with him later in the night." I shrug. "I did want to talk to you about him, and having dinner with him."

"Okay. When?"

"Next weekend. After Halloween. He'll be out of town from tomorrow until then."

"I thought he just got back?" she says over the popping and hissing from the frying pan as she flips the sandwich.

"He did."

"Why's he leaving again so soon?" she asks, turning to face me with the spatula in her hand.

"You remember how I said he works with troubled youth?"

"Yeah, why?"

"Well, that was a very generous interpretation of the truth."

"Okay. So what does he actually do? Is it something embarrassing?"

"No. I mean… I don't know. You're not going to like it, and once I tell you who he is, you're probably going to be mad at me."

"Why would I be mad at you? You're not dating one of *my* exes, are you? Even if you are, I don't care," she replies, turning back to the stove to remove the grilled cheese from the pan. She puts it on a plate and uses the spatula to slice it in half before passing it to me. She starts assembling the second sandwich as she continues, "It would be funny though. Please tell me it's Jeff. If anyone could unpack his mommy issues, it's you."

"Don't even joke. I never understood what you saw in that guy. Easily the biggest man-child I've ever known—personally *or* professionally," I mutter.

"Yeah, because you have such great taste in romantic partners. There was Jenny—who was channeling Angelina Jolie circa her Billy Bob era—and don't forget about Brent the cycling instructor—who didn't even know what the word 'zygote' meant. Besides, Jeff was really good in bed. Eager to please. Apparently, the mommy issues are good for something after all," Katie remarks with a grin.

"Yeah, what do you think I was so interested in Jenny and Brent for?"

"I bet Jenny was fun in bed," Katie says thoughtfully.

"I can give you her number if *you* want to date one of *my* exes," I tease.

"God no. She was insane. No amount of fun in bed is worth *that* hot mess express. Plus, she's not really my type. If you know a slightly more chemically balanced male equivalent of that, let me know."

"Why? Are you going to start dating again?"

"I don't know. Maybe. Joey Carmichael and Matt Davidson dying kind of makes me feel like the whole world isn't all doom and gloom and maybe I should stop hiding."

"Okay. Well, I don't know anyone who fits that description, but if I run across them, I'll send them your way. There was this server at the restaurant we were at last night…" I joke.

"Oh yeah, back to the original topic. Dinner with your boyfriend. What does he do, and when are we having dinner?"

I take a deep breath and then exhale it. "He's Mark Eriksson, Kay. The Black Bears' head coach."

She freezes, her entire body having gone rigid. After a handful of seconds, she takes a deep breath of her own, then turns to face me. "Excuse me?" she asks, the humor of a few moments ago having completely vanished.

"Yes. That's why I've been reluctant to tell you about him."

"You're dating the *enemy*?" she hisses.

"He's not the enemy, Katie, though I get that it might feel like that. But he didn't have anything to do with what happened. Even the other players on the team aren't the enemy, Kay. If anyone has your back—ever—you know it's me. And you don't have to meet him if you don't want to. I'm not asking you to hang out with him or to be friends, but I also don't want to take the decision of whether or not you meet him away from you."

"Does he know who I am?" she asks, sounding furious.

I nod. "I told him last night."

She snorts. "Oh good. At least you're keeping secrets from everyone then and not just me."

"Okay. That's fair, and I understand why you're mad at me."

"Don't fucking use your therapy-speak on me, Alyssa!" she shouts. "Of course you understand why I'm mad at you. You're not a fucking idiot! Don't talk to me like I'm one either!"

"Fine! I didn't tell you because I knew it would piss you off! Happy? I didn't tell you because I wasn't sure if my relationship with him would go anywhere, but I fucking like him and I want it to go somewhere!"

"How the hell did you even meet him? Why would you ever go on a date with him? How could you?"

"How could I? I've never criticized you for anyone you've ever dated, Kay! It'd be nice if you could extend me the same courtesy."

"I've never dated anyone who employs people who raped you, Alyssa! The circumstances are totally fucking different!" she roars.

"Okay. Okay. Fine. You're right. They are different. But it's not like he chose to hire them, and believe me, he would fire them if he could."

"Like that makes it better?" she asks, and I smell smoke.

"Katie, the sandwich."

"I don't care about the goddamn sandwich, Alyssa!"

"No, it's burning."

"Shit!" she snaps, spinning to the stove, grabbing the frying pan, and throwing it into the sink.

"Here," I slide the grilled cheese she gave me back toward her. I haven't had any of it yet.

"I'm not hungry anymore."

"Alright. I'm sorry. I didn't mean for this to turn into a fight, and even though it probably seems like it right now, this isn't me betraying you. And it's okay that you're mad at me. If our situations were reversed, I'd be mad too. I'm going to drop the subject for now, and if you want to talk about it more later, let me know. If you decide you want to meet him, I'll set it up, but if you never want to, that's fine too."

"Yeah, whatever," she grumbles.

I sigh but grab half of the sandwich off the island and head for my room to give her some space to cool down and process her feelings. I'm not surprised by her reaction. It makes sense. It's frustrating not to be able to tell her the full story, because if I did, she'd definitely understand how and why I started dating Mark, even if she wouldn't understand why I'm interested in him as more than a means to an end now.

I set the half of the grilled cheese I took from the kitchen on my nightstand and flop onto my bed. I'm not hungry anymore either, but I didn't want to leave the entire sandwich sitting on the island like another slap in the face.

*No-go on the dinner for now*, I text Mark.

*Okay. No worries. I assume you won't be coming by tonight and I'll see you when I get back?*

*Yes. I'll call you later though*

*Sounds good*, he replies.

"WHAT'S WRONG WITH YOU? YOU LOOK TERRIBLE," VAUGHN says when he sits down across from me on Saturday.

I suck down some more coffee prior to responding. "Seriously? No 'Hi Alyssa, nice to see you' before you launch into insulting me?" I sulk. "I did what you wanted, and it blew up in my face." I know I'm being unfair, but Vaughn can take it. Mark's out of town, and Katie's not speaking to me. There's not exactly anyone else I can talk to about this. Besides, he insulted me first.

"What I wanted?" Vaughn questions, taking a sip of his own coffee.

"I told Mark about Katie and Katie about Mark, and now Katie's not talking to me. She accused me of sleeping with the enemy."

Vaughn shrugs. "From the sounds of it, he didn't dump you, and she didn't move out. It'll be fine. You should try getting some sleep."

"Gee thanks, *dad*," I snap.

"If you were my daughter—" he begins.

"Yeah, I know. It's lucky for us both that I'm not."

Vaughn snorts. "Here's what I figured out about Brandon Miller," Vaughn says, handing me another folder to add to my collection.

I open it and begin flipping through it. "He slept with all these women just since I asked you to look into him?" I ask, glancing up to see Vaughn nodding. "That was only five days ago, and he's been out of town since yesterday. There are six names on this list."

"Yup. Five of the six are sex workers, though, so at least they're getting something out of it. The sixth simply has no taste in men, I guess," he replies.

"He must be a sex addict," I mutter. "What do these women look like?"

"Next page," Vaughn says, and I shuffle the papers around.

They're all white, which is good news for me. And they're all taller than average, which is also good news. Unfortunately, all of them have more curves than I do. Maybe I can buy some padding and a really good push-up bra and get close enough. It's worth a shot. Plus, if he is a sex addict, he's unlikely to say no even if I don't match his type exactly.

"Can you get me some GHB?"

"GHB?" Vaughn's brows are raised as he takes a sip of his coffee.

"At least one of them should die with date-rape drugs in their system," I reply, staring into his eyes.

He gives a small nod and says, "Yeah. I can do that."

I continue flipping through the pages. Brandon Miller doesn't have much of a life outside of hockey. It seems as though most of his remaining non-working time is spent with a rotating cast of sex workers. Fortunately, thanks to Mark's Halloween invitation, I know at least one time I'll be able to bump into Brandon to get him to invite me back to his house. Unfortunately, that means I won't be able to go to the party with Mark. Although if I time it right, I could spend the first part of the night with Katie—assuming she's talking to me by that point—take a couple of hours out in the middle of the night to kill Brandon, and then still make it to Mark's before the night is over. Maybe even still make it to The Rose Room before the party ends.

Yeah. It could work.

"The team gets back on Halloween. When they do, can you look into Rhys Steichen?"

"Sure. You need anything else?" Vaughn asks.

"No, not unless you want to hit up Spirit Halloween with me."

"I'm good," he comments drily.

"Alright. Thanks, Vaughn," I say, gathering the folder and tapping the edge against the table as I move to leave. "I appreciate the help."

"Anytime."

I'M WANDERING THROUGH THE AISLES OF THE HALLOWEEN store, looking for costumes. I need at least three. One for luring Brandon Miller away from The Rose Room, one to make my way back to The Rose Room without drawing attention after I've killed him, and one to wear when I'm with Mark. I'm going to be cutting all of my timelines really close. There's not much margin for error.

I check my watch. It's one in the afternoon, which means it's three for Mark. I'm pretty sure he has a game tonight, but I don't think that's for a few hours yet. I FaceTime him, hoping he'll have some time to talk.

"Hey Alyssa," he says as he comes into focus. It took him a minute to answer, and his back is to some sort of cinder block wall.

"Hey, if I'm interrupting and it's not a good time, we can talk later."

"No, it's fine. I needed to get out of that room anyway. What's up?"

"I was thinking about Halloween, and I don't know what time the party starts, but if I can meet you there around midnight, I'd like to."

A smile spreads across his face. "Midnight works."

"Okay good. Do you already have a Halloween costume?"

"No. Not yet. Why? Did you have something in mind?"

"How do you feel about couples costumes?" I ask. "Is it too nerdy? Too clingy? I've never done it before."

"Any chance I get to be a first for you, I'm going to take it."

I clear my throat but say nothing, trying to ignore the warmth spreading through my chest.

"Cat got your tongue?" he asks.

"God," I grumble, amusement threading through my voice. "You are *such* a dick."

"I know. I meant it though."

"Yeah. I know. So, what do you want to be? Fred and Daphne? Beetlejuice and Lydia? Morticia and Gomez?"

"Well, of those, there's only one right answer."

"Morticia and Gomez?" I ask, hoping he chose right.

"Yes. Can you tango?"

"No. Can you?"

"Maybe," he glances away from his phone, his mouth turning down as he does. He looks like he's listening to something. A few seconds later he runs a hand through his hair, and says, "I've got to go. I'll call you later tonight."

"Alright, bye," I reply as the screen goes black.

I toss the Gomez and Morticia costumes in with the Ghostface Killer costume. There's nothing slutty enough for the costume I'm going to wear to lure Brandon Miller away, so I settle with buying a wig and a copious amount of body paint. I'll have to stop by a lingerie store after this.

# Chapter 19
# Strip Club Rules

I open my office door and walk Henry Jackson out, setting my latest round of notes on the desk for Teresa to type up when she has a chance. Henry deals with moderately severe obsessive-compulsive disorder with a side of generalized anxiety disorder for good measure. He's been doing well lately, though.

"A Mark Eriksson is going to be stopping by for me soon. Can you send him back to the office when he gets here?" I ask Teresa as soon as Henry Jackson leaves. I need to give Mark his half of our costume before we meet at The Rose Room tonight and since I have a movie night—assuming Katie is willing to watch movies with me—and a murder lined up prior to that, this is the only time that worked for us both.

"Sure. I'm going to run to the post office during lunch to send out the billing statements for this month. Do you have anything that needs to go in the mail?" Teresa questions, adjusting the witch's hat she's wearing for Halloween.

"No. Thanks though," I reply at the same time Mark steps through the door. "Hi Mark," I greet, not bothering to hide the smile spreading across my face. "This is Teresa. Teresa, this is my boyfriend Mark."

He also looks stupidly happy—the smile he's wearing spreads all the way to his eyes, crinkling them at the corners as he walks to the desk and shakes her hand. "Hi, nice to meet you."

"Yes, you too. Well, I guess if I don't need to wait around for anyone, I'll run to the post office now."

"Okay, thanks," I say as she grabs her coat and the stack of mail, then heads for the door leading out of the reception area, locking it behind her, since she won't be here to keep an eye on the room.

As soon as the door clicks shut, I grab Mark's hand and pull him into my office, shutting and locking that door as well.

"You introduced me as your boyfriend," he says, sounding giddy.

"Isn't that what you are?"

"Yes, but you've never introduced me that way, and it turns out I like hearing you say it," he tells me, and then his hands are in my hair, and his lips are on mine, his tongue plunging into my mouth.

I groan, arching into him as his hands release my hair and run down my body. He reaches the waistband of my pants and pulls my shirt out, sliding his hands under it and across my skin. His palms are warm, and my cunt is already throbbing.

"I need you, Alyssa," Mark murmurs, pulling his mouth just far enough away from mine to get the words out as he takes my hand and places it on his cock.

I can't help but run my hand over him when I feel how hard he is. "We shouldn't," I say, not meaning it. Because even if we shouldn't, I really want to.

"She's gone. The office is empty." He's slipped his hand under my bra and is tracing circles around my nipple. "And I need this. I need you. Even if she were here, I would still want to bend you over your desk and fuck you until you were screaming my name. Please," he says, and it sounds like he's begging. It's incredibly hot.

I unzip his pants, freeing him and wrapping my hand around his dick. He's so hard, and his skin is silky smooth. He moans, his hips twitching as my skin makes contact with his. "Say it again," I demand, stroking him slowly as I stare into his eyes.

"I need you so much right now. I want to feel the tight, wet warmth of you squeezing my dick. Please. Please let me fuck you."

"Why? Has it been a while?" I tease.

"You know exactly how long it's been," he growls, as his hands slip out from under my shirt and begin undoing the buttons.

"Have you been imagining this moment since the last time we were together?"

"Yes." The buttons on my shirt are halfway undone now. "Say yes," he demands as I continue to pump my hand along his shaft.

"How many times did you masturbate to the thought of screwing me?"

"Every day I've been gone."

"Only once a day?"

"No," he admits, his eyes are locked on mine, and I couldn't look away if I tried. I want him in my mouth, and I want him in my cunt. I want him in every part of my body at the same time.

"How many times, Mark?"

The buttons on my shirt are all the way undone now, and he reaches around to unfasten the hooks on my bra, then pushes my shirt off one shoulder. As soon as my hand is free, he pushes the bra strap down my arm as well. I switch hands, gripping him with my other so I don't have to let go of him as he repeats the process, being careful with my elbow.

"At least once in the morning and once before bed. Say yes, Alyssa."

"My office, and my rules today. You do what I say when I say it."

"As long as I can have you, I'll do whatever you say. Anything you want."

"Okay. Yes," I agree, releasing him to yank his shirt off, then shoving him away. He staggers backward a step, his lower legs hitting the couch as he falls onto it with a look of surprise on his face. "Pants off. All the way off," I order with a smirk as I remove my remaining clothes and then straddle him on the couch.

He places his hands on my thighs, running them up the insides of my legs. I almost let him touch me, but I know if I do, this won't go the way I want, so I pull his hands away from me. "Strip club rules. No touching until I say otherwise."

Heat moves across his expression, and I can tell he wants to argue, but he already agreed to play by my rules. "Okay," he says with a nod. "Hands off."

"Good." I line up the shaft of his cock so the underside of it is pressing into my clit and then run my hand along the top from base to tip. The friction and the pressure of him pressing against me makes me groan, and I shift for an even better angle.

"I want to touch you," Mark moans, watching me intently.

"No," I say, and a frustrated rumble builds in his chest. "Tell me what would've happened in the restaurant if we hadn't been interrupted."

"You know what would've happened. Let me touch you," he pleads.

"No. Tell me anyway."

"After another minute or two, it would've been too much for me to take. I would've grabbed you from the table, dragged you into the bathroom, and fucked you from behind while we watched ourselves in the mirror. Alyssa, let me touch you." His skin is hot beneath my hands, and I can't wait to have him inside me, but I'm enjoying torturing him—torturing us both—too much.

"No. What if someone had heard us?"

"I wouldn't have cared. They could've been on the other side of the door shouting at us, and I would've kept going until we were both satisfied. Please. I need more."

I lean forward, bracing my left hand on his shoulder until my nipples are grazing his chest, and the extra stimulation feels amazing. My right hand is still on his dick, but it's pinned between our torsos. "How many times have I said that to you only for you to make me suffer? You can deal with having a taste of your own medicine," I whisper in his ear before nipping at his earlobe.

He growls.

"What were you thinking about the last time you jerked off to me?" He swallows as I trail my tongue down his neck and over the hollow between his clavicles. I resume stroking him as soon as there's enough room for my hand to move.

"It was in the bathroom on the plane on the way back."

"On the plane?" I question, biting one of his nipples. I'm rewarded with a sharp intake of breath.

"Yes. The team's plane. I was in my seat, thinking about seeing you, which led to thinking about being with you. I ended up so hard I had to go to the bathroom just to get a little relief."

"And did you? Get some relief?" I probe as I slide off the couch to kneel between his legs, licking my way down his stomach.

"Yes. I went into the bathroom and rubbed one out while fantasizing about being with you in the restaurant. I was imagining you slipping under the table with the tablecloth hiding you."

"What was I doing under the table?"

"You had your mouth wrapped around me, and you were sucking me off while I was trying to play it cool so no one would know what was happening," he says breathlessly.

"Do you want me to wrap my mouth around you now?" I ask, letting all the desire I'm feeling for him flood into my voice. I want him desperately, but teasing him is such a turn on for us both that it's going to make things even better when I finally fuck his brains out.

"God yes."

"Tell me what happened next. If you stop, I stop," I warn as I slide my mouth over him, engulfing his cock until he's deep enough in my throat that I have to fight my gag reflex.

"Alyssa, oh god," he moans, jerking against me. "I was imagining it felt just like this. And I wanted you to keep going, but I was also imagining pulling you up to ride me so that everyone in the restaurant could see how perfectly we fit together and how much I love being buried inside you. Please let me touch you." I wait until he's almost there—until I can taste the cum dripping from the head of his cock—before pulling my mouth away.

"Alyssa, please," he begs as I move to straddle him once more, gripping his shaft, lining him up with my opening.

"No, not until I say so," I groan as I slide down his length one slow inch at a time. The sensation as he fills me is so amazing that I'm already quivering around him. "Tell me what this feels like."

"You're so tight and warm, Alyssa," he says, and it's barely a whisper. "So soft, but you're squeezing me so hard. It's all I can do to sit here and hold still. I want to fuck you until you're hoarse from screaming my name. I want to make every part of you mine. Your mouth felt amazing, but this is everything I could ever want."

He's buried all the way inside me, and I squeeze his dick with my cunt as tightly as I can. I'm rewarded with a strangled moan that sets every nerve ending on fire, and I rub myself against him, in tiny motions, letting the tip of his cock stroke across my cervix, pleasure building until I'm coming on top of him, writhing in place, squirting all over both of us, a choked gasp escaping my throat.

Mark's eyes are wild, and he looks as though he's about to lose it.

"Touch me," I whimper. "Please fucking touch me, Mark."

He locks one hand in my hair, smashing our mouths together as his other goes around my waist, lifting me off him and pulling me back down onto him again and again. His motions grow more frantic until he's filling me with cum, pushing me into a second orgasm.

He's still hard inside me when our bodies stop moving and he pulls his mouth from mine. "What the hell was that?" he asks, sounding awed.

"Hmm?" I murmur as I slump against his chest, enjoying the feeling of him still buried inside me.

"You, squirting all over me. You've never done that before."

"Oh. That."

"Yes. That."

I shrug lazily, luxuriating in the heat rising from his skin to mine. "I don't know. Sometimes it happens, sometimes it doesn't. It's not correlated to how much I enjoy it, if that's what you're wondering, but it happens more often when I'm in control."

"That was amazing," Mark whispers, his hand stroking across my hair.

"Mhmm." I glance at my watch and then sit up abruptly. It's a quarter to one. "You need to get up."

"I just did that," Mark quips.

"Ha. Ha," I deadpan. "I have a patient coming in fifteen minutes. We need to get cleaned up. You can't be here," I tell him as I stand to sort through our clothes. The couch is a mess. I can flip the cushions for now, but I'll have to take them to the dry cleaners this weekend and… "I should ban you from my office," I mutter. "You're a menace."

"It was worth it." He grabs my wrist and tugs me toward him as he stands. "Thank you," he says, pressing a kiss to my forehead before heading toward the small bathroom off my office. "Besides, I had to pick up my costume," he comments as he moves away.

"Yeah, you'd better not forget it," I grumble as I pull on my shirt, then open a window and flip the couch cushions over.

"I WANT TO MEET HIM," KATIE SAYS, AMBUSHING ME AS soon as I walk into the condo. I have the distinct feeling that I'm the gazelle in one of those nature documentaries she's always watching.

"Hi, happy Halloween to you too, Kay. So you're talking to me again?" I reply, trying to keep my tone mild as I set the grocery bag I'm carrying on the counter. "I think that's the most you've said to me in the past week."

"Yeah, well you deserved it, springing the info on me like that."

"Should I have made you play Twenty Questions? Told you whether you were getting warmer or colder?"

"Fine. You're right. I would've been mad no matter what. But I want to meet him now."

"Okay," I agree. "I'll find out when he's free. What changed?"

"I've been researching him," she informs me.

"Okay. That still doesn't explain what changed."

"You don't know," she states, sounding confident as she pushes her blond hair back.

"Don't know what?" I probe.

"You should ask him what happened at college in Wisconsin," Katie states before turning and heading toward her room.

"Hey," I call after her. "You're not going to watch *Halloweentown* with me? I bought marshmallows on the way home!"

"Can't," she replies over her shoulder. "I have tutoring sessions with international students all night."

"Seriously?"

Katie stops and turns back to me when she reaches her door. She gives a small shrug, then says, "Sorry. I booked them when I was still mad at you."

"Does that mean you're not mad at me anymore?" I ask.

"I'm considering my options," she replies, but she smiles as she says it, and relief washes through me.

"Fine. But I'm going to watch them and make s'mores without you."

"We can watch them tomorrow if you want. An All Saints' celebration. Burnt marshmallows as an offering."

"I don't think that's a thing," I grumble. "What am I supposed to do tonight?"

"Don't you have a boyfriend?" she snarks.

I roll my eyes and huff as she goes into her room. Then I turn and head for mine. It gives me extra time to get ready, at least.

I start by putting on the hip padding I got to make myself look curvier than I actually am. Unfortunately, the lingerie I bought isn't going to allow for a pushup bra or any kind of cutlets—I'm already in danger of my tits popping out if I bend over too far—but my nipples will be on full display, which will probably make up for it. Plus, it'll be sure to get me past the bouncer at The Rose Room without having to give a name or show an ID.

Next, I pull on two pairs of shimmery tights to obscure the padding, and then two pairs of fishnets on top of those. It's ridiculous, but it hides the padding, and it'll help keep me warm, because the teddy I bought to wear for my costume is nothing but see-through black mesh embroidered with little pink flowers. It goes on next.

After that, it's the thigh-high stockings, which I tuck two small vials of GHB into. Each vial contains three milliliters of GHB. I measured the dosage out yesterday from the larger bottle Vaughn gave me. Technically, anything over two milliliters puts the victim at risk of an overdose, which is what I want, since part of an overdose is the loss of consciousness. These are street drugs, though, so the purity is questionable. And even though three milliliters should be enough to knock Brandon Miller out, it shouldn't be enough to cause respiratory distress. Probably. It's always hard to say with street drugs.

In addition to the vials, I slide six hundred dollars into my stocking—five hundred-dollar bills, with the last hundred being composed of a mix of tens and singles. I'll probably need cash for The Rose Room, since I can't risk using a credit card.

I wrap a robe around myself, twist my hair into a low, flat bun, pin it in place, and sit down to do my makeup. I begin by covering my face with white cake makeup, before outlining my eye sockets with black liner and filling them in. I do the same with my nose, and then over-line my lips with blood-red liner, and fill those in too. I continue applying makeup until my face looks like a very elaborate skull.

I fit two wig caps onto my head before carefully placing the dark red wig over those and securing it in place with eyelash glue rather than wig adhesive to make it easier to remove later, since I'll have to do a full costume change prior to reappearing at The Rose Room to meet Mark. I pin a few fake flowers in the hair at the front of the wig to complete the look.

The only thing left to do is to take off the robe and put on the thigh-high boots and black satin gloves that complete my costume. I stand in front of the mirror once I've done that, trying to decide how likely Mark will be to recognize me. I stare at myself for a while. I think if he's there early enough to see me luring Brandon Miller away, which he probably will be, the makeup combined with the wig and everything else should stop him from realizing it's me—as long as I don't go near him, anyway.

Finally, I leave my room. Getting ready took the better part of an hour and a half, and Katie is in the kitchen getting a drink when I come out.

"Whoa," she says, staring at me.

"Too much?" I ask.

"Well, aside from the nipples," she begins teasingly. "No. You look great."

"Thanks. Okay. I've gotta go."

"Knock 'em dead," Katie suggests as I move past her.

# Chapter 20
# Suffer Not a Rapist to Live

It's shortly before eight when I park on the street a few blocks away from The Rose Room and get out of my car, tucking my keys into the top of the stocking opposite the GHB vials. I'm relying on my looks and skimpy costume to get me through the door without giving a name, so I'm not wearing a coat.

The night is cold, and the chill seeps into my bones as I walk toward the club. There's already a line formed outside, snaking down the sidewalk and wrapping around the building. I ignore it and head straight for the bouncer. He's a big, tattooed white guy wearing a black hoodie, holding a clipboard. My name is technically on his list, but I don't have any intention of using it until I come back to see Mark.

I stop next to him and clear my throat, ignoring the three women at the front of the line as I wait for his eyes to lock onto me. He gives me a once-over as soon as they do, and his gaze lingers on my very visible boobs, which are currently showing precisely how cold I am, I'm sure.

"Hey," I say, leaning toward him, placing my hand on his arm. "I'm here with the Black Bears."

"Are you—" he begins, his eyes still on my boobs, but I cut him off.

"I'm with Brandon Miller. He's waiting for me."

"Okay," he replies, waving me through.

I saunter past, and another man closer to the club door pulls it open as I approach. Fog comes rolling out along with a burst of house music. Then I'm stepping through, into the din and chaos of The Rose Room at Halloween. Everyone is wearing costumes, and the place is already packed. The bass is blasting against me, making my whole body vibrate. Finding Brandon is going to be easier said than done. I'm taller than most of the crowd in my heeled boots, but there are so many people in here that it doesn't matter much. I still can't see well enough to have a snowball's chance in hell of finding him.

I snake through the crowd, twisting between groups of witches, fairies, and devils as I head toward the staircase leading to the second floor. A guy in a vampire costume gropes my ass as I slide past, and I'm tempted to turn around and backhand him, but I don't. Given that I'm planning on committing a murder later tonight, causing a scene and drawing attention to myself wouldn't be worth it. Finally, I'm climbing the staircase to the second floor. I push my way to the railing, ignoring the protests as I claim a spot against it where I can look down at the main floor.

I spot Rhys Steichen almost right away. He's wearing a Frankenstein costume, but his size combined with the missing tooth makes him easy to recognize. Plus, his makeup isn't that good. The grey-green face paint couldn't be more haphazardly applied. He definitely won't be winning any costume contests. He's in a raised section of the club, behind a velvet rope, in the middle of a group. I recognize a couple of the guys as players on the team—including Garret Fischer, who's wearing a cowboy costume. I assume the others must also be hockey players. The women are probably the players' significant others —or WAGs, because a lot of sports culture is so misogynistic that they believe it's acceptable to discuss women based solely on the relationship they have to 'important' men.

I don't see Brandon Miller, though there are a few guys wearing costumes that have full-face masks—a Jason Voorhees, a Spider-Man, and a triangle *Squid Game* guard. My money is on Brandon being Jason or the guard. He doesn't strike me as the 'great power, great responsibility' type. They'll have to take their masks off to drink at some point. I'll just stand here watching until they do.

About fifteen minutes have gone by, and I've ruled out Spider-Man. I'm not sure who he is, but he's not Brandon. The other two haven't removed their masks yet though, and I'm growing impatient. I can't stand around all night.

I spot a cocktail waitress dressed as a French maid with blood running down her neck. I remove two hundred-dollar bills from my stocking and hold them up in the air until I catch her attention.

She slowly wends her way through the crowd. "What can I get you?" she asks when she's near enough to be heard above the thumping bass and shouted conversations.

"Do you see the guys behind the velvet rope?"

She nods.

"Can I have thirty Jello shots delivered to them?" I pass her the hundreds, saying, "I don't need change."

"Sure," she agrees, heading for the stairs.

Ten minutes later, she's approaching the raised area where the players are sequestered, carrying a tray filled with neon-green Jello shots at the same time Mark is approaching, dressed as Gomez Addams. Damn. I was really hoping my luck would hold, and he wouldn't show up until after I'd managed to get out of here with Brandon.

Mark looks good. He stops for a moment to say something to the guy manning the velvet rope, who's pulling it aside for the woman carrying the Jello shots. After a few seconds, Mark is ascending the steps too, and I have to force my eyes away from him to watch the players as the woman begins handing out shots. Almost everyone takes one, including Jason and the *Squid Game* guard. But Mark holds up a hand, warding her off, when she reaches his spot near the back. Apparently he's not a fan, which doesn't surprise me. The *Squid Game* guard pulls his mask off first. Not Brandon. A second later, Jason raises his hockey mask, and it's him. Perfect.

Now I just need to get behind the velvet rope. Fortunately, Mark is sitting about as far away from Brandon as it's possible to be while remaining in the same enclosed area. I hope it's far enough that he doesn't recognize me.

I abandon my position on the railing and head down the staircase to the first floor. Then, I make my way to the bar at the rear of the club. The crowd is at least three deep all the way around, and it takes fifteen minutes before I'm able to get a bartender's attention.

"Hey love, what can I get you?" he asks.

"Can I get a bottle of Grand Brut with five glasses?" I reply, passing over three hundred dollars when he nods.

A minute later, he returns, handing me a tray with an already opened bottle and five champagne flutes. There's eighty dollars in change on it. I give him twenty as a tip, then I turn and head for the velvet rope.

I unobtrusively glance in Mark's direction as I approach, and I swear he's watching me. The guy charged with keeping people out pulls the rope aside for me without a word, probably assuming I'm one of the miscellaneous bottle girls hired to help out tonight.

I think Mark is still watching me, but I don't dare look toward him to check. Instead, I beeline for Brandon Miller as soon as I reach the top of the steps. Once I'm in front of the group he's sitting with—which thankfully doesn't include Rhys Steichen or Garret Fischer at the moment—I set the tray down, fill the champagne flutes, and begin handing them out.

"Compliments of the club," I say when I pass the first glass to a player I don't recognize. I save Brandon for last. I stare into his eyes, letting my fingers brush across his as he takes the champagne.

Almost immediately, he lifts his mask and smirks at me. I smile back coyly, and he reaches up to take my hand, tugging me toward him. "Stay and have a drink with me," he says. It sounds less like a question and more like a demand, but I nod and bat my eyelashes anyway, letting him pull me onto his lap. His eyes drop to my chest, and his right hand goes around my waist.

I force out a giggle, and he says, "You know you're very pretty."

I want to say, *'What I am is very naked. There's a difference,'* but I don't. I merely giggle again as I drop my eyes and murmur, "Thanks."

He takes a sip of the champagne and then holds the glass to my lips. I make myself drink. At least I know he hasn't put anything in it. He pulls me into him a little more, ignoring the people around us in favor of focusing all his attention on me.

I shift on his lap, which has the effect of grinding my ass against him, and he lets out a small sigh that sounds like a repressed groan of pleasure. I do it again as his hand creeps up from my waist to skim over the side of my boob and he makes the same sound, just a little louder. I fight down the desire to fling myself away from him out of pure revulsion and force myself to stay put.

I'm sure he's one of those guys who believes the fact that he can't keep his hands to himself should be taken as a compliment. It's not. It's simply disrespectful. Normally, I wouldn't stand for it. Right now though, it's exactly what I was hoping for.

We stay like that for another ten minutes, with him groping me more and more with each passing second. His dick is pressing into my ass, and it's anything but sexy. Eventually, it seems like I've been compliant and placid long enough for him to press his luck.

"Want to get out of here?" he whispers in my ear. He's too close, and I want to pull away, but I don't.

"Where would we go?" I ask, channeling my inner Marilyn Monroe, making my voice breathier than it's ever been in my life.

"My house isn't far. It's only twenty minutes from here."

"Okay," I agree. Before the word has even finished leaving my mouth, he's in the process of standing and bringing me with him.

Then he's headed for the exit, his hand on my wrist dragging me along behind him, and I hope I know what I've gotten myself into. I hope the drugs Vaughn got me work. If they don't, I'm not sure I'll get out of this in one piece.

The night is even colder when Brandon pulls me back into it, and goosebumps instantly prickle my skin. He heads toward the parking lot, aiming for a large black G-Wagon, climbing into the driver's side when we reach it, leaving me to go around to the passenger's side. I pull a vial from my stocking, unscrew the lid, and palm it, wedging it in my left hand between my pointer and pinky fingers with my others obscuring it. Then I climb into the SUV.

Country music blares to life a little too loudly when he starts the car. It's one of those artists that racist white people love. I'm not sure which one—they all sound the same—but the kind who blends country with rock and hip hop and spews bigotry every time they open their mouths.

Brandon turns the music down as I fasten my seat belt, eyeing the half-full Gatorade bottle sitting in the cup holder. If I can get him to drink it, that means I don't have to wait until we get to his house before I drug him. It's better than my original plan to tell him I need a drink when we arrive and try to distract him long enough for the GHB to kick in. It should also cover up the taste.

"You said it's twenty minutes to your house?" I ask, rotating my body to face him. I want to get the timing right. Too early, and he'll crash the SUV with me in it. Too late, and I won't be able to get away from him.

"That's right." He grabs my right arm, and it twinges as he pulls it across the center console to rest on his crotch. "You can keep me entertained until then," he says, leering at me. He still hasn't asked me what my name is, or shown even the slightest hint of interest in me beyond what I can do for him sexually.

*Yup. Definitely want to get the timing right,* I think as I unenthusiastically rub my hand against him.

We spend the next ten minutes with the horrible music as the only sound. Brandon seems content, either not noticing or not caring about my complete lack of enthusiasm.

Finally, I say, "You've got Gatorade!" as I remove my hand from his crotch, grab the bottle that's in the cup holder between us and unscrew the lid. I try not to gross myself out, thinking about his backwash as I take a few large gulps. Then I pretend to screw the lid back on, upending the vial of GHB I palmed prior to getting into the car, dumping it in the Gatorade.

I thrust the bottle at Brandon. "Here! Have some. We wouldn't want you getting dehydrated!"

He takes the bottle, finishes it without question, and returns it to the cup holder. I tuck the empty vial back into my stocking and remind myself that I'll have to grab the Gatorade bottle before I leave. It has my DNA on it. The rest of the vehicle should be clean, though. I'm wearing black satin gloves, so I won't leave fingerprints, and my hair is under a wig, so there won't be any stray strands left sticking to the headrest.

The clock is ticking now. In the next ten to twenty minutes, the effects should begin to show. Thirty minutes from now, he should be on the verge of passing out. I need to get him into bed before then and keep his hands off me as much as possible in the process. I'm not sure how I'll do it, but I'll figure something out.

Eleven minutes later, at nine-twenty, he turns into his driveway. His house is large, and the winding driveway allows enough of a view to determine there's a clear Mediterranean influence. It's all terracotta-tiled roof and stucco walls. The garage opens, and he pulls inside, almost hitting the wall. Hopefully that means the GHB is kicking in, and dealing with him will be easy.

He gets out of the car first, and I follow. As soon as he comes around to my side, he grabs me—one hand in my hair and the other on my hip, forcing me against the side of the SUV, pinning me in place. The hand on my hip moves up to my boob, which he squeezes. Hard.

"Fuck," I hiss. "That hurts." Brandon doesn't acknowledge that I've said anything, though. He simply squeezes harder as he grinds his hips into mine. He's going to leave marks.

I place both hands on his chest and shove him away. He staggers, almost tripping over his own feet. Surprise is written across his face. "Let's go inside," I suggest. "You can show me your bedroom."

He grunts something unintelligible but turns for the door leading into the house. I trail behind him. His feet are dragging with each step. I slide under his arm as he enters, and we ascend a staircase to the second floor together.

"You're really pretty," he says, repeating his words from earlier, sounding much more impaired this time. He leans over, trying to kiss me when we reach the top.

"Thank you. Where's your bedroom?" I ask, aiming to keep him focused on what I want rather than what he wants.

He leads the way to the second door on the right, flinging it open so hard it bounces off the wall. He takes several steps toward the bed and falls onto it, trying to pull me with him. I duck out from under his arm in time to save myself. He's not that out of it, though, because he rolls over faster than I expected, grabbing me to force me to join him on the bed.

"Wait, wait. I'll dance for you," I tell him.

His eyebrows knit together as he seems to consider the idea. After a tense moment, his hand drops from my wrist, and he nods.

"Do you have any music?" I ask.

He pulls his phone from his pocket, and I watch the code he enters as he unlocks it and passes it to me—one-one-two-two-three-three.

I have to remove a glove to get the screen to register my finger, which is unfortunate. It means I'll need to take his phone with me and throw it off a bridge or something—I don't want to risk some lab tech being able to retrieve touch DNA from it. I spend a second racking my brain, trying to decide what song I should put on. Eventually, I settle on Billie Eilish's *bad guy*. It seems appropriate. I tap the button to make the song repeat. Hopefully, he'll pass out quickly, but who knows. I set the phone down and begin oscillating my hips slowly from side to side, while he leans back on his arms, watching me hungrily. His eyelids are growing heavier by the second, and he slumps noticeably as I'm pulling my second glove off, finger by finger.

I stop and watch him as he falls back the rest of the way. I turn the music off, put my gloves back on, and count to a hundred before approaching him.

"Hey Brandon, are you awake?" I question.

He lets out a sound halfway between a moan and a grunt. That's good enough for me. I leave him on the bed and let myself out of the room, heading down the staircase, to the first floor, looking for the kitchen. I didn't bother bringing anything besides the GHB to kill Brandon. His kitchen should contain everything I need. While I could just press a pillow over his face and smother him, I'm going for something a bit more dramatic this time. It is Halloween after all, and I want to make a statement. It might be stupid. I might regret it. But Brandon will be the third player to die, leaving only Rhys Steichen and Garret Fischer—and I want them scared.

His kitchen is unnecessarily large. It's filled with lots of stainless steel, which doesn't fit the Mediterranean vibe at all, and there are two different stovetops on the kitchen island—one gas and one induction. He could run a catering company from this kitchen if he wanted. It doesn't seem like he does much cooking, though. Most of the drawers are empty, and I open one after another searching for the knives. Even if he doesn't do much cooking, he has to have a set of knives. I find them in the sixth drawer and choose the largest, pointiest one from the set. I briefly consider trying to find a pair of scissors to cut his clothes away, but I don't have that much time.

Instead, I go back to Brandon's room. He's on the bed with his legs dangling over the edge, exactly how I left him. I peel back an eyelid, and there's no resistance. He doesn't stir at all. He's well and truly unconscious, which is good news for him. I slide the knife under the hem of his T-shirt, using the tip to pierce the fabric. Once the slit is big enough to work my fingers into, I tear his shirt open. It rips all the way to the neckline, and I use the knife to slice through the extra fabric there. Then, I move the fabric to the side, exposing his entire torso.

I know I should feel bad for what I'm about to do. But I don't. Not really. This is karma. At least that's what I'm telling myself. If Brandon didn't want to end up drugged and at my mercy, he and his friends shouldn't have drugged and raped Katie. They shouldn't have drugged and raped *anyone*, because after seeing Rhys Steichen's address book, I'm certain that Katie wasn't the first, and I'm not certain she was the last. But I'll make damn sure there aren't any more.

I trail the knife down his torso. He's thin enough and his body fat is low enough that counting his ribs is easy.

One. Two. Three. Four.

I move the tip of the knife just past his fourth rib. To the intercostal space between the fourth and fifth ribs. I palpate his chest to find the left edge of his sternum and place the knife to the left of that. Then, I angle it slightly upward and a little more toward the left and press down. The blade should pass straight through both the left and right ventricles of his heart. He's not conscious, but if he were, he'd be dead before he knew it.

There's some initial resistance, and I lean my weight onto the knife. Once I'm past that, it goes in easily. I leave it in his body. His chest cavity is already filling with blood, but there's only the faintest bit of red rimming the blade. Gravity is working in my favor, and the knife is sealing the wound. It'll be a very clean crime scene.

I wait a minute, and then feel for a pulse. The satin of my gloves is thin enough that I'd be able to feel it if it were there, but it isn't. He was dead the second the knife slid into his chest. I glance at the time on Brandon's phone. It's nine-forty-three.

I've got a bit more than two hours to throw the phone off a bridge, make it back to my car, get cleaned up, and meet Mark. I'd like to look through the contents of Brandon's phone to see if I can find evidence related to any other women he and his hockey-douchebag friends may have raped, but I don't have the time.

# Chapter 21
# Coming Out on Top

THE ROOM IS EERILY SILENT AS I UNLOCK BRANDON'S phone, turn off location services, and then power it down. I search his body for his keys. They jingle as I fish them out of his pants pockets, and I wince. Even though I'm the only living soul in this house, I can't help but feel like I should be quiet, which is ridiculous.

The stairs creak beneath my feet as I head to the garage to retrieve the Gatorade bottle. I'm doing my best to ignore the unease pooling in my stomach. I'm sure the rest of my plan will work. I've run through the timeline every day during the past week.

My body is on autopilot while my brain is distracted by my own intrusive thoughts, and before I know it, I'm standing beside Brandon's SUV, looking in through the open door. I have his keys. I could take it. It's not part of my plan, but taking it would save me a lot of time. *It's Halloween, though,* I remind myself. Police will be out in force tonight. Saving half an hour isn't worth the risk of getting pulled over while driving Brandon's unnecessarily flashy G-Wagon.

I sigh, then grab the bottle, hit the button to open the garage door and walk out, tossing his keys in the bushes along the driveway as I move past.

The temperature is probably in the low fifties, but I'm barely wearing anything, and it feels colder. I only have to make it a couple of blocks, though. *Well, as long as no one found the bag I stashed in the park yesterday evening,* I think unhelpfully.

I fold my arms across my chest—empty Gatorade bottle in one hand, Brandon's phone in the other—and pick up my pace.

Ten minutes later, I'm on my hands and knees, reaching under the blackberry brambles. The ground is cold and spongy, and dampness is seeping through my tights. I'm fighting the shivering that's threatening to roll through my body as I search for the bag I left. If I start shivering now, it'll only make me more likely to slice my arms open on the thorns surrounding me. This was a lot easier yesterday when I had a jacket for protection.

After another moment, my hand lands on the bag. I have it almost all the way out when it catches on the thorns. I try to work it free, but it only catches more. Finally, I yank it toward me in frustration. The bag moves, but my forearm scrapes over the thorns, and pain flares across my skin.

"Fuck!" I hiss, dropping the bag as it comes free. There's blood welling from a long, thin scratch running down the inside of my left forearm, and I press it against my torso. The leering white mask of the Ghostface Killer from *Scream* stares back at me as I open the bag using my right hand. I pull out the black robe and put that on first. I need the extra warmth, and I'd rather bleed on the robe than the ground. After that, I slide the mask over my head and pull the hood up.

Once my new costume is in place, I trade the bus fare sitting at the bottom of the bag for the empty Gatorade bottle and phone that I've been carrying since I left Brandon's house. Then, I tuck the bag under my robe and walk across the park to leave opposite where I entered. If there are any cameras in the park, it may throw the police off if they check the surveillance footage.

By the time I'm back on the move, it's just after ten and the trick-or-treaters have vanished. The houses in this area are spaced far apart and set back from the road. Many of the windows are dark, and any jack-o'-lanterns have long since burned out. It's a five-block walk down empty sidewalks to the bus stop, which is only marked by a sign with a bus symbol on it. A flickering streetlight casts a dancing puddle of light around the sign. I should feel out of place in my costume on this desolate road, but the night is atmospheric enough that I don't.

Several minutes pass prior to the bus appearing. It lumbers toward me, its headlights slowly illuminating the night, before rumbling to a stop. When the doors clatter open, the middle-aged woman driving the bus doesn't give me a second look as I climb on and shove three dollars into the fare box. I take my ticket so I can reboard later and then find a seat toward the middle. There are about ten other passengers. Half are wearing costumes, probably on their way to a Halloween party, like me. Of course, when I signal the bus to stop near the Tilikum Crossing Bridge, I'm the only one—costumed or no—who gets off.

It's a ten-minute walk to the bridge. I stand against the railing at the midway point for a few minutes, pretending to admire the view, as I pull Brandon's phone from the bag concealed under my robe. Once I've got it out, I let it slip from my hands. It plummets almost eighty feet into the water, barely making a splash when it hits. The river is deep enough here that it's unlikely they'll ever recover it. Even if they do, the depth is well beyond any phone's water resistance rating.

I walk the rest of the way across the bridge to find the next bus. I'm back on the Eastside.

It's eleven-twenty, and I'm in my car, staring into the visor mirror, scrubbing the makeup off my face. These makeup remover wipes aren't working quite as well as I was hoping, but my skin is slowly emerging from beneath the face paint, and at least the bruise Matt Davidson's fist left on my cheek two weeks ago has finally faded to nothing.

By the time I'm nearing the end of the pack, it seems like the makeup is all gone. I tilt my head from side to side in the dim light, trying to get a full view of my face in the four-inch mirror. I think I got it all.

I shove the used wipes into a trash bag, along with the Ghostface Killer mask. Then, I gingerly pull off the red wig, using my fingernails to scrape away the adhesive. The wig goes in the trash bag too. I'm still wearing the robe, using it as cover to change under. My arms are pulled into the body, and I'm stripping off the teddy, the four pairs of tights, and the hip padding I was wearing for my original costume. Once I've got it all off, it also goes into the bag.

Putting my Morticia Addams costume on beneath the robe is more challenging than undressing was—but a naked woman changing in a car is memorable, and I don't want to be memorable, so I suffer through it. I'm on the verge of breaking into a sweat by the time I slip my arms into the sleeves of the dress and pull off the robe. Thankfully, the sleeves on this costume go all the way to my wrists, covering the scratch on my forearm. But Mark is bound to see it later, and the best excuse I've been able to come up with so far is that I caught it on an exposed framing nail, which isn't great but might be boring enough not to raise questions.

I finger-comb my hair, put on some blood-red lipstick, line my eyes with black liner and smudge it out a bit, then call it good. I take my phone from the glove box, turn it on, and start my car to look for a parking spot closer to the club. I don't need Mark asking why I parked three blocks away if I can avoid it.

I move the trash bag to my trunk once I've found a new parking spot a block-and-a-half closer and check my watch as I slam the lid closed. It's eleven-forty-one. I'll be early.

The same bouncer is at the door, only this time when I skip the line and approach him, I say, "Hi. I'm Alyssa Reed. My name should be on your list as a guest of Mark Eriksson."

He angles his clipboard toward the light, scanning the list. His eyes find my name. "Do you have ID?" he asks without looking up.

I pull my license from the pocket of the dress and hand it over. He takes a cursory look at it, glancing briefly at my face before handing it back. It's a very different reaction than I received when I was here earlier with my tits on display.

Fog still comes rolling out when I enter the club, but a trap remix of *Monster Mash* is playing this time.

I move to the wall beside the door and send Mark a text saying, *I'm here, where are you?* Assuming he's still in the same area, I know exactly where he is, but he doesn't need to know that. I look up like I'm searching for him, and half a minute later, he's at the edge of the raised platform, looking for me.

Movement behind Mark pulls my eyes away from him. Garret Fischer is about fifteen feet over Mark's shoulder, and he's definitely watching Mark with more than passing interest.

I tear my eyes away from Garret in time to see Mark's face light up as his gaze lands on me, and he steps down to the main floor, pushing through the crowd. I match his expression despite the sinking feeling in my stomach as I watch him walk toward me, trying to ignore the other thoughts competing for my attention.

The first is that as soon as Garret hears about Brandon's death, he's going to know someone is coming for him. The worry might already be there, eating at him in quiet moments, but what I did tonight will change worry to certainty. Garret Fischer is scum, but he's not stupid—he got away with a well-orchestrated gang rape scot-free. If Garret is watching Mark, that will inevitably lead to watching me. And the last thing I need is for him to remember I exist. To wonder about me. Unfortunately, there's nothing I can do about it.

The second is that Mark is going to lose his job because of me. I just killed the second member of his second line. That seems like the sort of thing that would be hard to recover from on its own. And when the team finds out he was murdered...? Well.

The third is that Mark will hate me if he ever figures out what I've been doing, and I hope he never does. Because while I was sneaking past his defenses, he was evidently tiptoeing around mine. It's only been twelve hours, give or take, since I last saw him, but relief washes through me anyway. It's getting harder and harder to pretend that I don't have serious feelings for Mark.

I think I might actually be falling in love with him, which would be a first. But even so, that's not enough to stop me from killing Rhys Steichen and Garret Fischer. Maybe I'm more like my dad than I care to admit. *At least what I'm doing contributes to the greater good,* I tell myself.

"Hey, you're early," Mark says, ducking his head to speak into my ear so I can hear him over the music when he reaches me, his arm slipping around my waist.

"Yeah, Katie and I finished up our movie marathon early. You look nice. I wasn't sure I got the right size costume," I reply, lifting my hand to run it across the fake mustache he's wearing. "I'm not totally sure you're pulling that off though," I tease.

He snorts. "What did you guys watch?" he asks, his mouth next to my ear as he leads me toward the bar.

"The *Halloweentown* movies."

"What?"

I repeat myself, assuming he didn't hear me above the noise, but he looks no less confused. "Have you not seen *Halloweentown*?"

"No. Should I have?"

"We might have to do a movie marathon of our own," I reply into his ear as we stand in the crowd at the bar, waiting for service. I want to glance over my shoulder to see if Garret is still standing near the edge of the platform, watching us, but I don't want to risk drawing his attention if he is.

"Only if we alternate who picks the movies," Mark counters.

"Deal," I reply as someone jostles me, sending me stumbling into Mark. His grip on my waist tightens, and he's glaring over my head by the time I look up.

I follow his gaze to find the offending party already retreating with a hastily muttered, "Sorry."

"I wish people ran away when I glared at them," I joke, and his eyes snap back to me.

"Is there any chance at all you might want to leave? I thought this could be fun, but we're just going to be shouting at each other and dodging assholes all night unless we're in the VIP section. But Fischer and Steichen are both up there."

"Yes," I agree, jumping at the opportunity.

He nods, and we turn and head for the exit.

"Where are we going?" I ask once we're outside and I'm finally able to speak to him at a normal volume.

"Have you ever been to Waffle House on a Friday night?"

"No. In case you haven't noticed, Waffle House isn't exactly endemic to the Pacific Northwest," I snark.

Mark grins. "Believe me. I've noticed. But Portland does have Jack in the Box, which in terms of the late-night clientele is almost the same thing."

I take his hand as we walk, and his skin is warm against mine. "Dining rooms close at ten, and it's after midnight."

"So we'll go through the drive-thru, then sit on the hood of my car in the parking lot and see if anything interesting happens. It's Halloween. It's bound to be entertaining."

"Alright. As long as we can stop by Voodoo Doughnut after that."

"Deal."

"KATIE DECIDED SHE WANTS TO MEET YOU," I SAY AROUND A mouthful of sausage croissant. Mark and I are sitting on the hood of his car, which is backed into a parking spot facing the drive-thru, watching people come and go. The air is cold, but heat from the engine is radiating into my body. It's nice. I never could've pictured myself here a month ago.

"What changed?" he questions, glancing at me as he pops a fry into his mouth.

"I don't know. She researched you, I guess." I pause before repeating her statement from earlier. "She said I should ask you about Wisconsin."

"How the fuck did she find out about that?" he mutters, looking away from me to toss a fry to a late-night seagull that's been stalking the parking lot.

"She has a master's in library science. She's good at research." I shrug. "So, are you going to tell me?"

"That was when I started dipping my toes into coaching."

"Why?"

"I went to school on a hockey scholarship."

"Okay. And?"

"My scholarship was revoked after I was removed from the team," he says, sounding annoyed, and I'm not sure if he's annoyed at having to explain it to me, or if he's annoyed that it happened.

"Okay. And?" I repeat.

"What do you know about the way the NHL draft works?" he asks.

"Absolutely nothing."

"Alright. Quick overview," he says, tossing another fry to the seagull. He hasn't taken a bite since I mentioned Wisconsin. "Players can be drafted in high school as long as they turn eighteen no later than September fifteenth of that year. And after being drafted, they're able to go to college and play in the NCAA. Basically, the drafting team holds the NHL rights for anyone they draft for a set period of time—for college players, that's typically four years. Between being drafted and signing a contract, you're just a prospect, and until the contract is actually signed, they can pull it."

"And that's what happened to you?"

"Yes."

"Why?"

"At the start of sophomore year, I put one of my teammates in the hospital."

"So what? Don't people get injured playing hockey all the time?"

"He wasn't injured playing hockey."

"Ah," I reply, taking a bite of my sandwich to see if he'll continue on his own. But he doesn't. "What happened?" I ask eventually.

"We were at a party, and he disappeared. I didn't think anything of it. But on my way to the bathroom, I walked past a door that wasn't all the way shut and saw him raping a semi-conscious woman. I pulled him off her. We ended up in a fistfight. And I won."

"And they revoked your scholarship for that?"

"Not exactly," he says begrudgingly. "I threw him out of a window, and he ended up in a coma for a few days. The woman he'd raped didn't want to go through a trial, so no charges were filed against him. And no one wanted the bad press that would come from filing charges against me. They settled on revoking my scholarship instead. Once my scholarship was gone, I tried to sign a contract with the team who'd drafted me, but apparently they heard about *why* my scholarship was revoked, and they were no longer interested. A month later, I landed an assistant coaching job with a rival school that either hadn't heard what happened or didn't care. Then, I realized I liked coaching more than I liked playing anyway." He tosses another fry to the seagull.

"Why is it still such a sore spot, then?" I probe.

"He's the one who should've had his scholarship revoked."

"Ah. The principle of the matter. I can understand that. It sounds like you came out on top, though. Literally and figuratively."

He snorts but says nothing.

"I can't believe you defenestrated a guy. No wonder I like you so much."

# Chapter 22
# Hat Tricks

It's a bit after two in the afternoon on Saturday when I step into my condo. Katie is on the couch, under a blanket. She hits pause on the documentary she's watching and turns to look at me.

"Hey," she greets.

"Hey. What are you watching today?" I ask. There's a guy on the screen lining up a slim-looking rifle to take a shot at a herd of elephants.

"*The Secret Life of Elephants*. They're trying to put a radio collar on one of the elephants. It doesn't work, though."

"How do you know?"

"I've seen it before. I was just killing time until you got home and we could start our *Halloweentown* marathon."

"Okay, good. Let me drop my bag in my room. I'll be back in a few," I tell her with a grin. I spent the night with Mark, and the bag I'm carrying now is only an overnight bag—not the trash bag full of costumes I was wearing during last night's activities, which is still in my trunk. I'd like to get rid of that bag sooner rather than later, but I didn't want to throw it into the dumpsters at my office. I've never gone there to throw trash away on a Saturday. It would be suspicious if I were to suddenly do so. And I don't want to put it into the condo's dumpsters—those won't be emptied until Wednesday. Dropping it into some random person's trash is a risk I'm unwilling to take, so it'll have to sit in my trunk until Monday, unless I can figure out some other way to get rid of it.

"You're home earlier than I figured you would be," Katie says, pausing the documentary again when I reenter the living room and drop onto the couch beside her.

"Mark had to work. Practice, I guess. It didn't make sense to stay at his place longer when I'd have to leave for our movie marathon before he got back anyway," I explain, not bothering to mention that he was hoping I'd spend the night. I declined, both because I had preexisting plans with Katie and because if he finds out about Brandon tonight—which seems likely—I'm not sure it'd be a good idea for me to be around.

They have a game tomorrow. Mark mentioned getting together afterward since I said no to tonight. Tomorrow is Sunday, which means their game takes place earlier than normal. We'll see if getting together actually happens, though. I expect that when Brandon doesn't show up for practice this afternoon, they won't take any chances given recent events. Either they'll call in a welfare check immediately, or someone from the team will go to his house and do it themselves. Maybe both.

When they find his body, it'll be obvious that he was murdered. I want Rhys Steichen and Garret Fischer wondering if they're next. I want them to be afraid. I want them to regret the things they've done. It's stupid because as soon as they realize they're being actively hunted, it's going to make killing them harder, but I don't care. I'll figure it out. Somehow, someway. Marjorie was right about that.

Finding Brandon might make the police reconsider the circumstances of Matt Davidson's death. But if they've already ruled his manner of death as accidental, even if they decide to give it a second look, the most they're likely to do is change it to undetermined. And even that... who knows? Bureaucracy is slow and unwieldy.

Either way, the Doomsday Clock that's been hanging above my head since all this started is currently about one second away from midnight —midnight being the moment that Mark starts to become suspicious of me and my involvement with the deaths of his players. I don't have long. If I'm lucky, I'll be able to kill Rhys Steichen before that happens. Mark likes me as much as I like him, which means he won't want to think I've been murdering his players. But eventually he will. He's not an idiot.

I've been telling myself we'll cross that bridge when we come to it, but if I'm being honest, I'm not sure there will be a 'we' after that point. Or even a bridge.

"What do you think about having dinner with Mark on Wednesday?" I ask Katie, picking up the remote from where she set it on the coffee table.

Katie glances at her phone, checking her tutoring schedule, I assume. "Yeah, Wednesday works. Here?"

"Up to you."

"Yeah. We'll do it here. We can get takeout, and you can show him where you live. I'm sure he's dying to see it," she replies with an edge to her tone that tells me she hasn't entirely forgiven me.

"I gave him a video tour a few weeks ago when you were out," I say as I select *Halloweentown* from the menu and press play.

"How does that work?" Katie asks, and I pause the movie.

"What?"

"Him traveling?" she provides.

"He gets on a plane and goes places…?" I say, confused. "How does traveling ever work?"

"No, Alyssa," she says, exasperation heavy in her voice as she turns to stare at me. "He's gone like half the time, right?"

"Not that much, but close," I agree.

"So, what do you guys do? Is it like a ton of phone sex? Video sex? How does that work?"

I burst out laughing.

"Please!" Katie says over the roar of my laughter. "Like you wouldn't ask me the exact same question if our positions were reversed?"

I wipe the tears from my cheeks. She's right. I totally would. "No. I mean, we've tried it a couple of times but... have you ever had phone sex?" I ask.

"Yes, it's the worst! Like the absolute worst!"

"Yes! Exactly!" I agree. "No woman has ever gotten off on phone sex, and you won't convince me otherwise. Video sex is even worse! Suddenly you're concerned about whether the camera is positioned right and how you look and... Yeah. No. If anything, it just made me *more* frustrated. After the second time, I told him I'd rather wait until he came back."

"And he was okay with that?"

"Yeah, why?"

"Just wondering."

"Are you done wondering? Or are we going to play Twenty Questions about my sex life?"

"Nope. I'm done," she says. "You can start the movie. For now."

I snort as I press play, and a jack-o'-lantern dominates the screen.

It's a bit after six, and we're about ten minutes into *Halloweentown High* with a bowl of popcorn on the couch between us when Katie springs forward and grabs the remote, pausing the movie.

"Holy shit! He's dead, Alyssa! Brandon Miller is dead, too!" she shouts, waving her phone at me. It's too far away to make out any details, though. "They're saying he was murdered sometime last night! They found his body a couple of hours ago!"

"By who?" I ask.

"It doesn't say. All it says is: 'Police are treating the death as a homicide. The investigation is ongoing. Authorities have scheduled a press conference for noon tomorrow. More details are expected to be released then.'"

I raise my eyebrows. A press conference. I should've seen that coming. "Damn," I murmur, not knowing what else to say. I'm sure they don't know anything. Most likely, the press conference will simply be to ask the public for help, and the public doesn't know anything either.

"It's a hat trick! October is my new favorite month!" she states, beaming.

I laugh. "One less creep in the world is always a good thing, and I'm ecstatic he's dead, but would you hate me if I sent Mark a text quick?"

"No. Go ahead! I'm going to get some ice cream! Want some?"

"Sure," I agree as I type out *Hey, I heard about Brandon Miller. Let me know if you want to talk,* and send it. My message doesn't show as read though, and eventually I set my phone down, wondering if it's already started—if he's already suspicious.

"Hello?" I say as I answer my phone. It's almost ten.

"Hey Alyssa," Mark says, sounding exhausted.

"Hey. I heard the news. I'm sorry. For you. Not that he died," I clarify. "Are you alright?"

"Yeah. Sorry it's late. There was a lot going on with the team's lawyers and the media spokespeople. I just got out of there."

"No. It's fine. Don't worry about it. It's not that late. What's going on?"

"Nothing right now. The police want to question all the players again, and the ownership is increasing security at the arena."

"Why? Do they still suspect someone on the team?" I ask. I doubt they do. There's no way I'll be that lucky twice.

"I have no idea. I don't think they have any clue what's going on. The players want personal security at this point, and the owners and the legal department were demanding the police supply it, but—and I quote—'Portland Police Bureau is not responsible for supplying private security.'"

"Are they going to hire bodyguards then?" I ask, hoping the answer is 'no' because some rent-a-cops could really throw a wrench into my plans.

"I don't know," Mark says. "Probably. The police were only there to question everyone again. The lawyers got them to agree to hold off on that until Monday, but…"

"You're worried you're going to lose tomorrow?"

"It's hard to imagine another outcome. We could really use a win," he says with a loud exhale. "I'm going to have to find someone from the AHL to bring up," he mutters.

"The AHL?"

"It doesn't matter. Anyway, I know you're busy tonight, but I was hoping you might come by tomorrow after the game."

"Yeah, that sounds good. I'm having dinner with Jeanette and Katie tomorrow, so I'll come over after that. Oh. Also…" I trail off. This timing sucks. It's my fault it sucks, but still.

"Also?" Mark prods.

I sigh. "I know it's not a great time, so if you want to reschedule, we can, but Katie agreed to dinner on Wednesday. She's officially invited you over, and we'll order some takeout or something. If you want." I hate bringing Katie up during this conversation. It seems like there's a good chance it'll only make him suspect me that much sooner, but there's not a lot I can do about it at this point. I have to keep acting as if everything is normal.

"Yes. There's no way in hell I'm going to pass up the chance to see your place."

"Okay. Great. Do you want to text me when you're on your way home tomorrow, and I'll come over?"

"Yeah, that works."

"Hey Vaughn," I greet as I sit down with a latte in hand and shrug off my coat, which is beaded with water from the incessant drizzle outside. It's nine in the morning, and we're meeting up in yet another coffee shop.

"Alyssa. How are things? I saw there's going to be a press conference," he says, propping his chin on his fist and looking more like The Most Interesting Man in the World than ever.

"Yes. It's... suboptimal," I agree.

"Do they have any information about you?"

"No," I reply, having the distinct impression he's trying to decide if he needs to figure out a way to smuggle me out of the country.

"You're sure?" He's staring me down as if I might be lying to him. I'm not though. No one knows anything. I was careful.

"Yes. But if you're concerned and want to be helpful, I have a trash bag in my trunk that you could get rid of."

"Yeah. I can do that. How are things with Katie and Mark?"

I take a sip of my latte, feeling like I'm being interrogated. "Are you checking up on me, Vaughn?"

He shrugs noncommittally. "Maybe."

I snort. "As good as they can be, all things considered. The three of us are having dinner together on Wednesday, so ask me again after that."

"Alright. I'm still nailing down Steichen's routine, but I do have information about the address book you gave me," he says, pulling a folder from the messenger bag on the seat beside him. He sets it on the table. "I'd wait to look at it until you're back at home. But long story short, not including Katie, I found six women that I'm almost positive were raped by him—and possibly the others—and three more that I suspect may have been, but I haven't been able to get enough info to be sure about."

"What makes you confident about the six?"

"It's all in there, but a combination of things depending on the specific woman. Either they moved shortly afterward, they visited a doctor for an STI screening, they were given DoxyPEP or visited a pharmacy to purchase Plan B, or they started seeing a therapist or attending a support group shortly after a time where they were likely to have been assaulted by him."

"How do you know that?" I probe.

"Once I figured out who lived at the addresses listed in the book, I was able to get most of the information from their social media posts. People share too much. The three that I'm not sure about either don't have public social media profiles or they don't update them regularly."

"Did any of them report it?"

"No."

I lean back in my chair and sigh. "How long have they been doing this?"

"It started about two years before Katie, as far as I can tell. But that doesn't really mean anything."

"Damn," I mutter. "You know, for a while, when all the 'Me Too' stuff was happening, it seemed like things might actually be different."

"Yeah. I know," Vaughn agrees softly.

"Can you get me a tranq gun? And some Telazol?"

"Telazol?" Vaughn asks.

"Yeah. It's what they use when they need to dart a bear."

Vaughn's eyebrows rise at that, but he merely nods and says, "I'll see what I can do. I'm going to be out of town for a few days next week. I'll call you when I have a tranq gun and enough info on Steichen for you to act."

"Thanks," I say. It took me forever to come up with the Telazol idea. It wasn't until I saw that scene from *The Secret Life of Elephants* yesterday that I thought of it.

I must've run through at least twenty ideas that would've only ended up with me dead. But when I saw them tranquilizing the elephant in the documentary, a lightbulb went off in my head. Rhys Steichen is so much bigger than me—he's got eight inches and close to a hundred pounds on me. I have no chance of winning a physical fight against him. It would be equivalent to a ten-year-old child trying to fight me. If I can't incapacitate him prior to interacting with him, I'll have to acquire a handgun and put a bullet in his head—anything else would be too dangerous. And a bullet to the brain is too fast, too clean. He doesn't deserve to get off that easily.

I spent a good chunk of last night reading into how they tranquilize big game for tagging and tracking. And the biggest game in this part of the country is bears. Telazol is used on all types of bears.

But it's most frequently used when interacting with black bears. I doubt they'll be able to nail down the fact that Rhys will have been drugged with Telazol during an autopsy because it doesn't have any human equivalents, but if they do figure it out... Well. Talk about poetic justice.

It's one in the afternoon, and I'm lying on my bed, shuffling through the pages in the folder Vaughn gave me this morning when there's a knock at the condo door, which is weird. I'm not expecting anyone, and I didn't hear the intercom go off for someone asking to be buzzed in. I'm trying to put the pages back into some kind of order before getting up to answer the door when I get a text from Katie that says, *Don't come out*

*What the hell,* I wonder, reading the message again. I shove the stack of papers and the folder under my pillow. *I'll sort it out later,* I decide as I move toward my bedroom door.

There's an indistinct man's voice, followed by an equally muffled woman's voice. I don't recognize either one, and I crack the door.

"We're just here for a couple of routine questions," the man says, the sound filtering to me more clearly now. It must be the police here to follow up with Katie.

We watched the press conference together when I got home, and like I told Vaughn earlier, it doesn't seem like they know anything. It lasted for a grand total of fifteen minutes, during which they asked for anyone who'd interacted with Brandon the night before last to come forward. They also asked for anyone who may have noticed suspicious activity around the time of Joey Carmichael's and Matt Davidson's deaths to call the tip line as well. Naturally, the first thing reporters seized onto was that Matt's death was being lumped in with the others. The police spokesperson was quick to say that his manner of death had not yet been reclassified, but noted that it could be if they received additional information. When it ended, Katie and I looked at each other and shrugged, and then I came back here to look through the files Vaughn put together.

I'm not sure why she doesn't want me to come out while the police are here, though.

"About?" Katie responds sharply. She's definitely not thrilled.

"The death of Brandon Miller." There's an awkward pause and then the man asks, "Where were you on Halloween night?"

"Here," Katie states.

"All night?"

"Yes. I don't leave the house often anymore."

"Can anyone confirm that?"

"I was tutoring students online all night."

"What time was that?"

"From six in the evening until one in the morning."

"On Halloween night?" the woman asks skeptically.

"Yes. International students. From China mostly. It wasn't Halloween for them."

"We'll need their contact information," the man says.

"Fine," Katie grates out.

*Fuck.* If they contact the parents of the students she's tutoring, she's going to lose those jobs.

"Do you recognize this woman?" the man asks.

There's a moment of silence before Katie says, "No. Are you sure this is a woman and not a man in drag?"

"What makes you ask that?" the woman questions.

"Well, Brandon is six-two. The person in this picture is practically the same height as him. There aren't many women that tall. Even most men aren't that tall."

We must be in the middle of a crowd in whatever picture they're showing her. Most likely all that's visible are our heads and shoulders. They must not be able to see the heeled boots I'm wearing.

"How tall are you?" the man asks.

"Five-three."

There's another pause, then, "Okay. Thank you for your time."

"Wait. Hold on," Katie says. "You're here because they raped me, right? The players who have died?"

"Yes," the woman says.

"Well, you should know that I don't think I'm the only person they did that to. You'd probably learn more if you asked for other victims to come forward than you will by doing… whatever this is."

The condo door thuds shut, and there's the distinctive sound of the deadbolt slotting into place. Then, Katie flings my door open as I jump back from it, narrowly avoiding being hit in the face.

"You killed them," she states.

# Chapter 23
# The Yips

"I..." I trail off.

"Say it, Alyssa. You killed them. Say it," Katie demands, her blue eyes feverishly locked on mine.

"I may have... perhaps... done the thing that you say I did," I haltingly admit, but Katie just continues staring at me. "Fine," I say, throwing my hands up. "I killed them!"

She crashes into me, her arms wrapping around me. "Thank you," she whispers.

"You're welcome. Did they show you the picture of me in my costume?"

"Yes," she says, releasing me and pulling her phone from her pocket. "I thought about saying you were here with me all night, but since they didn't mention you, I didn't want to put you on their radar, so to speak."

"Thanks. It was quick thinking to tell them you thought I could be a man. How'd you know I shouldn't come out?"

"Right before they knocked on the door, I was looking at the news, and they'd posted the picture. I guess someone leaked it," she says, turning her phone toward me. As expected, it's a close-cropped photo of us in the middle of The Rose Room's crowded main floor. A bit less than three-quarters of my face is visible in the image. "I knew it was you right away. I can't believe you didn't tell me! Is this why you're dating Mark?"

"Yes, but also no." She tilts her head questioningly, so I explain. "It started out that way. I asked Vaughn to put together—"

"Vaughn has been helping you? Vaughn? And you didn't even breathe a word of it to me? I was mad at you for a week! You could've told me!"

"Kay, you have to admit he's a little more equipped to help than you are. And it seemed like it was better if you didn't know."

She folds her arms across her chest and huffs. "Fine. Continue."

"After the verdict was read, I asked Vaughn to put together a list of people who could get me access to the team, and Mark was one of those people. Of everyone Vaughn suggested, Mark made the most sense. So I followed him," I say, taking a seat on my bed. Katie sits down beside me, and I explain how Mark and I really met. Then, I tell her everything that's happened since.

"And now you've actually fallen for him," Katie states after I've finished.

"Yeah. I have."

"Are you in love with him?"

"I don't know. Maybe."

"What about him? Is he in love with you?" Katie asks.

"I don't know," I repeat. "Maybe."

"And he has no idea what you've been doing?"

"I don't think so. But..."

"But?"

"I told him about you, and he's made a couple of comments since. They might not've meant anything, but..." I shrug.

"You are so screwed," Katie tells me.

"Yeah. I'm fully aware."

"So, what now?"

"What do you mean?"

"Are you done now that the police are getting suspicious, or are you going to kill Rhys Steichen and Garret Fischer too?"

"Oh. I am absolutely going to kill them."

"I want to help," Katie declares.

"No, Kay. You can't. You're the most obvious suspect. You need an alibi. You couldn't have killed Joey Carmichael because of where he was killed. They think someone on the team did it. You couldn't have killed Matt Davidson because I made it look like an accident. And you couldn't have killed Brandon Miller because you were in video tutoring sessions the entire night. You have to stay away from it. The media are probably going to show up and start hounding you for a comment soon, anyway."

"That just means that I can't be there when you kill them. I can still help, though. I can't just let you do this yourself. And nothing would make me feel better than killing Rhys Steichen and Garret Fischer."

I sigh. She's not wrong, and it's not like I'm in any position to tell her she can't be involved. "You already helped by telling the police that they should consider that the person who killed Brandon might have been a man," I try, hoping it will be enough and knowing it won't. "And by telling them you thought there were other victims. There were, by the way. Or at least Vaughn and I are pretty sure." I pull the folder out from under my pillow and hand it to her.

She opens it and moves through the pages, scanning each one silently. After twenty minutes have passed, she says, "All of them?"

I nod. "Yeah. Maybe you can do something with that. Maybe some of them will be willing to talk now."

"How did you find out about them?"

"There was an address book in Rhys's stall in the locker room. I took it, and when I was looking through it later, I found your old address listed in it." The color visibly drains from Katie's face. "I had Vaughn look into the other addresses in the book, and he believes these women were probably also raped."

"And none of them reported it?" Katie asks.

"No. It doesn't seem like it. I'm sorry, Kay."

She shakes her head. "Maybe they're the smart ones. If I'd never reported it, you and I could've killed all five of them, and no one would've ever even considered the possibility I could've been involved," she says softly. "I should've—"

I take the pages from her. "You did exactly what you should've done. It's not your fault the system is broken."

"No, but I should've known better. It was stupid."

"Hey," I snap. "I'm not doing this so you can beat yourself up over some 'should have' bullshit. You did the *right* thing. It's not wrong to try to do the right thing first. You should've never had to go to trial in the first place. They shouldn't have raped you, and the legal system should've punished them after they did. Those are the only 'should haves' that exist in this equation. Got it?"

"Yeah," she agrees, but I'm not sure she believes me. "What was your plan if I hadn't booked the tutoring sessions?" Katie asks, changing the subject.

"What?"

"On Halloween. You thought we were watching movies. You didn't know I'd booked the sessions. What was your plan to give me an alibi if I hadn't?"

"Oh. That. You're not going to like it," I say, but she's still waiting for me to tell her. "I was going to call your mom and tell her you were having a rough day, and ask if she could come stay the night since I had plans."

"You were going to *call my mom*? And say I was afraid of the dark? Alyssa! How could you ever think that was a good idea?"

"I wasn't worried about it being a *good* idea. I was just trying to make sure there was someone available to say, 'No officers, she was here all night.'"

Katie rolls her eyes. "I think I'm going to go back to not speaking to you," she comments as she stands to leave.

"Hey, what are you going to do?"

"I'm not sure yet. Ask me tomorrow."

"Hi Jeanette," I greet as I step into the house, following behind Katie.

"Alyssa!" she says, hugging me as soon as she releases Katie. "It's been forever since I've seen you." The rebuke in her tone is clear, which is fair, I suppose. It's been three weeks since I was last here. Between planning murders and being with Mark, I haven't had a ton of free time.

"Alyssa's been busy," Katie says at the same time I say, "I know. I'm sorry."

"Busy with what?" Jeanette asks.

"Her new boyfriend, mostly," Katie replies.

"Oh! That's right. You're still seeing him?"

"Yes!" Katie answers for me. "I'm going to meet him on Wednesday. We're having dinner together. Finally. Apparently he has a very full calendar, what with the troubled youth and all," Katie says, and I stop myself from rolling my eyes at her, but I can tell from the grin on her face that she knows I want to.

"That's wonderful," Jeanette replies as we follow her to the kitchen. "It's good to find someone and settle down."

"That's not—" I begin, but Jeanette continues talking.

"Did you see the news today? There's been so much crime recently."

"Yes, mom. The police already came to talk to me."

"Well, that makes sense. Two might be a coincidence, but three's a pattern. What do you think is happening?"

I shrug as Katie says, "I don't know, mom. It's not like I did it. And I also don't care. Maybe someone else they raped is getting revenge. I'm just happy they're dead."

"Katie," Jeanette chides. "I wasn't asking if you'd done it!"

"Are you sure? Because it kinda sounded like it. And for the record, I didn't. But whoever did has my full support."

"Jeanette, what are your plans for Thanksgiving this year? Do you need any help?" I ask before she can say something we'll all regret.

"No, dear. I already took the day off. You and Katie just need to show up. Of course you're welcome to bring your new boyfriend if you'd like. Just let me know. The more the merrier," Jeanette says, launching into her menu plans.

"Tell me what you think of this," Katie says, startling me as I'm pouring my coffee.

"What?" I ask, grabbing a rag to wipe up the spill.

"I was thinking I'd go visit Erica in California. I can do it under the guise of trying to get away from the reporters," she tells me. There were two who made it into the building and knocked on our door last night, looking to shout questions at her. Anything for a sound bite.

I shrug. "Sure. Why not?"

"It'll give me an alibi, only I'll make sure the reporters know I'm there."

"Why would you do that?"

"Because then they'll stop sniffing around here, and a couple of them are bound to try to get to me there. And when they do, I'll talk to them."

"And say what? They're all going to assume you're involved. That's what all their questions will be about."

"Yeah, only when Rhys and Garret die while I'm in California, it'll give me a better alibi than anything you've done so far. Plus, I can talk to the reporters about how I'm sure there are other victims."

I open my mouth to protest, but Katie continues talking.

"Don't worry. I'm not going to out anyone to the media," she says quickly. "But I can tell the reporters that Rhys told me they'd get away with it because they'd gotten away with it before. It might encourage the others to speak up, but even if it doesn't, it'll help muddy the waters here and broaden the suspect pool to include any number of unknown people."

"That's not a bad idea."

"I know," Katie says smugly.

"When will you go?"

"This weekend. That way they'll have time to find me before you kill anyone else."

"You know this is fucked up, right?" I ask.

"The world's a fucked up place, Alyssa. But I already talked to Erica, and she's cool with me coming to visit for a bit."

The reception area door clicks shut behind Conrad Clay, and I glance at this afternoon's schedule. There are four patients back-to-back. Three I've been seeing regularly over the past several months, and one new patient.

"What do you know about Nick Fischer—the new patient who's scheduled for one?" I ask, tapping his name in the appointment book. "Is he a referral? Do we have his medical history? Any notes about prior treatment or providers? I haven't seen them."

"No," Teresa informs me. "I called both Monday and yesterday to ask him to complete the intake forms. When we spoke on Monday, he said he'd do it right away. When I came in yesterday and saw he still hadn't filled them out, I called again, but he didn't answer or call back. Sorry. Do you want me to reschedule him?"

I glance at my watch. It's eleven-fifty-eight. Only an hour until his appointment. I sigh. "No, it's fine. I guess we'll be filling them out together as part of his session."

"Sorry," Teresa apologizes again.

I shrug. "It's his money. Don't worry about it. Did he happen to tell you anything about the reason he's seeking treatment?"

"He said he's been struggling with PTSD recently, but he didn't go into detail beyond that."

It's not much to go on, but it's something at least. Oh well. Like I told Teresa, if he wants to waste the session filling out forms, that's his business.

"I'm going to order a gyro for lunch. Want one?" I ask.

"Sure. Lamb, please."

I'M AT MY DESK, SCROLLING THROUGH RESTAURANT options for dinner with Katie and Mark tonight, when there's a knock on my office door.

"Come in," I respond, shoving my phone into the top drawer of my desk now that my new mystery patient has arrived. He's on time at least, even if he didn't fill out his intake forms. I stand up to introduce myself to Nick as I slide the drawer closed, my eyes landing on his face.

"Oh. You. Hi," I say, hoping my expression is steadier than my heart, which is currently beating so erratically that it's obviously forgotten what a normal sinus rhythm looks like. I take a breath and unclench my fists. *Fuck*. "I thought your name was Garret," I finish. At least my voice sounds normal.

I'd already asked Vaughn to start looking into Rhys Steichen before I killed Brandon. After that, when I saw Garret watching Mark at The Rose Room, I considered changing my plans and going after Garret next. I seriously considered it. But then there were the other women from Rhys's address book. And... if I'm being honest, a big part of me wants to make Garret watch his friends die. I want him to be afraid. I want him to feel the weight of his death as an inevitable conclusion. I want him to know what being powerless feels like.

But this is not good. Very, very *not good*.

"Hi. Yes, it is. I use my middle name, Nick—Nicholas—for these kinds of things. You know, for privacy reasons," he says, studying me like I'm a butterfly pinned under glass, his icy blue eyes boring into mine.

"Ah. Yes. I see. Well, I'm Dr. Reed," I reply, introducing myself in an effort to buy a second to regain my equilibrium.

"Yes, I know. We've met."

We did meet, but I never introduced myself, though I don't say as much. Ethically, I should tell him to get the fuck out of my office right now. He raped my cousin. I can't treat him. I shouldn't say another word. If I do, and he reports me to the state medical board, I'll have to fight tooth and nail to avoid having my medical license suspended. Hell, if I talk to him long enough, they'd have grounds to revoke it entirely. Really, I should be running for the hills.

Instead, I extend my hand and wait to see if he'll take it. Because fuck him. If he's here to rattle my cage, well. Two can play at that game. I've killed three of them already, and I'll kill him too. Just not yet. And if I'm willing to risk Mark's job, why shouldn't I be willing to risk my own? I'm already risking my freedom. What's a medical license in comparison to that?

The fact that Garret Fischer knows who I am and found my practice without me having ever told him my name, the name of my practice, or even that I was a psychiatrist means that however he learned it, he's almost certainly aware that Katie is my cousin. I wonder if he recognized me from the days I showed up to the trial. I didn't think so at the time, and neither did Mark. It's possible he got my name from The Rose Room's guest list after seeing me there with Mark, or maybe even the security guard who was on duty the day I went to Tofana Arena.

Garret smirks as his hand wraps around mine, and it highlights the cleft in his chin. I plaster a smile on my face. *He's definitely a psychopath,* my brain supplies. The superficial charm, the constant clashes with Mark that never quite cross the line, the manipulation of others to suit his goals. But he's used to being the predator, not the prey. I can see it in the hard, flat glint in his eyes as he gives me a once-over. And I can use that to my advantage.

"What brings you in today?" I ask, gesturing for him to take a seat on the couch and discarding my plan for us to fill out the forms he neglected to complete prior to his appointment.

"You've heard about what's going on with my team?"

"The deaths. Yes, it's been all over the news lately," I agree. "You all work quite closely with one another. I'm sure that's been difficult to deal with."

"It is. I've been feeling very anxious lately. I'm having a hard time sleeping, and I feel like I'm letting my team down," he says with no real emotion. I wouldn't be surprised to find out he'd Googled 'symptoms of depression' prior to walking into my office.

"How so?" I ask.

"A lot of players on the team look to me as a leader, and I'm having a hard time staying focused. I keep thinking about the guys who've died. One of them died on the ice during a game. At first we were told it was a heart attack, but later the police said he was poisoned."

"And you witnessed his death?" I ask, playing the dumb, clueless psychiatrist.

"Yes. I turned to pass him the puck, and he was down. I keep having flashbacks to that moment during games, worrying that it could happen to someone else."

"To you?"

"Yes," he replies too quickly, and it might be the first honest thing he's said since he walked into my office. "To any of us," he amends.

"How does that make you feel?"

He pauses as if he's considering my question, but I'm certain he's not. There's no introspection to his demeanor. His focus is solely on me, and he's trying to decide whether I'm as clueless as I'm pretending to be. He's likely of above-average intelligence and used to believing himself to be the smartest person in the room. And though I don't know for sure, I'm guessing he generally assumes the average woman is less intelligent than the average man. Now that I'm sitting before him, his cognitive biases have him second-guessing himself and wondering if I really could've pulled off killing Joey Carmichael, Matt Davidson, and Brandon Miller.

"Uneasy," he says finally, which may be true. Contrary to popular media depictions, psychopathy exists on a sliding scale in much the same way autism does, and most psychopaths experience the full gamut of emotions, just not quite the same way neurotypical people do. It takes more to rattle them and more to excite them. But having three of your closest hockey-douchebag friends die in close succession is enough to rattle practically anyone. Especially when you have good reason to believe you're next.

"Would you say anxiety is the primary symptom you're experiencing?" I probe.

"That and insomnia. I can't sleep."

"I see. How long has that been going on?"

"Since Carmichael—Joey Carmichael—died."

"That was at the start of October?" I ask as if I'm uncertain of the date. I'm not.

"The seventh. It was during our first game of the season. We should've won easily, but the game was canceled after his death."

I nod. "Prior to his death, were there any other recent traumatic events that occurred?"

"No," he says. "Everything was normal. The team was doing well. It seemed like we'd have a good shot at making it to the playoffs, but then my teammates started dying. Now, it feels like we'll be lucky to be alive come the end of the season."

"Is there any reason for you to feel like your life may be at risk other than proximity?" I question, pushing just a little.

His icy blue eyes narrow slightly, and the bland smile he gives me doesn't reach them at all. "Not really. Is that a normal question? No one should ever be murdered," he replies, doing the same.

I'd like to take the pen in my hand and bury it in his eye socket. I'd like to tell him that some people absolutely deserve to be murdered. I'd like to tell him he's one of those people. Instead, I say, "I'm merely trying to get a sense of your state of mind and the stressors you're experiencing." I pause, waiting to see if he'll respond, but he doesn't. He only stares at me with the same flat gaze. "So, to that end, what are you hoping to gain by meeting with me?" I ask, leaving the question open-ended and up for interpretation. How he chooses to answer it can tell me a lot about him as a person.

"I figured since you and Coach Eriksson are seeing one another, and you're a psychiatrist, you'd be a good person to talk to about this. The sports psychologists the team keeps on staff are a little busy at the moment, and I'm not certain they have the capacity to deal with something like this, but if I try to find a completely independent doctor, I'll be at risk of something leaking to the tabloids. And I'd rather not wake up to a headline about how I have the yips."

I nod. "It's important that our goals are aligned when it comes to determining the best treatment plan for you. But I can't do that if you're lying to me, Garret."

"I'm not—" he begins.

I cut him off and continue talking. "I asked if you'd experienced any other recent traumatic events, and you said no. But you were on trial for rape this summer, weren't you? That's pretty traumatic."

He leans toward me slightly, his hands blanching. I think he wants to hit me. Unfortunately, he's not that stupid, and he leans back a moment later, the tension vanishing from his body, the mask settling into place again. He's angry, though, even if he's hiding it right this second. I'm certain he showed up here expecting that I would be intimidated, and things aren't going quite the way he imagined they would.

"Yes."

"Do you know who I am?" I ask, deciding not to bother with the charade any longer.

"Alyssa Reed," he says.

"Do you. Know. Who I am?" I repeat slowly, and this time he dips his chin, giving the barest hint of a nod. "Then you know I can't treat you. So why did you make an appointment?"

He gives a half shrug, unconcerned with being caught lying. "I wanted to meet you. To actually speak with you. This was the easiest way to do that without Eriksson interfering."

"And?"

"And?" he replies, echoing my question.

"You've met me. You've spoken to me. What now?"

"I know what you've been doing," he states boldly.

"Likewise, Garret. Likewise."

He tilts his head, the question clearly written across his face. I don't bother answering it though, and eventually he says, "You killed them."

I snort. "Prove it."

# Chapter 24
# Carnivorous

"You look nervous," Katie tells me.

"I am nervous. Thanks for pointing it out, though. That's very helpful of you."

She smirks. "What have you got to be worried about? I'm the one who should be nervous."

"Yeah, well. I don't think there's a hard limit on who's allowed to be nervous in this situation," I mutter. "I'm sure Mark's nervous too." I glance at my watch. It's six-forty-five. He should be here in fifteen minutes.

I've only been home for about thirty minutes, having stayed at my office later than I normally do and then walked to my car with my head on a swivel. I might be paranoid, but now seems like a good time to vary my routine as much as possible. Garret Fischer knows what I'm doing. He can't prove it. But he knows. And he knows I know. I basically taunted him with the fact this afternoon, and the look on his face was murderous. He's smart enough to realize this is a zero-sum game. Either he dies or I do—and right now, I'm winning.

You wouldn't know that from my body's physiological response, though. My hands have been shaky since he left my office earlier, and

I'm not sure my heart rate ever fully returned to normal. The pressure in my chest definitely hasn't receded at all.

I wouldn't be surprised to learn that he's trying to figure out my routine, much the same way that I've been learning all his scumbag-rapist friends' routines prior to killing them. It makes me want to get rid of Rhys Steichen sooner rather than later, but I can't. Until Vaughn can get me the tranq gun I asked for, it's not worth the risk. For the immediate future, it's two against one. The odds are not in my favor, and it's making me jumpy. At least they'll be leaving for road games in a day and a half, which will give me a bit of breathing room.

That's assuming Garret bothers to share what he's learned with Rhys, and I'd guess the chances of that are about fifty-fifty. If he tells Rhys, they could try to figure out a way to kill me together. But Rhys is an idiot. He's the one who made the video of Katie. He's the one who had an address book containing the addresses of women he's assaulted mixed in with friends and family.

I sigh, trying to stop thinking about it. It's all I've been doing since Garret left my office, and there's no predicting what'll happen next.

I should tell Katie that he came to see me today. But if I do, she'll want to cancel her trip to Redding to visit Erica. And right now, it's safer for her if she's not here. I don't believe he'd go after her, but why risk it? I definitely need to talk to Vaughn. *Hopefully he's back in town,* I think, chewing on the inside of my cheek. He's not going to react well. Vaughn and I might not be related, but I know he considers me family anyway. He's going to want me to shut this whole thing down. He's going to be pissed when I refuse.

God. This would all be a lot easier if Garret Fischer didn't have a brain. I'm sure he connected the dots as soon as he realized Katie was my cousin, which, based on the timing, was probably immediately after he saw me with Mark at The Rose Room. I bet he initially wanted to figure out who I was simply to screw with Mark, but then—

"Why would Mark be nervous?" Katie asks, interrupting my slow descent into madness.

"After I told him you wanted to meet him, and explained who you were, and he got over being mad that I lied to him, the first thing he said was, 'What would I even say to her? Sorry doesn't exactly cut it.' So yeah. I'm pretty sure he's nervous."

I check my watch again. Ten minutes. There's nothing for me to do except wait. I already placed an order for half of the local Chinese restaurant's menu.

"You're going down to California on Friday?" I ask, checking that her plans haven't changed.

"Yeah. I was going to take the train, but if I did, I'd either get there at two in the morning or have to leave here in the middle of the night. So I decided to drive instead. I'll get there in half the time anyhow," Katie tells me.

"Okay. Good." The Black Bears have road games starting this Friday and going through next Thursday. They'll be out of town by the time Katie leaves. It'll probably be next Friday at the earliest before I can get rid of Rhys, which should give the reporters time to find her. After that, I'll just have to figure out how to deal with Garret—the sooner, the better.

The intercom buzzes, and I jump.

"Geez. You really are nervous," Katie says.

I huff and walk over to it. "Hey," I say as I press the button.

"Hey, it's me," Mark responds, and I buzz him in.

My heart is beating just as erratically as it was this afternoon when I looked up and saw Garret Fischer standing across from me in my office, only now it feels like it might explode for an entirely different reason. I glance back at Katie. She's chewing on her lip, and she looks paler than she did a few moments ago.

I take a deep breath and exhale it as Mark knocks. *This is going to be the most fun dinner of my life,* I think sarcastically as I open the door. Mark is there in faded, paint-stained jeans and a well-worn flannel. Apparently, he decided to dress down, and it somehow makes him even more attractive—highlighting the fact that he's actually gorgeous. His dark red-brown hair seems to glow with the reflection of the hall lights, and the hint of stubble along his jaw is begging for me to run my fingertips over it.

A smile spreads across my face. "Hi," I say as I step out of the doorway. He steps in and freezes when he sees Katie behind me. It's the first time I've ever seen him look unsure of himself. "Mark, this is Katie. Katie, this is Mark."

For a second, there's awkward silence as they stare at one another, each uncertain about what to say. Finally, Mark's chest rises. "I'm really, really sorry," he blurts out.

Katie gives a small nod. "Thanks. Well, um. Come in. Nice to meet you and whatever," Katie replies, also sounding confused. There aren't a lot of *meet your rapists' boss* moments to model. This is uncharted territory for us all. "Alyssa told me you pushed her off a step stool," Katie says eventually.

Mark's eyes flick to mine, his brow furrowing in confusion. "I didn't—" he begins, and Katie and I burst out laughing. "Ah," he murmurs with a sigh.

I loop my arm through his. "Come on. I'll give you a quick real-life tour before the food gets here. Katie's room is over there," I say, pointing to the closed door off the living room on the right, before tugging him toward the hallway on the left and opening the first door. "This is the laundry room," I say as I flip on the light. The room is about ten feet by ten feet and has the hot water heater in addition to the washer and dryer. Other than that, it's a completely undecorated room. I let him look around for a moment before I turn off the light and pull the door shut. "Half bath," I say when we reach the next door, which is already open. The walls are a light sage-green, and our reflections are peering back at us from the mirror above the sink.

"I like the color," Mark tells me, his eyes meeting mine in the reflection.

"Thank you. This was the first room I painted when I moved in four years ago. It used to be a very violent red. It was like being inside a blood bag."

His lips twitch, and I move to the next door.

"This is just a closet. Nothing exciting," I explain as I open the door to a small storage space that's about four feet by six feet. We glance in for a second, and then I shut the door. "This is my room," I say as we approach the last door in the hallway.

I drop his arm and shut the door after we step through it. Mark looks around, surveying my bedroom. He's seen it on video, but that has a way of distorting a room's dimensions while simultaneously failing to capture the actual feel of a space.

"There's a bathroom through there," I say, pointing to the door on the right. "Katie's room is more or less identical and also has its own bathroom."

"Your curtains are closed," he comments, looking at the dark blue velvet drapes that cover the sliding glass door and large windows opposite my bed.

"Yes, of course they are. It's been dark for over two hours, and I live *in* the city. I have lots of neighbors."

"Mmm," he murmurs, interlacing his fingers with mine. "And you have orchids."

"You sound surprised."

"I am."

"Why?"

He turns to look at me, lifting his free hand to tuck my hair behind my ear. "I've always thought carnivorous plants seemed more your style."

I grin, stepping closer to him. "I tried. They're too hard to keep alive."

"Ah. Yes, that tracks," he says, his mouth centimeters from mine. "I can see how that might be a problem."

I close the distance between us at the same time his arm wraps around my waist, tugging me toward him. His lips have barely brushed against mine when the intercom buzzes.

I sigh, and Mark steps away. "We should go back out there before Katie comes to find us," I say.

"You know, I like it."

"Like what?"

"Your place," he says, and I smile. "And how much you want me."

"Oh, get over yourself," I grumble, opening the door and heading back to the living room without bothering to look behind me. I know he's watching my ass as I walk away.

Katie is at the small dining table we never use when it's just the two of us, unboxing the food. "Hey," she says, glancing up. Her eyes move past me and land on Mark. "Did you have a nice… tour?" she asks him.

"It was revealing," Mark answers. "She has orchids."

"Yes. Alyssa is *full* of surprises," Katie says. "Apparently you found out about me before I found out about you."

I thought we were past this, but I guess she hasn't completely forgiven me for keeping Mark—and everything else—a secret.

"Only by a day. If it makes you feel any better, I was mad too."

"You got over it awfully fast."

"Yeah. Well, I like her."

"Me too," Katie agrees, her eyes flicking toward me. "She's annoying like that."

"If you could both stop talking about me like I'm not here, that would be great. Katie, I'm sorry I didn't tell you about Mark before I told him about you. You're right. I should have told you first."

"You guys really are like sisters," Mark comments.

"Yes. We are," Katie says. "So if you hurt her, I'll kill you," she tells him, pointing a fork at him.

To his credit, Mark merely nods and says, "Okay."

"Shall we sit down and have the most awkward dinner ever?" I ask, handing out the plates that are stacked on the table as Katie passes out chopsticks.

There are a couple of minutes of semi-uncomfortable silence where no one says anything under the guise of filling our plates and taking our first bites before Katie says, "So, Mark. How's the season going?"

"Kay," I chide.

"No, it's fine," Mark interjects. "It's okay, all things considered. We're six and six right now."

"That doesn't seem very good," Katie comments around a mouthful of lo mein.

"It puts us fourth in the division with most of the season left to go. It's better than we were doing this time last year," he says, surprising me.

"Why have you been so stressed then?" I ask. "Beyond the obvious," I add quickly.

"New jobs are always stressful," Mark says, deflecting.

"Oh, come on," I prod. "That's not why. I've been assuming you were worried about being fired or something."

"They can't fire me. Well," he amends quickly, "they could, but they'd have to pay me for the duration of my contract, so they're unlikely to, especially since we're not losing quite as badly as you'd expect considering we've had three players die."

"So why then?"

Mark taps his chopsticks against his plate, his eyes darting to me and then to Katie. "They were never supposed to be on the team," Mark says finally, his eyes locked on Katie. "Regardless of whether the trial ended in a conviction, they were never supposed to be on *my* team. That stipulation was part of my agreeing to take the job in the first place. But it wasn't written into my contract. It was a handshake deal. And player contracts with the NHL are fully guaranteed by the collective bargaining agreement unless the contract is terminated by breach," Mark explains.

"If the trial had ended in a guilty verdict, well. Terminating their contracts outright would've been simple enough. But it didn't. It shouldn't have mattered, though. They could've still made the case for terminating, or at the very least sent them down to the minors or bought them out. Only every one of those guys was a good enough player that when the GM and the owners saw the chance to keep them, they did, which was already enough of a pain in my ass," he says looking back to me, and I know he means Garret Fischer specifically.

"But now I'm having to deal with a GM who thinks the sky is falling and our franchise is crumbling, police who want to come back and question the players every other day, a team full of superstitious idiots, and a bunch of rent-a-cops standing around, pretending they're doing anything other than being in the way. Half of the team is acting like they're next, and the other half doesn't want to share the ice with

Fischer and Steichen for fear that they might be hit by a stray bullet or something.

"There's constant talk of canceling games, only no one wants to be the one to make that decision. I'm having to run interference between about forty different morons, and none of them will just let me do my fucking job. And that doesn't even touch on having to deal with Garret Fischer day in and day out. If someone is actually targeting those assholes, they should've started with him," Mark growls.

I look at Katie, eyebrows raised, only to find the same expression on her face. But at least that answers my question about the private security—Mark had mentioned it before, but it sounded like they were still only considering the option. I guess they decided to cover their asses. That's going to make things more difficult.

"Sorry," he mutters.

"I hear you threw a guy out of a window," Katie says.

Mark glares at me. "Yeah."

"That's cool."

The rest of the dinner goes by slightly more normally, and by the time we're done eating, Katie seems to have somewhat rescinded her grudge against Mark.

"Well, I'm going to go to my mom's for the night," Katie announces as I'm taking our plates to the dishwasher.

"What? Why?" I ask, looking back at her.

"I should go see her before I leave for California. Otherwise, I'll never hear the end of it. Plus, if I go to my mom's, he can spend the night without feeling weird about it, and I know he wants to," Katie says, her eyes locked on Mark, who looks like he's trying really hard not to squirm under her gaze.

"You're sure?" I question.

"Yeah. I'll be back at noon tomorrow, so if you're still here, be wearing clothes," she tells Mark before turning to head to her room.

"Are all the women in your family that direct?"

"Yes," I answer, loading the plates into the dishwasher.

"Ask me to spend the night," Mark says from immediately behind me.

I close the dishwasher and turn to face him, stepping into his space and looping my arms over his shoulders. "Would you like to spend the night?"

As soon as the words leave my mouth, his lips are on mine, and my hands are in his hair, pulling him closer. I've wanted him since before the intercom buzzed and interrupted us earlier. I've wanted—

"Geez. You could've at least waited until I was gone," Katie says, sounding amused.

Mark steps back from me, his cheeks flushing. It might be the first time I've really seen him look embarrassed. "Sorry," he mumbles, and Katie and I both laugh.

A few more minutes pass, and then Katie is out the door.

"Why is she going to California?" Mark asks.

"She's got a friend who lives in Redding, and the reporters have been circling around trying to be the first to get a sound bite from Katie since the news about Brandon's murder broke. We've had three make it into the building and knock on our door this week alone."

"Ah," he says, pulling me closer to him.

I keep waiting for Mark to ask me about Brandon. Or Matt Davidson. Or Joey Carmichael. Or even if I think Katie could have something to do with it. But he hasn't. If I thought he was stupid, I'd be less nervous about his disinterest in questioning the circumstances around their deaths.

I keep almost asking him about it. And I keep chickening out.

"I liked the windows in your bedroom," Mark says softly as he wraps his arms around my waist.

"The curtains were closed. You didn't even see them."

"I *liked* the windows in your bedroom," he repeats, a low growl in his voice.

"I... Oh. You want to open the curtains and fuck me against the window, don't you?" I drop my hand to stroke him through his jeans, and he rocks his hips into it.

"Yes. I've wanted to do that since you told me about your dream, and you've got better windows than I do."

I grin. "Want to record it?" I might not want to have FaceTime sex, but I have no issues recording us having fun together.

"Are you asking me if I want to make a sex tape?" he asks, a wild look in his eyes.

"Yes," I reply, pulling him out of the kitchen toward the hallway.

A soundless gasp escapes my lungs as he scoops me up, cradling me to his chest. "You weren't walking fast enough," he states before I can say anything. He turns sideways, stepping into my bedroom and setting me down.

The lamps above the orchids are still on, casting glowing pools around them. I reach for the light switch, but Mark grabs my hand, stopping me before I can hit it.

"This is fine."

"But—"

"If you turn on every light in this room, you're going to spend more time worrying about the neighbors watching us than you are enjoying this, and this is your fantasy as much as it is mine. You wouldn't have been dreaming about it otherwise. Besides," he says, cutting me off when I open my mouth to protest, "we can always turn on all the lights next time we do this."

"Bold of you to assume there will be a next time," I tell him as I stare into his hazel eyes, already having to restrain myself from winding my hands into his hair so I can drag his mouth to mine.

"Oh, I *know* there will be a next time," he replies with an annoying amount of confidence.

"Whatever," I scoff, although I'm pretty sure he's right. Lust has been racing through me since he mentioned my curtains, and it's tinged with just enough uncertainty to make things really exciting. I pass him my phone. "You set up our phones, and I'll get the curtains. The dresser is going to be your best bet."

The drapes snick along the track as I pull them open, revealing a sliding glass door that leads to a small balcony surrounded by windows on both sides.

"Stay where you are. Don't move," Mark orders over the sound of him shifting things around. "I need to make sure you're in frame."

"Okay," I agree, looking out the windows to the building opposite mine. Lights are on in at least half the units, and of those, there are a solid twenty whose occupants can see into my bedroom. I'm still fully clothed, but I've never felt more exposed.

Another moment passes, and then Mark is behind me, his body pressing into mine, his hands sliding under my shirt. They're warm against my skin as they move up my stomach and over my ribs. I lift my arms so he can pull it off.

"Nervous?" he whispers, his lips next to my ear as his hands undo the hooks on my bra.

"A bit," I answer as he strips it from me, tossing it aside.

The lights in my room are just bright enough that I can see his reflection if I focus on it instead of the world outside, and I watch him quickly strip off his own clothes in the glass. Then his chest is pressing into my back, heat radiating into me. His hands are on my body again, his fingers trailing across my boobs and down my stomach. My pants and underwear join the growing pile on the floor.

Mark is silent as he places his hands on my ass, separating my cheeks before stepping closer. Then he pulls them away, leaving his shaft trapped between my cheeks. He takes my hands in his and raises them above my head, pinning them to the glass.

I'm trying to focus on the warmth of Mark's body behind me, rather than the increasingly uncomfortable sensation that I'm being watched. My eyes have been dancing between his reflection and the windows in the building across from us, which is making it difficult to focus on the fact that I do actually want this to happen.

"First," Mark begins, the tip of his nose grazing my ear as his breath trickles over my cheek, "I'm going to spin you around and go down on you while I fuck you with the vibrator I took from your nightstand until you're coming so hard that the glass behind you is the only thing holding you up. After that, I'm going to turn you back around and pin you here, where everyone can see. I'm going to bury myself in you, and I'm going to make you come. But," Mark continues, switching his grip, so that one of his hands is holding both of mine to the glass above our heads as the other slowly moves down my body until it's resting on my hip, "they're going to be watching *us*. Not *you*, because I'll be right here too. And when you scream my name—because you will—anyone who's watching will see how much *we* like it when I come inside you," he says, and I hear the promise in his words.

I shift my hips against him, wringing a small groan from his mouth as I say, "Yes. And after we're done, when your cum is running down my thighs, I'll let you lick it off me."

"Deal," Mark agrees, releasing my hands.

I twist to face him. The glass is cool against my back, but the heat from his body makes up for it. I slide my hands across his jaw and into his mahogany hair as he sinks to his knees, his lips and tongue skimming down my torso. Then he's nudging my feet farther apart and reaching for my vibrator, which is resting atop his clothes on the floor. Seeing his hand wrapped around it erases any remaining concern I had about being watched, and the only thing I can think about now is how much I want this.

Mark's breath ghosts over my clit and along my labia. He pulls his face away just far enough to insert my vibrator into his mouth, and somehow my nipples harden even more. It might be the hottest thing I've ever seen.

"Do you know where that thing's been?" I tease, my voice a low growl of unmet need as I stare into his eyes.

"Nowhere my tongue hasn't already gone," he states when he pulls it from his mouth and holds down the button to turn it on.

The anticipation alone has me ready to burst, and I can't stop the moan that escapes when it buzzes to life, even though he has yet to touch me. I release my grip on his hair to grab his hand, ready to thrust it inside me myself, but he moves it out of my reach.

"Say please, Alyssa."

"Please get me off before I explode."

"Since you asked so nicely," he replies, sinking the vibrator into me as his tongue flicks across my clit.

My legs practically give way beneath me, and I bring my hands back to his head, twining them in his hair to hold myself up. I'm pinned between Mark and the glass, and there's nowhere else I'd rather be.

Time stretches and dilates as I lose myself to the dual sensations of the vibrator buried deep inside me and Mark's tongue moving over my clit, faster and faster. When I look down and find his free hand wrapped around his cock, stroking himself, the orgasm rolls through me, swamping me all at once. My head is buzzing like I've had too much to drink as my hips rock against his face, again and again.

By the time it ends, the vibrator is back on the pile of clothes, and Mark is holding me up as he rises to his feet. My body is still a limp, quivering mess as he spins me toward the window, pressing me against it, groaning as he slides into me.

A distant voice is chittering in the very back of my mind, reminding me that people could be watching. Normally that would be enough to give me second thoughts, but I can't bring myself to care.

"Is it as good as you imagined?" Mark asks, his voice a low murmur, his breath ghosting across my ear as he begins moving.

"Better," I pant.

"Good. Because I love that anyone can see us right now. I love that anyone who looks in this window is going to know exactly how much you like it when I come inside you. And how much I like it too," he whispers, his thrusts growing more urgent. "I told you how it felt in your office. Tell me what this feels like."

"It's…" I begin, struggling to find the words—to form a coherent thought—before blurting out the first thing that comes to mind. "Terrifying."

He freezes.

"Don't stop," I plead. "This is amazing. It's terrifying because when you're buried in me, it's like I lose track of the entire world, and everything narrows to how good things are. You're hard and soft, and half the time my body doesn't even know how to process the things you make me feel. All I know is that I want—need—more. Please keep going," I beg, and he finally starts moving again.

"Yes," I moan. "Yes. Yes, yes, yes."

"I'm getting close," he says raggedly. "What do you need?"

"Tell me the thing you said before. Please."

He doesn't ask which thing. "Anyone who's watching right now isn't watching you. They're watching us," he pants. "Because I'm here with you, and all they're going to see is how much *we* like it when I come inside you."

"Fuckfuckfuck, Mark!" I scream as I come, pinned so tightly between Mark and the glass that I'm unable to move at all as the orgasm hits me like a tsunami. Then Mark is coming too, shouting my name as his hips jerk against me.

We ride out the wave together, and then he continues lazily moving inside me as he holds me plastered to the glass. Eventually, he's soft enough that he slips out of me with a low, satisfied growl, and cum drips from my cunt, running down my thigh.

I turn to face him, my back to the glass as I take his hand, brushing his fingertips across the cum on my thigh before raising them to my lips and wrapping my mouth around one finger, and then the next, and the next, sucking it off each as Mark's amber-flecked eyes burn into mine.

"I could use a little help with the rest," I murmur, and he drops to his knees in front of me.

# Chapter 25
# Lotta Late Nights

"Hey kid," Vaughn says when I sit down across from him on Sunday morning. The lines around his eyes are etched deeper than normal, he's got the largest-sized coffee this place offers, and he's trying to stifle a yawn. He looks exhausted.

"Late night?"

"Lotta late nights," he agrees, gulping down some more coffee. "How was your dinner with Katie and Mark?"

"Not bad. No one died. No one even got stabbed. Katie's in California now, though."

"Why?"

"The police came to talk to her last Sunday after you and I met. They were trying to figure out if she had anything to do with Brandon Miller's death," I elaborate when his eyes narrow. "Anyway, since then, the reporters have been circling. So, she decided to leave town. It seemed like a good idea, so I didn't argue. But then after that..." I trail off. I haven't told Vaughn about Garret Fischer yet. Or that Katie knows everything. Or that she's got plans of her own now.

"After that?"

I let out a long, slow breath. "After that, on Wednesday, Garret Fischer made a new patient appointment and came to my office."

"Alyssa," Vaughn grates out, pinching the bridge of his nose with his right hand.

"And then it seemed like a really good idea for her to be somewhere else."

"Alyssa," Vaughn repeats. "What does he know?"

"Nothing he can prove," I state.

"You're certain?"

"Yes. Trust me, Vaughn. He sat across from me for the better part of an hour. He can't prove anything," I say, taking a sip of my coffee. "But he's going to try to kill me before too long. And it turns out the team hired private security to… I don't know. Sit outside their houses, I guess."

Vaughn closes his eyes, takes a long breath, and then says, "He's out of town now?"

I nod. "Until early Friday morning."

"What's your plan for when he gets back?"

"I'm still working on it."

"Alyssa," Vaughn chides again.

"When they get back, I'll stay with Mark. Katie's out of town, so why not? Garret won't try anything there. And I'll figure out how to work around the security detail. I won't do anything unless I'm sure I can get away with it."

"If you get yourself killed…"

"I won't. I promise."

"That's a lie, and you know it," Vaughn says.

I shrug. "What else am I supposed to do, Vaughn? There's no going back now."

"You know your father said those same words to me right before your house was raided?"

"No, but that doesn't surprise me. Was anyone trying to kill him?" I ask.

"No, he was just an asshole who didn't want to quit."

"And what about me?"

Vaughn sighs. "I already regret this, but everything you asked for is in there," he says, using the toe of his boot to nudge the bag at his feet toward me, seeming to agree that I'm in too deep to quit now. "There are instructions for everything."

"Thanks, Vaughn," I murmur as I hook the strap with my heel and pull the bag the rest of the way to me. "I'm going to go see him on Tuesday. Want me to say hi for you?"

"Sure. Why not?" Vaughn grumbles, but he's not very happy about it.

I'M SITTING IN THE PRISON VISITOR'S ROOM, WAITING FOR my dad to be brought out. The light from the windows is practically nonexistent due to the heavy cloud cover and drizzle that's been falling throughout the morning. The usual four-hour drive from Portland took closer to five hours last night, thanks to some snow falling in the mountains. It'll probably be the same on the way home, and I'm not looking forward to it. He'll be getting out in a few months, though. I shouldn't need to make this drive too many more times.

The room is emptier than usual. Only three tables are occupied, and there was no wait to get in today. The weather must be keeping people away. And the time of year, I suppose. A lot of people are probably saving their November visits for closer to Thanksgiving. I should talk to Mark about that. I have no idea what his plans are or if we'll be spending the holiday together. Assuming *we're* still together at that point. Assuming I'm still *alive* at that point.

I prop my chin on my hand and sigh. I could've just left well enough alone—except it wasn't 'well enough'—and I'm not built to sit around and watch rapists get away with it. And if I were, I never would've met Mark in the first place.

A second later, my dad sits down opposite me.

"Hey dad," I greet.

"Hey Alyssa. Why do you look so glum?" he asks.

"You've always been really good at that," I comment.

"What?"

"Knowing what I'm thinking. You'd think at some point you'd have lost the knack for it, with only seeing me once every thirty days or so."

He shrugs. "It's just one of those things. You're good at it too. It's probably half the reason you became a shrink. So, what's up?"

"Nothing. Just lamenting my decisions."

"You kept the hair. Does that mean you kept the guy?" my dad asks.

"I'm working on it," I tell him. "Why? Do you want to meet him?"

"Do you want to bring him up here to see me? It might not exactly make the best impression," my dad says, gesturing to himself and his beige DOC uniform.

"Eh. He already knows you're here. It wouldn't even be the first time he's been inside a prison visitor's room," I tack on with a smirk.

"No?"

"His older brother is in prison for murdering his dad. Sounds like his dad had it coming, though."

"Exactly who is it you're dating, Alyssa?"

"Mark Eriksson. He's the head coach for the Black Bears," I add since I'm not sure what sports my dad keeps up with.

"The coach for the guys who raped Katie?" my dad questions, eyebrows raised. "The team that's unexpectedly had three of those guys die in the past month and a half?"

"Yes."

"Alyssa," my dad mutters, pinching the bridge of his nose. Vaughn had exactly the same reaction yesterday. They like to pretend they're nothing alike, but they are. "What the *fuck* are you doing?"

"Righting wrongs? Balancing the scales?"

"And this guy—"

"Mark."

"Mark. You want to bring him here to meet me? Why?"

"I…" I take a long breath and exhale it. "I don't know. I guess because I'm in love with him," I admit, finally saying the words out loud.

My dad closes his eyes and sighs. "You and goddamned Vaughn.

How is it you're *my* child but you take after him?" my dad grouses, eyes still closed. He sits there silently for a moment. Finally, he opens his eyes and stares at me. "You fell for a mark named Mark." He bursts out laughing.

It's Wednesday night, and I'm alone in my condo, reading the instruction manual for the tranquilizer gun with a nature documentary playing in the background. I miss having Katie around.

The bag Vaughn gave me had the tranq gun in a neat, little carrying case with a set of ten practice darts and an equal number of real ones, five CO2 canisters—each of which is rated to fire a total of six darts—and a laser sight along with eight glass vials, each containing five hundred milligrams of Telazol.

Next time Mark wants to buy Vaughn an absurdly expensive bottle of bourbon, I'm going to have to let him.

The Telazol is supposed to be reconstituted at a ratio of five milliliters of sterile water per vial, rendering a solution containing a hundred milligrams of Telazol per milliliter. Rhys Steichen is six-five. I'd guess he's around two hundred and twenty-five pounds, but I'm doing my calculations based on a two-hundred-and-fifty-pound man. Or bear, since the closest dosing instructions I found for someone that size came from the Alaska Department of Fish and Game Division of Wildlife Conservation's *Wildlife Capture and Chemical Restraint Manual*. I figure since bears share the feature of being omnivores, the dosing guidelines for humans—not that Telazol is ever recommended for use in humans—should be similar enough. Fingers crossed. I could accidentally kill Rhys Steichen. Not that it really matters since I'm going to purposefully kill him anyway. I *would* like to ask him some questions before I do, though.

Also in the bag was a folder with documents summarizing Rhys's typical routines. Luckily for me, he has a late-night food-delivery habit. Based on the notes Vaughn gave me, I'm betting that as soon as he gets home tomorrow night, he'll put in a delivery order from one of the trucks at whatever food cart pod is still open.

His yard has a large hedge encircling both the front and the back. There's no seeing the house from the street. I checked. And assuming his security detail is sitting in a car on the street outside of his house, not inside with him—which seems likely—I just have to arrive before they do. The hedge will block their view of what's happening in the yard. Then I'll knock on Rhys's door, leave a bag of takeout, hide in the shadows when he comes to get it, and hit him with a tranq dart.

That's the easy part, because it'll probably take a few minutes until he's fully incapacitated. If he shouts for help during those few minutes, and whoever's sitting outside his house hears him... Well. I'm screwed. As long as that doesn't happen, once he's unconscious, I can drag him back into his house. Then I'll have a couple of hours to restrain him before he wakes up.

Once he's awake, I can question him. And once he's answered my questions, I can kill him. Between the practice darts and the laser sight, that part should be a walk in the park.

Assuming he doesn't shout for help. But I don't see any way around that as long as he has a security detail. I'll just have to roll the dice and run if he does. Live to fight another day, and all that.

If it works, there will only be one hockey-douchebag left. Mission almost complete.

I jump when my phone vibrates against my thigh, almost dropping the tranq gun as I reach for it. It's Mark.

"Hey," I say, accepting the call and pausing the documentary. He's in Texas right now, so while it's nine for me, it's eleven for him. "How's it going? Did you win?"

"I'm good. You could just watch the games, you know," he says with a grin.

"If you're threatening to torture me, I can think of more fun ways to go about it," I tell him, and he snorts. "Besides, the only reason I'd bother watching the game is to see you, and you might be disappointed to learn that the cameras don't show you that often."

"Yes, we won. Five to three."

"Nice. Hey, what are your plans for Thanksgiving?" I ask. I didn't get the chance to talk to him last night because I was on the road driving back from Walla Walla, and he was already asleep by the time I got home.

"I don't have any, why?"

"I was thinking maybe we'd spend it together. And normally I go up to visit my dad sometime that weekend, so if you wanted to come…"

"Are you inviting me to meet your father?" Mark asks.

"Yes. You'd actually be the first person I've dated who's met him."

"Yes."

"Are you sure? It's kind of a long drive and not the most fun way to spend the time," I say to give him a chance to consider it and change his mind if he wants.

"I already told you I'm going to take any chance I can get to be a first for you, Alyssa," he softly reminds me.

"Okay. Want to go on Black Friday?"

"Yes."

"Good. Normally Jeanette—Katie's mom—hosts Thanksgiving, and we go over there. So if you want to meet her too…"

"Count me in."

"Alright, good. What time are you getting back tomorrow?" I ask. Rhys Steichen will be on the same flight, so he'll arrive home around the same time.

"We should land around one-thirty in the morning. I'd invite you over, but I'm sure you'll be in bed by then."

"Yeah," I lie. "I will. I can come over after work on Friday afternoon if you want. And since Katie's in California for the next couple of weeks, I can stay until whenever you're next out of town. Feel free to tell me no, though," I add quickly. "I'm not trying to move in on the sly or anything."

"Or I could stay with you. I don't have glow-in-the-dark stars above my bed, after all."

"You're never going to let me live that down, are you?"

A smile spreads across his face. "No. But it's cute. You can see them in the video."

"Been getting a lot of use out of that, have you?" I tease.

"Yes. Thank you."

I grin. "Yeah. Me too. I'm good whichever way, so let me know what you prefer."

"Well, since I'm desperate to sleep in my own bed for a night or two, how about you come over?"

"Okay. Unless something on my schedule changes, I should be there a bit after five."

Mark and I spend another twenty minutes talking before he starts yawning, and I tell him to go to sleep. I still need to read the instruction manual for this tranquilizer gun and test it out. The manual is helpful enough to let me know I don't need a federal firearms license to shoot it. *I might go down for murder, but at least I won't have illegal gun possession charges added to my rap sheet,* I think with a snort as I load in a practice dart.

# Chapter 26
# Laser Tag

IT'S JUST AFTER ONE IN THE MORNING, AND I'M CROUCHED in the bushes outside of Rhys Steichen's McMansion, waiting for him to get home. It's in the fifties, and it's been drizzling all day. I'm cold and I don't like it, but at least it means there should be fewer people out and about. Not that there's much foot traffic in this neighborhood. Only the occasional dog walker, and there aren't many of those this late. But still. I'll take what I can get.

Right now, I'm trying not to freeze to death before Rhys gets home. I've been hiding here for three hours. I wanted to make sure that I arrived prior to the hired security detail that pulled up half an hour ago. My position in the bushes near the front hedge gives me just enough visibility to make out two figures in the car between the branches. Because of our positions relative to the hedge, I can see them, but they can't see me. It's like looking through a keyhole. They've been sitting there since they parked at the curb in front of his house. I don't know if they're supposed to get out and walk around to surveil the perimeter, or whatever, but so far they haven't. If I were them, I wouldn't want to get wet either. Hopefully the rain keeps up, and hopefully that's enough to keep them confined to the vehicle.

I'm wearing a long, new-to-me black raincoat I bought with cash from a thrift shop a few days ago. I have a couple of layers underneath it for warmth and a ski mask pulled over my face. Although the ski mask does have the added benefit of keeping me slightly warmer, both it and the latex gloves on my hands are solely to obscure my identity. Unlike the others I've killed, I'm actually going to talk to Rhys Steichen. Kind of. The duffel bag on the ground next to me is stuffed with equipment, because—also unlike the others—this death is going to be a production. Assuming I can pull it off, anyway.

There's a plastic bag stacked with containers full of food that has long since gone cold on the ground beside me as well. I could wait for the delivery driver to show up and ring Rhys's doorbell, but what if the driver is the sort who sits in the driveway for five minutes after delivering the food? Or what if one of the security guys out front decides to bring it to the door? I'd be screwed.

I'd rather wait fifteen minutes after he gets home, set the bag on his doorstep, ring the doorbell and run back to the shadows where I can shoot him with the tranq dart. If I'm lucky, when the dart hits him, he'll have no idea what happened or where it came from. Hopefully he'll be too surprised to raise the alarm. And hopefully the drugs will take him out before he can spot me.

It's a lot of 'hopefully's. The only other option is to wait until the team gets sick of footing the bill for the rent-a-cops and cancels their contract. Even if I wait two or three months until they're gone, though, Rhys's got eight inches on me, and his entire job relies on sprinting. It's a safe bet he's faster than I am. So this is still probably my best chance. As long as he doesn't realize where the dart came from, and as long as he doesn't start shouting for help, once he passes out, I just have to get him into the house prior to the real delivery driver showing up. I'm trying to tell myself that it's not really any different from laser tag, but it might be the biggest lie I've told myself yet.

I sigh and shift my weight from side to side, checking my watch for the thousandth time. *Their flight had better not be late*, I complain to myself as I fold my arms across my chest and think warm thoughts.

Thirty more minutes go by before a large, dark pickup truck pulls up beside the security detail's car. They exchange words for a few minutes, and then the truck turns into the driveway. I crouch into the shadows a little more, averting my eyes so that I'm not blinded by its headlights. The garage door clatters open. A minute later, a door slams and the garage closes. It's one-fifty. I give him two minutes to get inside and set his things down before starting a fifteen-minute timer on my watch. Throughout that time, my eyes keep moving between the car on the street and Rhys's house, but the security detail seems content to stay warm and dry.

When the timer goes off, I turn on the tranquilizer gun's laser sight and hold the gun along my right side. Then I grab the cold, sodden takeout bag and head for Rhys's front door. It doesn't matter if he has security cameras, because my face has been covered since before I got here—first by a scarf and now by the ski mask. Plus, I arrived on foot after walking a few circuitous miles and cutting through multiple parks to make it difficult for anyone to track my route. And thanks to Vaughn, I have a set of fake license plates on my car right now.

I take a deep breath and glance behind me to make sure no one has gotten out of the car. Then I set the bag on the doorstep, press the doorbell, and sprint back to the bushes. My heart is pounding by the time I turn to face the door with my finger on the trigger. Another ten or fifteen seconds pass, and then the door cracks open and light streams out.

I set the takeout bag at the very edge of his doorstep to force him to take a few steps out of his house to grab it. He opens the door wider and steps through, backlit by the interior light.

Adrenaline floods my system, and I consider leaving. He'll still be here in three months, and I'm not sure this is worth the risk. But if I wait... In three months, there could be a new address book with a new woman's name in it. And I can't spend the next three months looking over my shoulder, waiting for Garret and Rhys to kill me.

I wish the rain were heavier.

I take a breath and raise the tranq gun as he stoops to pick up the bag. The green dot from the laser races across the grass toward the house. Rhys must see it, because his eyebrows draw together in confusion as he stands, and then the dot is on his torso. I squeeze the trigger. There's a soft whoosh of air as the dart flies free, followed by a yelp, and the dart is embedded in Rhys's torso, to the left of his navel, just below his rib cage. He looks down and pulls it free. Then he holds it in front of his face, staring at it for a second before dropping it and the takeout bag to the ground.

I look at the car behind me. There's no movement. They're still focused on the street. They haven't noticed anything's amiss so far, and I return my focus to Rhys.

There's a funny thing about men. Once they reach a certain size, they have a tendency to think they're indestructible. If Rhys were smart, he'd run inside, lock the door, and call for help. But he's too big for that. He's probably never lost a physical fight in his life, and it doesn't seem to cross his mind that he might lose this one.

So he doesn't do the smart thing. Instead, he steps into the yard, his head turning left and right as he tries to determine where the shot came from. I whistle softly. I don't want him to decide that whoever shot him ran away. I want him to continue looking for me because if he goes inside before the drugs kick in, I'll have to break a window, and that would probably trigger an alarm. He looks in my direction, taking another step into the yard. I whistle again.

"Are you fucking hiding?" he shouts, and I flinch, looking at the car behind me. His words already sound a bit slurred, and no one gets out of the car. Either he wasn't as loud as the adrenaline coursing through my veins made him sound, or the drizzle on the roof of the car is too loud for them to have heard him. Maybe both.

He takes another step into the yard. I whistle once more, and he stumbles in my direction. The Telazol is kicking in faster than I expected. It's been maybe a minute and a half since the dart hit him. He takes one more step and trips over his own feet. His knees hit the ground, and he topples forward, catching himself on his outstretched palms. He's about ten feet away from me. He tries and fails to stand, muttering, "What...?" Then he crumples, landing face down on the wet grass with his arms awkwardly folded beneath his torso.

I check on the rent-a-cops again. They're both still in the car. They're not even looking toward the house. So far, so good.

I count to thirty before shoving the tranq gun into the duffel bag, exchanging it for the large tarp I brought with me. I approach him cautiously, waiting to make sure he's not about to spring up and grab me. When he stays motionless, I spread the tarp on the ground next to him and roll his body onto it. He's all floppy limbs, and he's huge. He's only a couple of inches taller than Mark, but he seems bigger than that. By the time I've got him centered on it, I feel like I'm about to break a sweat.

I grab the corners of the tarp, take a deep breath, and then start dragging him toward the front door. It's like pulling a sled through sand, and about halfway there, my right elbow starts protesting, reminding me it's still not fully healed. At this rate, I'll be lucky if it's back to normal by spring. Oh well.

I try to move faster, but there isn't much in the way of 'faster' when you're dragging two hundred and twenty-five pounds of dead weight across wet grass in the dark. Another minute goes by before my heels hit the base of the doorstep, and I momentarily fight to keep my balance. When I release the tarp to pick up the tranquilizer dart and the takeout bag Rhys dropped, my forearms are on fire. I toss them onto Rhys's motionless body and shake out my arms before grabbing the corners of the tarp and stepping onto the doorstep.

The step is only six inches higher than the ground I've been dragging Rhys across, but getting him onto it takes at least a full minute, and I'm panting by the time I manage it. I pause long enough to slip some shoe covers over my boots. And then I'm dragging the tarp into the house. Once we're all the way through the door, I shut it behind us. I'll need to go back for my duffel bag, but I'd like to let the actual food delivery person come and go prior to that. I don't want to risk running into them.

In the meantime, I leave Rhys's body lying on the tarp and survey the room. It's a formal living room that looks like it was decorated by a woman in her fifties. I wonder if his mom did his interior design. Weight settles on my chest, and I hope not. That would suck for her.

But considering the fact that he's been walking around the world, raping women and getting away with it for at least a couple of years... Well, he's only getting what he deserves. I know that won't make the loss any less painful for his family, though.

I push the thought away with a sigh.

I need to find a chair. A nice sturdy dining room chair. Preferably one with arms. The formal living room opens onto a large kitchen, and there's a formal dining room to the left of the kitchen. The dining room is dominated by a large table surrounded by eight sturdy-looking wooden chairs. I drag the closest one to the living room and lay it on its side next to Rhys's body.

The doorbell rings as I'm turning to go back to the kitchen. I freeze, hoping Rhys left instructions for the driver to leave the food at the door. I count to two hundred before I approach it to peer out of the peephole. There's no one visible on the doorstep, and there's no car parked in the driveway. I breathe a sigh of relief and return to the kitchen, figuring it won't hurt to give it a bit of extra time, just in case. That way, if the security detail noticed something amiss, and this is them checking up on things, they'll grow so concerned when no one answers the door that they'll bust it down, and I can make a run out the back.

I open drawers until I find the plastic wrap. There are boxes of it in my duffel bag outside, but I may as well start with what Rhys has in the house. When I return to his body, I roll him off the tarp until he's lying on his side next to the dining room chair. I position his body so that if the chair were upright, he'd be sitting in it. Then I pull the roll of plastic wrap from the box and wrap his lower right leg to the right chair leg. I do the same thing with his right arm. By the time I'm finished, the roll is almost empty. I leave him lying there, partially restrained but fully unconscious, and return to the yard to retrieve my duffel bag. The car hasn't moved, and it looks like one of the guys is napping while the other watches the street.

I bring the recently delivered takeout bag in, stopping long enough to wrap Rhys's hands around the bag before setting it in the kitchen. Maybe it'll help confuse the timeline a little and make it look like he wasn't attacked until after the food was delivered. I bet Rhys told them the delivery driver was coming when he stopped to talk to them, and they waved the person right past.

When I return to the living room, I finish wrapping him to the chair. Once I'm done, almost every inch of him is covered in plastic wrap. I even slid a long, thin breadboard I found in the kitchen between his back and the chair and made sure his head was affixed to it. He shouldn't be able to so much as rock the chair since I also locked his feet into a flexed position. He looks like a cling-film-wrapped mummy.

I slap a strip of duct tape over his mouth and set up the tripod from my bag with the camera I purchased in cash from a pawnshop earlier this week. After that, I go to his garage and find a screwdriver and a hammer. Then, I return to sit down on the floor with my back against the front door. There's no reversal agent for Telazol. All I can do is wait for Rhys to wake up.

It's three-fifty-eight when he begins to stir. It's four-seventeen when his eyes open and he blinks a few times. It's four-thirty-five when his eyes focus on mine and he seems to realize his predicament. His muscles strain against the plastic wrap, but aside from his face changing to a deep purply-red color, nothing happens. I wait until his muscles slacken. He's breathing loudly through his nose, and I want to make sure he's not going to pass out again. Once his face returns to a more normal color, I rise to my feet and hit the record button on the camera, being sure to stay out of frame—despite the ski mask I'm wearing—as I pull a stack of preprinted pages from the duffel bag. This part of the plan was Katie's. She thought it would help to muddy the waters. I'm sure she's right.

I hold the first page up, facing the camera, then turn it to face Rhys. It says, *Hi Rhys*. When I'm confident he's read it, I let it fall to the floor. It drifts down in lazy, swooping arcs, landing next to his feet. I show the next page to the camera and then to Rhys.

*You're going to answer my questions. If you're honest, I'll let you live.* I move to the next page. *Blink once for yes, twice for no. Understand?* He blinks once. *Good.* I let the page flutter to the floor with the others.

*Did you have an address book that went missing recently?* He blinks once. *Do you recognize the name Nina Capper?* One blink. I let the page fall to the floor. *Was her name in your address book?* One blink. *Did you rape her?* He doesn't respond, and I shake the page in front of him. Eventually, he blinks once. I shuffle through the pages, looking for a woman Vaughn wasn't sure about. *Do you recognize the name Janelle Hayes?* One blink. *Was her name in your address book?* He blinks once. *Did you rape her?* He blinks twice in quick succession. I sort through the stack until I find the page that says, *Are you sure?* He blinks once. Interesting. Maybe someone else was living with her. *Do you recognize the name Katie Stanton?* One blink. *Was her name in your address book?* One blink. *Did you rape her?* Another single blink.

I continue working through the names. Rhys blinks yes, admitting to raping each of the remaining seven women. Every person Vaughn had on the list except for Janelle Hayes. I turn off the camera, stopping the recording. I remove it from the tripod and set it on the floor next to Rhys's chair. Then, I gather the pages scattered across the floor. There's nothing on the video that the police can use to identify the type of printer that printed the pages I showed Rhys. But if I leave the pages, they'll definitely be able to figure that out. I pack the tripod away next and set the bag of takeout food I brought with me, as well as the tranquilizer dart I shot Rhys with, on top of the duffel bag.

Everything else is already neatly packed. It's five-eighteen. Sunrise will be shortly after seven this morning, but people are going to start waking up for work soon, and I need to get out of here. Part of me would like to remove every tooth from Rhys Steichen's mouth like I promised myself I would in the courtroom all those months ago, but I don't have the time. And if I'm being honest, I don't have the stomach for it either. I don't need to cause them pain. Not really. I just need to make sure they aren't alive to fuck up anyone else's life.

I pick up the screwdriver and the hammer I took from his garage and step toward him. Once more, he strains against the plastic wrap binding him to the chair, but it has no effect. I place the tip of the screwdriver on his forehead and drag it down his face. His eyelids automatically shut to protect his eyes. I rest the tip on his eyelid and drive the hammer into the base of the screwdriver's handle, plunging it through his eye, into his brain, fighting down the bile churning in my stomach. He makes a strangled gurgle, and there's a wet sucking noise as I pull the screwdriver out and repeat the process with his other eye.

Let them decide it's some weird ritualistic thing with not wanting to be seen or whatever. It's not. It's merely that the trauma from a single strike probably wouldn't be enough to kill him—and certainly not quickly. Look at Phineas Gage.

This time, I leave the screwdriver impaled in his brain and grab the stethoscope I brought with me. I place it against his chest, wanting to be sure he's dead. And he is. There's no heartbeat. No respiratory sounds. I put the stethoscope away, pick up the bag, and walk out the backdoor of Rhys Steichen's house, leaving only the camera and its recording behind.

# Chapter 27
# The End of the Road

It's five-thirty-two in the morning and still dark when I step into Rhys's backyard. The rain has stopped falling, and a thick fog has replaced it, which is good news for me. I remove the shoe covers and latex gloves before cutting through the hedge separating Rhys's yard from his neighbor's. Then I start walking back to my car, duffel bag slung over my shoulder.

The route I take leaving Rhys's house is different than the one I arrived by last night, but it's just as circuitous. To make it in time for my first patient, I have to be in the office by eight-twenty at the latest, and I need to stop by Vaughn's house to drop off the bag before then. Minus the tranquilizer gun, of course, because I'm keeping that until I've dealt with Garret Fischer. Vaughn volunteered to get rid of everything for me, and having him dispose of it is better than throwing it into the dumpsters at my office building—especially now that Garret knows enough to be suspicious of me. I also need to swap out the fake license plates that are currently on my car for the ones that actually belong on it.

Time is ticking, so I put my head down and walk faster. I'm sweating under my raincoat by the time I get back to my car and strip it off, shoving it into a garbage bag in my trunk. The duffel bag goes in with my raincoat, although I pull the case with the tranq gun out and tuck it into my spare tire compartment, next to the jack and my real license plates. Then I close the trunk and climb into the car.

Katie knows I was planning on going after Rhys Steichen this morning. As soon as I leave Vaughn's and am on my way into the office, I'm supposed to call her to let her know I'm still alive and everything went according to plan. Then she's going to talk to the next reporter who shows up outside Erica's house. I'm guessing they'll figure out Rhys is dead whenever the security detail's shift change arrives—probably around noon, since they showed up not long after midnight. It'll give Katie an ironclad alibi—there's no way she could've driven from Portland to Redding between when Rhys arrived home and when she'll be speaking to the press. It'll also confuse the situation even more.

After I talk to her, I should call Mark and say good morning to him as well.

I took a nap after work last night prior to going to Rhys's, but I'm going to be dead on my feet by the time this afternoon rolls around and I make it to Mark's place. And Garret Fischer is back in town now too, I remind myself. I have to move through the world behaving as if someone is actively trying to kill me because they are. Hell, I should keep a tranq dart filled with enough Telazol to take down a male grizzly on me at all times just to be safe.

The lights in Vaughn's house are already on when I park in his driveway at six-fifty-five. By the time I've grabbed the trash bag from my trunk, he and Marjorie are waiting at the door.

"See, I told you she'd be fine," Marjorie tells Vaughn once I'm within earshot. He gives her a brief glare but says nothing. "There's not even a scratch on her. Alyssa, come inside and have some coffee."

"Hi Marjorie, good morning. Coffee would be great. Vaughn, where do you want this?" I question, inclining my head to the bag in my hands.

"Just drop it there. Glad to see you're still breathing. Any problems?" he asks gruffly.

"No. None at all. The security detail never noticed a thing. He admitted to everyone except Janelle Hayes."

"Huh," Vaughn murmurs as we trail down the hall after Marjorie. "I'm glad you're okay. You're staying with Mark tonight?"

"Yes. Bag's already packed. I don't even have to go back to my condo."

"Good. Fischer is going to be gunning for you, Alyssa. It might not be the worst idea to cancel your patients until after he's been dealt with."

I shake my head. "I can't do that, Vaughn, and not only because it would be suspicious if I suddenly cleared my books for the next couple of weeks."

"How do you want your coffee, Alyssa?" Marjorie asks, interrupting our conversation.

"Milk and sugar are fine, thanks."

"Alyssa—" Vaughn begins.

"Vaughn. It's fine. The other four are dead, and I'm still here. I'll be fine."

He sighs. "I'll be out of town from Sunday until Thursday. You'd better be alive when I get back," he grumbles.

"I will be."

"Wait here. I'll get you everything I've been able to put together on Fischer. It's not as much as I would like, but I doubt it matters since the circumstances are different with him. You'd be better off if you let me get you a handgun. You could shoot him from ten yards away and be done with it."

"That's better than he deserves. Besides, it's also more likely to get me caught than anything I've been doing," I scoff. "The only reason they have no idea who's behind all this is because I haven't been doing things like that."

"Because your stunt on Halloween was so different?" Vaughn snaps.

I shrug, taking the cup of coffee from Marjorie as he stands and leaves the room.

"Don't mind him," she says. "He's cranky because he hasn't slept. He worries about you, you know."

"I know," I tell Marjorie. Vaughn and Marjorie never had children of their own. I'm the closest thing Vaughn has to a daughter.

A minute later, Vaughn returns carrying a folder. "Don't take what's in here as gospel. Now that he knows what you've been doing, he'll likely behave differently."

"I know."

Vaughn nods and then says, "Give me your keys. I'll switch your license plates back while you finish your coffee."

"YOU'RE ALIVE!" KATIE SAYS, ANSWERING THE PHONE ON the first ring like she was waiting for my call. She probably was. If our situations were reversed, I would've been awake all night waiting for hers, but it's seven-thirty in the morning now. Calling any earlier than this would look suspicious.

"Yes, I am. He's not," I reply as I turn on my blinker and move into the left lane to get around the city bus that's slowing for the stop up ahead. The fog has receded, but the gloom doesn't show any sign of dissipating.

"Good. When I get home, I want you to tell me everything."

"Alright," I agree. "Are you still going to talk to the press?"

"Yes. Once we get off the phone, I'm going to go drink my coffee on Erica's porch. I'll be ready and waiting for whoever shows up first."

"He admitted to everyone but Janelle Hayes, Kay," I tell her. "If nothing else, the police will know that it wasn't only you they hurt. Maybe the other women will talk about it once they're all dead."

"Maybe. Either way, thank you."

"You're welcome."

"What's your plan for Garret Fischer?" Katie asks.

"I'm still working on it. I'll let you know once I've figured it out."

"Okay. I'll stay here until the Monday before Thanksgiving, but after that I'm coming home. And before you protest, it would look way more suspicious if I'm not there for Thanksgiving than it will if I am."

"Alright," I agree. She has a point. That gives me ten days to sort out what to do about Garret. Hopefully, I won't need that long.

"Plus," she continues, "I'm going to try going back to work after that."

"That's great, Kay," I state. She's been considering it for a while. I'm glad she's finally feeling up to it.

"Thanks."

"How's Erica?" I ask as I come to a stop at a red light.

"She's good. She mentioned moving back to Portland, though. I guess she's sick of dealing with the wildfires every year."

"Who isn't?" I mutter. The smoke this summer from the fires in the southern part of the state was almost constant, but at least we haven't had to worry about fires close enough to destroy property or cause evacuations to the same degree California has. "Okay, well, I'll talk to you later. I need to call Mark before I get to the office. Good luck with the media. Let me know when you've talked to them."

"Alright. Remember to let me know as soon as you decide anything about Garret Fischer," she reminds me.

"I will. Love you. Bye."

"Love you, too," she says, ending the call.

"Hey, good morning," Mark greets as he picks up the phone. Unlike Katie, it took a few rings for him to answer, and his voice sounds more gravelly than normal. I probably woke him up.

"Hey, good morning. How are you?" I ask.

"Looking forward to seeing you."

"Yeah. Me too. I should still be there around five. How was the trip back?"

"Uneventful. Sorry, I just woke up. I promise to be a better conversationalist later," he tells me.

"No, it's fine. I'm sorry for calling so early. I just wanted to say hi before I got sucked into work. You'll be at the arena all day tomorrow, right?"

"Yeah, from ten in the morning until around ten at night, most likely. Sunday is completely free, though."

"Okay. Good to know. Well, I'm at the office now. I've gotta go. But I'll see you later," I say as I spot Teresa's car and park next to it. It'll make leaving easier this evening.

"Okay. Have a good day."

"You too," I reply as I end the call.

It's not quite eight, and the office building's lot is about half full. I don't recognize most of the cars in it. Why would I? Unfortunately, there's no way for me to say whether Garret Fischer is parked somewhere, waiting for me. Watching me.

The thought definitely makes me uneasy.

I'm so much taller than the average woman that I've never wished I were bigger, but now I do. Which is stupid. I've demonstrated four times now that size doesn't matter.

*Oh well,* I think as I take a deep breath and fling my door open, already surveying the parking lot to make sure no one else is suddenly emerging from their cars. Everything looks the same as I rush toward the building.

I'M ON MY SEVENTH CUP OF COFFEE. *OR IS IT THE EIGHTH?* I wonder as I take another sip. I'm trying to focus on Harold, who's telling me about how he spoke up for himself at work, which is a big accomplishment for him, but my mind keeps wandering. I'm both exhausted and feeling like I might climb out of my own skin. It's not exactly pleasant. There are only five minutes left in this session though, and it's my last one for the day.

"... And then I asked if there was anyone else who might be better suited to handling it!" Harold says, a smile stretching across his face.

"That's really great, Harold. I'm proud of you for asking the question," I reply. "How did you feel afterward?"

"I was worried they were going to hate me. I thought I might get reported to HR for being combative, but…"

I glance out the window, looking at the sky. It's four-twenty-five, and the sun is dipping low. It'll be setting by the time I'm leaving the building. At least Teresa will be walking out with me.

"…But he said he would look into it."

"That's fantastic, Harold. How do you believe you would feel next time you do it?"

"Oh. I couldn't do it again," he says, frowning.

"Why not?"

"They would think I was a troublemaker. Or that I wasn't a team player."

I nod. "I want to talk about that more, but we don't have time today. Prior to our next session, I'd like you to make a list of your coworkers. Under their names, I'd like you to note each instance in the past year where you can remember them asking for something, and bring it with you, alright?"

"Okay, Dr. Reed. I will."

"Excellent. Let's go talk to Teresa and get your appointment set up," I say as I stand.

Teresa patiently listens to Harold mumble his way through booking his next appointment before he's out the door.

"He's getting better," she tells me once we're alone. "He actually looks at me sometimes when he speaks now."

"I know. He spoke up for himself at work this week."

"Wow."

"Yeah. Are you ready to go? I don't want to get stuck in traffic any longer than I have to," I lie.

"Sure." She grabs her coat. "Any plans for this weekend?" Teresa asks. I'm already scanning the hallway as we step into it and she locks the door.

"Just spending it with Mark."

"How's that going? You seem pretty into him."

"I am," I admit with a shrug. The lock slides into place. "And good, I think. Katie's out of town for a bit, so I'm staying with him for the next week while he's here."

Teresa raises her eyebrows as we move down the hallway toward the elevators. "You're serious about him, then?"

"Yeah. I guess."

"That's new," she says, reaching for the elevator button.

"Yup. What about you?" I ask as the doors part and we step into an empty elevator.

"We're going to put up the Christmas tree."

"Before Thanksgiving?" I question, feigning shock. "Scandalous, Teresa. Scandalous."

She laughs. "If I do it now, then I can take family photos of everyone in front of the tree during Thanksgiving and send them to people before Christmas. It saves me the hassle of trying to corral them all twice."

"That's a good idea," I tell her as we step out of the elevator and head for the exit. I'm searching the parking lot, which is emptier now than it was when I arrived this morning. I can't shake the feeling that I'm being watched, but I'm not sure how much of that I should put down to paranoia and too much caffeine.

Nothing happens as we walk across it, though, and Teresa climbs into her vehicle as I climb into mine. I lock the doors and start my car.

THE WINDING ROAD THAT RUNS ALONG THE EDGE OF Forest Park leading to Mark's is cloaked in shadows as dusk settles across the city. The trees have lost most of their leaves, and the underbrush has died back enough that I can see flashes of light from the houses along the road that would've been completely obscured a month and a half ago, when I was first here.

As I come around the final bend before Mark's, there are two sets of headlights moving down his driveway, leaving his house, and I slow my approach to give them time to turn onto the road.

The lights are bright enough that I have to squint against them, but I catch a glimpse of the spotlight along the driver's side mirror as I move past the first car, and I lock my eyes onto the second. Not only does it have a spotlight beside the mirror, but there are lights on the roof. *Fuck.*

It's a cop car. Two cop cars.

I continue past them, not turning down Mark's driveway. I keep going until I reach the end of the road. The same spot I ended up the first time I tried to find his house and drove past it. Before I had ever spoken to him.

I cut my headlights, pull out my phone, and open an incognito browser. Katie called me during lunch while I was sitting at my desk, filling another dart with Telazol, to let me know she'd talked to a reporter from some news station down there. She said it went fine, but the interview wasn't online then. I search 'Katie Stanton' and click on the most recent article. It's from an hour ago, and there's a link to a video of her interview.

The reporter is offscreen, and the camera is only focused on Katie. Her blond hair is pulled back from her face, making her blue eyes look even larger than normal. "I haven't spoken to the media since the verdict was read because there wasn't any reason to. At the time, I said everything I had to say. But now that three of the men who've raped me have died, I want to say that the morning after the rape occurred, when Rhys Steichen forced me to make the video saying I wanted what happened to me, he told me I didn't have a choice. He said that they had done it before to other women, and they'd gotten away with it, so they'd get away with what they did to me too. And he was right. They did. I pressed charges. I testified. I did everything I was supposed to. And they still got away with it.

"I don't know what's happened to them, but I know I'm not the only victim out there. That's all I have to say," she finishes, before she turns and walks into the house, slamming the door in the reporter's face.

The article with the video speculates that an unidentified victim could be behind the recent string of deaths but offers nothing else of substance.

I search 'Rhys Steichen' to find out if they're reporting his death yet, since that has to be why the police were at Mark's house. Nothing on the first page mentions anything about it, though. I limit the search results to items posted within the past twenty-four hours, and the only articles are about some assists he made in the last game and Katie's latest statement. They've probably found Rhys's body but are keeping it quiet. I guess they could've been talking to Mark about something else. They could've been asking him questions about one of the other players. They could've been following up on something. But I don't think they were.

My heart seems to miss a beat as I shove my phone into my coat pocket and return the way I came. This time, I turn into Mark's driveway. The lights are on, and a warm, cheery glow leaks from the windows.

I feel nauseous.

## Chapter 28
# Running Out the Clock

MARK'S FRONT DOOR IS UNLOCKED WHEN I TRY THE handle. I take a deep breath, plaster what I hope is a neutral look on my face, and step inside. The house is silent. Normally there's music playing, but not right now.

"Hey, I'm here!" I call out as I slide off my boots and set my bag on the floor.

"Hey," Mark replies from the kitchen. "I'm making a drink. Want one?" he asks when he sees me round the corner.

"What are you making?"

"Double whiskey," he says, glancing up at me, his motions tight and controlled. It's the first time I've seen him in over a week, but despite that, he hasn't set the bottle of whiskey down or made any move toward me, and I hope I don't look as panicked as I feel.

"There's not much 'making' involved with that, but sure."

He lets out a sharp exhale as he turns to grab another glass. He fills it with ice from the freezer before pouring in a generous amount of whiskey and sliding the glass toward me. I pick it up and take a sip, waiting to see if he'll say anything. He doesn't, though, and the whiskey settles in my stomach about as comfortably as I expect battery acid would.

"So. What's up?" I question, aiming for a level of calmness I don't feel.

"Nothing," he says, raising the glass to his lips. By the time he sets it down, it's more empty than full.

I force myself into motion, leaving my barely touched drink where it's sitting and moving to stand beside him.

"Are you sure?" I ask as I place my hand on his and slide it up his forearm, tugging him to face me. Once he's looking at me, I step into his space until our bodies are pressed together. He hasn't pulled away, but he also hasn't made any attempt to touch me. "Because it's been more than a week since we've seen each other, and normally your hands would be all over me by now."

Mark's amber-flecked hazel eyes are boring into mine as he raises his hand to my face. His fingertips skim along my jaw as he tucks a strand of hair behind my ear. We stand there in silence, and each second that passes seems to put more and more space between us, although neither of us has moved.

Finally, Mark blinks, and the spell is broken. "Where were you last night?" he asks, his fingers lightly curled around the nape of my neck.

"At home," I lie, meeting his eyes, praying he'll believe me, and knowing he won't. "Why?"

His eyes narrow and his jaw clenches, and I know I was right. "Are you sure?" he probes.

He knows. I'm all but certain he's worked it out, and he knows that I'm lying to him. He's giving me the chance to change my answer and walk it back. In that split second, Marjorie's words from weeks ago echo through my head. *'Randall wouldn't have told anyone the truth. Ever. I guess you've gotta ask yourself who's the better role model. Vaughn or Randall?'*

I know what the right answer is. I know what I should do. But I can't. Despite my dad's assertion that I'm too much like Vaughn, when push comes to shove, I can't bring myself to tell Mark the truth. I can't bring myself to tell him I was out last night, killing Rhys Steichen. I can't bring myself to tell him I never told him everything about how and why we met. And I certainly can't bring myself to tell him I've killed them all.

I don't think more than a few heartbeats have passed when Mark softly questions, "Alyssa?" It sounds like an invitation to tell him the truth. Like maybe he would hear me out. But I can't. I can't do it. I can't bring myself to trust him enough to let him all the way in.

I choke out a strangled, "Yes, I'm sure. Why would you ask me that?"

He drops his hand from my neck and turns away from me, picking the glass of whiskey up and finishing off its contents. He sets it down with a hard thud. "No reason," he says flatly. "I have to go. I'll be back later."

"Where? I just got here."

"The GM called a mandatory team meeting for seven," he tells me, still not looking at me. "Everyone is required to attend."

"Why?" I ask, even though I'm sure I know the answer.

"No reason," he replies, repeating his earlier words.

"Okay. When will you be back?"

"I'm not sure," he says as he turns and heads for the door, leaving me standing alone in his kitchen. A minute later, the front door slams shut. I check my watch. It's five-thirty-five. He'll be at Tofana Arena at least an hour earlier than he needs to be. It's an unspoken message stating that he'd rather be there without me than here with me. I sigh as I reach for the whiskey Mark poured for me. The outside of the glass is slick with condensation, and it almost slips through my fingers. I empty it into the kitchen sink, watching at least fifty dollars flow down the drain.

"He knows," I whisper to the empty house. "He *knows*." I stand at the sink, staring at the drain as the realization hits me. *I should go. I should...*

I check my watch again. Only two minutes have passed since I last looked at it. Five-thirty-seven. I'll wait an hour and then leave. By that point, Garret Fischer should be on his way to whatever meeting Mark just left for. And then I can go to my office and shred every file Vaughn has given me without having to worry about being attacked. After that, I'll rent a hotel room somewhere until I work out how to get rid of Garret or the team leaves town again.

I sit down on the couch to wait out the clock, wondering if I should've told Mark the truth instead of saying I was home all night. But how could I?

IT'S DARKER AS I DRIVE DOWN THE WINDING ROAD TOWARD my office than it was when I arrived. And not just the night, I realize. My mood is darker too. Aside from the first time I went to Mark's house while I was stalking him, trying to figure out who he was, I've never left so quickly. It seems like I'm back at square one. I don't need Mark anymore—not for access to Katie's rapists anyhow—but I can't help but feel like I lost something tonight. It was always supposed to be this way, but...

I consider turning around and going back to his house. It's not like he told me to leave. It's not as if he said anything about not seeing me anymore. Unless I tell him the truth, though, there's not going to be any 'getting past this.' It'll only be a sore that festers until neither of us can stand to look at the other.

And I can't tell him. I just can't. Marjorie was right when she said I'm not Vaughn and Mark isn't her.

I want to cry, but I can't even do that. I always knew this was how it would end, even if I tried to let myself believe otherwise these past few weeks. This is merely the inevitable conclusion.

The drive back to my office passes in the blink of an eye, and before I know it, I'm parked in front of the building. There are only a few cars in the lot. People working late or overnight cleaners, maybe. *At least I don't have to worry about Garret Fischer ambushing me as I walk into the building this time,* I think as I get out of my car and head for the doors.

The main entry door is locked, but like every other tenant, I have a key, even though I don't normally need to use it. It takes a second to find the right one, and then I'm inside, walking down the dimly lit hallway, headed for the stairwell. It's faster than waiting for the elevator, and I don't really feel like standing still at the moment. I know the second I do, I'll start thinking about... everything.

The building has that empty, haunted quality that so often appears as soon as the people disappear. Or maybe I'm just anthropomorphizing the building and projecting my own worries on it.

I climb the three flights of stairs wondering what Mark is going to think when he gets home and I'm not there. Will he call, or...? Should I send him a text telling him our relationship has run its course? No. I should call him. That would be the adult thing to do. *Or,* the small voice in the back of my head suggests, *you could tell him the truth. It's not too late. Not really. He doesn't even know you're gone. You could shred the files and make it back to his house before he does. He'd never even know you left.*

I huff, trying to shut the voice up as I emerge from the stairwell and walk down the corridor to my office. It's a bit after seven, and the only time I've been here this late in recent memory was the first time Mark came to see my couch. And... *I'm doing it again,* I realize. I made it a whole second and a half before my mind wandered back to him.

*Fuck.* I should've told him. He already knows. I should've just admitted I wasn't at home last night. I should've just explained I was out killing Rhys Steichen, and said, *'Sorry about your team, but they all really deserved it.'* He might've understood. Maybe. Instead, I lied to him.

My mind is going in circles as I unlock my office door. If I told him... Oregon is a two-party consent state for private in-person conversations. Even if he recorded what I said, which I'm certain he wouldn't do, it wouldn't matter. It wouldn't be able to be used against me. And even if he were to dump me, he wouldn't record me confessing to their murders. I'm certain of it.

*I should've told him,* I realize, and it hits me like a ton of bricks. Maybe he would've ended things with me, but knowing for sure—trusting him and actually letting him make that decision—would be better than this.

I go into my office and unlock the filing cabinet, pulling the bottom drawer all the way out. I stuffed all the folders Vaughn has given me throughout this process into the very back of it after the police showed up to talk to Katie two weeks ago. I figured in the event they got a search warrant for my condo, it was better that the files weren't there. And it would be significantly more difficult for them to get a warrant to search my office considering the fact that patient records are confidential.

There are the files on Clark Thomas and Adam Klaussen as well as Mark—all from my first meeting with Vaughn, when I decided Mark was the one. Plus, there are the files on Joey Carmichael, Matt Davidson, Brandon Miller, Rhys Steichen, and Garret Fischer, of course. I've already memorized the pertinent details from Garret's file, and the others are dead, so there's no reason to hold on to them. Especially not now.

I set Mark's to the side, and start pulling the pages from the others, running them through the shredder. The blades make a humming snick as pages are pulled in and sliced to pieces. The sound does nothing to quell my anxiety. The thought of telling Mark everything makes me want to throw up, and the feeling continues to grow with each page I feed into the shredder.

When all the folders except Mark's are empty, I stare at his, considering the merits of shredding it too. Ultimately, I don't. I remove the pages from the file, fold them, and stuff them into my coat pocket before taking the remnants from the shredder and dumping them into the trash. Then I remove the bag from the trashcan so I can toss it into the dumpsters on my way out. I shut off the lights and walk out of my office, locking the door behind me and resolving to go back to Mark's. I'll tell him everything and show him exactly the information Vaughn gave me prior to our initial meeting. I'll tell him about the first day I followed him and about dyeing my hair. I'll tell him all of it and hope it's enough. It probably won't be, but at least I'll have tried. This way, I won't regret running away for the rest of my life, because I'm certain I will if I don't at least try to fix this.

The building is silent as I walk down the stairs to the exit. I check my watch again as I near the door. Seven-twenty-eight. Whatever meeting the Black Bears are having, Garret should still be tied up in it, sitting on his hands.

I push through the door and step into the night. There are even fewer cars now, and I detour around the left of the building toward the dumpsters. It's windier on this side, and I spend a minute fiddling with my keys as the wind rushes past my ears. Finally, I find the one that unlocks the dumpsters. I lift the lid, throw the shredded files in, and let it fall shut. The bang it makes echoes, bouncing off the building's concrete exterior at the same time a fist grabs hold of my hair and slams my head into the dumpster's hard metal side.

Pain explodes through my face, and white envelops my vision as blood gushes from my nose. I fall to my hands and knees, the grit of the asphalt biting into my palms. My mind flashes back to Rhys Steichen collapsing on the grass in front of his house last night. A foot drives into my ribs. I'm not sure if the crack I hear is real or imagined as my arms give way and my cheek hits the ground.

# Chapter 29
# Elbows Up

PAIN AND AGONY ROLL THROUGH ME, AND I'M FIGHTING TO breathe as my diaphragm spasms. A pair of boots steps into my field of vision, and one slides under my ribs, flipping me over. The agony turns into a sharp stabbing sensation, and I suck in a breath as my diaphragm finally relaxes. The breath turns into a choking cough that I instantly regret as the taste of iron, copper, and salt floods my mouth, clogging my throat, leaving me feeling like I'm being waterboarded with my own blood. My ribs are definitely broken, and I can't breathe. Can't…

Garret Fischer comes into focus above me. There's a brief moment where I think he's going to stomp on my face, and my mind supplies an image of my head popping like a water balloon before he drops to a crouch beside me. His blue eyes look glacial, and a sense of futility washes over me as my brain tells me I'm going to die.

"Does it hurt?" he asks, reaching out to poke at my nose, which is still pouring blood down the back of my throat.

His finger makes contact with my skin, and I gasp. I feel like I might throw up as a garbled groan escapes from my throat. I need to get away. I need to… He stands and moves to my feet. I feebly kick at him as his hands reach for me, but he just grabs my ankles. I try to shake them off, but they're vises, and he drags me back toward the front of the building.

*He's supposed to be at the team meeting. Everyone is supposed to be at the meeting,* I think unhelpfully as my head bounces over the asphalt, and my coat scrapes across the ground, filling my ears. The sky overhead is unfathomably black beyond the parking lot lights, and I wonder where he's taking me. Why he's taking me. He could just kill me here. The police would most likely assume it was a robbery gone wrong and blame it on the homeless population.

The lot is so empty that there's no one to see what's happening. No one to stop him from killing me or abducting me or whatever he's doing. I turn my head to the side, spitting blood onto the pavement as I try once again to kick his hands off me.

"Piss me off and it's going to go worse for you," he throws over his shoulder.

*Worse than what?* I wonder, struggling harder. *If I don't get away from him, I'm dead either way.* It doesn't do any good, though. I have no leverage.

I open my mouth to scream, and then decide against it. There's no one around to hear, and if I start screaming he might gag me, and then I'd choke to death on my own blood.

Instead, I try to get my elbows under me. I need to get his hands off me. I need to give myself a fighting chance. I need to put some distance between us. Only before I can do any of that, he stops next to a van emblazoned with the words *Rent Me!* and drops my feet as he turns to face me. I try to scurry backward, but I'm not fast enough, and he drops a knee to my stomach, sending the air whooshing from my lungs. Darkness floods my vision as pain ricochets through my abdomen and across my ribs. My ribs that are so, so broken.

He says nothing for a second, apparently waiting for the pain to recede enough that my eyes focus on him. "Hands," he orders, extending a zip tie that already has the tail looped through the opening.

"No," I growl.

He sighs as if I'm making things difficult. As if he's not the one trying to abduct me, because it seems like that's what's happening. He leans more weight onto the knee that's digging into my gut and grabs my left wrist, wrenching it toward him. I wait a second until he's focused on forcing it into the circle of the zip tie, and then I try to gouge his eyes out with my right hand. He lets go of my wrist and backhands me, sending my head rocking to the side before I can make contact.

By the time I'm capable of reacting, he's tightening the zip tie down on my wrists. It bites into my skin. Then his knee vanishes from my stomach, and I suck in a breath.

"If you so much as twitch, Alyssa," he hisses, moving to my feet, "I will knock you out, and we both know you don't want that. Be a good girl and nod if you understand."

I give a tight nod and make what I hope is the smart choice, deciding to bide my time because, unfortunately, he's right. I don't want that. As long as I'm conscious, I have a chance. Maybe not right this second. But soon. I hope.

A zip tie goes around my ankles, and the noise it makes as it tightens down sounds like a death sentence. He just cut off any hope I had of running, and I try to control my breathing as the realization slaps me in the face harder than his hand did a minute ago.

Then he's back at my side, digging through my pockets. He pulls out the folded pages I put in there who knows how long ago. The ones about Mark. And as he unfolds them, his eyes scanning across the paper, I want nothing more than to rip his nose from his face with my teeth.

But I don't. I hold still as he murmurs a soft, "Hmm." He refolds the pages, shoving them into his coat, and then his hands are back in my pockets. He takes my phone, shuts it off, and stuffs it in with the pages.

Dread wraps around my chest, but his hands don't return to rifling through my pockets. Instead, he grabs my wrists, yanking me upright. My right elbow screams in pain, and I don't know if it's from him wrenching it when he zip-tied me, or if I reinjured it when I fell, or maybe when he was dragging me across the parking lot.

Blood is still flowing from my nose as he opens the van's sliding door and shoves me through it. I land hard, my left hip taking the brunt of the impact, and I yank my feet out of the way as he whips the panel door closed. There's a metal grill separating the back—which is empty aside from me—from the front.

A few seconds pass, and then Garret climbs behind the wheel, slamming the driver's side door too.

"Where are you taking me?" I ask, sounding like I've developed a bad head cold, but he doesn't answer.

The engine starts, and the van lurches into motion, sending me rocking sideways, unable to brace myself. I pinch my nose shut, staring at my feet as I try to stop the bleeding. I know there's a way to break zip ties using shoelaces, only I'm wearing Chelsea boots, which doesn't help me at all. The blood has been confined to my face and coat, and I'd like to keep it that way, so my hands stay on my nose rather than trying to come up with some alternate way to get free. Luckily, my nose doesn't feel broken, even if my face really hurts.

Ten minutes later, he's turning onto the ramp for I-84 East, and I slowly unzip my coat as he merges into traffic, hoping he won't notice the sound of the zipper over the noise of the blinker. It comes undone just as the blinker switches off, and I breathe a sigh of relief.

"Where are you taking me?" I ask again as I try to work my zip-tied hands into my pants pocket. My pants pocket I couldn't get to because of my stupid coat.

As before, he offers no response.

"Where are your personal rent-a-cops?" I question instead. "Did you sneak away from your guards?"

I'm met with more silence. I let a few minutes pass before trying a different approach.

"You know Rhys told me about all the women you raped. He said it's the only way you can get off," I lie, hoping to get a reaction. But I don't, so I press a little harder. I know I can find the right buttons if I keep pushing, and it's not like anything I say is going to make this situation any worse for me. "Impotence is a real bitch. You could've talked to someone about it, though, Garret," I taunt, and he taps the brakes, sending me sliding into the metal grill behind his seat. I groan as pain flares through my body, leaving me feeling more beat up than a piñata right before it bursts apart. But I grin anyway. I found my button.

My fingertips brush against the tranq dart, but it's not enough to get a solid grip. I put it in my pants pocket so that I would have it on me regardless of whether I was wearing my coat, which in hindsight might not've been the best choice. I didn't anticipate winding up zip-tied, and it's hard to get my hands far enough in to grasp the dart. The edge of the pocket is biting into my hands, turning my skin a blotchy red-white. I ignore the mixture of pain and pressure—it's nowhere near as bad as my head—as I slouch and extend my legs, hoping to create more space between the fabric and my hipbone. Just enough to shove my hands in and grab the damn dart.

Finally, my hands move a fraction of an inch, leaving behind a layer of skin. But it's enough to curl my fingers around the dart. Relief floods through me. Things still aren't great, but I'm not going to die tonight. Or at least if I do, I'll be sure to take this asshole with me.

It takes a minute to work it all the way out, and I glance down. The darts didn't come with any kind of caps or covers, and I didn't want to walk around with an exposed needle in my pocket. Fortunately, I found that a Sharpie cap fit over the dart's tip nicely. I slide a nail against the edge of the cap, loosening it, but not taking it all the way off, just in case Garret decides to hit the brakes again.

"When did it start? The impotence?" I ask, trying to piss him off, hoping it will make him sloppy later. "Has it always been a problem?" I get no response, but I continue talking as he drives despite that. "Was it the first time you were with a girl? That must've sucked. Being sixteen with a limp dick. That's rough, Garret."

"Shut up!" he snaps.

"Did she laugh at you? Tell her friends? I bet she told all her friends. I bet *everyone* knew. Big, bad hockey player Garret Fischer couldn't get it up." I can see his jaw flexing in the glow of the lights, and I know the only thing preventing him from backhanding me again is the metal grate between us.

"I bet no one wanted to date you after that. God. How *embarrassing*. But you're kind of a douchebag. I'm sure you deserved it. I bet you were a total asshat before that even happened. She was probably only dating you because you're a hockey player anyway. I doubt you've ever learned where the clitoris is."

He continues clenching his teeth as he hits the blinker, taking exit eighteen toward Lewis and Clark State Park at a higher speed than he should. Inertia presses my back into the sidewall of the van, but then I'm slipping sideways, trying not to topple over, as he accelerates out of the turn. With both my hands and feet zip-tied, there's nothing I can do to brace myself. My right shoulder impacts the floor.

Pain flares down my arm, from my shoulder to my elbow, and all across my torso, overtaking every other sensation. It feels like Garret's kicked me in the ribs again as I slide toward the rear. There's a faint skittering sound—like a pebble rolling across asphalt. Only I've stopped moving and I can't figure out what's making the noise.

*Shit! My hands. My hands are empty,* I realize.

I'm scanning the back of the van, but it's dark. I can't see the dart, and the noise is gone. Fear wraps itself around my chest, squeezing tight. I have to find it. I need to have it in my hands before this van stops. If I don't, I'm dead. The tranquilizer dart was the backup plan. The 'In Case of Emergency, Break Glass' plan. I don't have another.

My lungs feel like they're seizing. *Where is it? Why can't I see it?*

Garret hits the brakes, and the blinker comes on, and I'm sliding toward the front. Away from the dart, wherever it is. My hips and then my back hit the metal grate, abruptly stopping me. The dart must be rolling around somewhere, but I can't hear it above the blinker, which is filling my head with a hollow clicking noise that's echoing louder than a drumbeat. *Fuckfuckfuckfuck!* my brain is repeating, keeping time in the most unhelpful way possible.

Then the van is turning right, and something hits me in the face, bouncing off the bridge of my nose. *The dart, the dart!* I know I need to move to grab it, but the world has turned to visual static around me. By the time I lift my zip-tied hands to where I last felt it, it's gone.

I shove myself upright, and my head swims at the change in position. I need to find the dart. I need to keep my eyes focused on the floor, searching for it. Instead, I'm glancing out the windshield, trying to determine how much time I have. It's like looking back in a race. It's stupid, and I can't stop myself from doing it.

Garret's following a dark, two-lane road. It looks like there's a parking lot ahead. I resume my internal scream of *Fuckfuckfuckfuck!* as I tear my eyes away from the windshield, raking them across the floor. I should see it. It should be easy. There's nothing in here. But there's no dart either.

*Where is it? Where is it? Whereisit? WHERE—*

*There!*

It's trapped in the corner formed by the van's wheel well and sidewall. About two feet away from me.

The van is slowing, and the dart shifts. I throw my body sideways to grab it before it can vanish again. Nausea rolls through me. I think I might throw up, and I'm not sure if it's from having my face bashed into the dumpster, or the kick I took in the ribs, or my head bouncing across the asphalt of the parking lot, or being thrown around the van like a piece of flotsam. It doesn't matter, though. None of it matters because my fingers are wrapped around the dart, and I'm not going to die tonight.

The van comes to a stop, rocking forward and then back before falling still. I force myself up, through waves of agony, to look out the windshield, only to be met with Garret's leering smile as he peers through the grate, studying me. It doesn't matter because the dart is in my hands, and I'm not going to die tonight.

"Enjoy the ride?" he asks, and I force my eyes past him to the parking lot.

It's totally empty, and the night outside is pitch black. If I fuck this up, I'm as good as dead. Most likely, I'll be left wishing I'd jammed the tranquilizer dart into my own thigh. I push the thoughts down, telling myself again that I'm not going to die tonight.

I should've stayed at Mark's house. Leaving was stupid. Assuming Garret would do what he was supposed to and show up to the 'mandatory' team meeting was even stupider. He probably told them he wasn't feeling well when they called. He gets to get away with murdering me while everyone believes he's home, sick in bed. Part of me can't believe I was that stupid, but I was so focused on Mark and the idea of my world with him falling apart that of course I was.

*It doesn't matter. I'm not going to die tonight.*

Garret parks, and I force my attention back to the here and now as he exits the van. As soon as his door slams shut, I pop the Sharpie cap off the tranquilizer dart and carefully tuck the dart between my hands so that it's hidden from sight.

"Get out," Garret growls when he slides the door open.

I stay huddled against the van's far wall. The thought of moving seems impossible. "What are you going to do to me?"

"Get out," he repeats, the warning in his tone clear.

"No," I say, shaking my head and taking my chances. If I can get him to throw me over his shoulder, he won't even see the dart coming when I ram it into his back. Assuming I can keep it together long enough to avoid throwing up all over him. Or passing out.

I take a breath. *I'm not going to die tonight,* I tell myself resolutely.

"Now, Alyssa!"

"No."

He leans into the van, reaching for my zip-tied feet, and I kick his hands away. Adrenaline floods through me as he steps in with a huff, grabbing for me, and I press myself further into the wall.

*I'm not going to die tonight.*

Then his hands are on my arms, and he's yanking me to him. I topple forward, unable to balance or fend him off, and he slings me over his shoulder. The agony of my ribs compressing against his body steals my breath and sends stars swimming through my vision. I'm upside down, and my head is below my heart. The pressure in my head is building, nausea and vertigo melding together as the nosebleed threatens to reemerge, and I hold still so that he can get us out before that happens. As soon as he steps out of the van, I flip the dart in my grip. I'm tempted to stab it into his kidney, but I'm uncertain what kind of effect that would have on the drug's absorption, so I ram it into his ass instead.

*I'm not going to die tonight.*

He yelps and drops me. I hit the ground with a hard thud, and the world goes black.

# Chapter 30
# Crime With Me

I WAKE UP ON THE GROUND, SHIVERING, WITH GRAVEL digging into my cheek and my arms pinned beneath my body at an angle that makes me question if they'll ever work right again. I roll onto my back, groaning as pain lances through my ribs. The night is unrelentingly dark, and I lie there, staring up at the sky, panting as I wait for feeling to return to my hands. I'm still zip-tied, and I have no idea where Garret is, but wherever he is, he's almost certainly dead. There was enough Telazol in that tranquilizer dart to knock out four adult men. There's no way he didn't go into cardiac arrest within minutes at most.

Eventually, my hands and arms begin to feel like they're on fire as blood flows into them and the nerves wake up. I bite my coat sleeve, using my teeth to pull it up enough to check my watch. Eight-fifty-six. Almost an hour and a half has passed since Garret ambushed me outside my office building. I was probably lying on the ground unconscious for over thirty minutes.

I need to find him. I need to get my phone. I need to get out of these zip ties. And I need to do it all before anyone shows up and finds me next to a body filled with Telazol. This is obviously self-defense, but there's a good chance they'll be able to connect this to Rhys Steichen's death, and if they do, the whole thing will unravel.

I roll back onto my side, clenching my teeth against the stabbing sensation in my ribs, and shove myself to my knees. It takes twenty or thirty seconds for the pain to recede. There's a human-shaped lump about forty feet away. It's got to be Garret. Unfortunately, the zip tie around my ankles makes that forty feet look closer to a mile. I can either bunny hop my way to his body or try to crawl over there. Both options suck, but I'll be less likely to injure myself if I collapse while crawling, and right now, I can't accept the idea of racking up more injuries. *If this were a video game, my health points would be flashing red on the screen*, I think with a snort that sends more pain rolling through me.

I inch my way toward Garret's body. Every time I move my arms, my abs flex, pulling on my ribs. It's like being shivved over and over. I have to stop every few feet. By the time I reach his body, I'm no longer shivering. I'm sweating.

But things could be worse. It could be raining. Or I could be Garret.

His eyes are sightlessly staring at the sky, and I'm pretty sure he's dead, but I kneel next to him, placing my fingers against his neck, checking for a pulse anyway. There isn't one, and a weight I didn't realize I was feeling evaporates.

I dig through his coat pocket for my phone and the pages about Mark that he took from me, setting both on the ground beside me when I find them. I go through every pocket on his body, hoping to find a knife so I can get out of these zip ties. He doesn't have one, though. I'm not sure if he was planning on bludgeoning me to death or strangling me, and once again, I'm glad he's dead.

I turn my phone on, waiting for it to establish a connection, trying to decide what to do. I could call Vaughn. He said he was going out of town on Sunday. And somehow, it's still Friday, so he's still here. *Or*, I tell myself, glancing at the papers on the ground beside me, *I could call Mark*. He's probably home by now. He would've returned from the meeting and seen that I wasn't there. Most likely, he assumed that was me ending things. It tracks with what he already believes regarding me not sharing information. *Fuck.*

If I call him, there's no hiding anything. And calling him to come here would be profoundly different from telling him what I was doing. Just telling him wouldn't provide him with proof of anything if he decided to go to the police. But this...? This is undeniable proof. *This* is me spending life in prison.

I try to unlock my phone, but apparently my face is so swollen and smeared with blood that it doesn't believe my face is really my face. I sigh and slowly type in my passcode. Then I go to my contacts and tap Mark's name.

The phone rings. And rings. And rings. It goes to voicemail. I hang up and immediately call back. He doesn't answer. I go to my messages. "Don't be a dick. Pick up your phone. Please," I say, dictating a text. I send it, count to fifteen, and call him again.

The phone rings twice. And then he answers. "What?" he growls.

"I need your help. Please."

There's a long stretch of silence. Finally, he sighs and says, "What do you need?"

Relief washes over me, and tears prickle my eyes. "I need you to load as much of that turpentine and stain that's sitting in your carport as you can into your car. Anything else you have that's flammable too. And then I need you to take I-84 East until you reach exit eighteen. Take the first right off the exit and follow the road until you get to me. And bring scissors. Or a knife. And matches."

"What's going on?" Mark asks, now seeming more worried than pissed.

"I'll explain when you get here. Please just come."

"Right off exit eighteen," he verifies over rustling in the background.

"Yes."

"I'll be there in forty-five minutes."

"Okay," I say, and the phone call ends. I momentarily consider trying to make it back to the van, but without being able to get these zip ties off, it's so far away that it's not worth the effort.

Instead, I lie on the ground and spend the next forty-five minutes staring at the sky, worrying about what's going to happen when Mark arrives. This is not a position I ever anticipated being in. I didn't expect that I would ever have feelings for him. And I certainly didn't anticipate being abducted or asking Mark to come help me while I waited zip-tied next to a corpse.

I'm wondering how I managed to fuck things up so colossally. Was it when I decided to act on the idea of getting justice for Katie after the courts didn't? Or when I poisoned Joey Carmichael? Or maybe when I fell for Mark. I've been trying to put my finger on precisely when that happened for days now, and I'm still not sure.

I told everyone again and again that I knew exactly what I was doing. And clearly I was wrong. I'd definitely fallen for Mark by the time I told him about Katie. But I'm pretty sure it was well before then. Maybe after he told me about his brother. Or maybe when I realized how nervous he was about the dinner with Vaughn and Marjorie.

It doesn't really matter, because here I am—on the darkest night, in the most fucked-up situation—having to deal with the consequences of my actions. I wonder if this is what my dad felt like when the police handcuffed him and shoved him into a cop car.

I should've asked Vaughn what telling Marjorie the truth was like. I got her perspective, but it would've been helpful to hear his too. To know if it felt this awful.

Eventually, the sound of an engine drawing closer fills the night, and when I tip my head to the left, headlights are illuminating the trees in the distance. Hopefully it's Mark and not someone else. Otherwise, I'm screwed. I can't move fast enough to get up and hide.

Twenty seconds later, the car pulls to a stop about fifty feet away. The door opens, but the headlights are on and the engine is still running.

"Alyssa!" Mark shouts, and I'm so relieved to hear his voice I practically sob.

"Over here," I yell, leveraging myself to a seated position. Pain rolls through me, and I gasp as I sit upright.

He jogs across the parking lot, backlit by the headlights. "What's going—" his words cut off as he drops to a crouch in front of me. "Jesus Christ. What the hell happened to you?" he asks, extending his hand toward my face before retracting it and letting it fall to his knee.

I jerk my head over my shoulder, trying not to feel rejected by his reaction. "Garret Fischer happened."

Mark's eyes move past me and widen when they land on Garret's corpse, apparently only now noticing it. "How did you...?" he questions as his eyes land back on me.

"I'll tell you everything. Can you just get these off me first?" I ask, raising my wrists.

"You killed Fischer while your hands and feet were zip-tied?" Mark pulls out a pocketknife and flips the blade open, sliding it between my wrists and through the plastic binding my hands.

"Yes," I answer as I rub feeling into my wrists.

"How?"

"With an overdose of an anesthetic they use to tranquilize bears."

Mark huffs. "I fucking knew it," he mutters.

"I know. Here," I say, picking up the folded papers that are on the ground next to me.

"What's this?" he asks as he takes them.

"Everything I knew about you before we met. Everything Vaughn dug up about you."

"Vaughn. Of course. How much does he know?"

I shrug. "Everything."

"So why not call him? You already left. Why call me?"

"You were mad earlier when I lied about being home all night last night. You clearly knew it was a lie. You wanted me to tell you the truth, and I didn't. I panicked, and I fucked up. That's on me. So this is me apologizing. Saying sorry. Trusting you. And also asking if you want to help me cover up a crime."

Mark's eyes are boring into mine, and the papers I gave him are clenched in his fist, seemingly forgotten. "Why. Call. Me?" he repeats slowly, enunciating each word.

"You're really going to make me say it?"

"Yes."

"Fine!" I shout, throwing up my hands, ignoring the pain that's just... everywhere. "Because I fucking love you, okay? I've been in love with you for weeks! That's why I told you about Katie! That's why I invited you to meet my dad!"

His lips twitch upward, but he only says, "Then why'd you leave?"

"Can we have this conversation later? After we've gotten rid of the body?"

"No."

"You left first, and you left so much earlier than you needed to, and I freaked out. You could've stayed and talked to me—demanded answers—but you didn't. And I saw the cop cars leaving your house. And you didn't mention them, and it was obvious you knew. I panicked, and I left. And then I got to my office and realized how badly I'd fucked up by not just talking to you. I shredded the other files I had, but I was planning to take yours back to your place. I was going to be there before you even got home, and I was going to tell you everything. Only—" I fling my arm back toward Garret's body. "But I'm in love with you, and I want to be with you!"

"Okay."

"Okay?" I shout at him. "Okay?"

"Okay. I love you, too."

"Oh my god! You're such a bastard!"

"Yeah, but I'm a bastard who's going to help you cover up a murder," he says, smirking.

"It was self-defense," I grumble.

"What about the other four?"

"I didn't say anything about the other four, did I?"

He snorts. "How hurt are you? Can I touch you?"

"Well, my face is..." I gesture at it. "My nose isn't broken, but I'm probably going to look like a trash panda tomorrow. And I've got a couple of fractured ribs, and—"

"I'd kill him if you hadn't already done it," Mark interjects, looking like he wants to spit on Garret's corpse.

"And my elbow is fucked again."

Mark glances at my elbow and then back to my face, raising his fingertips to brush against my cheek. "Davidson?" he asks, referencing the cut that was there weeks ago.

I sigh. "Yes. Matt Davidson."

"I knew that cut wasn't from that morning."

"Yes. Fine. You were right!"

"How'd you do it?"

"Help me up, and I'll tell you. I'll tell you everything, but we can't keep sitting here next to a dead body just chatting, Mark."

He nods as he gently wraps an arm around my waist. "Good?" he asks.

"Yeah." I grit my teeth as he rises, pulling me with him. I stand there for a moment, braced against Mark, swaying on my feet. Everything hurts.

"Can you walk?"

"I'll manage. Can you get him to the van? Toss him in the back? We'll leave our phones here and come back for them when we're done," I say. I had a decent bit of time to figure out how to handle this while I was waiting for Mark to show up. If we leave our phones here and get rid of Garret's body somewhere else, hopefully it'll look like we were never there. If anyone ever checks our cell phone records, we can claim we were out here having sex in the park.

"I'll drive the van, and you can follow in your car. We'll drive east thirty or forty minutes, find somewhere moderately secluded, douse the van with all the turpentine you brought, and set it on fire. By the time the flames die out, it should erase any trace of me having been inside. Then you drive back, and I'll tell you everything you want to know. Deal?"

"Deal," Mark agrees, grabbing Garret by the ankles and dragging his body across the lot. Better him than me, but I still look away, remembering the sensation of blood running down my throat. "You know, I've been on worse dates than this," Mark throws out as I hold my ribs and shuffle toward the van.

"Oh yeah?"

"One or two."

I TURN DOWN AN OLD LOGGING ROAD, DRIVE A FEW hundred feet and park the van, happy to be done. Every time I had to turn the steering wheel or check my blind spot, it hurt. The next several weeks are going to suck, and not only because of the broken ribs.

I can't show up to see patients looking like this. By tomorrow afternoon, I'm going to have two black eyes that no amount of makeup will be able to cover. The sparring excuse isn't going to fly with Teresa a second time. I'll have to claim I came down with the flu or something and cancel my patients for next week. Maybe the week after that, with enough makeup, I could do online sessions without it being too noticeable. And then it'll be Thanksgiving. When the following Monday rolls around, I should be able to get away with going into the office.

*Goddamn Garret Fischer. At least he'll never be a problem again,* I think as I get out of the van and lean against the side, waiting for Mark, who just came to a stop behind me. He gets out, leaving the engine running and the headlights on once again, and goes around to his trunk.

When he reappears, he's carrying a large jug of turpentine in one hand and a five-gallon bucket of deck stain in the other.

"You okay?" he asks when he nears me.

"I'll be better once this is done, but I'm okay."

"Good," he says, pausing long enough to lean in and kiss my forehead. "Turpentine or stain on the seats?"

"Which one's more flammable?" I ask, hoping he knows, because I have no idea.

"Turpentine."

"Put that on the seats, and then we'll strap Garret into the driver's seat and douse him and the rest of the van in the stain," I say, moving out of the way. I'm not going to be much help. It's going to hurt to lift anything heavier than a glass of water for the next few weeks. "When did you figure it out?"

"A couple of weeks ago. After Halloween. When they found Miller. Two's a coincidence, but three's a pattern," he says, echoing Jeanette's words from dinner two weeks past.

"And you've just been waiting for me to tell you I did it since then?" I ask, watching him pour turpentine onto the van's seats.

He glances over his shoulder and shrugs. "I dropped some hints."

"Yeah, well, clearly I didn't get them," I mutter. "What gave me away?"

"I had wondered after you first told me about Katie at Outsiders, but then it was only Carmichael and Davidson, and they were saying Davidson's death was an accident, so I wrote it off. But when we were sitting on the hood of my car after The Rose Room, you had a smudge of white paint on your jaw, next to your earlobe. I thought it was weird because I also thought the bottle girl who was wearing white face paint and sitting on Brandon's lap looked a lot like you."

"Damn," I huff. "I saw you watching me. I'd hoped you wouldn't realize."

"I tried to talk myself out of believing it was you initially, since she was curvier, but then there was the paint. And the very fresh scratch on your arm. Then Miller turned up dead after leaving with the bottle girl. When they showed me the picture, I was pretty sure."

"And you stayed."

"Yes."

"Why?"

"I didn't give a fuck about any of those assholes. You had a good reason for killing them, and the world is better without them in it. Just like the world is better without my dad in it."

"Yeah," I agree. It makes a twisted kind of sense considering that he has relevant personal experience. I'm sure there's more to it, but I'm so tired.

"Plus, I knew your feelings for me were real, even if you hadn't admitted it yet."

"What made you so sure?"

"You introduced me to Vaughn and Katie and invited me to meet your dad," Mark replies. "And I know you well enough to know that's not a thing you do lightly."

I nod, and Mark is silent for a moment before asking, "What about Katie?"

"What about her?"

"Was she in on it?"

I shake my head. "No. But she figured it out around the same time you did. She saw me in my costume before I left."

"Is that why she's in California? Giving interviews?"

"Yes."

Mark nods and resumes covering the seats in turpentine. A minute later, he's dragging Garret's body into the driver's seat for me, dumping stain onto it, and then coating the rear of the van. "Be right back," he says, heading to his car once the five-gallon bucket runs empty.

"What's that?" I ask when he returns carrying another jug and a paint can.

"Acetone and shellac," he says, as he tosses the unopened containers into the back. "The acetone is used for cleaning up the shellac. They're both also highly flammable." He removes a matchbook from his pocket and passes it to me.

"The line between potential arsonist and DIY home improver looks thinner and thinner by the second," I murmur, striking a match and holding it to the matchbook. The cardboard smokes, and the flame catches hold, twisting up it, racing toward my fingers.

I throw the matchbook onto Garret Fischer's corpse at the same time Mark's arms wrap around me, scooping me up. He turns and runs.

"Ow, ow, ow!" I shout. There's a loud whoosh as the fire catches hold and oxygen is sucked from the air.

He sets me down when we reach his car, and I wrap an arm around myself, trying to remember how to breathe around the pain.

"Sorry, but you wouldn't have shuffled away fast enough."

"A little warning would've been nice!"

"Yeah. It would have been," he says, glaring at me.

"You handed me a matchbook! What did you think I was going to do with it?" I grumble as he helps me into the car.

# Chapter 31
# No Damsels in Distress

"So. How'd you do it?" Mark asks as he peers out the windshield, creeping through the trees, down the logging road, back toward civilization.

"Which one?"

"All of them."

"Joey Carmichael was cyanide. Sorry about doing it during your season opener. I was angry, and I wanted to make a point."

"Remind me not to piss you off," Mark murmurs.

"The week before it happened, Katie was leaving the pharmacy and she saw him. He waved at her," I explain.

"He *waved* at her?" Mark questions, sounding appalled.

"Yes. I was going to kill Garret Fischer first, but after that... Well. Joey bumped himself up to the top of my list."

"So you used me to get into the arena and then hid somewhere overnight?"

"Yeah. I'm sorry. You were the easiest way to get close to them. If I could do it all differently, I would."

"Why me?" Mark asks. "Why'd you decide on me as opposed to anyone else who works with the team?"

I take a deep breath and exhale it. "Vaughn said of everyone he looked into, he found three people who would be likely to be interested in me enough to get me access to the team. Clark Thomas, Adam Klaussen, and you. It didn't seem like I'd have anything in common with Clark, and Adam seemed like he had commitment issues. You were unattached, but you'd been in a long-term relationship before coming here. It seemed like you and I would at least have things to talk about. And it's shallow, but you're way more attractive than either of them.

"I actually followed you for a day before we met. That's why I dyed my hair. You were having breakfast, and I saw you checking out a woman with black hair, so I dyed mine," I blurt out. Heat creeps up my cheeks, and I know he can't see it, but I still want to look away. If I don't tell him now, though, he'll hear about it from my dad.

"You dyed it because you saw me look at someone with black hair?" he says, sounding skeptical.

"Yes, and yes, I know how that sounds!"

Mark bursts out laughing, and I know he's laughing at me, but it's okay. I deserve it. "How'd you get past the door locks?" he asks eventually.

"The code was nine-nine-nine-nine, Mark. It wasn't hard."

"Okay. And Davidson?"

"Some pepper spray, a baseball bat, and a lot of luck. He had cleaners. I snuck in after them and waited for him to get home. I ambushed him with pepper spray—which wasn't quite as effective as I was hoping, leading to him punching me in the face. We struggled, I hit him in the back of the head with the bat, and then tossed his body in his swimming pool and waited for him to drown.

"I drugged Brandon Miller with GHB, waited for him to pass out, and then slid a knife into his heart. I shot Rhys Steichen with a tranquilizer dart, tied him to a chair, and asked him about the others," I say softly.

"The others?" Mark echoes.

"He had an address book. I found it in his locker room stall the night I poisoned Joey Carmichael. I took it and asked Vaughn to look into the names in the book after I found Katie's old address in it.

Vaughn found the names of nine other women he thought had been assaulted. I asked Rhys about them. He admitted to eight of the nine."

"Ah. That explains both Steichen bitching about someone stealing from him earlier in the season and the police reading me a list of women's names asking if I recognized any of them. I admitted to having met Katie. I told them you spent last night with me."

"You gave me an alibi?" I ask, trying to ignore the pressure building behind my eyes. "Why didn't you say anything?"

"Why didn't you?" he responds softly.

"I'm sorry. Please believe me when I say I know I should have." I clear my throat. "Anyway, after that, I put a screwdriver into his brain. You saw what happened with Garret."

There's a long stretch of silence. Mark turns from the logging road onto a paved road, and then we're getting onto I-84 West. "You going to kill anyone else?" he asks finally.

"No. I'm not planning on it. At least not as long as they keep their hands to themselves. What happened at your meeting? I was expecting Garret to be there."

"He was supposed to be. He made an excuse about having food poisoning, and then apparently ditched his security detail. They're going to lose their shit when they realize he's gone. Tomorrow is going to suck," he says, and I resist the impulse to apologize again.

"As far as what happened... Not much. There was talk of postponing tomorrow's game. But they discarded that idea pretty quickly. No one wants to lose the money. Our games have been averaging higher than normal ticket sales and television views since Carmichael died in the season opener. I think people are hoping it'll happen again and they'll be there to see it when it does.

"They're increasing security at the arena. The team has been told to limit any extracurricular activities. The owners volunteered to install new state-of-the-art security systems for anyone who wants one. And the private security is going to stick around until at least the beginning of next year, despite being completely ineffective."

"Good old capitalism," I murmur. It was reason enough to let a bunch of rapists continue to be venerated, and it's good enough to overlook a murder or five. "He came to see me a week and a half ago."

"Who?"

"Garret Fischer. He figured out that Katie was my cousin and put two and two together. He told me he knew. And I knew it was only a matter of time before he tried to kill me. So I told him to prove it."

Mark's hands clench on the steering wheel. "You told him to *prove it*? What the fuck were you thinking?"

"I was thinking that if he'd figured it out, I had nothing to lose by taunting him."

"And you didn't bother mentioning this? Any of this? Even just that he'd shown up at your office threatening you?"

"I thought about it. I almost told you more than once. But…"

"But?"

I sigh. "You threw a guy out of a window, Mark. At a party full of people. If you'd thought Garret fucking Fischer was threatening me, what would you have done?"

"I…" he trails off.

"Yeah. Exactly. And I can take care of myself. I ask for help when I need it, and I'm sorry I didn't ask for yours sooner. I'm sorry I didn't talk to you sooner. I love you. But I don't need you to protect me. I'm not a damsel in distress. I'm not telling you about it now so that we can argue. I'm telling you so that you'll trust me when I say there's nothing else about this that I haven't told you."

He takes a deep breath. "Okay."

"Hey Alyssa, what's up?" Katie asks when she answers her phone. It's a bit after ten in the morning, and Mark left for the arena about half an hour ago, after making me promise more than once that I wouldn't leave, which is fair. He's still freaked out after last night, and seeing the state of my face this morning didn't help matters. He asked me if I was *sure* my nose wasn't broken at least half a dozen times and suggested taking me to have my ribs imaged nearly as many, but I wouldn't let him. The last thing I need is a paper trail documenting my injuries.

Instead, I'm propped up on Mark's couch. He put everything I could possibly need within arm's reach, and I promised to move as little as possible. It wasn't a hard promise to make. Everything hurts. The bruise on my ribs covers the entire left side, and it's just beginning to form. It's going to be purple by tomorrow. It hurts even to breathe. Moving is worse. I had to have Mark wash the blood and dirt out of my hair last night, so I had no issue promising to be exactly where I am now when he gets home.

"Where are you? Can you talk?"

"Yeah, just give me a sec," she says. "Okay. We're good. What's up?"

"Garret Fischer is dead, Kay. They're all dead."

"He's— You— Alyssa, what the fuck happened? I thought we agreed you'd tell me before you went after him!"

"I didn't go after him. He ambushed me last night. The Black Bears called a mandatory team meeting after the police found Rhys's body, and everyone was supposed to be there. I assumed it was safe. But he skipped it and grabbed me instead. I look like I got hit by a Mack truck, but he's dead." I wait a beat and then add, "Mark knows everything."

"You *told* him?" she questions, her disbelief clear.

"Yes. He'd already figured it out and… I'm in love with him. I told him everything."

"How'd that go?"

"He helped me cover it up. Turns out he'd already told the police I spent all night with him. He gave me an alibi, Kay, but admitted to knowing you as part of it."

"Okay. That's good to know. He *might* be worth keeping around."

"Yeah. I know you're eager to come back, but you should stay there until they find Garret's body."

"Alright. Are you okay, Alyssa?"

"The next couple of weeks are going to suck, but it was worth it. I'll be fine. Promise."

"Thank you."

"You're welcome. I'm still sorry I didn't go with you that night."

"I'm not," Katie says. "You know as well as I do that there's no guarantee it would've changed anything. They probably would've raped us both if you had."

I sigh. I know she's right, but knowing and feeling are two different things. Getting past the guilt is always the hardest part.

Katie and I talk for a few more minutes before she tells me she has to go. We hang up, and I call Vaughn.

"Hey kid, what's up?" he asks when he picks up my call.

"Hey Vaughn. I just wanted to let you know that Garret Fischer is dead. You don't have to worry."

"How? When?"

"Last night," I say, recounting the events, explaining what happened. "What was it like telling Marjorie the truth?" I finally ask.

Vaughn laughs. "Terrifying. You know the *Jaws* theme song? It felt just like that sounds."

"Yeah. That's how it felt telling Mark too. You knew about Wisconsin, didn't you?" I accuse.

"Yeah. I knew," he agrees.

"So, what? You decided you could be a matchmaker in addition to being a fixer?"

"I'm not a fixer, Alyssa. I only fix things for you because I like you. And because I owe Randall."

It's my turn to laugh. "Please," I scoff. "You might be licensed as a private investigator, and you might not be some crime boss's fixer, but you're definitely a fixer."

# Chapter 32
# A Soft Touch

It's five-forty-five in the morning when I wake up next to Mark. The curtains aren't the best—letting the glow of the streetlights seep in around the edges—but it's dark outside, and the small wall heater is humming away. It's the morning after Thanksgiving, and the hotel parking lot was nearly empty when we got here last night. We made the drive to Walla Walla following our Thanksgiving dinner with Jeanette and Katie, arriving a bit after midnight.

None of us bothered to tell Jeanette that Mark is the Black Bears' head coach. Like me, she doesn't follow sports at all, so she didn't make the connection, and Katie and I both decided that Thanksgiving dinner probably wasn't the best time to explain it. I'll tell her eventually—out of necessity more than anything else—but I'll bring him around a few more times and let her get to know him before I do. I'm hoping it'll spare me some of the snide, but ultimately well-meaning, remarks she's bound to make.

And today, I have plans. Plans beyond introducing Mark to my dad. After going to the bathroom and brushing my teeth, I wake Mark up.

"It's still dark," he says, rubbing the sleep from his eyes.

"I know. But I have something I want to show you. Get up."

He flings an arm over his face as I turn on the bedside lamp. A few minutes later, he climbs out of bed, muttering something about the time.

Ten minutes after that, we're in my car, driving north, coffee in hand.

"Where are we going?" Mark asks.

"There's a state park near here. It's a good spot to watch the sunrise."

"We're awake to watch the sunrise?" Mark questions with a noticeable lack of enthusiasm.

"Not exactly."

"I'd rather be sleeping," he grumbles.

Twenty minutes later, I pull into a small trailhead parking area and get out of the car. We're the only ones here. Mark follows me as I go around to the trunk, grab a blanket and hand it to him.

"Here. Carry this," I say before walking down the trail. Sunrise is about half an hour away, but it's bright enough for us to slowly make our way to the overlook—which is fine because slowly is the best I can do. My ribs still constantly hurt, but this trail is mostly flat, and as long as I don't have to take too deep a breath, the pain is manageable.

A mile and a half later, we come to the overlook. It's a grassy hillside, and I veer off the trail, down the slope until we come to a somewhat flat area. I pluck the blanket from Mark's grasp, spread it on the ground, and then step onto it, tugging him with me.

"What—" he begins, but my hands are running through his soft mahogany hair, pulling his lips to mine, my tongue caressing his. He tastes like mint and coffee, and I plunge my tongue deeper into his mouth as I drop a hand to the front of his pants, stroking him. He's already hard, and my cunt is already throbbing as I think about him sliding inside me.

His hands skim over my sides, slipping under the hem of my sweatshirt. I didn't bother to put anything on underneath it, and he moans into my mouth when his fingertips encounter nothing but skin. It's the sexiest noise in the world.

He pulls his mouth from mine just far enough to ask, "Are you sure you're up for this?"

"We could both benefit from blowing off a little steam," I murmur, my eyes locked on his as I slide my hand into his pants and wrap it around his shaft. His eyes flutter shut, and he makes the same soft moaning sound.

"What if someone walks by?" he asks, giving me an out.

But I don't want an out. "There's no one here except us. If someone should happen to walk by ten minutes from now, though, when you're buried in me, we'll put on a show."

"You're sure?" he asks, his fingertips running back and forth across my nipples.

"Yes."

The word has barely left my mouth before he's taking my sweatshirt off, leaving me standing topless on an open hillside. The air is cold, but I've never cared less.

"You're fucking beautiful," he whispers, grabbing my ass and pulling me toward him with one hand as the other moves to cup my boob.

"I'm glad you think so," I reply, moving my hands under his shirt, caressing his body. He lets go of me long enough for me to yank his shirt off, and then his hands are immediately back on me, pinching my nipples and making me gasp. I kick off my shoes and then shove my sweatpants down my legs. There's also nothing beneath them, and I take Mark's right hand from my boob, placing it between my legs and his fingers inside me. "Yes," I moan, and he thrusts them deeper and deeper as I bring my hand back to his dick, matching the rhythm his fingers are thrusting into me.

"You're so wet."

"I've been fantasizing about this—about being on my knees, face down in front of you while you fuck me—for days. I want you buried in the back of my throat and then pounding into me while my ass is up in the air. I want you to make me scream your name," I tell him, watching his pupils dilate as his fingers press into the walls of my cunt, leaving me gasping. He wants this too. He's been so careful with me lately. Too careful. "Please."

His left hand drops from my boob to ghost over my ribs. "It'll hurt," he warns.

"I like a little pain sometimes. You have permission to hurt me."

"You're sure?"

"Stop trying to talk me out of this and fuck me. If it's too much and I want you to stop, I'll let you know."

He kicks his shoes off, and then I'm pushing his sweatpants down his legs, following them until I'm kneeling in front of him. The sun hasn't risen yet, but the sky is so bright that if anyone walks by and glances in our direction, they'll get an eyeful. That realization just makes this more fun.

Mark's hand fists in my hair as he rams himself into my mouth. The head of his cock reaches the back of my throat well before my lips are anywhere near the base of him. He pushes deeper until my throat is molding around him, and then he holds my head there, groaning as my throat flexes around his dick and I fight my gag reflex. He draws back, repeating the process again and again. It's exactly what I wanted. Eventually, he increases the pace. My eyes are watering, and I can taste him more and more with each thrust. I drop a hand between my legs, running a finger over my clit in time with his thrusts.

I'm almost there when he pulls out and shoves me away. He drops to his knees. "Turn around. Ass up," he orders, his hand on the back of my neck, pushing my face into the blanket. "Keep touching yourself," he growls, the tip of his cock teasing my opening.

I return my fingers to my clit. "Please, Mark. Please."

"Tell me you want this," he demands, barely sliding into me.

"I want this. I want you. Please. Fuck me," I plead, but he's still just barely inside me. I struggle to figure out what he's waiting for, my brain unable to think beyond the fact that I need him *now*. "You have permission to hurt me," I say, repeating my earlier words. Apparently, that's what he was waiting for because his hands wrap around my ribs, squeezing as he slams into me. The angle is perfect, and he's so deep. My ribs hurt, and the pain makes every thrust even more amazing than the last.

"Keep going, Mark, please. More," I beg, and he steadily increases the pressure on my ribs, thrusting harder and faster. I continue stroking my fingers across my clit, the orgasm building. Then I'm coming, screaming his name.

He makes it another minute, and then there's the warm burst of him climaxing, and he bucks against me, growling. He loses all rhythm as he folds over me, panting, holding our bodies together.

"You're okay?" he asks after a moment.

"Yeah. I'm great. Thank you. That was amazing."

"I love you," he whispers before pulling out of me.

"I love you too," I reply, turning to find him lying on the blanket. "Feeling better?" I ask as I gingerly lie down in the space between his arm and his chest, pulling the blanket over us. The sweat coating my skin is evaporating quickly in the morning air, and it won't be long until I'm shivering.

"Yes, actually. How'd you know?"

I shrug. "It's kind of hard to miss the fact that family shit makes you nervous. Just like it's equally hard to miss the fact that this calms you down."

He snorts, and I rise and fall against his chest. "Well, this does top my list for the best sunrise."

MARK IS SITTING NEXT TO ME AT THE TABLE AS WE WAIT for my dad to be brought out. This is the first time anyone has come with me in years. It's nice. Even though Mark's knee is bouncing next to mine.

I place my hand on it as I say, "Relax. He'll like you. And even if he doesn't, who cares?"

"He's your dad," Mark murmurs.

"You know after he got locked up, and I went to live with Jeanette and Katie, Vaughn moved down to Portland?" I ask. Mark is looking at me curiously, so I explain. "Vaughn used to live in Seattle. He and my dad worked together."

"No, I didn't know that. Why?"

"He moved because I did," I answer with a shrug. "He and Marjorie put their house on the market and moved to Portland a few months after everything happened. There hasn't been a single month in my life where I haven't seen Vaughn at least once. Usually more often."

"Okay. What's that got to do with anything?"

"Vaughn's at least as much my father as my dad is. And he already likes you. That's all."

The door clatters open, and my dad comes through. He spots me right away, and his eyes linger on Mark as he approaches.

"Hi dad, this is Mark. Mark, this is my dad, Randall," I say, making the necessary introductions once he reaches the table.

"Mark. The hockey coach. So you're the one my daughter dyed her hair for."

I roll my eyes. I knew he would mention it. Better that than something about Katie, though.

"Nice to meet you," my dad adds, extending his hand across the table, and as Mark takes his hand, I can't help but notice that my dad's hair looks more styled than it usually does when I show up to visit. Apparently, Mark's not the only one who wants to make a good impression.

I smother a laugh as I say, "Vaughn sends his best. He told me to tell you he'll give you a real job when you're done. If you want one."

My dad huffs, dismissing Vaughn's offer without response. "I take it your trouble down in Portland is done?" my dad probes, glancing at Mark.

"Yes. And yes, he knows."

My dad shakes his head, sighing. "You and Vaughn," he mutters. "Like peas in a pod."

I snort. "Say it. I know you want to."

"I love you, Alyssa, but you and Vaughn are both soft touches."

"There are worse things to be, dad."

He grins. "That's true. Do you play chess?" he asks, turning his attention to Mark.

"Congratulations," I say to Mark, as I stand to get the chessboard. "He likes you. He only plays chess with people he likes."

# Afterword

You made it to the end, and you're reading the afterword. That's cool! So here's the deal. This book is a work of fiction. However, I was inspired to write it as a result of some real, very-uncool events. If you are not already aware of those events, you can search the internet for "hockey + rape" or "hockey sexual assault" or any other combination of similar words to find the events in question (and I strongly encourage you to do so).

I'll state for the record that I don't believe the justice system did what it was supposed to. When it comes to cases of sexual assault, it seems like the courts—in pretty much all countries—get it wrong more often than they get it right.

I hope this story entertained you, but I also hope it made you think. I especially hope it made you think if you're a sports fan—and not just hockey—because there's so much shady shit that is swept under the rug at all levels of sports.

Bad people are bad people, but when sports' governing bodies routinely sweep incidents of sexual assault under the rug, it becomes a systemic issue. And when sports fans don't care, there's no reason for the governing bodies to care either. They'll only ever do better—*be* better—if fans demand it. Boycott teams that hire shitty people. Boycott leagues that turn a blind eye. Make them do better.

Okay, PSA done. Thank you for your attention to this matter. Now, while I've still got you here, I need you to pull out your phone.

Have you done it?

Yes? Great! Next step. I need you to text at least one friend (or enemy, if you hated the book) and tell them to read it.

Have you done it?

Yes? Fantastic. Now, one last teeny-tiny favor. Go to goodreads, Amazon, StoryGraph, or whatever your review-place-of-choice is and leave a review—love it or loathe it. Reviews are the lifeblood of indie authors.

If you're interested in my goings-on, and for more details about what's in the works, make sure you're subscribed to my newsletter (sign up at www.sam-evans.me)! Plus, you get a free prequel chapter for one of my other books when you do—and other freebies as they become available. But wait! There's more! Every newsletter includes a dog tax. All the coolest people are subscribed. You should be too!

Bye!

# Acknowledgments

Thank you to both Tyler and Allyson, for your alpha-reading services. Additional thanks to Tyler for being the Pinky to my Brain (or vice versa?).

Thank you to Krys M for being interested in the insanity. I'm glad it's more than just loud.

Thank you to Dani D for the constant cheerleading.

Thank you to Dean S for the chapter title. You know which one.

Thank you to Dani K for being my subject matter expert and verifying I got the details right.

Thank you to Mark P for catching two things no one else did. I appreciate it more than you realize (I *hate* being wrong).

Thank you to Laura CW for *all* the suggestions. You always help to make my books better. Also, thanks for not thinking I'm insane when I bring up clearly insane ideas.

Thank you to everyone on Threads who said I should write this book. I probably wouldn't have if you weren't equally pissed about how things worked out. Fuck those guys. Each and everyone of them.

Thank you to all the people who know that pressing charges is often a losing battle but do it anyway. I'm sorry there's not more justice in the justice system.

# About the Author

Sam Evans has lived all over the US but currently resides in the upper midwest. She's a software engineer by day, but letting her imagination run wild is her full-time occupation. She lives with her partner, a high-strung border collie, and an insane kelpie. She routinely drinks too much coffee and gets too little sleep.

- instagram.com/sam_evans_writer
- threads.com/@sam_evans_writer
- tiktok.com/@sam.evans.writer
- bsky.app/profile/sam-evans-writer.bsky.social
- amazon.com/author/sam-evans

www.ingramcontent.com/pod-product-compliance
Lightning Source LLC
LaVergne TN
LVHW010310070526
838199LV00065B/5504